Alamo Rising

A Novel By
Josh Rountree & Lon Prater

White Cat Publications

Cover art by Zagladko Sergei Ptetrovich
Cover design by Scott Wilson
Interior design by Vasha Lewkowicz and Scott Wilson

Edited by Charles P. Zaglanis

SECOND EDITION
Published in March 2014

White Cat Publications, LLC.
33080 Industrial Road, Suite 101
Livonia, MI 48150
www.whitecatpublications.com

For Shelley, Emma, and Amy–
See? History can be fun!

and

To Kristin–for showing me Davy Crockett's tomb, and for everything else,
And To Beckett and Gibson, Texas Boys.

ACKNOWLEDGEMENTS

Few accomplishments in life are the work of just one person. The authors would like to thank the people who gave us support along the way with this novel, from its birth as a simple short story challenge on an out of the way writers forum to the cavalcade of steampunk zombie western action it is today.

From the disbanded Critical MS writers group, a rogues gallery with a rotating cast where it all began: Samantha Henderson, Joseph Paul Haines, Eric Marin, Karl El-Koura, Andrew Nicolle, Mikal Trimm, Abby Goldsmith, Annetta Ribken, Brian Rapatta, Peggy "Brutal Dreamer" Shumate, Dave Duggins, L. R. Snow, Simon Owens, Pam McNew, Carina Gonzales, Dave Bowlin, Amy Tibbetts, and Charles Tuomi, and Joe Cummings.

Non-writers who read the whole thing in draft, hunting typos and plotholes like there was a bounty on them: Chris Glasgow, Bob Monaco (who also provided a helpful casting list for the movie–Danny Trejo as Santa Ana's head, young Jody Foster as Willie–yes, please!)

Editors and Publishers who believed in this story and gave it the boost it deserved: Christine Purcell, William Jones who worked on the book originally at Elder Signs Press, and Rick Moore, who keeps White Cat running and made it possible for Charles P. Zaglanis to quite literally bring this book back to life during a time of extreme personal hardship. You have no idea how much respect and gratitude we owe you, buddy.

We especially appreciate Mark Rossmore (performing as Escape the Clouds), who found inspiration in our story enough to put together an amazing EP of steampunk music, and Alamo scholar and gunfight re-enactor Rich Curilla of Bracketteville, Texas' very own Alamo Village filming location and museum.

And last but never least, our families and friends who believed in us, supported our crazy ventures into fiction, and convinced everyone they knew to go buy this book. Like those brave souls at the Alamo, you will always be remembered and your sacrifices were not in vain.

Josh Rountree
Austin, Texas

Lon Prater
Pensacola, Florida

ALAMO RISING

PART the FIRST

❯❯❯❯❯<❮❮❮❮❮

TRAILING SMOKE

CHAPTER 1

TROY TANNER STUMBLED ACROSS SMOKE'S TRAIL ten days out of Austin and deep into Comanche country. The air smelled like Indian magic, and the wind blew hot as a whore's bed sheets across the cactus-scarred desert.

Gunshot men stiffened in the sun, a scattering of brown bodies and painted faces, bloody leather and rusted rifles. A few still clung to their weapons, as if even in death they might need protection from a man like Jebediah Smoke. For all Troy knew, they might.

A pair of steam-mare carcasses suggested they were part of Lightning Dove's outfit. Steam tech was hard to come by in Texas, and even more so out here on the Llano. Lightning Dove was known to have a few steam mares that he'd scavenged from murdered settlers and British solders who'd wandered too far from the California Colony, and he was one of the only war chiefs who'd figured out how to keep them running in such an extreme environment.

Troy removed his hat, wiped his forehead with a dusty shirtsleeve. Last thing he needed was to get caught by the Warhawks in Indian country. He wouldn't have to worry about excuses or a by-your-leave. Wouldn't live that long.

But what the hell was Smoke doing way out here in the Comancheria? The man had a lot to run from, admittedly. But riding out alone this way amounted to little more than suicide. Yet here Troy was, doing the same damned thing. Smoke's daddy had good money on the table for the return of his wayward son, but was it worth tangling with the Warhawks?

Apparently so.

Troy spit tobacco at the cracked earth and was half surprised it didn't sizzle when it hit. Crabapple whinnied, and Troy patted his flank. "Easy there."

Crabapple snorted and backed away from the carnage. Hot wind stirred up dust and the stench of death. Thunder rumbled in the cloudless sky. The horse reared up, then sidestepped a few paces. Something more than just the dead bodies had his dander up.

"Settle down."

Crabapple snorted again. Then the dead began to rise.

Not their bodies, like Lord Presidente Moctezuma and his zombies. Just their souls. Wispy columns of blue smoke rose from each corpse, billowing from mouths and nostrils to form the blank-eyed animal forms that some used as proof of the Indians' subhuman status. The ghosts held together for several seconds before the wind tore them apart. Carrying them off to join whatever heathen god gave the Comanche their magic, if the tales were true. The sight disturbed Troy; every description he'd heard of soul migration failed to do it justice.

He spurred Crabapple's flank and left the dead Indians to rot, wondering for the hundredth time why the hell Smoke was riding into such dangerous country. Troy decided it didn't matter, as long as he could keep clear of the Comanche. He'd been sent to bring back Smoke and he meant to do just that. Nothing more.

Troy wasn't a Ranger anymore. Smoke and his foolishness had seen to that. So he had no problem letting someone else deal with this bunch of hoodoo Indians.

Troy rode up on another dead man not far from a freshwater spring. This man was white, and he was strapped to the trunk of a wiry mesquite tree with rough lengths of rope.

Troy had encountered more than his share of settlers who'd fallen victim to Comanche torture, and it was almost enough to prepare him for the sight. But while scalping and other mutilations were common enough west of the larger Texas settlements, those fates seemed kind in comparison to this man's death. What flesh remained on his bones was seared a strawberry red, slick with weeping blisters. Much of his skin, though, had simply sloughed off the bone, and that left little doubt what had caused the damage. The man had been steamed to death–with a U.S. manufactured heat rifle most likely. Just point the barrel, pull the trigger and let the superheated air do its work, slowly burning away the victim's skin until not enough remained to matter. It was a particularly barbaric weapon, and typical of U.S. cruelty.

The Yanks often used heat rifles to chase peaceful Indians onto reservations, but this one must have fallen into other hands. Scorched bits of blue uniform clung to the body and marked the man as U.S. Cavalry. Probably an American scout, trying to get a handle on what Lightning Dove was up to. Could have been Comanche, Kiowa, or even some Indian-friendly bounty hunter that did him in. It didn't matter to Troy, as long as they didn't come for him next.

A warm breeze stirred the dust and tugged at the dead man's singed hair. Then the man's eyes flew open and Troy flinched. *Jesus, lord! The man ain't dead.*

"Red," said the man, his voice a tortured rasp. "Redjacks."

Troy dropped from the saddle and pulled a canteen from his saddlebag. He held it up to the cavalryman's lips and dribbled some water down the man's chin. "Who did this?"

"Redjacks. Queen's men."

Troy shook his head. "Mister, the sun's burned your mind. Ain't no Queen's men out this way. Nothing but settlers with no sense, a bunch of meaner than hell Indians, and fools like me who should know better. Hell, even Moctezuma leaves this godforsaken part of the world alone."

"Redjacks and Injuns. Hell, it's not right it's...you got to tell someone." The cavalryman coughed blood and thrashed against his bonds. Troy thought about cutting him loose, but was afraid the ropes were the only thing keeping him together. "They'll kill us all, mister."

"You ain't making sense," said Troy. "Listen, I'll ride out and bring somebody to help me get you back to civilization." Even as Troy spoke, he knew he was giving the man false hope. It was a miracle he was still breathing. He wouldn't last another few minutes.

"Leave here now!" the man said. "Tell somebody."

An arrow whispered through the air a split second before it appeared in the cavalryman's forehead.

Troy scampered around the back of the tree, looking for cover, but the blasted landscape offered little more than scraggly bushes and a few rocky gullies for protection. A volley of arrows feathered Crabapple's flank. The horse screamed and bolted for the horizon, leaving nothing but a dead man and a sickly tree to shield Troy from the approaching band of Indians.

Troy drew his pistol and considered his chances against their superior numbers. He might get one of them, but the others would do him the same as they had Crabapple. He knew he should start shooting anyway, but his instincts told him that was the quickest way to death.

The Indians advanced slowly. Their clothing marked them as Comanche. They rode toward him, the hindmost riders on pale sorrels, the one in the lead on a painted colt. Two of them held feathered lances; the other leisurely notched a new arrow in his bow. A prisoner walked behind them, hands bound at the wrists and tied to one of the sorrels' saddles. He'd either lost his hat or been foolish enough to venture out onto the Llano without one, and his face was nearly as blistered as the cavalryman's. He jabbered a few Indian words to his captors and the lead rider stiffened. The Indian spoke and the prisoner nodded.

"Put away that gun and get yourself over here, Troy," said the prisoner. "And come slow or they'll plant you in the ground with them lances."

Troy was shocked to recognize the voice.

"Smoke?"

"You know who it is. Now I suggest you get moving. These fellers ain't much for patience."

Fighting his better judgment, Troy holstered his pistol and left the protection of the tree. He wasn't sure what Smoke had told the Comanche to keep them from killing him, but if he didn't come as they asked, he'd be dead for sure. He walked slowly toward the halted riders. One of them dismounted when he neared and bound his hands with a strap of buffalo hide. He took Troy's pistol and tossed it to one of the other men. This close, Troy could see the broken cross that was Lightning Dove's sigil painted on the horses' flanks.

It would be suicide to struggle, so he allowed the silent Comanche to bind him to the same rope that pulled Smoke.

"What are you doing out here?" asked Smoke.

"Nothing that concerns you," Troy lied. "You're the last person I figured would help me out. Not that this is much better."

"You ain't dead, are you?" snapped Smoke. "Probably should have let them feather your ass."

"Why didn't you?" Troy couldn't feel grateful to Smoke. Not after what had happened outside of Laredo.

"Two against three is better than one against three. Ain't likely, but you might be of some use."

"Figured you'd be getting something out of it."

"You ain't changed, have you? Still as self-righteous as ever. Tell you what, maybe I'll just kill you myself and save us all the trouble of–"

Smoke lunged forward and Troy went with him. Pain shot through his wrists and he realized the riders were in motion. Troy almost lost his footing, but managed to scramble forward and keep pace with the horses. Fortunately, the Indians were riding slowly, which meant they intended to keep him alive a bit longer. Troy occasionally came across men who'd been dragged to death by Indian horsemen, and didn't care to wind up one of them.

"What kind of sway you got over them anyway?" Troy asked, jogging behind the horses. "What'd you say to them?"

"Told 'em you were with me."

"And why ain't they killed you?"

"Because I got business with Lightning Dove."

"What sort of business?"

"*None-o-your* sort of business."

Troy chuckled. "Yeah? Well I doubt he'll give you much of a welcome the way you kilt all his buddies."

"Who? Them ones riding steam mares?" asked Smoke. "It was cavalry killed them. Friends of that guy tied to the tree. I seen 'em ranging a few days back."

"So where are they now," asked Troy. "We could use some rescuing."

Smoke shrugged. "Probably wound up like their friend there."

As the day stretched on, Troy's thoughts lingered on the doomed cavalryman and his last words. What the hell had he been babbling about? Queen's men on the Llano? That was foolish talk. First, the Indians didn't have any more use for the Brits than they did the Texans. They'd just as soon kill either one. Second, any sizeable force of British soldiers east of the Rocky Mountains would raise the war call in the U.S., Texas and Mexico. Was the cavalryman just suffering from heatstroke?

That was a question that could wait. Troy's more immediate concern was how to break free from the Indians and get Smoke back to Austin so he could collect his fee. And maybe, so he could clear his good name. Troy doubted he could ever ride with his old crew again, but at the very least he'd like them to know the truth about the botched rescue. The way Smoke had killed that little girl.

As the sun began its descent, they reached a gentle rise and Troy knew from the landmarks that a small valley lay less than a mile ahead. Plumes of smoke rose above the edge of the hill and at first, Troy assumed it was from campfires. But as they drew nearer, he saw the smoke was white and billowy, and far too thick to be a product of campfires alone.

"Aw hell," said Smoke, and Troy understood the sentiment. Someone in the valley was operating a serious cache of steam machinery. More than any ragtag group of rogue Indians could muster. More even than a chief like Lightning Dove could scrounge up.

"That ain't just an Indian camp in that valley," said Troy. Then they crested the rise and saw what lay in the flat plain between the rocky grouping of hills.

"Aw hell," said Smoke again.

Troy turned his head and spat as the Indian leading them kicked his horse into a canter. The cord jerked tight and it was all Troy could do to keep himself upright and running behind Smoke.

CHAPTER 2

THE MOON CREPT INTO A CLOUDLESS SKY above Smoke's cactus pen, and it was all he could do not to beam back at it. He looked over at Troy. Still sleeping on his side and breathing regular. And the Indians and Brits were all too far away to see him examine the envelope he'd been paid to carry into the Comancheria.

With Lightning Dove and a select few of his top men gone from camp till tomorrow, he had one more chance to see if he could figure out what exactly it was he'd brought all this way. There hadn't been a chance earlier, not since the Indians had dragged him and Troy into the Comanche side of camp, both of them gawking at the dozen or so steam angels tethered to the ground along its eastern edge. Beyond those stood a squad of ten legged behemoths, gun barrels wide as whiskey bottles sticking out from their iron hulls. Redjacks pranced around the steam gear, saluting each other every other second and wrinkling their noses whenever they came within a stone's throw of an Indian. To Smoke and Troy they gave no more than a passing glance, betraying neither curiosity nor pity.

But the Indians hadn't put the pair of them into a tipi, and for that Smoke was glad. He didn't like being closed in, never had. So sleeping under the stars was plenty fine with him. And besides, the nearly full moon gave him a chance to take another glance at the envelope that Eastern dandy had paid him to deliver. Smoke had a sinking feeling it had something to do with all this Queen's gear hiding out here in the Texas wilds.

Not too long after a meal of grilled peppers and some kind of lizard, Troy had grown tired of glaring at him and rolled over to sleep. He hadn't said a word since this afternoon, apart from thanking the woman that brought their dinner. Now that Smoke was sure he was asleep, he reached inside his shirt and pulled out the sweat-stained envelope.

The wax seal was still in place, only because the little man in the derby hat had made it perfectly clear that he wouldn't get the rest of his money if the seal was broken. But now he was a Warhawk prisoner, and learning what this was all about might be his only chance for survival. He picked under the wax with his fingernails until it came unstuck and slid out the paper within.

Smoke unfolded the single page and cursed. What kind of Yankee horseshit was this? A blank letter. Smoke knew there was something off about the job when he let the man hire him back in Austin, but he'd needed an excuse to get the hell out of there and it had been a convenient one. Now that bird of doubt had come home to roost and here it was shitting right in Smoke's dinner bucket.

Somewhere in the night a coyote yipped, and before he could tuck the letter away, Troy sat up.

"What you got there, *Ranger?*"

Being called Ranger made the peppers burn in Smoke's gut. Troy knew that, and it was exactly why he'd said it.

"I don't see you wearing a star no more, either. Shit, Troy, I was the one gave you the peso coins you stamped your star out of–"

Troy was on his feet and in Smoke's face. "And you're the one lost it for me, too."

Smoke held the paper out to one side, but didn't back away. "This is the reason I'm out here." He poked Troy in the chest with one finger, sending the slighter man back a step. "And maybe if you tell me why you're out in the Comancheria this time of year, I'll consider discussing it in more detail with you. But till then, I suggest you keep your manners."

Troy's eyes narrowed and he seemed to be making up his mind about something. "Won't do any good to lie to you, Jeb. I come to bring you in so I can get my star back."

"What makes you think you're going to get back in the Rangers if you bring me back? And how'd you know to find me?"

"There's folks willing to discuss it." He reached for the paper, but Smoke snatched it away.

"What folks?"

"One or two of the older Rangers."

"Which ones? And that don't answer how you knew to find me."

"Got lucky finding you. Been looking for two months or more and finally heard tell of an old boy in San Antonio bought himself a steam mare cash money. He fit your description and the rest is everyday tracking."

Smoke stared at him a long time before he spoke, still keeping the paper out to one side. "It was my Daddy said you'd get your star back, wasn't it?"

Troy said nothing.

Smoke shook his head from side to side, his face tight like the skin on an Indian drum. Finally, he let himself scowl. "Take it. We got bigger problems to worry about than making up for Laredo, though. Look around."

Troy took the paper and squinted at it in the moonlight. "This some kind of joke?"

"Ever know me for the laughing type?"

The corners of Troy's mouth almost curled up, but lucky for him they didn't finish. "Then what the hell is this paper supposed to be?"

"A message for Lightning Dove. Probably got something to do with all these Redjacks and their iron hiding out on the plains."

"You reckon?"

Smoke nodded.

"So where's the message?"

"Hid by some kind of Indian hoodoo for all I know."

"You going to give it to him?"

"Don't see why not. Might get me out of this pen. Reckon I could use a head start if you're of a mind to take me back to my Daddy and the rest of the Rangers."

They looked at each other, measuring. As the coyotes yipped again, Troy handed Smoke back the paper and he put it away.

"I'm not too sure it's in the best interests of Texas for Lightning Dove to get that letter," Troy said, his voice real soft.

"You may be right. But it ain't in my best interest to go face a courtroom full of Rangers, either. Texas ain't got no use for you. What do you care?"

Troy lay back down on the dry, packed earth. "You never could see the big picture."

Smoke paced the circle made by the overgrown cacti, too smart to kick one and set off the Indian magic they were possessed with and wishing for all the world he still had his guns on him. He kicked a rock and it skittered to a stop just inches from Troy's back.

"Get some rest," the man carped at him, not even bothering to turn around.

Lightning Dove arrived with the sun, and a pair of his shamans did their dancing magic to make the cacti open up a crawl hole for the captives. Smoke wiggled out and stared up at the weathered, stony faces of a half-dozen Comanche with rifles. He might have mistaken the great chief for any other Indian if it wasn't for the legendary fall of milk white hair that draped his bare shoulders. Lightning Dove's eyes held cold malice, and Smoke knew the promise of information was the only thing keeping him alive.

Smoke stood and Troy rose with him. They were both a good six inches taller than Lightning Dove, but neither of them could look him in the eye for long.

"You say you have been sent with a message," said Lightning Dove in perfect English. "You will give it to me now."

Smoke shoved his hand in his pocket and the Indians surrounding them raised their rifles. He yanked out the letter and waved it in front of him like a flag of surrender. "Hold on, gentlemen. I ain't planning to knife you. Just giving the boss what he wants."

"Traitor," said Troy.

Smoke ignored the jab and handed the note to Lightning Dove. The chief examined the broken wax seal, gave Smoke a look of quiet disapproval, then opened the letter and stared at the blank surface. "You seem to have lost the words. You are obviously unfamiliar with the punishment I offer to fools. Have they not heard of Lightning Dove's wrath in the proud Republic of Texas?"

"I didn't do nothing to that letter," said Smoke, insulted. "I promised to bring it here to you and I'm a man of my word."

Troy snorted.

"Close your mouth, Tanner! Look here, the man that gave me that letter paid good money for me to bring it. And I don't fool around when money is involved. So how about you take your letter, or whatever it is, and let me go home? We're just two sides of a business transaction, you and me, and now our business is done." Smoke was horrified. He knew better than to speak so freely to a man like Lightning Dove, but the words wouldn't stop. His short temper had caused him more trouble than he cared to remember. This time it would probably get him killed.

Lightning Dove showed no signs that Smoke's insolence had offended him. He ran his fingers across the letter's blank surface and sniffed it. "Who gave this to you?"

"He didn't tell me his name. I promise that's the truth. But he paid good money."

"You're a damn fool," said Troy. "Coming into this part of the world just 'cause some stranger gives you a few rusty coins."

"More than a few!" snapped Smoke. "Besides, you–"

"Describe him." Lightning Dove's voice was calm, but it immediately silenced the prisoners' exchange.

"Squat little guy with a bowler hat. He had a whole lot of wax in his moustache. Made it curl up on both ends."

Lightning Dove summoned one of his shamans. The shorter man crept up beside him, silent as a shadow, his wiry body shrouded in feathers. Lightning Dove instructed him in the Comanche tongue. Smoke had picked up the language over the years well enough to understand what they said.

"Lift the veil," said Lightning Dove. "This is from the Texan."

The shaman took the paper from Lightning Dove and began to chant in a language Smoke couldn't understand. After several seconds, he blew roughly at the letter and Smoke was surprised to see a sandy mist spew from his lips. It settled on the paper and words began to appear.

"Son of a bitch." Smoke leaned forward, trying to get a look, but Troy yanked his shirt collar back.

"You've got us in enough trouble," said Troy.

Smoke shook off his hand and watched intently as the old chief read the letter. When he'd finished, Lightning Dove turned to a tall young man at his side and began barking commands.

"Summon the General. I need to speak with him. And assemble the men. The time for our war is come, and we must pray. The moon will soon swallow the sun, and that will be the signal for our strike. If we hope to reach Austin by that time, we must gather our strength and leave by tomorrow's nightfall.

The young Comanche nodded and left to carry out his chief's wishes. Lightning Dove considered his prisoners in silence, and Smoke couldn't stand the tension.

"I'm supposed to deliver your reply," he said, pointing to the letter. It was a lie, but Smoke knew his chances of leaving this place alive were shrinking by the second. "The guy said he wanted to know if you agreed. Not sure what he meant, but that's what he said."

"And your friend?" asked Lightning Dove, a hint of terrible amusement in his eyes.

Smoke shrugged. "An old acquaintance. He ain't no part of this."

Troy kept silent, but Smoke could almost feel the other man's disdain. All things being equal, he wouldn't leave even a bastard like Troy to the mercy of Indians. But all things weren't equal. There was a slim hope Smoke could still make it through this alive, and he wasn't going to ruin that for someone who hated him.

"But you are both a part of this," said Lightning Dove. "You are both Texans. The supposed victors of this land?"

"I was born in Tennessee," Smoke lied.

"The Comanche are not fools. Nor are we savages. We are a people who've had our world stolen from us. And now we are in a position to take it back."

"I'll tell the man that for you!"

"No, you'll return to your prison," said Lightning Dove. His warriors herded Smoke and Troy at gunpoint back into the circle of cactus and mesquite. "You will listen as we sing our war songs. You will watch as our allies prepare the metal beasts for battle. You will smell the dirt and shit and oil of a thousand angry men, riding to take your country from you. And you will spend the remainder of your life in this place, wondering what's become of the people and the land that you love, until at last you become so hungry you devour one another, just as you Texans thought to devour us."

The shaman spoke the words that caused cactus and mesquite to knit together, growing into the sky until all Smoke could see was a raging circle of sunlight overhead. There was no way through the spiny walls, and nothing below them but hard packed earth, void of vegetation and water.

Smoke dropped to the ground, lowered his head and waited to die.

CHAPTER 3

AUSTIN IN THE LATE SPRING wasn't much to Titus Smoke's liking. Some days he wished he'd never given up his free-ranging days for a seat on Ed Burleson's Texas Justice Board. But back then his only son was on track for leaving a mark on the Rangers that they both could be proud of. And now, what was he up to? Dodging a possible murder trial and, if Tanner's hasty messenger bird from San Antonio was to be believed, running courier duty out to the Comancheria. The Smoke family name was falling on hard times.

Through the mayor's steam carriage window, Titus could see that the blue bonnets were still blooming. Not that he could smell them beneath the layers of horseshit, steam carriage grease, and the stink of Mayor Addison T. Dundee's assistant's hair oil.

"...and so I fired two more shots at it, then and there, and the thing finally fell over sidewise and the guides butchered it on the spot. I highly recommend Jackson's buffalo hunting excursion, Titus," the Mayor blathered.

"Never cared for the taste of it myself," Titus said diplomatically.

"Oh, mercy me, I didn't eat any of it!" The Mayor took up his hat from his lap and set it firmly back on his head as the steam carriage hissed to a stop. "Well, here we are. President's House. Showing her age, isn't she?"

Titus grunted and followed the mayor out into the street, leaving his assistant to tend to the carriage master. Showing her age was a kind way to say it, Titus thought. The house wasn't even ten years old yet, but already the wooden veranda was starting to sag and the floors inside all creaked something fierce when there was a ball or a dinner there. President Burleson had already purchased a tract of land and intended to have a proper mansion built on it one day, but so far he hadn't found the right architect–or funding for that matter.

"Do you think he's going to be amenable to our proposal?" Titus asked. The steps felt loose and spongy under his feet as they made their way up to the carved wooden door. A stained glass insert let them see the approach of a manservant on the other side.

Mayor Dundee's eyebrows bobbed on his forehead like a pair of stubby cigars. "Amenable? Certainly. The question is whether he'll follow through. Our President isn't cut from the Sam Houston cloth, and he'd as soon shoot an Indian as treat with one. But he has to realize Texas is extremely vulnerable right now. Since Moctezuma–"

The door dragged unevenly open before them and the mayor grew silent at the sight of the pair of livid letters FF burnt into the wrinkled black skin of the manservant's forehead. "The President has another caller, gentleman, and will receive you momentarily," he said in a thick West Indies accent. Titus and the Mayor acknowledged him with a nod and the spoken thanks due all those who'd turned back Santa Anna and his army of walking dead men at the Battle of the Alamo.

When he was gone, Titus spoke in a low tone that only Mayor Dundee could hear. "But we need an ally. The United States is too set on keeping its cotton gins spinning to go in with a haven for escaped slaves, Moctezuma sure as hell ain't a friend of ours, and the Indian tribes are the only ones who'd suffer worse than Texans if either of them decided to call us out to battle anytime soon."

Mayor Dundee tutted, inclining his head toward the drawing room door where President Burleson, pot-bellied and sporting a wavy mop of salt-and-pepper hair, beckoned them to join him within. Titus noticed that whomever he had been speaking to earlier must have exited some other way, though the room smelled faintly of perfume. A woman, then.

The President reached for each of their hands in turn. "Mayor, Brigadier-Justice, I apologize for keeping you waiting," said the man who'd freed the West Indies slaves and saved the Alamo. "To what do I owe the pleasure?"

"The Mayor and I have completed the review and inspection of Austin's defenses," Titus said, taking one of the cheroots and a light when offered. "And I've read the reports from our northern and southern border outposts. Ed, we're like a ranch with no fences."

Burleson swiped a hand back through his hair almost boyishly, but his voice was hard. "And you're worried them damn Indians or zombies are going to come through and steal all our women and chickens, is that it? Is that what I'm paying a Brigadier-Justice to do? Wring his hands over a pack of redskins?" He glared at Titus, then at the mayor.

Dundee paled and cleared his throat. After a beat, Titus responded. "No, sir. But you left off the United States. We can't go up against them if they decide to come back and collect all the runaway slaves we've let slip in. And that's a real possibility these days."

Burleson blew out a cloud of clove-scented smoke at the pair of them and fixed Dundee in his sights. The mayor found his voice. "What Brigadier-Justice Smoke means to say, Mr. President, is that we have nothing but enemies on all sides, and he and I"–he looked around as if he could badly use a strong brandy–"Well, we think that perhaps the time has come to make peace with one of them. At least until we rebuild our armies and get some decent artillery on our side."

"We're broke, I know," Titus broke in. The mayor thanked him with his eyes. Titus continued, "So it might take awhile 'till we get our feet back under us. If we were to sign a treaty with the United States–"

"Not a damn chance in this world!" Burleson exploded. "Texas will remain independent as long as I am President." He pointed a quivering finger at the ground, punctuating each of his next words: "And every black man in Texas will remain Freed Forever. Let 'em come!"

"They will," Titus said. "They'll come charging down the Mississippi and through Louisiana. Have us annexed before we can so much as get off a shot. You mark my words."

Burleson was silent, his face set.

Mayor Dundee cleared his throat again, playing his part to perfection. "We could always go in with the Mexicans, then," he offered timidly.

Before the President's face could redden any more, Titus said, "Moctezuma and all his zombies are just chomping at the bit to come back and carve off another little slice of the Republic. We don't need Laredo much, do we? Or anything south of the Nueces for that matter."

At that, Burleson scowled. "I know you'd like to forget all about what happened to your son in Laredo, Brigadier-Justice, but I'm not about to let our people fall back under Moctezuma's reign. Sooner lay down with a...I see where you're going with this, gentlemen. I see."

Titus tried to speak but Burleson interrupted him. "This meeting is adjourned, gentlemen. Adjourned. Reginald will show you out."

Mayor Dundee scurried toward the door, but Titus held his ground. He pulled a sheaf of papers from a breast pocket and laid it on the President's desk.

"What's that?" Burleson asked. The manservant Reginald was already opening the drawing room door and handing the mayor his hat.

"It's the death of Texas, Mr. President. And my resignation on top of it."

"Resignation!" Burleson cried, picking up the sheaf of papers. "I never figured you for a quitter, Brigadier-Justice. Never." He stared Titus in the eyes for a long moment then turned his attention to the papers in his hand. He tossed the first one, Titus's resignation, to the ground and stared at the ragged columns of figures written up in the former Ranger's unschooled hand.

"That's what we have for troop strength, horse, steam, and munitions, side by side with what all our potential enemies can bring to the field."

Burleson scanned the pages, shifting back and forth between them every so often. "Are these numbers reliable?"

"The best we have, but close enough to see how bad it could go. Worse, they're spread all over the damn country. Couldn't bring them all to bear on one enemy without a great deal of advanced notice. If we were to offer the Comancheria recognition and ally ourselves with them, we might have a chance to keep what we've won. We may call that land out there part of Texas, but we damn sure couldn't back up the claim if we had too. Why not give it up if it brings them to our cause?"

Burleson gave the pages one last glance then set them on the mantle of a cold and vacant fireplace. The mantle canted just a hair toward the door where the mayor's assistant stood waiting. Both he and the mayor stared at President Burleson expectantly.

"You serious about resigning if I don't consider treating with the redskins?"

"Yep. I'll take up a gun against whoever attacks us first. And if we're all real lucky, against whoever attacks us next. But I won't go down in history as the man responsible for killing the Republic of Texas."

"Let me think on this, Brigadier-Justice," Burleson said. "And in the meanwhile, your resignation is *not* accepted and I expect the next time I see you, you'll have set a plan on paper to make Texas a strong, independent military power."

"You think on it, but consider me resigned until you decide to treat with somebody." Titus nodded politely, put his cheroot out, and strode across the squealing floor. The mayor and the smell of his man's hair oil followed Titus out of President's House and into the midday sun. He didn't let himself smile until the steam carriage ground itself back down the cobbled drive into Austin.

CHAPTER 4

LIGHTNING DOVE STARED THROUGH THE FLAMES at the British General seated across from him. He could tell the man was uncomfortable, sitting cross-legged in the dirt, his bulk straining against a stiff red uniform. Brown dirt clung to the sweat on his face and colored his graying hair. Lightning Dove could not imagine a man more out of place on the frontier, and the thought gave him pleasure.

He could still scarcely believe that the Europeans had managed to take this land from its rightful owners in so short a span of time. What were they but worshipers of science and false gods? Soft men with more ambition than love. Indian magic had scared them off for a time, but it had not taken them long to realize that the source of magic was not an endless well. The land had to be nurtured, respected, or there would be no further gifts.

"We could not meet in the tents?" asked General Thackeray. "We must instead bear more of this damnable wind?"

"It is the wind that drives our endeavor, General. And the soil, and the water, and what's inside our souls. If that connection is lost, then so is this battle before it even begins."

"It doesn't take wind to power my army," the General scoffed.

"And yet it is the wind that carries your steam angels aloft. And the earth's own fire that drives your infernal machines."

"You were not so quick to insult our infernal machines when you came to us, begging for our help."

"The Comanche do not beg," said Lightning Dove. The wind sang the song of night, and the soil began to dance. "Your offer of support was timely, but you know as well as I that this *alliance* benefits your nation every bit as much as mine."

General Thackeray gave an unctuous smile. "Perhaps." He lifted a mesquite branch from the ground and stabbed at the fire. Sparks rose with a crackle. "Just remember that this alliance does not end when we've helped you take the rabble calling itself Texas. You can have this godless land, but you will lend your full support to our strike against the Americans. And I'll hear no more nonsense about the limited extent of your magic. I've seen what your shamans can do when they turn their minds to it. I trust your support of our cause won't become half-hearted."

"Is your soul so void of trust that you must badger me about Comanche support at every opportunity? You will have what magic the earth allows us, and no more. How much we are gifted is not for me to say."

The General leaned closer to the fire and leveled a hard stare at the old warrior. "Just know that it was not my choice to throw our fate in with your lot. I'd far rather sweep you from the plains like the dirt you are and attack the Yanks with the whole might of New Britannia. I'd rather side with the Texans, or even the Mexicans, but instead the Queen has commanded that you shall be our allies. I am not one to question Her Grace, but I cannot help but wonder if she has been deceived with regards to the extent of your powers."

"Speak to me with such contempt again, and you will find out."

Lightning Dove did not want to admit that his people needed these pale fops to win back their land, but he'd been unable to muster all of the tribes, and as mighty as the Warhawk tribe was, it was no match for the entirety of the Texan defense. Yet the Comanche spirit had only been attacked, not defeated. Lightning Dove would suffer no more of the General's slights, consequences be damned.

He returned the General's heated stare, and as expected, the man lowered his eyes and leaned back from the fire. He might wear the rank of General, but he was still no more than a common thief. All of them were. The English, the French, the Spaniards. Their kind had declared this land ripe for the taking. It was this turmoil that had splintered Lightning Dove's ancestors from their old tribe and driven them onto the hard plains. Forced them to learn the ways of the horse and the weapon. Turned many of them into wanton killers and insatiable horse thieves. And yet they'd been content for a time.

Until the Texans began moving into what small bit of land they had left.

Thieves, all of them. And what land had a more purloined history than this one? These Texans, so proud of their Republic, had originally settled amid the region's numberless rivers to live under the grace of a resurrected Moctezuma and his army of dead men. He had stolen the land too, but he was just another in a long line of rulers who'd claimed it for his own. And yet the Texans had not been satisfied. They'd bucked against Mexico's bridle, and ultimately risen to steal the land for themselves. Had that been enough to slake their thirst for land? No. They insisted upon having the lands to the west, the Comancheria. Lands they admitted were too harsh for them to live in. But still they wanted them.

So many of the People had given in to the whites, but not Lightning Dove. His tribe held the old ways. And because of this, the Great Spirit had sent them the tiny one. The girl. Others hadn't the faith to care for her, or the love to coax the magic from her being. Others would not understand what a momentous gift she was. She was a source of power undreamed of by his ancestors, and so long as the girl blessed them with her presence, the Warhawks would still have a chance to triumph.

"The irony of our situation is not lost on me," said Lightning Dove. "We intend to steal back what the thieves took from us. What your people originally took."

"England made no claims on this region."

"You are all the same, you men from across the ocean."

"Just as all of you redskins are the same?"

Lightning Dove considered this and waved the man's comment away with an aged hand.

The General grinned. "So why Texas? Why don't you want revenge on Mexico, or America? I would think they are both counted among your staunch enemies."

"We do not want the world. We only want a place to live. Make no mistake. This is not about revenge. It is about survival."

"So your source tells us that the attack must come with the eclipse?"

"No, we choose to attack during the eclipse. My source only confirmed that it would be an acceptable day to attack."

"Acceptable? When are you going to tell me who this source is?"

It was Lightning Dove's turn to smile. "That is unimportant information. It has no bearing on your quest for America, only on the Comanche defeat of Texas. When that is finished, then you shall choose our direction."

"So give me our current direction." The General looked uncomfortable again, his smugness temporarily reined in. He was not a man accustomed to taking orders from anyone, let alone those he considered no better than savages.

"We strike Austin during the dark day. Then we march on San Antonio. My source allows that the Texan's defenses are withering. Our combined might should have little difficulty taking them. If we hold those cities, we hold the Republic's heart. They will have a difficult time retaking what has been lost, especially when their neighbors hear of their sudden weakness."

"And if Mexico decides to march on us?"

"We will drive them back as well."

"And if the Texans muster their warlocks? The Freed men?"

"I do not fear their magic," said Lightning Dove.

"Neither did Santa Anna until he faced them at the Alamo."

Lightning Dove simply smiled wider.

Santa Anna had not been prepared for them.

Because Santa Anna did not have the little girl.

CHAPTER 5

TROY FELT THE FIRST DROP OF RAIN on his face and looked down at Smoke. "It's going to take you all damn week to dig us out of this pen, Smoke. And even then we won't be out of this." Smoke stared up at him in silence, all the while continuing with the heel of his boot, scuffing up handfuls of crumby dry soil with every kick and leaving them in a neat pile alongside. All just inches away from the woven organ pipes of their prickly cell.

And Lord help them both if he touched one of the cacti and set them off. Troy figured Smoke would ask him to help, but the son of a bitch hadn't so much as spoken since the Queen's men and the Warhawk tribe set off that morning.

"Why don't you just admit you done got us both killed, Smoke?" Troy felt himself crossing a line even as the rare desert rain began falling in earnest on Smoke's pitiful little hole and dirt pile. "Or do you only crow about shooting little girls?"

Smoke shot up from the ground, his eyes wild, teeth bared, two fists both cocked far behind his head. And then he stopped himself. Troy was ready for a fight, and a good one, but Smoke was skylarking at the clouds above him.

"Later." he snarled at Troy then dropped back onto the ground and began scuffing up more dirt from his hole. Troy watched Smoke work. He was breathing heavy and doing his damnedest to dig an escape hole, scooping out handful after handful of the dirt and in the parson's own hurry to get it done. Every so often he would stir up his growing mud pile and slap some of it onto his face or his hands.

The Llano does strange things to a man, Troy thought, slumping to the ground on the far side of the cactus ring. He opened his mouth and let the rain quench his thirst, one little drop at a time. No doubt about it. He was going to die out here on the hard plains with the same lunatic who had cost him his place in the Rangers.

She-Who-Is-Alone did not like the smells of the men in the red shirts, or of their machines. They made her nose clog up and her head feel like Coyote had put it sideways on her neck as a prank. She and her mother were the only females on this long hard ride and She-Who-Is-Alone missed spending time picking flowers or grinding the blue green stone into beads with her friends.

But Lightning Dove insisted she come with them into the white man's lands. She caught herself at that, glad she had not been speaking. Lightning Dove would strike her face if he heard her calling it the white man's land. He told her once that because she was young, she was especially dangerous to the tribe. *You do not remember how free the land was in the time before the Great Spirit put you into her belly. But we Elders must remember for the sake of the tribe, and teach you children also, that you might one day restore things.*

But he did not explain why the tribe needed white men to set the land free from white men, and when she asked, he merely scowled at her and reached for his pipe. *You are special among us. You have no father but the Great Spirit. One day you will understand.*

That day was no closer, even a year after he had said those words to her. At least as far as she could tell. The only thing that had gotten closer were the giant steel monsters the men in red shirts rode on, and the ones that had flown ahead of them to the end of the day's march to begin setting up camp. What had the elders called them? Steam Angels? Neither word made sense to her. It would have been more fitting to call them *Stink Metals*, a thought that made her cover her giggling mouth with her braids.

At last the ride came to an end and She-Who-Is-Alone gingerly dismounted from her mare between a ragged shelf of rocks and the small tipi her mother was already beginning to set the poles up for. She patted her mare on the nose, saying words of thanks to it for its service and rushed up to help, dodging the travois-dogs to get there.

Dancing Clouds smiled at her, setting her back to the task and grateful for the help. Before too long, they had the skins in place around the poles and the opening situated to let the morning sun greet them.

"I could go look for brush and wood for a fire," She-Who-Is-Alone said to her mother.

Dancing Clouds nodded and told her also to gather anything good to eat as well. "Look for the eggs of the lizards and anything to make this pemmican taste better, if you can."

"I will, Pia," she said.

"And return before the Great Spirit allows the sun to rest this time. The war chief is very concerned when he cannot look upon you."

"I will, Pia" she repeated.

She-Who-Is-Alone set off with her buffalo hide sack to see what gifts the desert would provide. Barely a hundred paces from the war party and all the Stink Metals, she realized she had already been given a gift: sweet, fresh air untainted by the red-shirted whites.

As the light began to fail, she found some bitter red berries beneath a stone sitting upon another and was surprised to see a single bluebonnet growing in the shade of the other side.

She plucked it with nimble fingers. "I thank the Great Spirit for giving me something to smell besides the white men!"

She did not feel the spider bite into her flesh at first, just wondered at the sudden dreamy sensation. Was Coyote playing with her head again? The world began to tilt farther and farther to one side and in that moment, just as all the light faded from the skies and her nose was full of dirt, she heard again the blue bird who cries "Jay! Jay" and a flutter of wings.

The shaman Broken Lance had told her that this bird had stood watch over her umbilical, keeping any creature from molesting it for seven days, and that when it flew away on the seventh day it took her umbilical with it, and that when the season turned, that place suddenly grew bluebonnets where none had grown before. *That is how we know what you mean to the Comanche and the future of the land, little one.*

Somewhere in the blackness, the bird was crying and her hand was aching and nothing Broken Lance or even Lightning Dove said mattered very much anymore. The tiredness stole upon her too quickly. The farther she fell into sleep the colder she felt inside.

The rain stopped as suddenly as it began and Troy gawked at Smoke. Hatless, the man had covered every inch of his face with mud and then did the same to his arms and his neck. Then he'd stripped off every stitch of clothing and folded it all neatly next to the hole he'd had dug in the ground. Smoke continued caking himself in desert mud.

When he appeared to be satisfied, Smoke lay on his back in the sun like he was waiting to die.

"What'd you go and get all dolled up for? Just me here and I don't care what you look like. I still ain't gonna dance with you."

Smoke grit his teeth and gave his head one controlled shake. "Later" was all he said. Then he lay there letting the mud bake and harden to him, apparently content to nap until death came to claim him.

Troy walked in tight circles, dodging his naked cellmate as much as he could. *He ain't crazy already, is he? The Smoke I knew never would give up and quit like this. So he's got to be up to something.* Troy had no idea what, but he stayed up half the night trying to figure it out.

Titus Smoke was reading a news sheet by candlelight when the Mayor's man rode up, dismounted, and stepped onto his porch. Titus peered through the window at him. Since his wife's death, dust was the only thing curtaining the window, and Titus preferred things that way. In such uncertain times, he liked to know what was coming before it had a chance to surprise him.

The Mayor's man–a Mr. Adolphus Pincher, late of Derbyshire, England–was said by his employer to be the finest manservant west of the Atlantic Ocean. His resume supposedly included service to a minor cousin of Victoria herself, though Titus often wondered how anyone could stand Pincher's unpleasant company for long.

Mr. Pincher saw Titus watching him through the window and inclined his head a fraction of an inch in greeting. The man was pale as a sheet, as if the blistering Texas sun was no match for the memory of London fog. An abundance of wax coiled his moustache into a pair of matching wings, and it looked like the well-tamed facial hair might break away from his lip and take to the sky at any moment. A starched shirt peered from the cuffs and collar of his black suit, and he held his bowler hat in both hands against his stomach.

Titus knew from experience the man would stand there motionless until invited in. He sighed, folded his paper and waved. "Get in here, Pincher."

Pincher opened the door by the window and stepped into the cabin. His eyes darted from a pile of unfolded blankets, to a fallen chair with two broken legs, to the crooked family photo with a crack in the glass. His nose twitched like a rabbit's, and his lips pressed together in a tight, false smile.

Titus didn't appreciate the man's silent disapproval of his home. His financial situation had certainly improved in the years since Cecilia's death, but he had no need for a larger place to live. And he had no desire to live in the city proper. His cabin was several miles west of Austin, and though the Comanche still raided in the region, Titus considered that more something to be excited about than something to be feared.

"Good evening, Mr. Smoke," said Pincher. "I apologize for the hour, but the Mayor was quite insistent that I call upon you tonight."

"What for?"

"I've a message for you, sir."

Pincher reached into his coat pocket and handed Titus a folded piece of paper. Titus pressed it flat on the table and squinted through his spectacles at the Mayor's loopy handwriting. He read it through. Then read it again.

Titus,

Burleson has delivered his verdict. Texas must stand alone against those who would ruin her. Please call on me tomorrow morning to discuss alternate courses of action.

Yrs. in honor,

Addison Dundee

"Son of a bitch!"

Pincher did not react to Titus' outburst. He simply stood in silence as Titus balled up the note and hurled it harmlessly at the window. Why was it that fools always rose to the power positions? There were no other courses of action and the Mayor knew that. If only Burleson had that much sense. Without allying itself with at least one of her foes, Texas' nationhood would be short-lived.

Pincher remained impassive.

"Why are you still here?" said Titus. "You've delivered your damned message. Now get!"

"Mayor Dundee has asked me to confirm your appointment for the morrow. Nine o'clock is his preference, but if you are unable to attend, an alternate time can be negotiated."

Titus pushed back his chair, grabbed Pincher by his stiff shoulders and ushered him through the door. He gave the man a shove and sent him stumbling off the porch. The unflappable Pincher gathered himself and turned an unconcerned expression toward Titus.

"Nine o'clock, sir?"

"Tell Dundee he and Burleson can discuss *alternate courses of action* until Moctezuma and Lightning Dove come to fight over their bones. I ain't having any part of it. When the history books write about the men who destroyed Texas, my name won't be among them."

"I will deliver your refusal, Brigadier-Justice."

Pincher placed his hat on his head, climbed into his saddle and turned his horse toward Austin.

"That ain't my title anymore!" Titus yelled after him. "And tell him not to come looking for me. I'm quitting Austin for good."

The sky was still dark as an undertaker's jacket when Troy heard Smoke getting up from the ground. Troy watched from beneath the hat he'd propped across his face as Smoke stretched carefully. It was odd the way he was doing it. Like he didn't want the hardened mud on him to brush off. Troy pretended to be sleeping.

Smoke stood before the hole in the ground and began filling it with piss. And as he did he kept repeating a phrase or two of one of the Indian languages. Nothing Troy could make out.

The smell of Smoke's piss overwhelmed Troy's nostrils and he kept making the same words over and over again. *Man has lost his mind.*

Troy was just about to tell him so when the pillars of cactus before Troy began to swell and bob. It was hard to make out at first, but then they just kept on bending like there was a stiff breeze about to knock them over.

No-about to part them like the Red Sea.

"Hot damn!" Troy shouted, jumping to his feet and tossing his hat into the air impulsively. "We're getting out of here!"

But his hat came to rest on the prickly wall behind him and as soon as it did, the opening that had been forming in front of Smoke's piss offering closed up tight as a schoolmarm's legs. Moonlight reflected off the pool of urine, until odd shadows of waving midnight green sewed themselves together above their heads, sealing out the moon and advancing down upon them.

"What the hell?" Troy started, but Smoke already had him by the back of his shirt collar and his empty gunbelt.

"You know what time it is?" Something in Smoke's voice made Troy's innards run cold. He felt Smoke shift his naked mud-caked body and tried–too late–to break free of the bigger man's grip.

"It's *later*," Smoke said, hurling Troy at the place where the cactus had been opening, using Troy's body to keep it from closing. Troy felt the hundred, no thousand stabs of cactus needles jabbing into every part of his body as something rustled overhead.

He felt something heavy on his back then. Smoke scurrying across him, Smoke, free of the cell and most of the cactus needles just bouncing off the mud caked to him like he was half-armadillo. He could barely keep his eyes open, the pain was so great, and the cactus was already closing up around him even more.

Smoke clambered to his feet outside the cacti and tore off running.

No goddamn way he's getting away from me now.

Troy mustered up his courage and burrowed his way out of the cactus, feeling the blood already oozing around his fingers, making them slippery as he forced himself to grab on to the next spiny plant and pull his body farther along.

He could feel the sting of the plant everywhere and knew he would be finding burrs in his clothes for days to come. But no way was Smoke getting away. With a burst of blinding pain and raw will, Troy yanked himself free. He looked up to see the cactus looming overhead and even the ground beneath him seemed to be trembling in anger.

"If you're coming, Tanner, you damn well better get moving," Smoke bellowed at him from somewhere in the distance. "Stand that big has probably got a root system over a hundred feet long."

Troy swallowed his surprise and sprinted in the direction of Smoke's voice. With every step he could feel the cactus needles rubbing against each other and driving themselves deeper into his skin. He ran until he caught up with Smoke's bare ass and then they both kept on running together until they were good and damn sure the ground was no longer rumbling beneath them.

CHAPTER 6

TRAVELING THROUGH THE LLANO barefoot and naked was preferable to rotting in the cactus prison, but not by much. Smoke wasn't sure how far they'd run to avoid the cactus' wrath, but by the time they'd pulled up, lungs heaving, the sun was creeping over the flatland to their backs. Now, it hung fat in the sky, and his shoulders were already beginning to redden.

"Heck of a plan you had there," said Troy, grinning.

Smoke had expected Troy to be mad, but the unlimited opportunities for taunting a naked man seemed to have mellowed him. Troy had always been an asshole.

"Weren't for me having bartered my way out of that fix once before, we'd both be stuck."

Troy's gaze seemed to reappraise Jeb. "Did you give any thought to what you'd do without your clothes?"

Smoke was embarrassed that he hadn't. "All I was thinking was to get out of there before we had to resort to cannibalism. You ain't got much meat and I figured you'd be too damned sour for my taste."

"Well, eating you wouldn't exactly be a treat either."

"I'll get some clothes in Austin. I can make it out here a few days."

"A few days by horse, maybe," said Troy. "Course, we ain't got any. I'm less worried about you burning up than I am getting to Austin before that army. Town will be burned to the ground by the time we get there."

Smoke sulked. He'd never been more uncomfortable in his life. His body was stiff with dried mud and hunks of the stuff cracked and fell from him as he moved. Each step drove more stickers into the soles of his feet, thirst was beginning to sting his throat, and to top it all off, he smelled like piss. Even worse, Troy was right. Texas might not have any use for him anymore, but it was the only home he had. And Lighting Dove meant to take it. His daddy was in Austin, what few friends he had left were in Austin, and above all else, Audrey was probably still in Austin. No matter what Troy thought, he wasn't a traitor, and he didn't care to see his country fall. All he'd set out to do was deliver one god damned message and now he found himself the middle of another uncomfortable situation that wasn't likely to end well.

Not to mention he was concerned for his own well being. It could take a week or more to get to someplace where he could find clothes, and the sun wasn't getting any cooler.

"At least we won't get lost," said Troy.

That was a fact. Lightning Dove's war party left a trail that a blind schoolgirl could follow. It wasn't the Indians – they could move a thousand men through this land without leaving so much as a bent stalk of grass. But the Redjacks' steam tech wasn't nearly as stealthy. The earth was grooved from the passage of the land vehicles and steam angel exhaust still hung in the sky like billowy arrows pointing the way east. Many stands of cactus and wide swaths of mesquite trees were flattened, and the air smelled unnatural. This was a land not used to machines.

They walked in merciful silence for at least an hour before Troy spoke again.

"More I think about it, the more I think we can catch these Indians."

"How do you expect us to do that?" asked Smoke.

"We move fast, get around them and get word to Austin before they can attack."

Smoke shook his head. "Hell, we could whittle us a pair of wings and fly there. What do you think?"

"I think you're a jackass."

"Yeah? You're the jackass if you think we can catch them Indians on foot."

"Think about it," said Troy, ignoring the insult. "Those big ground units they have move like snails. I bet they don't travel much faster than we do through rugged country like this. And getting all them Indians and all them Brits moving at the same time has got to be a chore. We walk fast, we might catch them by nightfall."

"Yeah? Well *you* walk fast," said Smoke. "I have burrs in my damned feet."

Troy grinned and picked up the pace.

Smoke cursed and hobbled after.

She-Who-Is-Alone woke to the sound of mesquite branches cracking in the wind. Her hand throbbed with pain and her throat was dry from thirst. A bed of bluebonnets lay crushed beneath her. She sat up slowly, disoriented by her situation and the blowing sand that painted the sky brown.

What had happened to her?

She remembered leaving her mother to search for firewood and hopefully for something to eat, and she remembered the Jay-bird, calling out at her with the Great Spirit's voice. Then the pain in her hand.

She studied her hand and grimaced. The back of it was swollen and purple, and she recognized it as the bite of a spider. Not deadly, but painful enough. Yet this should not have caused her to fall into an unwanted sleep. Surely this was the will of the Great Spirit.

She struggled to recall what the bird had been trying to tell her, yet the memory would not come. For some reason, the Great Spirit wanted her to bide her time in this place, and so she'd been stricken.

She stood and tried to gauge the time of day. It had been approaching dark when she left her camp, so this must be the following day. A suffocating sand storm raged around her, and the sun was only visible as a pale circle of light in the west, rendered a soft shade of gold by the storm. It would be late afternoon. She had slept a full day.

Her heart raced. Whether this was the Great Spirit's will or not, she was frightened to be so alone. Why hadn't the tribe come looking for her? And if it had, why hadn't they found her? Certainly the storm would hinder the search, but she hadn't traveled more than half an hour from camp.

She-Who-Is-Alone calmed herself and allowed that if the Great Spirit had delivered her into these circumstances, he would provide a path out. She had traveled due south of camp, so she began walking north.

Less than a hundred paces from where she'd started, a pair of figures appeared in the gloom. For a moment, they were dusty brown ghosts floating across the grass, then their voices carried to her on the wind.

"You just need to look at the positive side of things."

"And what the hell is so positive about a sandstorm? I can hardly see my damned hand in front of me."

"This sandstorm will probably save your hide from being cooked by the sun. You better hope it lasts all the way to Austin."

"That might be the case, but unless this sandstorm figures out how to whip us up a mess of biscuits, it ain't gonna matter."

Suddenly the figures came into focus and they were white men. One wore a nearly shredded shirt, and pants shot through with cactus thorns, and the other was naked and half covered with dried mud. The first white men she had ever seen had been the ones who traveled from beyond the mountains to the west to make war with their Stink Metals. They liked to wear outlandish clothes with golden ropes hanging everywhere and hats and boots as shiny as one of Raven's eyes. These two were nothing like that. She wasn't even sure they were real. The young men in her tribe often wandered the plains in search of visions, and she wondered if that's what was happening to her. It wasn't something that women did, but if the Great Spirit willed it, who was she to fight it?

She-Who-Is-Alone rubbed her throbbing hand and began walking quickly in the direction of the Great Spirits' peculiar messengers.

Jeb Smoke wondered for the thousandth time why any amount of money had compelled him to venture this far from civilization. Even in his Ranger days, he'd hated this place. Nothing but bitter cold, inhuman heat, scarce food and scarcer water. Rattlesnakes, cactus, sandstorms. He'd never understood why the Republic of Texas was so dead set on taking this godforsaken part of the world away from the Comanche anyway.

As far as he was concerned, the Indians could have it.

The blowing sand collected in his eyes, his teeth. Troy at least had a shirtsleeve to put over his face; Smoke had nothing but his bare arm. The dirt was so thick in the air, he wouldn't have been surprised if they walked right into the Indian camp they were trailing before they even caught sight of it.

When the little girl appeared suddenly from the haze, Smoke's heart nearly stopped.

He froze in place and Troy followed suit, immediately alert to Smoke's sudden tension. They'd Rangered together for a long time, and some habits never died.

"What is it?" Troy whispered. He obviously hadn't seen her yet.

"It's *her*," said Smoke, growing cold. But it couldn't be, could it? *That* girl was dead. Guilt grabbed him like the devil's fist and squeezed. Smoke had spent most of the last two years trying to forget Annabelle Sheppard and how still her body had been that day in the South Texas sage. The way her pale blue dress blossomed red from his bullet and the slow crawl of blood from one side of her mouth as the death rattle shook her. Jeb Smoke should have been a goddamned hero. Would have been if that bullet had been a fraction of an inch to the left. But instead, he was a ruin, and there wasn't anything in the world that could repair the damage. Dead or alive, that little blonde headed girl was with him every day, laughing and screaming and chattering inside his head until sometimes he wanted to shoot himself with the same gun that had done for her.

And now it appeared she wasn't content with that sort of torture any more. She was here in the flesh, and God knew what she had in store for him.

Smoke pointed at her and Troy spotted her at last.

"It's a little Indian girl," said Troy. "You think she wandered off from Lightning Dove's outfit?"

Smoke squinted at the approaching child and realized Troy was right. She was younger than Annabelle had been, and her wind-tossed hair was the color of starless night. She walked boldly up and greeted them with a smile. Relieved that his nightmares weren't manifesting themselves after all, Smoke couldn't help but smile back.

"Where'd you come from?" he asked in his broken Comanche.

"The Great Spirit," she said. "He sent me to you."

"What's she saying?" asked Troy.

"Shut up a minute," said Smoke. He resumed speaking to the girl. "Were you with Lightning Dove's tribe?"

She nodded. "Yes, but I think I'm on a vision quest. Don't you have any clothes?"

"I did have, but they're long gone. I mean to get some more."

"That's good," she said. "Even spirits need clothes."

"I ain't no spirit," he said, confused. "I'm Jeb Smoke."

"Where are you going, spirit?"

"Austin."

"I recognize that word," said Troy. He knelt down and peered into the girl's eyes. "Did you tell her where we're headed? I figure if she's wandering around, Lightning Dove can't be far. We need to move on."

"We can't leave her here," said Smoke.

"Course not. Especially now that you told her where we're headed. If she tells Lightning Dove we're out here, we won't be long for the world."

"I ain't talking about taking her prisoner," said Smoke. "Don't matter what she might tell, we can't just leave a little girl out here to wander alone."

"So you're interested in the welfare of little girls all of a sudden?" Troy scowled.

Smoke bit back a retort. They'd argued over his guilt or innocence in the death of Annabelle Sheppard a hundred times and Troy was never going to see the right of it. He'd rather condemn a man than help him find redemption. It was the kind of person Troy was. But Smoke *was* interested in the girl's welfare. No matter what men like Troy thought of him, he felt a certain responsibility in situations like this. Good men didn't leave little girls to die on the plains, not even Indian girls.

And despite all the evidence to the contrary, Jeb Smoke considered himself a good man.

"We'll take her to Austin," said Smoke. "I'd take her back to Lightning Dove, but I'd just as soon keep my skin."

Troy snorted. "You may not get a much better welcome in Austin."

"I didn't figure I would," snapped Smoke. "I know you've got the hangman's noose tied and fitted for me. Promise me at least you'll get me a decent pair of pants before you string me up in front of Audrey."

Troy laughed, and there was genuine amusement on his face. "You still holding out hopes she'll marry you after you run off? You never did have a lick of sense."

"Not much sense," said Smoke. "But I got hope."

The little girl watched their exchange with wide-eyed interest. "What are you arguing about?"

"Well, Troy here is an idiot," Smoke said in Comanche. "I'm just trying to help him understand that."

The girl nodded, as if that explained everything.

"My name's Smoke. What's yours?"

"She-Who-Is-Alone."

"Lord, that's a mouthful. You mind if I call you Darla? You look like a Darla to me."

"I don't mind," she said.

"Well then, come on, Darla," said Smoke. "Let's go to Austin."

CHAPTER 7

TITUS LEFT THE HOUSE AND FURNISHINGS in the care of one of Cecilia's older brothers, promising to write once he found a place to settle and have the things he wanted packed up and brought over. All he took with him was a bedroll, the rifle and pistol his Daddy had given him when he earned his star, plenty of ammunition, and enough rations to last him a week or so if he couldn't shoot enough to eat along the way.

The hot air was tinged with sage, but even so, it stung his nose just a little, like the mentholated rub they used at the barbershop after a shave. It was a good sting, and Titus savored it as Nebuchadnezzar clopped along the busy trail from Austin down to San Antonio. He patted Nebuchadnezzar's neck, trying not to think about how similar it was the color to Cecilia's long varnished mane. What was that old trail song? *A Good Woman's Like a Good Horse, Except When She's Better?* Something like that. Jeb would know it.

At the thought of Jeb, he clucked quickly to Nebuchadnezzar and touched spurs to his flanks. The stallion knickered and stepped up into a lopsided gallop. It wasn't fast enough to outrun the thoughts of his only son, the self-made fugitive out ranging the Comancheria for no reason worth owning up to.

Titus let his mount have its own way, hardly mindful of the wagons and horses and entire families passing him by on foot for the better part of an hour. Jeb ate up his thoughts like Sunday dinner. He considered heading west into the Comancheria to look for his son. No sense counting on a mildly capable man like Troy Tanner to bring him back. And even if Tanner was able to, at this point Titus had resigned his position and there was no looking back. Not to mention no chance of getting Troy reinstated.

He pulled Nebuchadnezzar to a stop, wheeling around behind a wagon full of children getting schooled by a stern little woman sweating beneath her bonnet. Titus pulled off his hat and came alongside the wagon. A big man with a burned red pate and no right leg sat on the bench beside the teacher but facing forward. He flicked a long switch against the haunches of two gray mares. Beneath him lay a knobby, polished crutch of sun-bleached wood.

"Hate to interrupt lessons," he said to the man with the stick. "But where's everybody headed?"

Nearly a dozen young faces gawked at Titus from the back of the wagon. The schoolmarm came to an abrupt stop in her arithmetic quizzing, her face set into a pruny scowl that looked to be permanent.

The big man tapped his switch against each of the horses before answering. He seemed to be weighing his words so as not to upset the children. "As far north as we can get before Moctezuma decides it's time to come callin' on the south of Texas. They been massing just south of the Rio Grande for the better part of a week now."

"You're sure of this?"

"Sure enough. Old Sylvester, one of the Forever Free that lived just off the river, he come into town and told everybody it was time to get the women and children out to safety. He figured Austin would be safe for now, but maybe up north of that if things get to looking ugly."

Titus swiveled his head to take in the scene on the trail. The wagons and horses were overloaded with women and children and old folks. He had three thoughts then, none of which he gave voice to. The first was that Austin wouldn't be safe for long if Moctezuma got the hankering for it. The second was that Burleson would likely send someone looking for Titus to press him back into service. And the last thing he thought was a word he hadn't felt compelled to use since Cecilia died. *Fiddlesticks.*

"Did Sylvester stay behind? Are they assembling a volunteer army?"

"Yes, sir. And yes, sir. They're callin' for all able bodied men to muster up at the Alamo mission." The man gulped. "Like before."

The schoolmarm did a good job of keeping her alarm from showing through her scowl. Titus had heard enough. He tipped his hat again. "My apologies for interrupting lessons, ma'am," he said as he rode off the western side of the trail. He could feel the eyes of the children and dozens of the other refugees on his back as he struggled with his own desire to go tell Burleson *I told you so, you damn fool.*

He nudged Nebuchadnezzar to keep angling southwest into the scrubby brown plain. His heart felt torn in too many directions, so he'd split the middle till he came to a decision. Maybe a foolish one, but a decision nonetheless. A renegade son up in the Comancheria, nothing to hold him in Austin, and a pack of zombies threatening Texas again from the south. *Fiddlesticks.* He turned Nebuchadnezzar south then north then south again. Did he really aim to enlist in the Texas Volunteer Army and hope nobody recognized him as Brigadier-Justice? Titus kept Nebuchadnezzar trotting a steady course against the flow of people streaming out of South Texas. The sage wasn't smelling so menthol sweet anymore and he was already reconsidering his resignation. *Fiddlesticks, Fiddlesticks, Fiddlesticks.*

Troy spat on the ground away from the Indian girl and away from Smoke's mud-caked nakedness. The temptation had been great for both of them to take a dip in the river not too far back, but with the turquoise eyes of the Indian girl on them every second neither Troy nor Smoke felt it would be the most Christian thing to do. Even so, the filthy brown water looked inviting.

It only got worse when they came to the place where the Llano joined up with the rushing Colorado. From here the river would wind its way down to the Gulf, and from the looks of it, the Queen's men and Lightning Dove intended not to stray too far from the river, their steam gear needing a constant supply of water to keep covering ground. Troy snorted. More like plowing and aerating ground, the way their broad, chewed-up track looked.

"What's so funny, Tanner?"

"Never mind, Smoke. Just thinking about the way this river runs."

Smoke started, then an indifferent look passed across his face. He had an idea but he didn't aim to share it. Fine. Let him keep his secrets. Probably had some un-Christian thoughts about the Indian girl, too. Walking around bare-ass in front of her, like that. Not that he had much of a choice at the moment.

But what kind of idea could Smoke have? Apart from jumping into that river and washing the dirt off his sorry carcass. The river was full and clear, apart from the occasional clump of dead wood rolling along its slow course past the big hill of Austin and out into Matagorda Bay.

Troy stopped in his tracks. He looked up at Jeb Smoke cackling. "I'm on to your–"

Smoke was shaking his head, his body a tense crouching mountain cat. One hand waved a warning. It was all Troy needed to shut up and save his remarks for later.

"Darla, you stay here," Smoke whispered to the Indian girl. Then he said something in Comanche which was probably the same thing. The Indian girl said something back to him and he glared at her. Another brusque interchange followed and Smoke beckoned for Troy.

Troy scrambled over to Smoke's side, low and agile enough to surprise himself, given all the cactus burrs still stuck in his clothes. "What?"

Smoke nodded past the stand of riverside trees ahead of them. A narrow trail of white vapor made a hazy line into the sky. "Somebody fell behind," Smoke said.

Troy let his voice drip with sarcasm. "Well, by God, I guess we ought to send Darla on up to them and they'll get her safely along to Lightning Dove. I'm sure she won't say one word about us two escaping from her chief's cactus trap."

Smoke bit his lower lip a moment before speaking. "She don't want to go. Says the Great Spirit means for her to stay with us."

Troy laughed. "Well, I don't give a damn what she wants, but it's nice when it coincides with what I want. *We* are going to sneak past them on the Colorado tonight–You didn't think I'd think of that, did you?–and she is going to be gagged the whole time, and *we* are going to warn Austin that Lightning Dove is on the way with a pack of Redjack steam gear." He spat again, this time right at Darla's feet. "No offense, Miss Darla."

Smoke gave him a look like a summer thunderstorm brewing on the range. "Supposing we were able to sneak past whoever's up ahead there...what about the main force? How do you plan to sneak past the entire war party? And what do you intend to use to float on, anyhow?"

Troy scowled at him, but had to admit he hadn't thought it through all the way. "So what do you recommend, crack shot?" The jab was unnecessary, but it hit Smoke just the way Troy wanted it to. Took some of the cockiness out of Smoke, being reminded of the one time he should never have missed. Troy felt justified bringing it up, if only for the way it took some of that looming storm out of Smoke's eyes and replaced it with–what? Sadness? Regret? Troy doubted Smoke was capable of either one of them, but regardless, he found he had to look away from Smoke's sunburned face.

Smoke cleared his throat and sighed through his nose a time or two. Finally, he spoke. "One, don't you *ever* call me that again, you hear?"

He said it so loud and deep that Troy worried about the Redjacks down the river hearing him.

When Troy said nothing, he repeated it. "Do you hear?"

The Indian girl watched the pair of them with interest.

"I hear."

"Good," Smoke said. "And second, I ain't going another day without a bath, some boots and fresh clothes on my back. A good hat would be too much to ask for. We're going to take them Redjacks up ahead one at a time if we have to, and we're going to get us some weapons and maybe a ride."

Troy shut his own gaping trap, opened it, and shut it again. Smoke was crazy. This went beyond piss and Indian magic by the light of the moon. This was life-threatening lunacy.

"And Darla's going to help us do it, aren't you Darla?"

The little Indian girl blinked at him, clearly not understanding a word of it. But Troy was starting to get the idea.

"I sure hope she can swim," he said.

She-Who-Is-Alone listened to the plans of the naked white man, whom she had taken to calling Wind-at-Night for the way he barely made a sound when he chose not to and the soothing effect his words had on her. She understood now that he was the one sent by the Great Spirit, and she could tell that the Great Spirit wanted her to help Wind-at-Night as he would help her. She could tell by the way the birds who cry "Jay!" had begun swarming into the trees above them as he spoke, calling at her in a way that left her certain she was meant to trust the naked white man and his spitting friend. She had named that one Barking Spider in her mind.

She plunged herself into the water and felt the current begin to pull her almost immediately. It was less than a bowshot from shore to shore here and it only took a dozen strong strokes to bring her out to the middle of the river. Overhead, the blue birds kept crying "Jay!" almost as if they were in a frenzy, or trying to warn her. But what could there be to warn her about? She was doing the Great Spirit's bidding. Then she realized: the Great Spirit must have ordered the birds to help her with Wind-at-Night and Barking Spider's plan. They were making so much noise so that the white men in the red shirts would be sure to see her.

She swam hard with the current toward the white trail in the sky, surprised at how quickly her hand had healed from the day before. Occasionally, her feet would brush the bottom or a turtle would dive away from the commotion she was causing in the water. Random bits of dead wood and soft strings of vegetation brushed against her legs. She was grateful the water ran mostly clear in this river.

She-Who-Is-Alone felt the river's voice lulling her softly downstream like a mother crooning to a fretful child. Ahead the plumes of white grew larger. Lightning Dove had told her that this was the breath of the Rain God's children, free at last from the white men's stink metal. But Lightning Dove had told her many things.

The jays above her were calling louder and louder, doing the Great Spirit's work for her. Already, the commotion had brought a pair of red-shirted soldiers to the river bank. They had their thundersticks aimed above her head at the circling swarm of birds, but had not seen her yet.

She-Who-Is-Alone took a deep breath and prepared to scream. Her arms thrashed in mock terror and then real as she felt a sharp pain in her right foot. She reached out with one hand at a bit of floating debris to help keep her head above water despite the overwhelming urge to curl herself up into a little ball. Her throbbing foot bounced along the river bottom, and she saw a long skinny shadow moving away from her in the depths.

She had been bitten by a snake. Even as the realization sunk in, she felt her brain becoming cloudy and dark and all of her senses muffled as if by an enormous hide blanket. Her eyes squeezed shut in pain, even as she heard a rumble nearby. A second later, the crashes of thunder began in earnest. There were no flashes of light to go with them all, or none that made it through her closed lids. She could not understand why she felt no rain on her face either, just dozens of talons tugging at her hair and the soft batting of little wings all around her. She would surely ask Broken Lance about this miracle, whenever she saw the shaman next.

"Just like old times, ain't it, Smoke?"

"Shut up, Troy. She's going to be making that distraction any second now."

The pair of them edged closer to the Redjack camp, wriggling on their bellies through the sparse vegetation so as not to be seen. Smoke would have preferred it if they were to come at the Queen's men from different angles, and even more preferred it if his pecker wasn't dragging in the dirt, but neither of those could be fixed. Troy was too damn stubborn and suspicious to split up, and when you were crawling naked as a jaybird across the ground that's just what happened.

Jaybirds. Smoke did not want to think about how they'd started filling the trees as he explained to Darla what he wanted her to do. There was something spooky about that girl, about the way she had just shown up out of the desert, the weird bond he felt with her, like he was meant to protect her. And it wasn't just because of Laredo, was it?

Ahead, Smoke could just make out the gray metal of the Queen's steam gear through the skinny cedars and mesquite. Lazy soldiers moved about the camp, and the smell of beef and onions cooking permeated through the stink of oil and steam. All it would take was a little noise from Darla to focus their attention on the river... That and a whole lot of luck.

Smoke adjusted his privates again and scooted a little farther away from a large red ant hill. Troy snickered.

A second later, a shot rang out, and after that, a half dozen more. Horses knickered and whinnied in fear. One galloped past them, nearly running Troy down. Without thinking,

Smoke stood and ran straight for the camp. He heard Troy curse and the sound of the faster man's heavy footfalls and breathing catching up.

"It damn well better not go like last time," Troy huffed, passing him.

And just like that Smoke was among them, reaching around a surprised Redjack and grabbing his rifle. Smoke swung the rifle like a club, knocking the soldier out. Two more went down the same way. None of them were even looking in his direction. But they weren't looking toward the river either. Smoke stared past them, incredulous, even as Troy opened fire with an English pistol on everything in sight. Well, almost everything. He didn't waste any bullets on the trio of men with bloody chasms where their hearts used to be. The Redjacks had already used up enough ammunition on that worthless prospect.

Zombies! What were they doing this far north of Tenochtitlan? The only Redjack with a sword was the officer, hardly more than a scared boy who held it all wrong for the kind of work zombie killing called for. He was already sobbing and sniffling as he swung his blade wide.

Smoke felt bad for him, but worse for himself. Naked, dog-tired and now zombies? Troy shouted, grabbing up a rifle with a bayonet on it from another downed Redjack. "What the hell did you get us into now?"

Smoke gave a grim little smile and ran toward the officer. The harried man froze at the sight, as if a naked Texan was more to be feared than a trio of undead. He may have been right at that. "Take off their heads, you Limey sonofabitch! Take off their heads!"

The Redjack officer hacked viciously to the left and right but the distraction had given one of the zombies a chance to get around behind him.

Smoke ran and jumped feet first, knocking one of the zombies down and grabbing another by the head, baring its neck for the officer's blade. Troy galloped toward the river, where two more Queen's men were busy making all kinds of noise and not at all interested in what was happening to their fellow troops.

The officer understood what Smoke had in mind but didn't follow through in time. The zombie behind him reared up and tore off the man's ear with its sharp dead fingernails. The officer went white and panicked, fluttering his sword behind him like he was twirling an umbrella over his shoulder.

Smoke twisted the zombie's head in his hands, feeling the gruesome pop of gristle leaving bone. The smell of death bubbled up from the zombie's neck. Smoke would have vomited then and there, if he had anything in his stomach. Instead he threw the torn-off head at the creatures behind the officer, distracting the pair of them.

Out of the corner of his eye, he saw the zombie he had knocked over struggling to its feet. Damn, they were awful fast for dead folk. Troy fired off two quick shots and hollered something Smoke could not make out.

The officer went down, white eyes blinking like a frightened deer, and the zombie on him turned its grisly attention to Smoke. One in front of him, one in back of him. And what the hell was taking Troy so damn long? Were there more zombies by the water? Would Darla know to keep on swimming?

Smoke felt the wind blow against his sweating skin, chilling him. He felt slick and dirty and chewed up. He stung from the cactus in a thousand little places where the mud had not protected him.

But he was still better off than the dead Redjacks.

He grabbed at the officer's sword and realized the man was still alive, just lying there too scared or low on blood to move. And the man wasn't letting go of his sword.

Smoke took his pistol instead, jerked it clean from the holster. He pulled the trigger four times before the empty clicks registered. The zombie behind him was upright now and turning his way. The one in front leered at him as it advanced.

Smoke threw the useless gun at the officer's head and snatched the sword out of his hand when it hit him. He jumped and scrambled up a set of metal rungs onto the huge tracks of the steam conveyance, a detached part of him noticing the moniker LEVIATHAN 212 stenciled in neat black letters onto the finished steel. He felt a cold hand on his ankle and kicked it off, feeling satisfied at the crunch of bone and sickened by the rip of flesh under his bare foot.

He wiggled around to see the two zombies trying to climb up after him. From this higher vantage point, it was easy to see Troy, surrounded by bluejays and Redjack corpses and huddled over something by the riverbank.

Smoke felt fury building in him like a hot water geyser. As the first zombie hand reached above the treads at his feet, he chopped it off. Then the other. The zombie fell backward, unable to hold on to the rails anymore. It turned in Troy's direction, sniffing like a coyote. Smoke arced the sword down hard at the other zombie's neck as it came up the ladder, one worried eye cast toward the curious scene on the riverbank even as he did.

The officer's saber was more a ceremonial blade than a utilitarian one. The flesh and bone that held the zombie's head in place took five more good gashes before it finally slipped to the side, hanging by a leathery strip of skin like a smokehouse ham. The zombie fell to its knees. Smoke jumped on it, knocking the thing down for good and charged the handless zombie as it blundered its way toward Troy.

Smoke made short work of that one. In the silence that followed, he ran to the water's edge. Troy was crouched next to Darla. The girl was unconscious, with an improvised tourniquet made from one of the soldier's belts wrapped just below one knee. He had her heel in his mouth, sucking.

Sucking and saying nothing.

The sour man looked a little green, and his black pebble eyes were cloudy and distant. Overhead, hundreds of voiceless blue birds waited, holding their breath. Darla lay too still, reminding him of another little girl whose time had run out on Smoke's watch.

Troy spat, and didn't say a word. He didn't have to.

CHAPTER 8

OUTSIDE LAREDO, 1848

Smoke lay flat on his stomach, peering through the sage at the men around the campfire. A few of the bandits were living men; a few of them were zombies. Not that it mattered. They rode together and they'd kidnapped the little girl. Every one of them had an appointment with a bullet or a noose. It didn't matter that they were a few miles south of the border. Texas law had a long reach.

The living men laughed and told stories in Spanish while the zombies sat apart, watching the shivering little girl with their customary empty expressions. Their eyes were milky pools, and it was impossible to tell if they even knew the girl was there. One of them moaned, scratched a leathery patch of loose skin on his cheek. The little girl whined and struggled against the ropes binding her wrists and ankles.

Her name was Annabelle Sheppard and she was the daughter of Andrew T. Sheppard, the enterprising owner of four livery stables in three different South Texas towns and more cattle than any one man had business owning. A man like that had the President's ear; that's why Smoke and his crew had been pulled away from their normal life of hanging horse thieves and chasing off Mexican bandits to bring back his daughter. But he also had plenty of enemies south of the border, particularly the Mexican ranchers whose farms he raided for livestock, and they'd apparently grown tired of losing their animals. The men sitting around the fire, heedless of their surroundings and apparently unafraid they were being followed, didn't seem like the most capable sort, but they'd managed to slip through the girl's window and steal away with her before Mr. Sheppard could find his rifle and chase them through the streets of Laredo in his dressing robe.

"That's her," whispered Troy. "The little girl."

Smoke sighed. Troy was over fond of saying things that went without saying, and that was the least of his annoying habits. While Smoke had approached the camp in near silence, he was surprised that the noise Troy made crawling behind him hadn't alerted Moctezuma himself. But somehow the bandits hadn't heard them, or at least they were doing a good job of pretending they hadn't. Smoke had his pistol out ahead of him, waiting for the rest of the crew to ride in from the South. They were supposed to be circling the camp. The rest of the boys would whip up some noise with their horses riding in and Smoke and Troy would take them unawares from the North. It was a poor plan, but Smoke knew from experience that Captain Calloway wasn't much of a planner.

"Where's the Captain and the boys?" asked Troy.

"How the hell do I know?" said Smoke. "Keep your voice down. They'll be along directly."

"You can't order me to shut up. You're just as low on the totem pole as I am."

"I ain't ordering, I'm strongly suggesting. Unless you want them bandits to figure out they have us outnumbered by more than a couple."

Troy snorted. "You're supposed to be such a damn good shot, why ain't you already just killed 'em all?"

"Because I don't own no damn rifle and the country don't pay me enough to buy a good one," said Smoke. "I might could hit 'em from here with my pistol, but it would be tough."

"Bullshit! You couldn't hit them Mexicans with no damn pistol. Not from here."

"I said it would be hard, didn't I? Why the hell–"

Gunshots cracked in the Mexican night and hooves thundered against hard packed soil. It sounded like an army was coming, but Smoke knew better. There were four other rangers in all, and Captain Calloway hardly warranted that affectation. His brother was some big-wig in Austin and for that he'd been given a command he was utterly unsuited for. Still, his plan had the desired effect. All attention in the camp was lured to the south. Smoke rose from hiding and bolted toward the camp. Troy followed him with far less enthusiasm than the situation warranted.

The chief problem with Calloway's plan, as Smoke saw it, was the fact that it all but invited the bandits to murder the girl. Scaring the hell out of them and attacking from all sides might win them the battle – if they were lucky – but what was to stop them from putting a bullet through the girl's frilly yellow dress before the Rangers could liberate her? So Smoke ran at top speed, got a bead on the closest bandit, and fired. The bullet punched through the back of the man's head, spun him sideways and into the campfire. His clothes caught at once and the terror in the Mexican camp turned to full-fledged panic.

These men worked for money, not loyalty, and whatever they'd been paid wasn't enough to tackle unknown enemies firing at them from the darkness beyond their camp. The three living men remaining ran for their horses and Smoke took one down, shooting from the hip. Troy rained bullets into the camp, but there was no accuracy to it, and Smoke yelled at him to stop before he shot one of the other Rangers, or worse, Annabelle Sheppard. The horsemen rode hard into camp, scattering the zombies and stirring up a screen of dirt that blinded Smoke as he reached the circle of firelight.

Men cussed and called out, and he recognized Calloway's gruff voice yelling for someone to grab the girl. Smoke had tried to keep his eye on her, but the arrival of the horseman had disoriented him. Troy came up behind him, screaming in his ear about zombies. Then Smoke saw them, attacking the horsemen with sabers, hacking at legs and ankles as the startled men struggled to shoot. Bullets passed right through the zombies and they didn't slow. It was well known that you had to hit their brains or spine, yet Calloway and the others seemed to have forgotten all of their training. There were at least seven zombies, and three of them pulled the inept Captain from his mount before he could loose his special issue saber and defend himself. They slit his horse's throat then went at the Captain with their swords. By the time Smoke dropped his pistol in his holster and drew his saber, the Captain was dead.

"Find the girl!" he yelled at Troy, then launched himself at the suddenly ravenous zombies. They squealed like squashed kittens as they gorged on the Captain. Others were trying to dismount Sonny Blue and the new kid, Little Bo. Clyde Flowers hunched dead in his saddle, run though with a blade. Smoke beheaded the closest zombie, and the others reluctantly pulled away from their feast and came at him. They were fast, almost impossibly so. Smoke's strong suit was shooting, not sword fighting, and he figured he could hold his own against one of them for maybe a minute. Against two at once, he was in serious trouble.

Smoke parried a clumsy hack and fought back with a howling strike that caught the enemy on the forearm. The second zombie was trying to circle around him, jabbing with the point of his sword, and Smoke slashed to the side, forcing the creature back a step. The blow he'd landed on the first zombie's arm wasn't serious, and the monster renewed its attack. Its blade crisscrossed the air, and Smoke hissed in frustration as he was backed into a defensive posture, fighting with all of his agility to keep up with the zombie's raw speed.

His boot heel hit a rock and he stumbled. The ground came up fast to meet his ass and he barely managed to block his opponent's aggressive downswing. The thing raised its blade again, and Smoke could read the utter satisfaction in its grin, the pure savage triumph. Then a silver streak crossed its rotted throat and its head fell away. Little Bo watched in wide-eyed terror as the rest of the zombie's body followed the thing to the ground.

Smoke climbed to his feet. The kid had apparently killed the two zombies who'd been trying to unhorse him then came after the ones chasing Smoke. He'd taken both unawares, not only beheading the meaner of the two, but severing a leg from the other one. Little Bo was a mess of bloody gashes and looked like he might start crying before long, but he was alive.

The one-legged zombie clawed through the dirt, dragging its sword in a desperate attempt to kill whichever one of them came the closest. But his supernatural speed was useless from such a compromised position, and Smoke ended the monster's un-life with a few quick cuts.

That left only two, and both of them were busy eating Sonny Blue. The Ranger had joined Clyde and the Captain in death, ripped down from his horse, hacked up by zombie swords and claws, reduced to little more than meat and shredded clothing. Smoke indicated that Little Bo should follow him and together they moved quietly into position and killed both zombies before they had a chance to finish their grisly suppers.

Troy appeared beside them, his sword a clean swath of steel catching the firelight. He had a few dime sized drops of blood spattered against his shirtsleeve, but otherwise he looked like a man who'd managed to avoid yet another conflict in close quarters.

"Where is she?" asked Smoke, fighting to get his breath back. Captain was dead and Little Bo wasn't yet old enough to rate a straight razor. That left Troy or Smoke to take the reins of the mission, and Smoke knew where that responsibility would doubtlessly fall.

"I can't find her," said Troy, looking put out. "She was there, then the dirt got all kicked up and the zombies came running and hell if I know which way she went. She's probably run off in the darkness somewhere."

"Damn it!" said Smoke. If Troy couldn't fight, the least he could do was keep track of one god damned little girl. "She can't have gone far. Spread out and call for her. Take heed, though. Them other bandits are likely still out there."

"Won't have to do that, Mr. Smoke," said Little Bo, pointing out past the campfire. "There she is."

Beyond the camp smoke, a lone bandit had Annabelle Sheppard tucked under one arm and he was trying to get a foot in the stirrup of Little Bo's spooked horse. The girl thrashed, but the man had a good grip on her and she had little hope of wriggling free. Smoke broke into a run just as the man's leg swung over the saddle. He was a strong son of a bitch, carrying the girl like that. She kicked and squealed but the man just ignored her, snatched up the reins with one hand, and spurred the terrified horse into the darkness.

Night began closing around them like the devil's fist, and Smoke knew if he didn't take the bandit down before they disappeared completely, they'd have little hope of finding the girl before morning. If he went for his horse, he'd lose them to the night, so the only option left was to drop the bandit from his saddle with his pistol. He was a celebrated shot; even Troy admitted it, though with no small amount of irritated jealousy. But hitting a rider moving away with only a campfire to guide the eye was no mean feat.

There was no time left to think. Smoke pulled his pistol, took a second to aim. Then he fired.

Lesser hands with a gun wouldn't have noticed the slight pitch in the wind, the way the night seemed to sigh just as he pulled the trigger, a mocking exhalation that assured his shot would go just wide of the target, somewhere to the side of the man's rapidly disappearing back. But Smoke knew all of this, before the bullet even left the pistol's barrel.

Annabelle Sheppard screamed and the bandit dropped her to the earth. Smoke ran toward them both, putting more bullets in the air as he did so, each one hitting the bandit square in the middle of the back. The rider pulled rein and spun around, and only then did Smoke realize he'd been shooting at a zombie. He fell to his knees by Annabelle's side, choked back his horror at the fount of blood pouring from the bullet hole he'd put through her chest. The other Rangers screamed something at him from the campsite, but he couldn't make out the words over the stamping of the horse's hooves and the girl's raspy coughs as she struggled for breath.

The zombie could have fallen on him then, taken his head and his life, and that might have been for the best. But instead it watched the scene play out, thinking god-knows-what behind it's hollow, impassive stare. The boys put a few more bullets into the thing, but it didn't move. Smoke raised his eyes and stared the monster down, making mental entreaties to either leave him alone or put him to death.

"What the fuck are you looking at?"

A smile broke across the zombie's face, the only hint of emotion Smoke had ever seen one of the creatures wear.

He lowered his head and prayed he'd never see a smile like that again.

The horse stepped into a trot and by the time Troy and Little Bo worked up the nerve to approach, the zombie was lost in the darkness. Little Bo knelt beside Smoke, took off his hat.

Troy stood over the scene like the shadow of death, pistol hanging limp at his side, face slack with shock.

"God damn, Smoke. You went and killed that girl."

CHAPTER 9

LIGHTNING DOVE KNELT IMPATIENTLY by the edge of the river, watching as Broken Lance communed with the earth. The old medicine man emitted an atonal hum as he pushed around a pile of bones and snake rattles with a chipped arrowhead. The river conversed with the leaves, and Lightning Dove listened intently, as if he might divine the girl's whereabouts from the secrets they shared.

But he was a war chief, not a shaman, and to his ears the wind was just the wind. Broken Lance cocked his head, hummed deeper. A rangy, gray man who'd been old before Lightning Dove had first drawn breath, Broken Lance awed the elders and terrified the faithless. His one cloudy eye and eerie ways caused some to think him a witch, but Lightning Dove knew better. He knew how rigidly the man adhered to the old ways. Broken Lance had told him he'd be war chief before he'd ever taken up a bow. He'd predicted the Texan's victory over Mexico and how they'd set their sights on the Comancheria. And it often seemed he could speak with the animals. If anyone in the tribe could find She-Who-Is-Alone, it would be him.

When Lightning Dove had learned of the girl's disappearance, he'd struck Dancing Clouds across her teary face in his rage. Hadn't she been tasked with taking care of the girl? Certainly She-Who-Is-Alone was an extraordinary child and the responsibility for her care was great, but a mother must be able to look after her daughter. Particularly when that mother is a virgin and the child was put in her womb by the Great Spirit. Few in the tribe understood the girl's importance, but Dancing Cloud did.

Dancing Cloud wailed her sorrow, but her voice had fallen silent against the rush of blood in Lightning Dove's head and his furious barking of orders. How many young men had he sent to search through brush and gullies and the seas of grass that began growing this far to the east? A dozen or more. And yet there had been no trace of her, not even a track to follow, and these were men who would have seen one if it existed. She'd simply disappeared, and that worried Lightning Dove more than anything else. It supported his notion of supernatural interference in his plans, and he could not fathom the Great Spirit's motives for such a game.

Ultimately, he'd had no choice but to move on, leading his people and their damnable white conspirators closer to the Texan settlements. Waiting any longer might cause them to miss the dark day, and that couldn't be countenanced. If the Great Spirit had seen fit to deliver the girl to them, then there was a reason he'd taken her away again. He was there to protect the People, not toy with them. And as everything Lightning Dove had planned was in service to the People, he would trust that the girl would find him again in his time of greatest need. It could be no other way.

Still, he could not help asking Broken Lance to seek the girl with his ghost mind. And though he'd passed several evenings watching the old man toil at his magic, he'd been disappointed every time. Broken Lance would lift his hazy eyes and focus them on Lightning Dove, shake his head slowly and retire to his tipi. The Great Spirit kept the girl well hidden. Lightning Dove began to wonder if he was being punished for siding with the British and relying on the strength of their war machines rather than the pure power of the deity's gift.

Never in his years had he felt such fear and indecision.

Broken Lance whistled and his head snapped up. A wide toothless smile broke the serenity of his features and he stood at once. Lightning Dove climbed to his feet and stared into the old man's inscrutable eyes.

"I have your answer," said Broken Lance.

"You know where she is?"

"No. But I know that we need not seek her. She will find us when the Great Spirit wills it. She follows her name and walks alone, though perhaps there are spirits to guide her steps. You have known this in your heart all along, have you not? Trust in the Great Spirit and he will provide. You lead these men and let him lead their souls."

With that, Broken Lance returned to his tipi and Lightning Dove stood at the river's edge, feeling at once relieved and slightly chastened. The simple act of commanding Broken Lance to search for the girl showed how unworthy he was of the Great Spirit's charge. Losing the girl was a test, but he would prove in the coming days that he was the great man they all thought he was.

He knelt in the hardened mud and prayed, begged for forgiveness. Then he returned to the fire and began making his final preparations for the sack of Austin. The loss of the girl's power would certainly hinder him, but the war mages had enough spirit in them to make short work of the untrained resistance they were likely to meet in their first battle. The Texans feared the Mexicans far more than they did the Comanche and the bulk of their military would be looking to the south, stationed in San Antonio. It was there they would need the girl and her strength. But that gave Lightning Dove plenty of time to prove his worth, to reclaim the gift he'd allowed to be lost. He would take Austin and deliver it to the Great Spirit. Surely then the girl would be returned.

Dusty outriders rode into camp as they did every night with news of yet another outlying settlement. They were mostly lonely farms and ramshackle cabins. Rarely did one find two buildings within sight of one another so far from the cities. The farmers and hunters that made their livings on the edge of the plains offered no threat to Lightning Dove and his people, but they had to die nonetheless. They could not be allowed to warn Austin.

As he had with the few other farms they'd encountered, Lightning Dove ordered them burned, their occupants slain. The heart of Texas would not know it was being cut out until the last possible minute, and Lightning Dove would hold it in his hands until the blood ran down his arm and the pitiful thing finally refused to beat.

CHAPTER 10

MAYBE NEBUCHADNEZZAR COULDN'T KEEP UP the same rapid pace all day like a steam mare, but when it came to warning a man of things sneaking up in the dark, Titus would take a flesh and blood mount any day of the week. It had to be at least a few hours past midnight, from the look of the stars overhead, a time when every law abiding man and decent creature ought to be snoring cozy in their beds and dens. Whatever had got the horse's dander up wasn't likely to be either law abiding or decent.

Another soft snort from the stallion and the sound of one hoof stamping. No owls hooting, no coyotes yipping or peccaries rooting around. No night bugs buzzing, not even a hint of wind. Titus listened so hard his ears rang and the sound of his own quickening heart nearly deafened him. Too quiet, and that meant whatever was out there was a predator, and most likely a hungry one.

Titus reached slowly for his pistol, grimacing as the bones in his wrist and elbow popped like burning mesquite. He felt as wooden as the polished cherry handle of his six shooter, but he took comfort in the familiar way it fit his hand anyway.

He squinted into the dark, forcing himself to take deep breaths and just wait. A tease of a breeze kicked up and he caught a whiff of something sickly and sweet like night flowers gone putrid. It was a smell he knew well from over twenty years of wearing a Ranger star. Flesh long dead, but still moving.

And this far north already. Goddamn Burleson. Titus was sure he could take one or two zombies, but not knowing how many were out there he wasn't about to call attention to himself and bring down a pack of twenty. He waited for a tense half hour or so, never catching wind of the dead men again. Even Nebuchadnezzar had finally settled down. He was just about to close his eyes again when the night exploded into gunfire.

Two shots in quick succession somewhere off to the south, then before the echoes had even died down, two more. The stillness of the night after that was even more deafening than before. Then a hoarse voice began shouting something incomprehensible. Before he knew it, Nebuchadnezzar was saddled up and galloping off with Titus hardly aware of the cramped muscles he'd gotten from a night sleeping on a thin doubled-over blanket.

It was a strange scene that greeted him as he crested a miniature ridge and charged down the other side, dodging cacti and scrub brush as best he could in the starlight. The first things he noticed were the bodies of four zombies sprawled out on the ground, each of their strung-together bone gorgets in shattered pieces around their necks. A long haired figure stood looking up at Titus from the shadows, a little four-shot gear pistol quivering in both hands. It was pointed straight at Titus.

"I mean you no harm, stranger," the former Brigadier-Justice said. "I'm a – Well, I heard the commotion and thought I ought to come help."

The figure's upraised little gun did not waver.

"And besides, don't you think I know how to count four bullets when I hear them?"

At that, the tiny handgun went down. The figure kicked the closest zombie's head. As Titus got closer he could see that the shot had torn right through the zombie's neck, severing the spine from its skull. Just like all the others. The figure hauled back a slim-booted foot and gave it a few more kicks, until finally the head separated from the body.

Titus climbed down from Nebuchadnezzar. "That was a fine piece of shooting, getting the spine like that."

The figure grunted at him and turned away.

"Were there any more of them than these four, you'd be a whole lot more grateful for someone with a saber to show up, mister."

The figure wheeled on him so fast that Nebuchadnezzar nickered, and before he knew it Titus had a ten inch knife pressed to his throat.

"I can take care of myself," a raspy voice said. "But I ain't no mister, *mister*." The knife disappeared as fast as it had come out. "However, I do appreciate you rushin' out to save a lady, Mr. Smoke."

Titus boggled. If he didn't know better, he would have guessed he'd heard that froggy voice before. "Wilhelmina Wontshee?"

The figure took off her hat and let him get a good look at her face. It certainly was. The years had taken their toll on the girl, who'd always looked a touch manly anyway, but underneath the dirty clothes and tough set of her face, Titus recognized the sweet girl who used to moon over Jeb every Sunday and chase him around with threatened kisses during church picnics. Now she'd grown hard.

"Nobody really calls me that no more. Willie is good enough from now on. And what brings a Brigadier-Justice out to the middle of nowhere?"

"Willie?" He cleared his throat distractedly. "Willie it is," Titus agreed, more than a little confused by his feelings on the subject. "I'm headed south to shore up San Antone. You?"

She laughed, and it was not raspy at all. Off in the distance, the sky was beginning to redden with dawn and clouds. That girl always did have a pretty laugh to her, Titus thought, for all that no right minded person would allow her to sing in a church choir.

"Headed up from that way. You probably shouldn't be going there, unless you aim to die for nothing." She eyed him narrowly, then began loading the muzzles of her four-shot from a sack hanging from her waist. She wore a gun belt, and it had bullets on it, but she didn't touch them. "You know I had you, right?"

Titus admitted nothing.

"I was pretending to be scared. I figured if you were up to no good you'd want to get close up on me assuming I didn't count my shots. But I was ready with that knife."

"Is that so?" Titus asked. "Well then, I guess you had me, fair enough."

Willie Wontshee grinned. "Damn straight."

"If you don't mind my askin', why are you out here by yourself instead of riding with the rest of the folks headed north?"

Willie spat on the ground like a man would, but to Titus it still looked like a very feminine thing she had done. "Was just going to escort my cousin Sam, she's a school marm, and a mess of kids up halfway to Austin where they'd be safe, but once I turned back and got off the roads I run into these zombies going north. Figured they was up to no good, so I followed them."

She reached down and picked up the ugly head in front of her by its bone and shell decorated hair. She made a face at it, a mockery of its own death expression.

"But you didn't do anything interesting did you?" She said to the head in a hoarse kind of sing-song. "No you didn't do anything interesting at all, except double back and try to kill me. But let me tell you something Mr. Moctezuma Man. I only carry a four-shot because those six guns make you over-confident. The day I need more than four shots is the day I forgot how to make 'em count."

Titus grimaced and looked away. Not so much away from the corpse's head as from the way she was baby-talking to it. Something really unsettling about Wilhelmina Wontshee. But the girl could shoot. The four blasted out neck bones on the ground proved that.

"Sun's about up," he finally ventured. "Want to share some bread and the last of my bacon?"

"Sure thing, Brigadier-Justice. You cook, I'll keep watch."

Titus didn't correct her assumption about his rank, but saw no harm in putting her a little off balance if he could. Her odd ways were starting to grate on him anyway so it'd be no skin off his knuckles if they went their separate ways sooner rather than later.

"You heard anything from my boy, Jeb, lately?" he asked, not looking up as he began laying a fire.

It took her a long time to respond, and when she did, there was a little extra frogginess in her reply. "Nope. Not for years."

Titus leaned back, satisfied he had a good fire going. "So you headed back to San Antonio?"

"I am. Figure they'll need all the help they can get with that Mexican army marching."

"Someone needs to let Austin know what's coming," said Titus, knowing that someone couldn't be him. He was done with that town and everyone in it. If he returned, they'd find a way to lure him back into his old routine, and he was tired of fighting those battles. Politics were all well and good, but Titus preferred enemies he could look in the eye.

"I reckon they know already," said Willie. "Sam's there by now I guess. And more folks are headed that way."

"Well, someone needs to tell Burleson. I don't suppose I could convince you to do it. He's a stubborn fool. He won't listen to nothing I have to say."

"Then he damn sure won't listen to me," said Willie. "I'm riding south."

They ate in silence. Titus would have ordered a man to go, whether he had rank over him or not, but what call did he have to send a woman off on his errands? Still, he couldn't go back to Austin, not now.

Willie finished her meal and made to mount her horse, not even bothering to say thanks. Titus stood hurriedly, taken aback by her brusqueness and lack of all civility.

"I reckon old Burleson would pay you for your time," he said, desperate to convince her. If she didn't go, he'd have no choice. He couldn't leave such important news undelivered.

Interest sparked in her eyes. Titus could tell by the way she was dressed that she hadn't had more than a couple of coins to rub together in some time.

"How much is my time worth?"

"I suspect you can set your price. Texas is good for it."

"Fifty dollars?"

"That's reasonable." She could have asked for a thousand and he would have agreed. He doubted Burleson would be forthcoming with payment anyway. Titus felt guilty for lying to her, but at least he'd be getting her out of harm's way. She might fashion herself a tough one, but he remembered the girl she'd been.

"How do I know he'll pay me?"

"Tell him I've authorized it."

Willie didn't seem convinced, but Titus could tell she'd taken the bait. A chance at fifty dollars was worth a day's ride north. If she was determined to fight the Mexicans, she could still make it back to San Antonio long before they arrived. Titus hoped she'd reconsider.

"Be careful, Mr. Smoke," she said, drawing up reins. "Bad days are coming." She turned her horse and spurred it into a gallop.

Titus watched her until she was nothing but a dot on the horizon. Then he packed his saddle bags, mounted Nebuchadnezzar, and headed south.

CHAPTER 11

TITUS SAW THE RAGGED GREEN LINE OF JUNIPERS and grand old cypress trees that meant the San Antonio River was close ahead. He kicked his horse into a gallop. They were still barreling full-bore across the rusted out earth when the town of San Antonio, such as it was, rolled into view.

It had grown up quite a bit since the last time his travels had brought him this way. Whereas before there had only been a few dozen broadened dirt tracks and not many more chinked log houses and stores, now the town was bustling like a small city with horses and soldiers, and even a few steam carriages and mares had made their way down here. The San Antonio River, waters the color of buckskin, flirted its way back and forth across the valley like an Indian princess, from the buzzing hive of Military Plaza in the west, to the hallowed ground of the Alamo mission in the east, and then back again around a huge stand of cottonwood, before meandering on south toward massacred Goliad and the Gulf of Mexico.

The Alamo. The sight of that mission always brought a lump to his throat. He had been there that night, when Moctezuma's general, Santa Anna, had unleashed unholy hell upon the Texans who had taken shelter inside it. There had been rumors, of course, that the Lord of Mexico had somehow forged himself an army the like of which had not been seen for over a thousand years. If you believed what he had to say on the subject, it was an army of living dead men all with their hearts torn out atop a ragged pyramid in Tenochtitlan and kept beating one and all in a vast copper pot at the heart of the Temple of the Sun. The same kind of army Moctezuma claimed to have used against Cortez way back when.

Titus didn't believe that. No one did. And how could it have been true? Dead Mexicans didn't walk and Cortez and his men had been stricken by Diphtheria or the Bloody Grippe. That's how the stories went when white men told them, anyway.

And how they had joked at first, seeing the ramshackle horde of them all holding muskets and atl-atls both in disjointed lines. They staggered like drunks, at first, till the smell of blood quickened them.

He closed his eyes, taking several deep breaths to clear his mind of the images of that night, of the realization that no one was coming to help them. Not one damned soul. The day and the night went on forever with shots exchanged and Texan men shouting insults across the adobe walls and hearing only stony silence in return.

It was true what Sam Houston had said, that every man there took down eight or more of the zombies. But it had not been enough. Not nearly enough, when every single one of them got right back up and started fighting again. Back then, no one knew about cutting their heads off, or at least breaking their necks really good. The men took long tired shifts on the battlements, pushing down ladders and cutting ropes. Moctezuma's army kept rising again and again.

It had been the Tennessean, Davy Crockett, who had got the idea to listen to one of the crazy old slaves. "Nothing else seems to be working, Sam," Titus remembered him shouting. "Why not let them try. He said they have something like 'em on Haiti."

Sam Houston had been against it, as any upstanding Christian would be. But Burleson was in his face next, with one of the slaves in tow. "It may be the devil's work, Sam, but by God, Santa Anna's devils are the ones I'm more worried about right now." Titus smiled when he remembered the way Houston had pretended it had been his plan all along, after.

But the idea of making Texas a republic free of slavery forever more, that had been all Edward Burleson. Titus felt Nebuchadnezzar slowing and he began to pay more attention to the clatter of a black work detail and their squeaky-voiced sergeant, who was busy directing them in the task of extending a dried out irrigation ditch and fortifying it.

Did they expect Moctezuma to come from the north?

Well, if the four Wilhelmina killed had gotten that far past San Antonio as to approach Austin, maybe it wasn't such a bad idea. But even so, it seemed not to make too much sense to Titus. The two most defensible locations in the valley were Military Plaza and the Alamo.

"You coming to join up?" the sergeant asked, wiping one damp woolen sleeve across his sweating forehead.

"I am." The other soldiers, if you were generous enough to call this rabble of mismatched uniforms soldiers, laughed.

One of them hollered out, "Welcome to the last paying job you'll ever have, mister," and they all laughed again. Titus liked the good natured sound of their laughter after so many dark thoughts. He checked the men's foreheads, but not as surreptitiously as he had hoped.

"None of us was here the first time," the sergeant squeaked at him.

Titus looked him in the eye. "Well, we're all here now, and that's what counts, isn't it?"

"That it is. You looking to enlist? They have an officer standing ready to swear you in up in the Plaza."

Titus tipped his hat and thanked him. "One more thing," he said, tugging a little on Nebuchadnezzar's reins to keep the excitable horse from heading off. "Are there any of the Forever Free still here? Maybe one named Sylvester?"

The men grew silent at the mention of that name. "You the one with the son killed a little girl?" The words spilled out of the sergeant's mouth like jackrabbits surprised from their burrow.

Titus just stared at him, his mouth hanging a bit too open for a bit too long and the ache in his soul nearly as piercing as the one in his heart. The soldiers' broad smiles had disappeared.

The sergeant pointed one finger at a tiny island a few miles down river. "He said when somebody come asking for him with a child-killing son, send him there."

Titus looked past the grassy island with its handful of trees and up above it into the cloud-stricken sky. He clucked at Nebuchadnezzar and slapped the reins lightly on the horse's gray neck. He didn't hear what exactly the black soldiers were calling to him as he rode off, any more than they could hear what he had to say on the subject.

"Fiddlesticks," he swore. "Fiddle-fucking-sticks."

As he forded the river at what looked like a shallow enough spot, Titus held his ammunition satchel and gun belt up high in one hand to keep them from getting wet. He kept a steady grip on the reins with the other, but he hardly needed to. Nebuchadnezzar didn't balk, even when the river breasted him. When they'd made it to the little scrub grass and stunted juniper island, Titus slapped him fondly on the neck and treated the horse to a pair of gnarled carrots, the last of what he'd picked up in New Braunfels. Then he hitched Nebuchadnezzar to a low hanging branch with his customary "one good yank" knot, making sure he'd be able to graze on the grass and leaves close by.

And here was the part he wasn't looking forward to. There were just enough trees to obstruct a clear view of the little shack set back thirty yards or so from the muddy shore, but the wind brought him the bitter smell of strange herbs and organ meats burning together. Little islands like this one were the sort cattle thieves might hide out on, if they knew a Ranger was on to them. The thought made Titus scowl at himself, feeling ridiculous.

He felt even more ridiculous when a pair of squirrels bounded after each other in the trees, startling him. He's just a man, Titus told himself. Even with his weird ways and the things he can do – did do, to save the Alamo that day – Sylvester was still just a man. He put on his britches one leg at a time, when he chose to wear any.

But there had been a moment, when Santa Anna's zombies were raging up the southern face and Sylvester had gathered up all the black folk who remembered their old ways that he could find and set some of them to dancing and some of them to rapping on the tanned skins covering the full rain barrels. There had been the craziest sort of yelling and carrying on and they were calling him Hoon-gan and screaming and writhing like they was all having the exact same kind of fit. There had been a moment when Titus had looked away from the ravenous zombies with their bone necklaces and towering headpieces, and looked right square at Burleson and Houston and the rest of them, all looking on except for Crockett, who was dancing with them in a most un-Christian way.

And in that moment, he had seen the thought he was having jump across the faces of those others and any of the men too distracted to be aiming and shooting and reloading like they were supposed to at the Mexicans. *Are we any safer in here with them?*

Titus shivered, and made himself stop remembering. He strode on waterlogged boots up to the Hoon-gan's sod shack and squinted into the smoky dimness. A centipede ran across one boot and Titus kicked it away. A dozen other critters called the dark little shelter home as well: spiders, caterpillars, sow bugs, and horseflies all seemed to be living in harmony under Sylvester's crumbling roof. There was a narrow slit on the downriver wall that didn't let in near enough light or fresh air. A mound of bricks lay arranged in such a way beneath a hole in the ceiling that it could almost be called a mantle if a man was feeling particularly charitable. Beneath it, a fire blazed around a row of sticks speared with some sort of meat.

"You done come back for more, Mistuh Smoke?"

Titus wheeled around to see the old black man, virtually unchanged from that day thirteen years ago. Age had not softened Sylvester's raspy voice any more than it had smoothed over the livid bubbled up brand he had placed upon his own forehead, and the forehead of every other slave who had danced that day. Crockett had wanted one, but was not allowed. *A piece of you is always goin' be dancing with the loa, Mistuh Crockett,* Titus remembered hearing him say. *Brand or no, you was born Forever Free, and don't you forget. But the only ones wearing this brand is going be the ones who sold they souls to the loa to get that way.* It had come as some shock to polite society when Davy Crockett, a former Congressman, branded himself not long after with that same pair of letters anyway.

Titus felt himself staring at the FF on the man's forehead and brought his eyes down to meet Sylvester's own river-pebble gaze. "I hear tell Moctezuma is coming back for more."

Sylvester mongoosed his bony carcass through the doorway, not bothering to allow Titus to move out of the way. The stink of hard work and river mud assaulted Titus as the man came far too close for comfort in the process. "You think you know what's going on, but you don't. You most like the cat who thinks he snuck up on a mouse, but you ain't, because that mouse is dead."

Titus was confused. "Are you talking about Moctezuma's armies? Of course they are dead."

"Them zombies ain't the only thing dead, unfortunately, Mistuh Smoke. Moctezuma's godhood be dyin' too. And his ain't the only one neither."

"What do you mean?"

"I mean he's losing his power to keep them zombies alive, and that's making him desperate. He done killed off a dozen of the Free. But that's 'cause he don't realize the loa dyin' off too. And there's others."

Titus stared at the soggy end of a fat bloodworm squirming gradually out of a sod brick wall like the tail of a patient cat. He wondered how it was he got suckered into such a conversation about heathen gods when he had always gone out of his way to avoid talking about the Christian one with his own beloved Cecilia.

He rose to his feet, a bit stunned to realize he had come in and sat down upon the loamy floor with Sylvester without even realizing it. "I don't want to hear about this," he said evenly. "I just want to get up there with my pistols and my rifle and my cutlass and I want to kill them zombies when they come, and the only way to make them stay dead is you doing that thing you did again so that they'd stay dead from the gunshots long enough for us to get out there and whack their heads off."

He took a deep breath to steady himself. His voice had risen over that last outburst to a near panicky shout. The smoke tickled his throat and made his eyes water. His head swam and he could have sworn he heard Nebuchadnezzar whinnying in alarm.

Sylvester, crooked one finger and as it bent, so did Titus, till he was back on the ground again. His own heartbeat sounded like drums, like Indian drums. Not them other, he didn't want to hear them other drums ever again.

"The gods not raining their love on us any more, Mistuh Smoke. None of them. But your boy and the one you sent after him, they coming with a thundercloud, a gift, and a whole lot of trouble."

"Jebediah's coming here?" Titus croaked. "Wait, a gift? A gift for who?" But the spiders and flies and worms and dirt and smoke and the burnt-liver stink of the room overwhelmed him before he heard an answer.

"Blue Norther coming in," said a grizzled soldier with a trumpet hanging from a strap around his neck. The voice jarred Titus from what felt like a long and feverish sleep. He didn't remember leaving Sylvester's sod shack, didn't understand why he had so much dirt inside his clothes and in his mouth and ears and nose, or why his moustache smelled like toad piss. But here he was in San Antonio atop Nebuchadnezzar.

"What's that?" Titus said, taking in his surroundings. He was coming up on Military Plaza by way of Dolorosa Street, if the carved wooden sign the man was standing next to could be believed. But he was coming from the west for some reason. How long after talking to Sylvester had he wandered before finally coming out of the state he'd been in? A smaller, messier sign beneath the street name read: NEW ENLISTEES SEE SGT. WALLACE IN MILTY PLAZA.

"I said 'Blue Norther coming in,'" the man repeated. Titus turned in the saddle to see that what the man said was true. The sky behind him was bruising faster than a blacksmith's apprentice and the temperature had already dropped a good ten degrees. The air had that thick, dreamlike quality that trapped light and sound in its sticky molasses grip and refused to let either of them go very far without a fight. "Better get to shelter, it's liable to be a dandy."

Titus nodded and touched his spurs to Nebuchadnezzar's flanks, even though the horse was already trotting a little faster. He wasn't far when the man called out to him. "Hey mister, do I know you?"

Titus didn't turn around. The last thing he wanted was to be recognized as the Brigadier-Justice. There'd been too many big men barking orders for him to be in charge of anything other than his gun and powder when he'd last defended the Alamo. It'd be fitting for him to go out that same way. But if they figured out who he was, they'd want him in charge of something, resigned or not. He couldn't remember much of what Sylvester had told him, but it sure sounded like there wasn't going to be much hoodoo help this time around and Moctezuma was more desperate than ever for some reason.

He yelled back over one shoulder, "Don't reckon you do," then rode on past the plaza. Fast rain was already driving everyone inside the town's crowded little hotels and bars and barns. By the time Titus got Nebuchadnezzar stabled up in an empty steam mare berth (one he'd had to pay fifty cents extra for), he was cold and miserable and in need of a hot bath for all that he was already soaking wet. He shook his hat off at the door of a saloon and waited patiently for the barkeep.

Folks were talking in brave loud voices, men mostly, only a handful of bar girls were in attendance and they seemed to be turning fast business, heading up and down the stairs to the second and third floor as quick as their petticoats could bustle.

Titus thought of Cecilia. She wouldn't mind, she knew he had needs, but in his heart, Titus would mind. When the barkeep came over finally, he ordered up a whiskey, a hot plate of biscuits, beef and fried potatoes with chilies, a bath, some barbering, and a bed for the night, in that order.

While he nipped at his whiskey, he tried to pay attention to what some of the folks were saying. It was mostly young men's talk about the mess they would make of any dead Mexicans so much as got near San Antone, but some of the older ones–the ones who'd been around long enough to understand the real threat and stay here anyway–those folks were doing just as Titus was, quietly working at their drinks or their meals, listening.

He felt lucky no one recognized him. Not that he would have recognized himself at this point. He made a note to have the barber shave off his lamb chop whiskers as well, hoping it would aid in the cause of his anonymity.

"Hear what that Polk has to say?" the man next to him at the bar asked.

"Polk?" Titus responded, confused until he realized the man meant the United States President. A plate of food materialized under his nose while he was looking at the man and Titus nodded his thanks at the barkeep.

"Yeah, Polk," the man said, almost gruffly. Titus counted the empty shot glasses in front of him. Eight. Not too bad for a man of his size. "Polk says the U.S. has a manifest destiny to cover the land from one coast to the other. Says whatever they do to take it from the red man is justified. What do you think of that?"

Titus sampled a bit of the food before speaking, unable to delay his hunger any longer. How long *had* he been wandering around after talking to Sylvester?

"I think he's going to have his hands full when he tries to take the Comancheria. If it could be taken, the Republic of Texas would have already claimed it. And the British colony in California aren't going to just walk away from their gold mines."

The man lifted his glass as if to toast Titus, but then realized it was empty. He signaled to the bartender for another. "Do I know you?" he said, eyeballing Titus like he'd been the last one to touch a light collection plate in church.

"I don't think you do."

"Guess not." The man switched subjects rapidly. Titus considered buying him as many shots as it would take to make him pass out. Looking again at the eight–now nine–empties, he decided against. "Do you think the U.S. is going to want to come lay some of that manifest destiny down in Texas, make us a part of the Union? They'd probably have us allow slavery again if they did."

"I don't know about all that," Titus said, forking more roasted beef into his mouth. "But I would hope that maybe Texas has a destiny all of her own."

"Here, here!" the man said, raising his next shot into the air.

Titus reluctantly clinked his glass to the drunk's and drained it. Hungry as he was, the thought of Texan destiny had suddenly soured his appetite. He left money on the bar next to his half-eaten plate and went upstairs in search of the baths.

CHAPTER 12

"LIFT HER ON UP HERE," JEB SMOKE SAID.
Now dressed in a bloodied uniform he'd scavenged from one of the dead Redjacks, he stood on the treads of *Leviathan 212*, one hand holding onto the iron rungs set into the machine's steel side, the other reaching out for Darla. Her breath came in shallow gasps and all color had fled her face. Troy had done what was needed, attempting to suck the snake venom free from her heel, but that wasn't always good enough. Darla needed a doctor.

Troy lifted Darla and Smoke took her against him. She was hot and her hair was slick with sweat. Tightening his grip on the motionless girl, he began climbing the ladder rungs, intent on getting her inside the Leviathan and getting them all to civilization.

The Leviathan was a massive cylinder of steel about twenty feet long with three sets of treads on either side. A great boiler was attached to the back and three small structures rose from the body: the operations cabin, the coal cabin, and a gunnery cabin. Smoke had made a cursory examination of the conveyance while Troy was ministering to Darla, and though his experience with steam vehicles was limited mostly to steam mares and wagons, he understood the concepts well enough that he felt he could get the Leviathan moving the direction he wanted.

The coal cabin was well stocked with coal, and a steady fire blazed behind a fire grate. A shovel stood at the ready. The top of the Leviathan was flat enough to provide a path between the three cabins, and the next one he'd found had been the gunnery cabin. Like the other cabins, it was a squat box of steel with a few windows, but these windows were outfitted with chain driven guns unlike anything Smoke had ever encountered.

The operations cabin housed all the mechanisms necessary for steering the vehicle and managing the boiler pressure. This was the most important part of the driver's job, in

Smoke's opinion. He'd seen enough neglected steam mares blow their guts open, and often blow their riders' legs off with them, to understand that boiler pressure was not a thing to take for granted.

The bulk of the Leviathan's body was a cargo hold, and Smoke had determined that with such light armament, that must be the thing's primary function. A quick peek in the hold had elicited a strained hiss from Smoke. It was full of gunpowder. A great deal of gunpowder. Now, as he scaled Leviathan's side, with a dying little girl in his arms, he cursed the universe for its cruelty. It was bad enough that if he couldn't manage the skill to drive this thing she would die. But now he'd have to contend with explosive cargo on top of it all.

"Get up here and start shoveling coal," said Smoke as he reached the top. Heavy British boots that didn't exactly fit his feet clomped against steel as he strode along the catwalk. He passed through the gunnery cabin and made for the operations cabin where he laid Darla gently on the metal deck. He shoved one of the soldiers' wadded up red jackets under her head, made sure she was still breathing, then turned to study the controls.

"Fire's already burning," called Troy from the back of the vehicle.

"Make it hotter!" said Smoke. "Get to shoveling."

Troy mumbled something that Smoke couldn't hear over the whistle of the wind through the cabin windows and the slow creep of the river nearby. But the chink of steel told him that Troy was shoveling, and within seconds, the largest of the pressure gauges in the cabin began to climb.

It was Smoke's theory that the solders had stopped to add water to the boiler, then were set upon by the wandering zombies. So he was gambling they had plenty of water to make it the short distance to Austin. It couldn't be far. The relentless plains had given way to gentle, sloping hills, and they were close enough that Lightning Dove's men might already be setting the town ablaze.

Smoke pulled the throttle lever and *Leviathan 212* lurched forward, then slammed into a tree.

Troy cursed. "God damn! Tell me next time before you do that. I nearly cracked my damn skull."

"Just hang on," yelled Smoke. "We ain't got time for you to be delicate."

Before Troy could reply, Smoke found a second lever, reversed the treads, and hit the throttle again. Leviathan moved more slowly this time, back into the river a few feet. Smoke yanked it to a stop and reversed treads again. The cabin was stuffy and Smoke was already beginning to sweat. He had no idea what most of the gauges meant, but he kept a constant eyeball on the one in the middle that was creeping toward the red. He found a valve release handle, muscled it slowly counterclockwise and heard steam begin to bleed off from several ports at the rear of the vehicle. The needle settled comfortably in the middle of the gauge, and Smoke throttled forward slowly. He gripped the iron levers with both hands and just managed to turn shy of the tree. The Leviathan plodded forward, and once they'd cleared the heaviest of the trees, Smoke gave it more steam and it lurched up to a respectable speed. Somewhere faster than a running man but slower than a good horse. He thought it might be capable of more. But he had to weigh the need for haste with the need for not blowing themselves into tiny pieces.

Smoke had taken one of the solder's canteens as well, and he tipped it to Darla's lips. She didn't drink, but he wiped some of the cool water across her face and forehead.

"Next stop, Austin," he said under his breath.

But what would they do when they got there? The Brits in charge of the Leviathan had fallen behind, and based on the size of the English contingent, Smoke doubted they'd even missed it yet. Lightning Dove and his men were too far ahead of them to catch, and by the time they made it to Austin, there might be no one left to warn, let alone a doctor to tend to Darla.

Smoke thought briefly about turning for San Antonio, but that would mean giving up entirely on Austin. And worse, giving up entirely on Audrey. Not that she hadn't already given up on him. She claimed to believe him, but something in the way she kept him at a distance told him she'd bought in to at least some of the lies that had taken root around his deeds in Laredo. But he still had a huge empty place for her in his heart, and abandoning her to her death wasn't an option.

Smoke had insisted that Troy trade his clothes for British red too, and he fostered some hope that there might be a delay, that they might be able to join the ranks unnoticed and somehow sneak word ahead so the city could prepare.

"Did I tell you I was gonna get married once?" Smoke didn't expect a response, but he thought maybe the sound of his voice would help Darla keep touch with the world. "This beautiful woman, she moved to town just after I'd joined the Rangers. Red hair and these freckles all over her face, and lord I'll tell you, she was a pistol. I think that's why I liked her so much. She had sass. She wasn't one of them ladies with the gloves and umbrellas and all. She worked with old Mr. Burnell, shoeing horses. You believe that?

"Well I liked her straight off and told her and she laughed at me. And, of course, that just made me all the more sure she was the one for me, no matter what my Daddy liked to think. See, Audrey ... that's her name. Audrey was married but she run off cause her husband was a mean son of a bitch and her parents wouldn't help her. I think her family came from Ohio but I don't recollect for sure. Either way, Daddy wasn't too keen on me courting a married woman.

"Well, we got on like two peas. And as far as I was concerned, she wasn't rightly married anyway. So I asked her myself and she told me yes and then I rode off for Laredo and ... well, nothing has quite gone my way since Laredo."

"What are you babbling about?" yelled Titus over the hiss and groan of the Leviathan's forward progress.

"Nothing! I'm just talking to Darla."

"Well, case you ain't noticed, she ain't listening. Why don't you just drive? You pay more attention and we might stand a better chance of getting there."

"Why don't you just shovel?"

"Damn thing is full. If it gets any hotter back here my skin's gonna melt off."

Smoke glanced over at the main pressure gauge and saw that Troy was right. He cursed, released some steam. "Quit shoveling then and go see if you can figure out those chain guns."

The shovel clanged when Troy dropped it, and Smoke could hear him moving toward the gunnery cabin. Smoke kept his eyes forward now. They darted from the landscape before him, to the pressure gauge, then back again. Daylight was beginning to break and orange light crept up between the cedars and dirty scrub brushes, and it gilded the scattered rock formations like cleansing fire.

Try and figure out the guns? Troy wondered just who Smoke thought he was talking to. Sure, he'd never spent much time riding shined-up steam mares like some pretty boy from back east, but one thing he knew inside and out was firearms.

Fighting the lurching in his stomach, which somehow managed to be perfectly off-rhythm with the jerking gait of the Leviathan, he made his way across the deck, grateful to escape from the heat of the coal furnace and rear-mounted boiler. The vehicle hit another uneven piece of ground, and Troy only prevented himself from falling face first by grabbing onto both ends of a loop of sooty chain. It gave a little and after checking that Smoke hadn't seen him nearly fall, Troy followed it with his eyes.

The chain seemed to be part of a dumbwaiter arrangement for bringing coal up from the Leviathan's hold. He gave the links a yank and watched the empty scoop clatter up. Probably had a crewman filling the scoop below and another up in the fresh air shoveling coal into the flaming maw of the furnace. Troy wiped his hands on the Queen's pretty red uniform, taking a shameful amount of pleasure in seeing it soiled. He noticed a pair of thick leather gloves tucked into a nook behind the coal lift; it wasn't too far from where he'd found the shovel. Troy spat.

Chain guns, huh? We'll just see. Troy looked up past the little enclosure that held the three rapid-fire guns. Two smaller ones were mounted on either side on a swivel that allowed for firing all but directly forward and behind, with just enough vertical mobility to fire at men on the ground as close as twenty feet or a decent pie-slice above the horizon; the other was nearly twice the size of the side mounted guns and built for firing straight ahead. The five-barreled turret jutted just above the pilot house, where Smoke was still busy finding every divot and soft stretch of soil in Texas. An arrangement not so different from the one that operated the coal lift served to spin a set of five barrels around like a revolver, but a part of the chain also drove a set of gears that pulled a fresh round into the empty chamber.

He had seen one of these fired a few years back. Part of the Alamo Day festivities in New Braunfels. The trick was getting the speed right, according to the town's English grocer and premier gun collector. Anyone could make it fire once or twice, but if you didn't have your speed just right and constant, the chain would seize up, or the rounds would get cocked and never enter the barrel. That's why it was primarily an English weapon, he had insisted; the soldiers of other countries lacked the steadiness under fire, the *resolve* to keep one firing long enough to do any damage.

Troy inspected the forward mount, working out how the bullets made it from their belted troughs into the firing chamber. He heard Smoke up there babbling to the next little girl he'd likely be responsible for killing. The taste of venom he'd sucked from her foot lingered on Troy's lips. His stomach started rolling again even though the Leviathan was for once riding fairly smoothly. That had been the first time he'd ever sucked venom out of somebody, and he hoped it was the last. But somehow, having shared the thing with the little Indian girl, he felt a little closer to her.

He lined up the red-painted square of metal—the reticule, that Limey grocer had called it—on a stand of cactus two or three hundred yards ahead of the Leviathan, and gave the chain a solid tug and kept right on tugging. The boom that followed, and the succession of them right after that, left Troy's ears ringing. It must have had some effect on Smoke too, because the Leviathan lurched hard to the left and then swung back on course. Troy heard Smoke cursing him and whooped.

"Who's being delicate now?"
In the distance, the tops of a half dozen cacti had splattered clean off.

Willie stood on the President of Texas' front porch, waiting for the irritating little man in the bowler hat to announce her arrival. He'd taken a dislike to her at first glance, and she'd done the same. He was too slick for her tastes and he talked in some sort of funny foreign accent. He'd been about to close the door in her face when she told him that no less important a man than Titus Smoke had tasked her with this visit to the President. That he had, in fact, entrusted her with a message of great importance to the Republic. No, she would not relay the message through him, but would deliver it to the man himself.

In truth, Willie had no idea how much pull Mr. Smoke had in these circles, but she knew him to be a man of reasonable importance, and the look on bowler man's face told her that at the very least, he'd have to run the request by the president. He'd asked her to stand put, then closed the door.

Now, she stood on the porch, scraping mud off her boots and onto the warped wooden planks, wondering why the hell she'd even agreed to come here. Fifty dollars was fifty dollars, but she wasn't entirely convinced that money would be hers. And she was needed in San Antonio. Anyone with a gun and a beating heart was needed. She'd been too young to fight at the first battle of the Alamo, but she wasn't going to miss her chance this time. Once she'd delivered Mr. Smoke's message, Willie intended to head south straightaway.

A few minutes later, and the President still hadn't appeared. Willie was put out enough that she'd arrived in the middle of the night and had had to wait until morning to call on the man, but she'd bided her time and managed to catch an hour or so of sleep on the outskirts of town. Now it was five o'clock and still she was being made to wait. The thought that Burleson might be lazing away the morning in bed while she had pressing things to attend to irritated her beyond reason. She spat on the porch and paced impatiently.

Finally, the man in the bowler hat grudgingly opened the door and ushered her in.

"Please wait here," he said, indicating a sitting room just off the entry hall, choked with far too much furniture. "The President will be with you shortly."

"Nice of him to get out of bed for company." Willie dropped into an overstuffed chair, judged it too soft for her tastes and decided to stand.

"The President is not accustomed to receiving guests so early in the morning. Certainly not emissaries from *former* employees of the Republic. You seem to think that being associated with Titus Smoke somehow credits your visit with a sense of importance. Believe me, it does not. That man turned his back on this country and frankly I am amazed the President has deigned to meet with you. It seems he still holds some manner of regard for the man. Understand; I do not share his opinion.

"You waste everyone's time with your rude visit. And if the news you bring is of any importance at all, why would he not come himself? Why would he instead send a ragged, smelly little girl dressed up in her father's cattle rustling clothes?"

Willie was not aware that she'd drawn her pistol until the barrel was pressed against the man's chin. His heavily waxed moustache twitched once, but otherwise he seemed unconcerned at her sudden action. He was a bastard, but he was a cool one.

"You might consider changing your tone, Mr.–"

"Pincher."

"Mr. Pincher."

"I thought my tone was quite reasonable, given the circumstances."

"You keep thinking that. Let's see what my gun has to say about things."

"You won't shoot me," he said, smiling now. "I've known killers, and you are no killer."

Willie snorted. "You ain't known no killers. You might know how to answer the door and be a pain in my ass, but that's about all you know."

"This is stimulating conversation," he said. "But I must be going. My employer awaits my return."

Willie began to feel foolish and holstered her gun. This man needed to be knocked down a few pegs, but they both knew she wasn't going to shoot him.

"I thought your employer was on his way to speak with me," she said.

"The President is on his way," said Pincher. "I work for the Mayor. You are not the only one with early business, dear lady." He chuckled, then turned for the door. He was gone before the full realization of what had happened dawned on her. He wasn't the President's manservant, tasked with filtering out unwanted company. He was unwanted company himself, and he'd been having sport with her. Angry again, she considered following him into the yard and hitting him in the face a few times, then decided to be done with the man.

She found a wooden bench nestled between all of the expensive furniture and took a seat to wait for Burleson.

Assuming he planned to see her at all.

Titus woke the next morning refreshed and more than a little eager. The idea of slipping into the enlisted ranks enticed him nearly as much as the smell of sweet cornbread and honeyed butter that seemed to follow him down the street to Military Plaza.

The plaza itself was wide and square, surrounded on all sides by a boxy wall of clay bricks. Every wall suffered from enough gap-toothed gateless openings to ensure that the plaza would never be put to much more martial use than as a parade and mustering ground. Even so, skinny men and boys in mismatched uniforms that might well have been salvaged from the last battle here perched and marched and smoked along the top of it, lounging on their rifle butts, or holding up light cannons with their rear ends.

Another gaggle of ragtag soldiers stood baking in the morning sun, eyeballing the half dozen or so men already in line to join up. Titus fell in behind a potbellied man with long red whiskers. He rubbed his own newly shorn face, still not quite used to the lightness of it, the heightened sensitivity. It was like he could feel the smoke and insects of Sylvester's mud hut crawling across his face with every rare gust of wind.

At the head of the line, a short desk had been constructed from two whiskey barrels and an irregular plank of knotty pine. Titus wondered briefly how full or empty the whiskey barrels were. Behind the desk on an uncomfortable looking three-legged stool sat one of the largest men Titus had ever seen, and one he wasn't exactly happy to see again, under the circumstances. The giant's legs were too long for him to bend his knees, even under this makeshift desk, forcing him to keep them extended straight out. The man currently signing up and swearing in had to step around a pair of boots large enough to feed a horse from. As Titus had actually seen him do on more than one occasion.

Titus pulled his hand away from his face, trying not to feel defeated already. Fiddlesticks. Of all the Wallaces in Texas, the one in charge of new enlistments turned out to be Bigfoot. They had ridden together on a few occasions in the early days, before Goliad and the Black Bean Affair. Titus had been years younger and wore only a wisp of a moustache then. He held little hope that Bigfoot would not recognize him.

So much for enlisting incognito. But wait a minute, maybe not. Bigfoot had left the Rangers himself after the Black Bean Affair, after all. And he never showed up to fight at the Alamo, claiming it was all over by the time he came into a town to hear about it. Word was that the big man had been out living off the rough of the desert alone for two or three months at a time. But now here he was, enlisted, when it would have been nothing for him to un-resign and put his Ranger star back on. So maybe he would not raise a stink about Titus doing the same. It would all depend on how he approached him. And whether or not Bigfoot called him by name so anyone could hear it.

Titus shuffled up a step as the man who had just been sworn in was rushed over to uniform issue by a tall black man with only one eye. There were already three more formed up behind him, and some officer with a Back East accent was busy shooing the onlookers away and setting them about whatever passed for a day's work. Titus pulled his hat down low and stared at his own boots, wondering which way Bigfoot would fall.

In the space of thirty minutes, it was time to find out. He pretended to be dozing on his feet until the one-eyed soldier was out of earshot and the restless men behind Titus started muttering. Bigfoot Wallace squeaked out at him in that unsuited voice of his, "If you want to play dead, mister, you're on the wrong side."

Titus let himself smile under his hat as he approached the desk, keeping his eyes hidden. His lips curled up even more when he saw that the plank Bigfoot was using as a writing surface wasn't so irregularly cut after all. Atop those two whiskey barrels, planed and sanded as smooth and flat as any *mesa*, lay a coffin lid.

"I reckon I'm on the right side, and in the right place, for a man wanting to just put up a good fight and not have to think about it much." Titus let his gaze rise to look Bigfoot Wallace right in those almost inbred-looking eyes. "My name is"–he hadn't thought about this before hand, and kicked himself silently for the pause–"Jeter . . . Jeter Brown, and I want to enlist."

Bigfoot Wallace had always been much brighter than folks liked to give such a large, slack-jawed man credit for, but it showed in the simpleminded common sense he brought to bear on things. He squinted and shut his hanging lower lip, then shut it once more. The big man gave him a confused look.

Titus heard the one-eyed soldier returning, the jingle of some idiot in the line behind him still wearing his spurs. Sweat trickled down one hairless cheek, but Titus did not reach up to wipe it. "You going to sign me up, Sergeant? Or would you rather I head over to join Moctezuma and the Mexicans?"

Bigfoot's Adam's apple bobbed once before he spoke. "We can use every live man can pull a trigger, Mr .... What was it again, Brig-something?"

"Brown. Jeter Brown."

Bigfoot nodded his gigantic head, and wrote it down on the next contract. "Pay is $4 a week. Held in abeyance for the first week to pay for your uniform and kit. Another two weeks if you didn't bring your own rifle and shots."

"I have them, Sergeant Wallace."

The contract hissed across the wood as Bigfoot slid it toward him. "Sign here and put your hand in the air."

Titus did as he was told and passed the paper and writing stick back.

Bigfoot put his own hand in the air and spoke to the one-eyed soldier. "My stomach ain't right this morning, Hadley. I think I need to find me an outhouse and sit a spell. You mind taking over here a while? I'll take this one over to get his kit. Tell Slippery Dave to come help out."

Hadley snorted. "That one's about as much help as my left eye. But sure, you go. I can handle this."

Bigfoot thanked him and rose to his near seven feet, his arm now so high in the air that its shadow stretched all the way back to the end of the line of new recruits.

"We don't have an actual Bible this morning. The chaplain took all of them out to Ol' Sylvester for blessing."

"That's alright," Titus managed, blinking over the eastern wall of Military Plaza into the morning sun. Cecilia would be double mortified, if she'd lived to see this day. "I guess every little bit helps," he said, pushing her ghostly condemnation out of his head.

"That it does, but it doesn't make your oath any less binding, Private Brown."

"I understand you, Sergeant."

Hadley cleared his throat and settled onto the stool. The desk made out of death and whiskey seemed to fit the gruff one-eyed man better than it had its former occupant. The look on Hadley's face made it obvious he was ready for Bigfoot and Private Brown to move along and let him get to work.

Titus repeated the oath of enlistment in the Army of the Republic of Texas word for word after Bigfoot, and when that was finished, he followed the only survivor of the Black Bean Affair outside.

They were only alone for a second before Bigfoot loosed a grin. "A private, huh?"

"Yeah."

"You really think you can enlist in the army, a man of your stature, and nobody's gonna know?"

"Probably not, but it's worth a shot. I'm tired of responsibility. Tired of making decisions. I'd appreciate you keeping this secret."

Bigfoot nodded. "For what that's worth." He cast a curious look at the sky. The moon had begun its slow pass across the sun. "Here's that eclipse they been expecting."

"There's something wrong about darkness in the day."

"That there is," said Bigfoot. "Let's get you a uniform."

He picked up the pace, and Titus hurried to match his long strides, on the way to the Bursar's building to collect his soldier blue.

Though it was barely past eleven, the shadows were already growing long.

It was nearly noon by the time President Burleson, dressing robe loosely tied around his sizeable gut, came into his study and found Willie snoring on his bench. He had a morning's growth of graying stubble and his hair was tangled and flattened against his head. When he saw Willie, he froze, then hurriedly pulled his robe around him tighter and backed into the adjoining corridor, harrumphing with an affronted air.

Willie jolted awake.

"Who are you?"

"Willie Wontshee."

"How the hell did you get inside my house?"

"Mr. Pincher let me in. He said he told you."

"Pincher? Woman, you'd better be straight with me."

"I *am* being straight with you," said Willie. It was irritating enough that she'd had to waste the morning waiting for him. She didn't intend to let him accuse her of lying too, President or not. "I came here to deliver you a message at the request of Brigadier-Justice Smoke and when I got here, that Pincher man gave me no end of grief. He told me you were on your way down to talk to me then he left."

"Pincher was in this house?" said Burleson. "This morning?"

"That's what I said."

"Well, why the hell–"

Two women, one wearing a fancy lace dressing gown, the other wearing absolutely nothing at all, peeked out from the stairway behind Burleson. Willie blushed, though not as brightly as the President. He turned around in the doorway and waved them away. "Go on, now! I have company!"

"Go where?" asked the naked woman. The other just grinned, and she looked to Willie like she'd had more than her fill of liquor.

"Anywhere. Back to the bedroom. Just go!"

"C'mon, Belle," said the naked woman, throwing an arm around the other woman and pulling her gently toward the stairs. "He's in a foul mood this morning."

"And put some damn clothes on!" said the President as they disappeared up the stairs. He then hurried into the sitting room and closed the door behind him, shutting off any other secrets he might not want Willie being privy too. The President sat across from her on a flowery couch, angry now, as if it was her fault his whores had come stumbling in. The smell of liquor and harlot's perfume lingered on him.

"I'll thank you to refrain from commenting," said the President.

"I wasn't going to say anything! What do I care what you do with yourself?"

"Well, okay then." Burleson relaxed a bit, then leaned forward to address her. "Before we were interrupted, I was telling you that Mr. Pincher does not work for me, and I have no idea what he was doing in my home. Frankly, I intend to visit the mayor this afternoon and ask him. Pincher works for him."

"Well, god damn!" said Willie. "I'm gonna whip that man if I see him again, running me around like this."

Burleson blushed again, apparently unaccustomed to hearing a woman swear. Willie didn't care. She'd had her fill of Austin and everyone in it.

"Well, then I guess you will." Burleson studied her, like he was trying to figure out if she was really a woman. Willie had seen that stare before. "Listen, then. Do you mind telling me whatever it is you came to tell me? I don't mean to be rude, but I've got a full plate of business to attend this afternoon."

"Zombies are marching on San Antonio."

"Pardon me?"

"That's my message. I come up from there and they're mobilizing. I guess Moctezuma is back for more. I didn't figure he'd stay put south of the river for long."

"You mean to say you barge into my house before I've even risen from bed to tell me this nonsense? Do you know how many people have carped on me about Moctezuma over the years? I've had three separate riders *this week,* all with conflicting stories. If I had one cent for every time I've heard that, I'd have a double eagle by now!"

"Well, you can believe me or not," said Willie. "That's what I come to say. The Brigadier-Justice says you'll give me fifty dollars for my trouble." She held out a hand, as if he might produce the money from beneath his robe.

Burleson pushed up from the couch and stood over her shaking his fist. "I'll have you leave this house, now. You hear? Titus Smoke no longer holds any sway around here. He saw to that when he quit. I see what this is now. He's rooked you into sharing his madness. Zombies coming from the south, Indians from the west, Americans hiding in every woodpile. If you believe him, everybody in the world wants this ugly bit of earth we've carved out for ourselves. Have you looked outside? Why the hell would anyone else want it?"

Willie stood, put on her hat and pushed past the President. She stepped into the hall and made for the front door.

Burleson followed her. "You tell Titus Smoke he can leave off on trying to scare me. I helped build this country into what it is and I ain't afraid of anyone taking it from me! Let them come if they're so bold. We whipped them once, we'll do it again. You tell him to quit sending women to fight his battles. He used to be a good man. What the hell happened to him?"

Willie spun around and punched the President in his face. She didn't hit him hard, but he gasped as if he'd been shot. She'd been needing to hit someone since the minute Pincher poked his lying face out of the President's door, and the President obviously needed someone to knock some sense into him. It was a fair trade.

If Burleson would have taken the time to just peek out the window, he'd see the streets were running with people moving north, getting away from the approaching horde. Obviously, Mr. Smoke had seen this coming and he'd tried to warn Burleson. She'd thought the President was someone to respect, and maybe he had been once, but complacency had reduced him to a frightened old man. She could see it in his eyes as he backed away from her, and read it in his inaction. It wasn't that Burleson didn't believe. He didn't want to believe. He'd rather hide out than face the fact that the Republic he'd helped build might well crumble around him.

Willie lunged at him, faking a second punch, and Burleson leapt back. She spat on his floorboard, opened the door and looked back at him from the threshold. "I've known Titus Smoke since I weren't no taller than a stick of grass, and he's a sight better man than you. I'll allow he ain't perfect, but at least he ain't dallying around in his pajamas with a couple of whores while the whole country goes to hell."

Burleson didn't speak. He just watched her like he would a rattlesnake that was a bit too close for comfort. He was breathing hard, and Willie decided if she didn't leave soon, his heart might give out.

"You should get dressed and figure out what that man was doing in your house," said Willie, then she stepped out into the street and left the President of Texas wide-eyed and fuming in his foyer.

The day seemed too dark for noon. Willie cast a look up and saw the moon beginning a slow creep across the surface of the sun. An eclipse. Her grandmother took great stock in signs, and best as Willie could remember, an eclipse meant some sort of trouble was coming.

Good thing Willie didn't believe in signs.

The hilly terrain and rain-softened brown clay ensured that the white man's beasts–great hissing, clunking, groaning, stinking things made of metal and boiling water–could not go much faster than a mounted brave for most of the way to the Texan capitol. Nor could they go far without water, or the occasional caches of coal that had been deposited in stealth months ago by what General Thackeray described as "giant floating air-filled bladders" which somehow used the air spirits trapped within to push them into the Great Spirit's open skies.

The white man was one for his maps and coordinates. Which had come in good stead, once Lightning Dove understood them. It was difficult, even with the time he'd spent learning the white man's ways and their words and their number magic, to connect in his mind that a bending blue line on the General's paper represented the Poshoshono, which the white men called Colorado River. But did it matter what anyone called it? The river had become but a trickle of its former magnificence since they had departed from Broken Lance's holy peak. No, it did not.

It mattered only that the General had said the land would be flatter here, and that the river would be rejoined there, and it was so, despite biting skepticism from both Lightning Dove and Broken Lance. Much as he resented these men who took orders from a woman across the long water, he had to admit a grudging respect for the way they could know the land without ever having walked upon it.

Broken Lance said that the white men were all afflicted with a sickness placed upon them by their god; they were able to understand the Earth with their head more than any other race of men, but their hearts were cursed to be forever numb. Their kind could only rape the land, and never love it.

And where was Broken Lance now? He had so far not fulfilled his promise of truly powerful medicine for the Warhawk braves on this, the day of the People's first vengeance. The old man was nowhere to be found. He had promised victory on the day that the sun was swallowed and vomited back up, but that had been when She-Who-Is-Alone rode with them. When she was taken, he had changed his counsel, saying that it was the Great Spirit's desire, and for him not to lose hope. Lightning Dove pushed his hand through long white hair, bound it behind his head with a bit of tanned mountain lion pelt as he surveyed the war party.

In the very rear of the formation lumbered the machines that used steam spirits to catapult the angels and the men who rode them into the sky. Each catapult was followed closely by a powered carriage containing four of the long white angel wings, all but one of them broken in half and trailing behind the carriage one upon the other. They resembled nothing so much as the scales of a great white lizard, or perhaps the nested wings of mating flies.

The General had forbidden the dozen or so men he called "pilots" from launching their great white wings into the sky, for fear that the Texans would see them and be warned.

Dejected at first, these goggle wearing men rode awkwardly and with long faces, like punished boys forced to work the corn and plants instead of joining the men on the hunt. But their dejection had not lasted very long. The pilots of Her Majesty's Wing Corps were such a high-spirited lot that often the other red-coated soldiers would joke that their brains were affected by breathing too much of heaven's own air. That could very well have been true. Even as he watched, one of the older soldiers with much yellow dangling from his shoulders loudly chastised a shame-faced trio of them for their habit of juvenile discord and "ass-grabbing."

Lightning Dove did not understand the white men.

Alongside the catapults, the storage galleons creaked. Enormous ribbed and pitch-coated wooden vessels designed to roll along on dozens of cantilevered sets of iron wheels. Some carried food and bullets and oil, but most were overflowing with coal. Every galleon had spaces for holding water throughout, even just beneath their pitch-coated wooden skins.

"The sun is getting high, Chief Lightning Dove."

Lightning Dove turned his horse at the sound of General Thackeray's voice. "Are you so quick to slaughter other white men?"

From atop one of the metal horses, the general made a strangled, grunting sound that reminded Lightning Dove of a regurgitating buzzard. "I am merely following the direction of my Queen," the general said.

"It is strange to me that you are led by a woman. And stranger still that she calls you to war." Lightning Dove swept his hand out to indicate the ranks of red before them: infantry men in neat lines with a forest of bayonets at their shoulders, interrupted occasionally by a wide-mouthed launcher of the steam grenades, the mechanical cavalry with their broad-brimmed hats and cutlasses and oil cans, and beyond them, the steaming metal Leviathans and fast-rolling jack-cars. Circling in their midst, and sending the red-jacket leaders into spasms of annoyance, Lightning Dove's own braves rode where they would, often stopping in the path of one hissing metal vehicle or another only to gallop out of the way seconds before the steam gear would need to slow down or turn this way or that.

Thackeray bristled. "I warn you, sir. As a peer of the Realm, I will tolerate no disrespect of my monarch or Her Empire."

"I mean you no disrespect. Only to understand. To what end, taking Texas? How does it serve your woman-chief's ends?"

Thackeray stared at Lightning Dove, then flicked one of the levers at the base of his metal horse's neck. It began to canter away toward the front of the line. "It does," he called back. "And that is all your people need to know. You should ask as many questions about how you aim to assist in this battle at all, without your magic princess."

Incensed, Lightning Dove galloped around him twice then slowed to match the general's pace riding alongside him to the left. He rode there silently for a while, watching Thackeray shouting loud commands to his army that did not appear to result in any change at all.

How had the man learned of She-Who-Is-Alone? No doubt his own men had spoken of her disappearance, and now Lighting Dove lamented their lack of discretion.

Finally, he spoke. "You will see the power of Comanche magic on this day, white man. The People will fight by your side and expel the Texans from their leader-city. But that does not mean that we will allow you to rule in their place." He spat on the ground, seeing Broken Lance's swaybacked stallion, nearly as old and grey as the shaman himself, grazing on the green limbs of a buckeye tree far to the right of the formation.

Thackeray said nothing. His busy blue eyes surveyed the horizon as if he were looking for dark clouds to match the sound of thunder.

"Your Queen is not the only leader worthy of respect," Lightning Dove said, then urged his horse through the rumbling war party toward Broken Lance, feeling the creature's beating heart and honest sweat as if they were his own.

Distantly, he heard Thackeray begin shouting again for more speed, that Austin was less than an hour away, and calling for reports from the vanguard, departed well before the morning sun arose with orders to slay any they could not detain who might warn Austin, and now strategically camped just out of sight of that doomed town.

Lightning Dove found Broken Lance in the shade with his back against the tree, bony legs crossed. The shaman's aged eyes remained closed and peaceful as if he were gazing straight through those thin, closed lids at the limbs and leaves and white geysers of flowers to the sky above him. A soft breeze whispered, disturbing what was left of the shrunken man's graying hair. Nothing else moved as Lightning Dove approached; even the shaman's horse was still.

Lightning Dove felt a cry welling up in him. To have come so far. With the girl and her mysterious gift of magic now lost to him. And now this. Four of his braves approached from the outskirts of the advancing war party. Lightning Dove waved them off, not trusting himself to speak.

When they were far enough away, and no longer looking back at him, he fell to his knees in front of Broken Lance. A sob escaped him.

He hated himself for it.

What now? The younger medicine men, even added together, were as tiny springs beside the fountainhead that was Broken Lance. They could not decipher the Great Spirit's intent, or channel the plant and animal spirits to aid the Warhawk tribe. They were too young, and not yet wizened by the sun and moon.

Lightning Dove bellowed then, an inarticulate howl of despair and damnation. Broken Lance's tired horse knickered once and continued to eat the foliage it could reach on the tree. For a moment, all he could hear was his own breath jerking in and out of his throat, though his face was dry. He beat the ground with his open hands unmindful of the miniature dust storms he created.

He raged like that he knew not how long before the sound of his own sobs began to fade and he heard another sound below them. A dry, rattling chuckle. He looked up to see the old man staring at him with one bleary eye, and smiling, but with only the right half of his face.

"Are you then all anger and no tears, Lightning Dove?"

"You!" Lightning Dove's heart raced. He felt his voice rising, the word scratched in his throat because of the shouting he had just been doing. "I thought you had abandoned the People!"

His cries had not gone unnoticed. Several of the braves were already riding back to see what the commotion had been about. Overhead, the sun was approaching its highest point. Less than an hour. And Austin was close enough Lightning Dove thought he could smell it.

The old man shook his head, that ridiculous half-smile still on his face. "You are not rid of me so soon, white hair." He rose awkwardly to his feet, using the tree to support himself. Broken Lance called to his horse.

"Help me, Lightning Dove. I have paid a great price for our victory today, and I am not sure I will see the stars over Comanche lands again."

Lightning Dove propped him into place, grunting despite how insubstantial the old man felt. It was as if he were nothing more than cattle pelt laid over twigs. "These are Comanche lands," he told the old man. "And surely you will see many things come to pass, before you smoke your last pipe."

It was the old man's turn to grunt. "If you would not see me trampled, you must tie me to my friend's back. Already, I am starting to lean too far to one side."

Lightning Dove gestured to the braves. They had kept their distance, but watched everything that transpired with a sense of earnestness. "Bring me rope. And the younger shaman to attend to Broken Lance."

Two of the braves broke off at a gallop. One toward Lightning Dove with a length of thin wound fiber stolen long ago from a white rancher, and the other in the direction of the disappearing war party. Lightning Dove took the rope and sent the worried-looking brave and his horse away with a sharp slap on the flank.

Working the rope around Broken Lance's thighs and the horse's neck and belly, Lightning Dove did his best to secure the old man, with his weird half-smile and bleary eye, to the gray horse. When he was finished, he asked, "What magic did you trade so much for, that you cannot even hold yourself upright or make your face behave as one thing?"

"Something truly powerful, Lightning Dove. Our fighting men will be forever changed. She is not with us, but not so far away either."

Even as he explained it to Lightning Dove, the war chief cried out with exultation even mightier than his earlier shouts of despair.

After, they rode as swiftly as the shaman's condition could allow, and massed the entire Warhawk Council down to the youngest untested boy. They rode together, oblivious to the desires of the white men, whooping and chanting like all the spirits of the Comancheria had been set loose upon them, each watching the sun and the shadow beginning to cover it.

Alamo Rising

Smoke maneuvered the leviathan without speaking for several hours, until he judged by the familiar scenery and the trail of destruction left by the advancing army that they were nearing Austin. He allowed hope to blossom within him and he urged the metal monster forward.

When he noticed the shadows beginning to creep and grow, Smoke cast a look up at the sky. The sun was slowly disappearing as the moon slid in front of it. Already a quarter sliver of the sun was gone.

Suddenly, Darla began screaming in her sleep, and Smoke knew they were too late after all.

PART the SECOND

➞➞➞❬❬❬❬

BURNING AUSTIN

CHAPTER 13

AUDREY HEARD THEM coming as the moon eased halfway across the face of the sun. She was sitting with her skirt pulled up to her knees, feet in the muddy river water, composing a mental list of all the places she'd rather be than Texas, when the unified howl of a hundred and more voices rode the thick summer heat through the streets of Austin and found her on the banks of the Colorado.

There was no mistaking that sound. Mr. Engle had told her numerous times that when the Comanches came, they would ride like avenging angels sent to scour the earth clean of white men, and they would announce their fury with the agonized screams of all those who'd been robbed of their lives and their homes. Most people in Austin thought the Indians would be content to exist on the hardscrabble plains, content to leave the Texans to their progress. But to Mr. Engle's mind there had never been any question the Indians would come. Mr. Engle was firmly convinced it was only a matter of time until the natives, or the desert, or the floodwaters, took back everything the Texans had built. As Audrey climbed hurriedly to her feet, dress sticking to her wet legs, the only thing she could think was the old man was right. *They've come for us. We were just borrowing this place and now they've come to take it back.*

Beneath the growing river of wails was the dull thunder of horses and a low rumbling drone that sounded like the hills themselves had begun to moan. Audrey couldn't reconcile that sound with anything familiar, and all the stories she'd heard about Indian magic suddenly leapt to her mind, no longer willing to be dismissed as simple cautionary tales to keep fools from wandering out west.

Lord, woman! Don't be an idiot. No time for that.

She hurried up the sloping banks, pulling herself up with handfuls of scrub grass and rock. The few streets that formed Austin proper were just downriver to the east. She ran that direction, not certain what she would do when she arrived, but unsure where else to go. The

Indians' cries intensified, and she could see them now, coming from the west, coming for her and for everything she knew. And something else. God, what was it?

Audrey reached the place where the streets began, screaming to anyone who'd listen about Indians and death and whatever the hell those gray lumbering shapes were that followed the Indians like creeping nightmares. But the people of Austin were already in motion: mothers pulled their children from the streets and locked them behind doors that would very soon be useless; merchants threw closed their shops in fits of similar futility; a few men with rusted rifles called for anyone willing to join them, insisting that if they didn't fight everyone would be killed; others milled about in utter shock, unwilling or unable to decide how best to preserve the last fleeting seconds of their lives.

Shadows crept, the day rapidly turning to night.

A woman with a gaggle of filthy children had parked a wagon in the middle of the street, and she whipped the old mule drawing them with a limp piece of rope, urging the stubborn thing into motion. A one-legged man stood beside the wagon, leaning on a cane and slapping at the beast to coax it forward. The mule took a few steps, then stopped to pick at a patch of dandelions. The woman swatted the animal again, but it only swatted back with its tail in response.

A few other wagons plodded up the street; they'd been coming all morning, wagons and horses and people on foot, many claiming that San Antonio was under attack by zombies. That seemed unlikely to Audrey, but whatever the case, these people had ridden into *real* danger.

"Indians!" yelled Audrey. She reached the wagon load of children and shook the one-legged man to get his attention. "You've got to hide these kids!"

"What the hell you think I'm trying to do?" he said. "This mule is staying put."

"You can't outrun them in a wagon anyway," she said. "You've got to hide." Without waiting for an invitation, Audrey stepped on the sideboard and began lifting children from the back of the wagon. The sour-faced woman with them wore a checked bonnet overstuffed with red hair, and she clutched a writing slate to her chest as if it would shield her from harm. She watched as Audrey sat three children down on the street with a mildly affronted look, as if Audrey was taking far too much liberty with her charges. Then understanding lit in her eyes, and she broke free from her shock like a frightened plow horse snapping its reins.

"You heard her," the old woman said, slapping at the man now with her bit of rope. "Help her with these kids. We've got to hide them."

"Can't hide from Comanches, Sam. We got to run!"

"You run and they'll have you before you reach the far edge of town," said Audrey, not pausing in her labors. The woman, Sam, climbed from her seat and into the back. She ushered the kids toward Audrey. They all wore confused expressions, and Audrey prayed they didn't understand what the wailing meant. Finally they all stood beside her on the ground save for a tiny blonde girl with one pig tail. The other had come loose and that side of her head looked like a bird's nest of straw. Sam coaxed her forward and Audrey took her gently from the wagon.

This one she held in her arms; the other children she shooed in the direction of Mr. Engle's stable where she worked. Sam helped corral them into a manageable group and Audrey led them all up the street, knowing any second that the Indians would appear between the crowded row of building and begin picking them off with arrows.

The gunshots began when they reached the stable and wrenched open the door. Mr. Engle had passed on nearly two months back, and Audrey had been doing her best to keep the place going in his stead. Not every man was willing to do business with a woman, and fewer were willing to let her shoe his horse, but she'd built a reputation in Austin as a steady hand and a fair minded business woman. So far she'd managed to keep the doors open.

Not that any of that mattered now. Austin wasn't well-armed; most of the country's military might was stationed in San Antonio, had been for years. Audrey's business, her home, her city–none were long for the world.

Still clinging to the little blonde girl, Audrey followed Sam, the one-legged man, and the rest of the children into the stable. A pair of roans she was boarding for the Rangers occupied the back two stalls, and the horses paid them little mind. Audrey slipped the little girl down to the earthen floor and turned to close the door behind them. She caught a glimpse of movement between the houses, and then there they were. A pair of painted Indians galloping up the street, more joining behind. Arrows flew and Audrey heard someone scream. She wrestled the door shut, desperately hoping she wouldn't find out who the scream had belonged to.

Sam hurried the children to the back of the stables, admonishing them in a whisper to leave their hands off everything. Audrey found her hammer, seized it and took comfort in the weight of it. Then she knelt beside the little blonde girl and eased her further away from the door. The girl trembled.

"What's your name?" asked Audrey in a low tone that she hoped encouraged silence from everyone.

"Gretchen," said the girl with a hint of a German accent.

"Well, don't be scared, Gretchen. They won't find us in here." Outside, the wails and gunshots were joined by more screams and the crackle of flames. Audrey wondered how long before the building they were in was burned to the ground.

"Klaus said they're going to cut off my hair," said Gretchen.

"Did not!" said a little boy that could be Gretchen's twin. His voice sounded as loud as a thunderclap. Sam hushed him with a hand over his mouth

"Yes he did," whispered Gretchen. "He says Indians always cut off people's hair. They aren't really going to do that, are they? I've been growing this hair all my life."

Audrey smiled in spite of herself. "No, honey. Your hair's too pretty to cut."

Then the wood plank door jerked open and a Comanche stood framed in the darkness of midday. Gretchen squealed. Sam hissed and gathered the children to her. The one legged man stepped between Audrey and the Indian. Audrey felt a coldness creep through her. They were all about to die. The one-legged man would buy them a second perhaps, and she felt immeasurable gratitude that he was willing to stand for them. She hadn't even learned the man's name.

Audrey clutched Gretchen tightly, and suddenly remembered the little girl in Laredo. The one Jeb had shot. What kind of world was this that little ones like that kept coming to such harm?

"You ain't welcomed here," said the one-legged man. He flexed his hands, as if imagining they held something to hit the Indian with. But they were empty, and the Indian carried a tomahawk. It dangled loosely in his grip, as if he couldn't even be bothered to raise it. He studied the terrified children with a blank expression, face streaked with paint, bare chest taught with flexed muscles.

Would he leave them alone? They weren't threats to him.

Audrey waited for him to move. If he came at the one-legged man, maybe she could get in a good blow with her hammer before the man killed them.

The Indian smiled then, and his head burst into flames.

Gretchen screamed, and Audrey dragged her to the back of the stables, unable to believe what she was seeing. The one-legged man lumbered after them, cursing, keeping his eye on the unnatural blue flames that now engulfed the Comanche's upper body. He didn't scream, didn't move. Just stood there and burned. Then slowly, the intensity of the flames began to wane, and ash began falling, staining the man's body, collecting on the ground. As the flames died down, they could see a new face emerging, as if the fires had consumed the old one and left another in its place beneath the coating of ash.

It wasn't a human face.

A coyote head had taken its place, and it stared at them from the Indian's body with a fierce, human intelligence.

The Comanche howled, and Audrey joined Gretchen's screams.

General Thackeray cursed.

The sun had only half darkened, yet the savages were already galloping across the hill and almost certainly into view of the town. Had they no sense of discipline? Did their lack of civilization preclude them from participating in an ordered attack? Regardless, Courtney Thackeray was a Queen's man through and through; no pack of primitives was going to ruin his attack, his first definitive moment of glory in what the Empire's historians and poets would surely rhapsodize for decades–no, aeons–to come.

And they certainly were not going to be the first to draw blood.

He turned to one aide and then another, ordering Her Majesty's Wings into the air post-haste to soften up the town with their array of Chinese style rockets attached to tins of combustible gas. Even as the first few satisfying thunks told him the initial wave was aloft, he heard the catapult crewmen shouting orders and stoking the boilers and muscling the next wave into place. They were a gorgeous sight in the air, truly a sign of Her Majesty's superiority over both the savages and upstarts of the American continent. It would be his name, Lord General Courtney Thackeray, that upstanding Britons remembered whenever the supper talk turned to how England had won back her too-long-errant colonies, how they'd used the hard won California colony as a launching point to take the whole of the continent. And how, in true conqueror fashion they had used the inhabitants against each other until there was no native military might left to object.

He quietly cheered as the grenadiers of Her Majesty's Mechanical Cavalry rode off toward the town, gears clicking in perfect time like God's Own Pocket Watch. The leviathans and jack-cars continued their gradual ascent up the hill as he rode up alongside his flagship, *Indomitable*. The bosuns were ready for him and in no time at all had the winch and davit in place to haul him and his metal steed aboard at one of the open gunnery sponsons. A private, buck-toothed and grinning, bore a hand and pulled him the rest of the way aboard.

Thackeray returned both the grin and the salute and headed purposefully to his command center on the highest deck, where he knew a slew of aides and officers were standing by to communicate his orders.

One soldier piped attention to announce the general's arrival, and the noisy chaos of his men and maps became instantly silent. "Carry on," he said, taking the spyglass offered him by an ensign. As he focused the lenses, he asked, "Reports?"

From this elevation, Austin was already in view. It was as described in his intelligence. Little more than a few dozen log homes and false-fronted businesses scattered like toys left around a sandpit by one of his sister's obstreperous brats. All but a scarce few of the dwelling places and establishments clung to the ground in simple one-story shambles. Why, it hardly merited being called a town.

And there upon the hill, whitewashed and towering over all those lesser buildings below it ... President Burleson' Mansion, or so his spies reported. Thackeray would sleep there tonight.

He moved the spyglass about before him, holding his other eye shut. "Reports?" he called again. He found one of the steam angels circling overhead, bobbing queasily in the half-light. Tiny parcels dripped from it like tears. Below it, red and orange bursts. He could just make out the occasional rattle of small arms fire. Were those shots being fired by his dragoons, or had the Texan rabble already begun to mount their futile defense?

He searched the grounds until he saw not red-jacketed soldiers, but red-skinned Comanche swarming on and off horse, with rifle and hatchet and knife and spear. It was hard to make out what was going on because the noontime sun had all but disappeared, plunging the attackers and the attacked into a preternatural darkness. His men conveyed battlefield information and occurrences into both ears at once, while he smiled and watched the combustibles fall and explode on Austin, while the assault carriages, mechanized cavalry, and all the other units pillaged the unprepared capitol.

And what of the Indian's heathen magic? On holiday at best, a sham more like. But he had to applaud their courage. These red devils fought as if they had a stake in the spoils. He chuckled, about to put the spyglass down since he could barely make out anything useful in the darkness. He put it back up again quickly, compensating for *Indomitable's* rolling and bumping as it heaved itself across the dry grass ever closer to the fighting.

What had he seen, there by a flaming wagon? The spyglass wove in tight little circles around the woefully small field of battle until he found it again. One of the Indians, hatchet raised and threatening a woman and her babe in arms. He would in no way be sorry if the entire race were wiped from the face of England's newest dominion. He squinted at the scene before him. Uncertainty created a panic in the pale woman's face. For just a moment ... there, flame-limned, he had seen it. That Indian was no longer a wiry man at all, but something horrifyingly different altogether. Thackeray let the spyglass fall, distantly grateful for the wisp of an aide who grabbed it midair, saving it from certain breakage. Chills wracked him, body and soul, as he struggled to understand what he had seen. Voices shouted information and requests to turn the *Indomitable* into a better firing position. He stood there dizzy and shivering until his natural Briton stoicism restored itself.

He gave the permissions, attended to the orders, waited eagerly for this unnatural night to become day again. All the while thinking: To what satanic magic has Her Majesty allied herself?

Lightning Dove rode with his warriors down the main street of Austin, hacking at the whites with his tomahawk, screaming a song of death and victory.

The earth's magic chilled his body, and he relished the sensation of power that gripped him like the commanding hand of the Great Spirit itself. His muscles quivered and strength flooded him. All around, his men were taking on aspects of the Great Spirit's other children. Coyote heads howled from human bodies; men wore bear claws like winter gloves; others clothed themselves in scales and hissed through venomous fangs. Lightning Dove's flowing white hair and his headdress had burned away and now the feathers he wore were his own. He bit at the air with his raptor's beak and flexed the great wings that grew from his back. The wind pulled at him, pleading for him to take flight. He wasn't sure how long he could resist.

Broken Lance's communion with the earth had reaped unimagined consequences.

Lightning Dove was accustomed to the tiny powers the earth gave his people over the plants and animals, the ability to grow vegetation and form it to their needs, the ability to call fish to the baskets and buffalo to the bow. But this new power surpassed everything he'd imagined. Even without the blessing of She-Who-Is-Alone, they'd managed this. What a formidable tribe they would be when she was returned to them.

The whites scattered, screaming, as the Comanche changed before their eyes. Many who'd been offering modest resistance simply fled in the face of what was happening. Not even the general's dragoons could hide their wonder and their terror, though they did an admirable job of continuing the fight once they realized these were simply their Indian allies in new forms.

Lightning Dove hefted his spear and drove it through the chest of a filthy man wearing only a torn pair of white man's undergarments. All around him, Comanche warriors burst into flames, and emerged as new, better, creatures. Totem spirits. The least of them became coyotes in full, or panthers. Enormous bears, indistinguishable from real ones save the intelligence in their eyes, lumbered through the streets, showing the white men their teeth and urging their allies forward with their fearsome presence. Greater warriors were rewarded with improved versions of their own bodies; these were still men, though far more fearsome. Lightning Dove was among them, and even as he rode, he felt his feet burning away into talons. His chest was painted with the blood of his first kill, and his legs gripped the stallion beneath him with renewed vigor. Lightning Dove had seen many summers, but he was not infirm. The earth had seen to that.

The wind gusted again, and this time Lightning Dove did not resist it. It carried him from his saddle into the air among the unwieldy contraptions that Thackeray had called his steam angels. They flew, that could not be disputed. But they did not soar as Lightning Dove did. Their power came from mechanical mysteries, but Comanches power came from the soul of the earth itself.

The people of Austin scattered below him, running from burning houses, rampaging Comanches and the slow crawl of English war machines that harried them with bullets. The battle had hardly begun–the sun was only now blackened in full–yet the Texans were already routed. If Lightning Dove had known how easy it would be, he'd never have joined forces with the English. They could have taken this sorry rabble themselves.

Lightning Dove screamed again, and circled the skies like Thunderbird protecting his People's lands.

CHAPTER 14

WILLIE NEARLY BEGAN SCREAMING when the Comanches caught fire and started changing into animals, then she remembered she wasn't a frilly girl. She'd never cared for dresses or painting her face; she'd never thought about being a school teacher or somebody's wife; not seriously. She loved her pistol, but other than fleeting thoughts about Jeb when they were kids, she'd never cared much about any man. And she certainly hadn't thought about cooking them supper or mothering a bunch of squalling babies. Once, she'd even shot a man in the arm in Galveston for trying to put his hands on her. No, she wasn't a girl. She was Willie. And so she swallowed her terror and pulled both her pistols.

The man who'd been standing in front of her emerged from a dying blast of flames, reborn as a panther. The panther stared at her and howled. Hair stood up on Willie's arms. She hated panthers. Always had. A panther had carried away one of her little cousins before it was old enough to walk, and ever since, she hated the sound of them calling to each other between the trees on moonless nights. But this wasn't real night; it was just an eclipse. And it certainly wasn't a real panther. Willie lifted her pistol and shot the thing in the face. Magic or not, it hit the dirt and didn't move again.

She hurried out of the main street and took refuge behind a rain barrel between two stores that hadn't yet caught fire. She needed some time to get her bearings, to figure out how to get the hell out of Austin without being killed. The Comanche had fallen on the town less than twenty minutes after she'd left the President, and that had been surprise enough. But she didn't understand why the Redjacks rode with them. What were they doing here, and why would they ally themselves with the Comanche?

Men flew overhead in winged contraptions, dropping fire on the city. One of their burning canisters had fallen not ten feet away from Willie and her horse, and the resulting explosion had knocked her to her ass and killed her mount. Since then, she'd been prowling through the city, keeping an eye to the sky while she tried to avoid Indians. She hadn't seized on any plan for survival other than to keep moving south, away from the President's broken down old house and toward the river. If she could cross at the ford down east, she'd be able to ride hard for San Antonio. Of course, that was assuming she found a new horse.

She peered around the rain barrel and spotted the stable directly across the street. The sign read: Engle and Associate, Stable and Shod. Est. 1839.

Willie's grandmother's voice crowed in her head. *The Lord will provide.*

"Shut up," whispered Willie, then she froze. She'd been about to emerge from between the buildings when a river of Redjacks poured down the street, pursuing a fleeing band of pitchfork and scythe wielding farmers with gunshots and bayonets. Animals–Indians, they were Comanche Indians–mingled in the fray, enjoying the chase. Willie pressed up against the wall, waited for the soldiers to pass. One of the Indians, this one as yet unchanged, yanked open the stable door and peered inside. Bastard was probably planning to steal all the horses. That sure as hell wouldn't do.

Willie risked a peek in both directions and saw that everyone in the battle was mercifully engaged. She took aim at the Indian just as his head burst into flames. She watched him change, staring him down over her pistol sight. When the flames receded, most of him was still like it had been, but his head looked like that of a coyote. Willie didn't like coyotes any more than she did panthers. They were low creatures, scavengers. And they were mean.

Willie bolted from cover and ran across the street in a crouch. Incendiary bombs fell around her, and one hit the building next to the stable. She never flinched. Willie reached the far side of the path, drew up to her full height and raised her pistol.

"Adios, coyote," she said, and shot the man in the head.

Gunfire barked from the east, and Chinese firecracker flashes lit the darkness. Troy imagined the wind brought the sounds of crying women and shouting men along with the all too real smell of gunpowder and burning homes. Up against the light-rimmed black disk in the sky, steam angels swooped and spun, their pilots dropping little specks of flame on the rooftops of Austin.

Smoke yelled something back at him that he almost didn't hear over the noise of his own anger. "Stoke the God damned fire!"

Troy swallowed his spit, tasting Darla's snakebite all over again, and turned his back to the fray long enough to fill the furnace with a dozen shovelfuls of fresh coal. He had brought up a lot of coal already, and had the lift all set up with a fresh load. Hot, sweaty work if ever there was any. Troy wasn't quite sure how the Queen's men put up with it. But Smoke was dead set on driving, and so long as that meant Troy would be the one pulling those gun chains, he wasn't going to ask for a turn in the driver's seat. No matter how hard Smoke tried to rattle everyone's teeth out.

Leviathan 212 had finally lumbered its way out of the valley and alongside a handful of other English units, strange contraptions pointed at the twilit sky and surrounded by handfuls of smoking crewmen, all their eyes on the steam angels and their hellish work. Troy shoved another heaping helping of coal into the hungry furnace. Hoping it was hot enough Smoke wouldn't be carping on him for a minute or two, Troy staggered along the tilting deck to the gun enclosure.

The guns were set up with plenty of ammunition standing by. Troy had even found a bit of oil and lubricated the moving parts of all three chain guns earlier while Smoke had been up there warbling to Darla about God knows what.

Three guns in the open air cabin, most likely each manned by two Redjacks: one to aim and another to pull the chain. Troy snickered as he adjusted the left chain gun until a handful of the skylarking Queen's men were captured inside its reticule. Then holding it as steady as he could with Smoke's driving, he reached one arm over and gave the firing chain a long sustained pull. The chain gun reacted with a series of satisfying bangs and three of the four soldiers went down. By lucky coincidence, the recoil from the shots had pulled the barrel up despite Troy's attempt to keep it aimed at the soldiers. Bullets tore into the steam gear behind the Queen's men, and steam began whistling through the breaches. A moment later, it was pluming like a tea kettle and the men still alive around it were going anthill crazy trying to figure out who was firing on them and how bad the damage was to their steam angel launcher.

Troy snorted and bounced over to the other side.

"Nice work!" Smoke shouted back at him. Troy smiled but didn't respond. He was too busy lining up a shot on the other side, where a gigantic steam vessel waited with all kinds of streamers and pennants flying from its iron mast.

He fired another burst from the chain gun, whooping as the bullets pinged against the metal-plated hull, even though it did not appear to be doing any actual damage. Troy looked ahead of them, eager to find a target on which to turn the largest of the guns.

Smoke kept the Leviathan surging toward the town, coming alongside some of the Queen's finest war machines and even passing a few. Using the darkness to their advantage.

"How's your steam?" Troy hollered up at Smoke.

"Going south!"

"I'm on it."

"We got bigger problems. That big son of a bitch with all them flags just sent a fellow on a steam mare our way. Bet he's going to tell us hang back."

"Hang back, Hell!" Troy was already headed to the furnace. He shoveled more coal and brought up the next lift-full, all the while keeping one eye on the steam mare and the puffed-up looking messenger straddling it. When the man was close enough, Troy pulled a Redjack pistol from his belt and fired one shot. The courier clutched his waist and rolled off the side of his mount. The steam mare plodded two dozen more paces before falling over on one side, mechanical legs kicking at the air as if they were galloping across an invisible and oddly tilted landscape.

It seemed Queen's men weren't any better at dodging bullets than anyone else.

Troy grinned and went back to shoveling. It might take a whole crew of Redjacks to run that gun cabin, but Troy was ready to show the Queen how much damage just one Texan could do.

The Indian's head exploded.

Once second he was lifting his tomahawk and taking a step toward the one-legged man, who still leaned valiantly on his crutch between the monster and the children, and the next his coyote head tore apart in a roar of gunfire. The bullet that ended his life thudded into a wood plank on the back wall and bits of his bone and blood spattered the room.

The children shrieked, and Audrey clutched Gretchen tighter to her chest. The one-legged man backed away as the Comanche's body hit the ground and a long-haired man in a riding coat stepped into the stable and swung the door shut quickly behind him. He dropped his pistol back into his holster, then turned to face them.

And Audrey saw then that *he* was a *she*.

"Well, I wasn't expecting this," said the woman, leaning against the stable door, as if doing so might keep out any other Indians who decided to investigate. She was a tall woman with two pistols and bullets belting her waist. She was bowlegged and stooped, as if she spent far too much time on horseback, but there was touch of beauty in her face, all but buried beneath road dirt and the hard mannish air she affected. The woman spat, peeked out a knothole. Then she strode boldly up to the one-legged man and addressed him.

"Hello, Mr. Marin. I reckoned ya'll was dead by now, but I'm glad to see you ain't. Where's Sam?"

"I'm here," said Sam, emerging from the darkness at the back of the stable. The horses knickered and several of the children were crying. These people knew the wild woman who'd come to save them?

"And all the kids is safe?" asked the woman.

"Yep," said Sam. "Every one, thanks to this kind lady and her stable. Though I reckon that's only a temporary state of affairs. How bad is it out there?"

"Plenty bad." The woman gave Audrey a look that didn't seem terribly convinced of Audrey's ability to save anyone from anything. "Austin's in more trouble than it can fight off. And there's Englanders too. Bunch of men with guns and flying machines and Lord knows what all. We got to leave as fast as we can."

"We can't," said Audrey, standing. Gretchen clung to her legs, whimpering. Audrey stroked the girl's hair. "We run and we'll die for sure."

"No, we stay and we die for sure. Every building in this town's gonna burn."

"What do you suggest?" asked Mr. Marin. He leaned on his crutch and ran a nervous hand through what remained of his thinning gray hair. The bare parts of his head were burned red and life had only left him with half the teeth he'd been given by God.

"Hell if I know," said the woman. "We just got to get." She turned to Audrey again and pointed at the horses in the back stalls. "Them animals yours?"

"Yes, this whole place is mine."

"*You're* the proprietor?"

"Yes. Don't look so surprised. There are plenty of women suited for man's work, as you no doubt can attest to."

"How many horses then?" she asked.

"Four."

"Wagons?"

"I don't own a wagon. And I doubt the one these children rode in on is a safe bet. It's bound to be overtaken by now."

"It surely is," said Sam, looking rueful. "That was a good wagon too. Can't stand the thought of Comanches and tea-drinkers wheeling it around town. I'd rather they just burn it, to tell you the truth."

The woman waved her off. "Can't be worrying about no lost wagons. We need to find one that we can get to. Do you know of any?"

Audrey realized the woman was speaking to her again. "I don't know. I mean there's folks that have them but they're like as not burned up or taken by now. I know a few farmers that come in from time to time with their animals. A few of them live south of town. South of the river. I don't know how we'd get there, but if they haven't already run off then maybe we could catch a ride. At least maybe they'd take the children. Do you think the Indians have got that far yet? Past the river?"

"I don't know," said the woman. "But the longer we wait around, the slimmer our chances. You have a back door?"

"Not a door, but there's a window I throw open to let the heat out. Back there near the horses."

"Then let's go. We'll sneak out that way. Though I don't know how we can move on the sly with a bunch of crying kids. I reckon it'll have to do. Sam, tell them to hush. You're the teacher, ain't you?"

"They're just kids, Willie," said Sam, moving back among her charges, trying to sooth them with soft touches and lies about everything being okay and there being nothing in the world to worry about.

"They are that," said Willie, and she made her way to the window.

Audrey stood motionless beside the fallen Indian. War raged outside, and she did her best to block out the horrible sounds awaiting them if they went through that back window. Surely they'd be dead in an instant if they tried to drag all these kids through the streets. But ultimately, the wild woman, Willie, was probably right. If the invaders were razing the town, the building around them wouldn't stay safe for long.

"Mr. Marin?" Audrey said, offering her hand to the one-legged man. He stood staring at the headless man at their feet, refusing to ask the same question the rest of them were trying to ignore. What had happened to him? One moment he'd been a man, then a few fiery seconds later he was something else. Something far from human. And judging by the sounds outside, he wasn't the only one. What sort of deviltry had fallen on Austin?

Mr. Marin pulled his gaze away from the body and nodded to her. He took Audrey's hand and she helped Gretchen and him move away from the fallen Indian and toward the band of children massing against the back wall. Sam bobbed among them, doing a remarkable job of quieting them and bolstering their courage. Audrey had never had children, and she'd often wondered if she'd have the right gifts of spirit to tend to them. She suspected she would, though she'd never anticipated being put to the test in this sort of way.

Willie pulled the latch from the window, waved a quieting hand at everyone and opened it just a crack so that she could peer out. Audrey wondered again how this woman knew Sam, Mr. Marin, and her children. She supposed it didn't matter. The woman had saved them and now she was ready to help lead them to safety.

"It's quiet back here," Willie whispered. "There's been some fighting but I think it's moved on along. You might want to shut the children's eyes when we go out, though. There's some bodies around and they ain't been treated well. And there's other things besides bodies out there I don't suspect they'd need to see."

With that, Willie opened the big shutters until they were wide enough to pass through and slid out onto the back street. She put her arms back in and Sam began passing children through the window.

"Line up against the wall," said Willie, gently. "Stay flat as you can and keep quiet."

"Willie," said Audrey, her heart suddenly tight in her chest. "Are you sure this is the best course of action? Maybe we should wait it out. The Rangers are sure to come quick. And the President probably has the whole army headed this way by now."

Willie shook her head solemnly and hefted another little boy out the window. "Most of the Rangers are out patrolling God knows where. Probably hanging bandits and chasing whores and having a good old time. As for the President, I can guarantee that man ain't doing nothing worthwhile.

"We've got to get the hell out of town. Ain't nobody coming to save us. We got to do it ourselves."

CHAPTER 15

NOISE AND FIRE AND DEATH ERUPTED all around him, regiments in red surrounding and laying waste to the capitol of the Republic of Texas. Once upon a time, Smoke had sworn to put the infant nation before himself, had carried a Ranger's star and rode from one end of the sparse landscape to the other putting an end to cattle thieves and steam carriage bandits and zombies and whatever else the scrubland threw at him. One fouled shot had put an end to that, set him on a downward course as sure and mud-spattered as any rain spout. Hell, even with the quick dip in the Colorado, he was pretty sure the mud-spattered part still applied. He could feel dirt caked up on his scalp and behind his ears. Even in the crack of his ass.

But at least the Redjacks weren't shooting back at him yet. He had the Queen's uniforms to thank for that. Behind him, Darla lay in a puddle of Comanche leather at his feet, barely giving him room to stand. Her screaming had not so much stopped as ... diminished. Her mouth gaped open and Smoke imagined she was still screaming, just not out loud anymore. Her stricken expression and shuttered eyes reminded Smoke of the way his Mama looked in her death picture, the shadows leaking from around those parted lips like the last vapors of forgiven sin wafting from her earthbound vessel.

He worried about the girl. Too much of his own soul was tied up in keeping her alive. Troy was right to cuss him, damn his bones. It had been his idea to send her into the water, and the water was where the snake got her.

But worrying about that didn't get them out of the fix they were in right now. Austin burning, a pair of ex-Rangers in Limey-suits sneaking through the ranks and no hope of escape if the battle kept going the way it was. The big gun boomed a dozen times in a row over Smoke's head and he ducked involuntarily. Off to the left, by the President's mansion, a row of marching Redjacks convulsed and went down. If his ears weren't ringing so much he would have sworn he heard Troy chortling. The shots stopped and a moment later the Leviathan's speed kicked up a notch.

"Keep shoveling!"

But shoveling for what? This was going to end badly. Any second the Queen's Men would turn on them, or some lucky son of Austin with a rifle and a hiding spot would start sniping at the pair of them, and then where would they be? Smoke was starting to feel like a rat in a roomful of bull snakes. *Damn it, I need a plan or we'll be hanging from that turret before the sun goes down.*

He ratcheted the speed controls for the treads on both sides of the metal beast to the FULL setting and began barreling toward Austin.

"We're in the thick of it now, Darla!"

If she made any response at all, it was lost in the noise of the Leviathan's boiler, the wind whipping past and the grinding rush of rocky soil beneath them. As long as Troy could keep the coal fire burning hot enough to keep pressure up, they'd be in the middle of all those Comanche and Redjack cavalry and dragoons in a matter of minutes. But where to then?

Smoke scanned the town. Everywhere he looked, roofs burned with all the tenacity of one of Audrey's Sunday morning teetotaler lectures. If Audrey was still in Austin, she was no doubt secretly pleased that the row of saloons seemed to be taking the most damage. *Alcohol, gunpowder, dance hallsl and French perfume*, she used to say, *The Four Horsemen of Our Modern Apocalypse*. Smoke smiled at the thought of her, hands on hips as she laid it out for him.

The President's mansion wasn't burning yet, but it was about the only place that wasn't. Smoke realized with a start that none of the paltry Austin return fire was coming from Burleson's Folly. Surely if there was any part of the capitol that would be heavily defended, it would be where the President of the Republic held office. Squinting as the last of the weird gray tinge went away from the noontime sky, Smoke tried to prove himself wrong.

Try as he might, he couldn't see even one single sign of a defense at the President's big house on the hill. In fact, as he stared, he saw, impossibly, the English flag going up the flagpole on the other side of it.

"Son of a bitch," Smoke said. Darla stirred behind him, grabbed on to one boot. Smoke checked her quickly. Her eyes were still closed, her mouth still open, but there was a peaceful air to her now. She finally looked more like a fevered child holding on to a doll than a botched death portrait.

Troy was at the guns again and Smoke heard him shouting something over the steady *chunk-chunk-chunk* on either side. Smoke adjusted the speed on one side of the treads or another to maneuver them around shattered steam mares or the occasional wounded Comanche. Why were there not more Comanche? Had they all gone into the burning buildings to terrorize the weak and scalp the helpless? All across the vista of war, it seemed many of the Comanche had disappeared from the battle. Those that remained wore fearsome animal masks that looked horribly real amid the darkness and smoke of battle. They howled and raged at those they pursued. If it hadn't been madness to think it, Smoke would have believed they wore actual animal heads on their shoulders.

Stranger still, real animals roamed the streets in packs. Coyote mostly, but a few big bears and a scattering of panthers ran among the Brits, leaving them alone in favor of attacking the city's defenders. Smoke could make no sense of it. It had to be Indian magic.

He and Troy had seen firsthand what power they had over the plants. Maybe they had a similar ability to command animals. If that was the case, Smoke was glad he was riding high in the Leviathan. He'd come a little too close to a bear once up near the Red River and he had a good understanding of just how large their paws were and what sort of violence they could command. He didn't care to relive the experience.

Darla squeezed his boot harder in her sleep. God only knew how that child could be snoozing with all these exploders dropping from the steam angels and the way those animals were yipping and carrying on. Not to mention the terrible noise of all these engines of destruction rolling into the capitol. Smoke felt a knot in his stomach and the ends of his mouth pulling down of their own accord.

If Audrey was still in Austin, she was surely dead, or worse.

He looked out across the town, saw the long white wings of the English angels curling overhead, the increasingly rare plume of gunsmoke from some valiant Texan's return fire, the haphazard carnage of Troy's improving skill with the chain guns. The Union Jack flapping stiff-lipped in the breeze over a victorious army of Redjacks and redskins.

It was at that moment that Troy poked his head into the cabin behind Smoke. "Both the side guns are jammed up and we're just about out of coal up here. It'll take me a good fifteen, twenty minutes to get enough up on the lift to be worth the effort. You got any bright ideas?"

Smoke didn't say anything, just pointed at the English flag.

"Yeah, it's a goddamned travesty. But there's just the two of us and only one chain gun left, and the handguns and rifles we got by the river. We can hold them off for a little while, but we'll be out of bullets before they let up."

Smoke shook his head. "Not quite what I'm thinking."

"You aim to swing that pretty sword at 'em while they're shooting us both full of holes?"

"No I don't."

"Then what are you dancing around, Jeb?"

Smoke didn't let his face react to hearing his first name come out of Troy's mouth. It was probably just the stress and excitation bringing out the old days in his former partner. He pointed at the Union Jack and then let his finger drop lower, to the assembled troops massing around Burleson's Folly.

"Yeah, there's a lot of them." Troy pursed his lips to spit, saw Darla laying beneath him and swallowed it instead. "And we're getting closer every second."

"Exactly," Smoke said. "And if we play our cards right, they'll let us get right up next to 'em."

"Then what?" Troy was almost shouting now. "Wander off without so much as a 'by your leave, sir?'"

"Nope, we'll already be off her by then."

Troy's eyes lit up. "Holy shit, Jeb. You're crazier than I thought. Let me go down below and take care of a thing or two." He made to run back to the cargo ladder, but Smoke stopped him with a shout.

"Hey! Give me one of your suspenders before you go."

Troy balked, gave him the eye like Smoke had asked him to paint his face and run naked among the Indians. "What for?"

"Need to make sure these throttles stay all the way up. Behind you!"

Troy looked over his shoulder but Smoke was already firing past him at another Redjack messenger. One shot, right between the eyes. Troy whistled and began stripping off his jacket to get at his suspenders.

Smoke took it from him and wrapped it around the pair of controlling levers and the iron they were mounted to.

President Burleson had seen them riding from the west. The Comanche were not unexpected; after all, Titus Smoke had warned him on numerous occasions that they'd make a grab at this land again some day. But the Redjacks took him utterly by surprise, and as he watched the united force approach, he thought about the warnings he had minimized about Mexican forces mounting to the south. He knew in his heart that his beloved Republic was doomed.

He closed the door to Reginald's room, shutting away the view of the man's ruined, bloody body for the last time, and wiped a tear from either cheek. After his girls had left this afternoon–after he'd kicked them forcibly out the door–he'd gone about the house locking every door, almost calling Reginald for some small task or another then, stopping himself as he remembered. His manservant was dead. Cold and stiff, neck hanging at an awkward angle, the result of a knife-opened throat. Pincher had done the deed, and the odds are he would have killed Burleson too if that horrible Willie person hadn't come to call. The thought made him sick. A traitor in his home. Not just this morning but over and over for weeks. No doubt feeding his tea-swilling countrymen all the information they needed to coordinate a swift and surprising attack on the capitol of Texas.

Had the mayor known his man was a spy? It hardly mattered anymore. The damage was done.

When the Comanche and the English had drawn close enough that Burleson could hear the din of their approach, he'd hammered a neatly inscribed sheet of stationery to the front door with a nail from one of the hanging portraits and the heel of one of his boots. It read: THE PRESIDENT OF TEXAS IS OUT. FOLLOW ME SOUTH TO THE ALAMO!

Not long after, the sound of gunshots had begun, and then horses and steam mares gathered outside the door, brave Austin men coming to protect him, slapping rugged open hands against the door, cursing in confusion as one of them read the sign to the others. None had tried to enter, though. They had at least that much respect for the office of President and the man they presumed Burleson to be. It was more than he deserved.

The portrait he had taken down to get the nail lay abandoned against the lopsided mantle, the face of Sam Houston turned toward the cold fire grate so Houston would not have too see what was about to transpire. He wondered how the old jackal was making out in Paris, whether he was having any luck convincing the French to open trade and immigration with their colony on Haiti. More likely getting him a taste of the City of Lights' feminine charms.

And why didn't Austin have a nickname like Paris did? He'd have to leave that to the next President of Texas. If there was one.

Burleson tied off one end of the rope into a lasso, the only knot he was any good at, and climbed the stairs in near utter darkness. A few forgotten candles guttered in the gloom. He fastened the other end to the railing and jerked it until he was sure it was snug. There were more shouts from outside, and odd animal noises could be heard every so often amid all the explosions and gunfire. Something was scratching at the door, like a dog trying to get in. Burleson could not make out what it was through the glazed glass.

He let one hand linger on the banister until the sounds at the door got more insistent. He heard a man with a distinctly English accent–too deep to be Pincher's–read the note he had left in a near shout. Laughter followed. They were right on his doorstep.

Burleson rushed down the steps, retrieving his pistol and a chair. He placed the chair below the dangling lasso, stepped up the wooden chair's ladder back and wrapped the homemade noose around his neck. He tightened it and positioned himself balanced with his pistol pointed squarely at the door just as they began ramming it with their shoulders.

Burleson fired the gun twice into the door and heard a yell. That would slow the bastards for a minute. Time enough for what he had to do. His last official act as President.

He tipped the chair and fell. The rope bit into his neck but it wasn't a far enough fall to snap the bone. It wasn't even cutting off the air very well. Burleson clutched at his throat. His tongue lolled out of his mouth, and the rope began burning his skin. The front door burst open and a junior officer in Queen's red followed a trio of musket-bearing dragoons inside.

Quickly assessing the situation, the officer smiled at Burleson's choking embarrassment. "Get him down," the man said in a clipped formal tone. The men sprang toward Burleson to obey, but before they could reach him, his own mansion betrayed him. The railing he'd used as his makeshift gallows groaned like an arthritic old woman getting up from her privy stool and then gave way with a crack. The President of the Republic of Texas found himself in a sprawl on the floor.

How fitting, Burleson thought, right before something heavy crashed down on the back of his head.

It was the damnedest thing Willie had ever seen, the skinny blonde woman, Audrey, leading a procession of children up the street, their hands linked to form a crooked train, each of them with their eyes pressed shut. Sam held up the rear of the line, shooing them silently forward with her mere presence, and Mr. Marin limping alongside them with his crutch in one arm and Audrey's hammer in the other. Around them, the darkness and smoke were still thick, and Willie prayed it would stay that way. It was the only hope they had of fleeing the city unseen.

The battle seemed to be tapering off, though she suspected that was more a result of most of the Austin defenders already having died than anything else. Houses continued to burn and the occasional explosion still sounded, causing them all to jump. Willie had both of her four-shot pistols drawn, all cylinders loaded. Half of her wanted nothing more than to get these kids, her cousin Sam, even the irascible old Mr. Marin, to safety. But the other half hoped she got a chance to kill a few more of whatever those monsters were the Indians had become.

Willie caught one of the little boys opening his eye a crack and she shot him a look that scared it back closed again. No sense them being scarred by all this. Not if she could help it.

Willie wasn't much for kids, but she'd taken to a few of them on their ride up from San Antonio. Her cousin, Sam, was a saint for carting all those farmers' kids out of harm's way. Some of the parents planned to follow as soon as they could close up their affairs, others intended to stay, but regardless, they trusted Sam with their children and she didn't take that trust lightly. But she was a school teacher, and though she was more than willing to take the children in her care, it would have been unwise to set out without some more experienced help. The kind that could discourage bandits and zombies.

Mr. Marin claimed to have lost his leg fighting alongside General Jackson in New Orleans, and though he was old enough to be Sam's father, he'd been sweet on her for some time. He'd offered his services as a driver and protective escort, and Sam had been too kind to turn the old man down, even though it was obvious he had no business protecting anyone. Willie on the other hand, could take care of things. And when Sam had asked her along, she'd joined them. Ever since, she'd been itching to get back to San Antonio and join the fight. She'd never anticipated the fight coming to her.

Audrey led the procession toward the river banks, doing her best to keep them in the shadows and out of sight. Sam helped her herd them around the corner of the now abandoned Hoover Shipping and Post building.

Comanche wails kept Willie's nerves taut, and she listened for the tell-tale signs of approaching hooves in the dimness and haze. Would the Indians ride them down or sneak up on them? And would they take mercy on the children? Willie had heard plenty of stories from those living on the outskirts of civilization, and if they were to be believed, the children would receive no special treatment.

"Get on in there, children," said Sam, shoving the last straggler into an alleyway. At the far end, Audrey looked to be searching for a safe route past the last row of buildings and to the outskirts of town. Mr. Marin swung his hammer through the air a few times, nervous. Willie tried to ignore the crackle of burning buildings and the terror that gripped her. She needed to keep her cool. She was in charge and that meant not losing her head.

"Come along, Mr. Marin," said Sam, tugging the old man's arm and coaxing him into the alley. "Pretty soon this dark's gonna lift and then–"

Sam's voice broke off, like she was trying to figure out what to say next. It wasn't until she resumed speaking that Willie noticed the arrow lodged in the woman's chest.

"I been shot," she whispered, gaze dropping to the fletched shaft protruding from below her collar bone. Another arrow tinged off the hammer Mr. Marin was holding up in front of him and before a third could fly, Willie fired blindly into the night with both pistols. The smoke was thick, and though that was likely the reason the arrow shots hadn't been fatally placed, it also prevented Willie from seeing their attacker. She knew loosely what direction he was, but by the time his horse punched through the smoke and the dark, her pistols were empty.

She had just enough time to chide herself for being a frightened fool before the Indian rode up on them and backhanded her with a long-bladed knife. It bit into her cheek and the force of the blow knocked her to the ground. It felt like her jaw was broken, the side of her face flayed. She'd dropped her useless pistols, and her hands patted absently at her gunbelt, fingers touching the reserve of cold bullets that she had no time to use.

Mr. Marin swung his hammer and it struck the horse in the flank. The animal hardly seemed to feel the blow. Its rider slid from the saddle, silent as death and quick as dread, and he took the knife to Mr. Marin's forehead. The skin split with a rush of blood and the old man howled, tumbled back into the alley where the children had begun screaming again. The Indian loosed his lance from his saddle and Willie saw for the first time he had the head of a rattlesnake. Part of her wondered why this one wasn't a coyote, but mostly she focused on regaining her footing.

The rattlesnake hissed, then drove the spear into Sam's chest. It settled into the wall behind her with a hollow thunk and Sam's eyes found some distant point on the horizon that likely only she could see. Willie was on her feet now, her big Bowie knife free from its scabbard. She unleashed a scream and drove the knife into the Comanche's shoulder, then yanked it free and stabbed him again as he whirled to strike her. This one caught him in the scaly throat and she jerked the blade sideways, slicing away a good portion of the creature's neck.

The Indian's forked tongue licked the air, and it's horribly human eyes went dim. He dropped to his knees, then keeled over sideways. His war-painted horse scampered away a few steps, but Willie took gentle hold of the animal's mane before it could bolt. It wore a world-weary saddle, likely scavenged from some unlucky Texan foolish enough to venture out onto the plains. Willie held out her hand to Mr. Marin, who was bleeding profusely from the forehead. He approached, eyes conspicuously avoiding the dead woman still pinned to the wall by the spear.

"Take your shirt off and wrap it around your head," said Willie, trying to ignore the pain in her cheek. Mr. Marin's worried expression told her that perhaps she should do the same thing. He did as she asked, and Willie reckoned he'd be well enough for travel.

"I'm bleeding like hell," he said.

"Head bleeds worse than anything," said Willie. "Can you sit a horse?" She asked partly because of his injuries, and partly because of his missing leg. She'd seen him drive the buckboard, but had no idea how he handled himself in the saddle.

"I surely can," he said. "Stump's long enough that it ain't too hard."

"Then saddle up," she said. "Take this horse and ride to San Antonio. You need to find a man named Titus Smoke and you need to tell him what's transpired here. He'll know what to do."

"I ain't leaving you with these kids."

"You sure as hell are. Me and Audrey can tend to them. River's there. We're almost out of town and talking about it ain't gonna make that any easier. The ford is a mile or so down. You ride and don't look back."

"But Sam—"

"Sam is dead. You ain't. And these kids ain't. Let's keep it that way."

Mr. Marin nodded, then used his crutch for support as he mounted his horse. He had a far easier time of it than Willie would have guessed. He lifted his crutch up after him and stowed it under one arm. With the other, he seized the reins. Willie slapped the horse's flank and it bolted. Mr. Marin steered it toward the river.

Willie stepped into the alley and took in the sight of a dozen crying children, and Audrey, who was so far proving to be little help in their escape. They all looked stricken. Their teacher was still in a standing position, held in place by the spear, and Willie must look a sight with half her face cut open. She wanted to take her cousin's body somewhere and tend to it properly, but there was no time for that. Not if they intended to leave Austin alive.

She settled for pulling the spear free and letting Sam slip to the ground. She tossed aside the bloody length of wood and closed her cousin's eyes.

"Don't worry," she said. "We'll get these kids back home."

Willie stood and turned back to the children who were now her charges. "Let's go," she said, softly. She shot Audrey a hard look that got the woman moving. Together, they herded the weeping children toward the river, away from the fire and smoke and sudden death.

Away from what remained of Austin.

Leviathan 212 rolled ahead of most of the other steam gear, chewing its way up the hill toward the President's mansion. As Smoke scooped Darla up he figured they would reach the building in a matter of minutes. The path ahead looked clear, and as long as they could keep any Redjacks or Comanche from boarding her they would be okay.

He made his way carefully to the rear of the lumbering war machine and set Darla down. Troy had left a handful of rifles on the deck, loaded and waiting, but Smoke ignored them and grabbed for the shovel instead. He dug the wide blade of it into what remained of the coal Troy had sent up and heaved it into the open furnace. It was a wonder the entire vehicle hadn't caught fire, with Troy leaving the lid wide open like that. As the coal hit the flames a wave of acrid burning air hurried up at him. Smoke started to sweat as he sent another shovelful into the furnace.

Darla seemed as unaffected by the heat as she had by anything else. Smoke kept shoveling till the fire threatened to smother itself out, then leaned out over one side rail. Burleson's Folly was looming ever closer. It was time to get off this glorified steam carriage while the getting was good. With any luck at all, they could make it into the stand of trees off to the west and keep running while the Redjacks tried to figure out how to stop a runaway Leviathan.

Not that Smoke ever counted on luck.

Troy bobbed up the ladder and scurried across the shifting teak deck toward Smoke. He grabbed Darla by the waist and hoisted her over one shoulder. "Them fuses are burning fast. You got your running boots on?"

Smoke nodded, about to tell Troy that he would take Darla down the steel rungs and jump with her. But he didn't get the chance. Smoke knew Troy was quick but the man could have been a monkey, or a sailor, the way he snatched the girl up and darted down that ladder. He carried Darla between the rear two sets of treads and rolled out onto the ground without losing his grip on her.

Smoke threw an armful of rifles and then himself over the side. At the bottom, he hung for a second, watching Troy limping briskly away, not even looking back. He unsheathed the English officer's cutlass and threw it as far as he could, watching how far behind the ladder it actually landed.

Smoke licked his lips, thinking of what a fool idea this all had been. There was no way in the world they'd get far, two men in the uniform of Her Majesty's Finest, and lugging around an unconscious Indian girl. Even so, like Troy had said, the fuses were burning, and there was no telling how long before all that gunpowder in the hold of *Leviathan 212* went up.

Smoke resisted the urge to close his eyes as he jumped, managed to land on his feet like a cat, and kept running after Troy's retreating backside. He slowed down only long enough to grab the cutlass and one of the rifles from the dry Austin ground.

At the edge of a cedar thicket, Troy stopped to watch his handiwork. Smoke had snatched Darla from him soon as he got close enough, and Troy had let him. Way his ankle was throbbing it was a wonder he had made it this far. If Smoke wanted to carry the girl, then let him.

They stood there panting like a pair of coyotes. A breeze brought the smell of ashes and the sounds of frenzied gunshots from all the Redjacks trying to stop *Leviathan 212* from running them over. Troy snorted. It was a ridiculous thing for them to do, staying all pretty and ranked up like that, guarding the President's back porch for him.

The huge machine kept right on toward them, in a line as straight as a cardsharp's face. As Troy watched, a blackbird touched down on one of the five-barreled turrets. He was beginning to get a pins-and-needles feeling in his face. What if the fuses had gone out? He had fashioned two good long ones that should have taken only about five minutes at the most from when he lit them. Why hadn't they gone off yet?

Smoke must have read his mind. "How many did you set?"

"Two."

Troy chewed the ends of his moustache, waiting.

General Courtney Thackeray stood proudly beneath the flapping banners of his command carraige, staring down at the glorious victory his solders had claimed for Victoria. The Texans were routed. The vast majority of the city's buildings were in flames, and the fools defending her had either fled, died, or been captured. Were it not for the sight of the heathen monsters sharing the glory with his good English men, the day would be perfect.

It was a grand victory, but it was tainted. What sort of monsters had they thrown in with? It had never been Thackeray's intention to honor any of his promises to these people. They hardly qualified as human, and after seeing their horrible transformations he was even less inclined to believe them anything but beasts.

Thackeray disliked the nervousness in his troops as the monsters moved among them. The time would come when he would order their weapons turned on these Comanche, and he did not need fear breeding hesitation. His soldiers could kill men; indeed it was their only function. But battling these monsters was outside their realm of experience.

Still, if this was all the sorcery the savages could bring to bear, Thackeray's men were all but assured victory. Terrible though they may be, the Indians could still be felled with bullets. They could not resist the crushing weight of landship treads or the burning wrath of Victoria's steam angels. They were animal men, but that afforded them no special protection against the superior might of England in her fury.

Thackeray allowed himself a smile.

The President's house loomed just ahead, and his command carriage approached with steady speed. The Union Jack over the house demonstrated England's claim on the city. Reports had already reached him of the President's ignoble capture. Thackeray had only to negotiate a surrender–what other choice did the beaten man have *but* surrender?–and the country would belong to his Queen.

Then he would deal with the savages and their parlor tricks.

As he drew nearer the house, Thackeray saw a Leviathan-class landfrigate speeding toward it at full speed. No men manned her guns or steered her progress. She was a runaway, barreling up the gentle hill behind the house, gaining speed.

Collision was imminent.

"Stop that landship!" he yelled, though even as he spoke, he knew his command was impossible.

Leviathan 212 sped steadily onward. The Redjacks scattered before the clanking monstrosity as it bellied its way over a small rise and seemed to speed up as the ground flattened. The blackbird that had taken the front turret as its roost lifted into the sky, seemingly bored with the experience of commanding its own English war vessel.

A second later, Leviathan struck the back of the President's mansion and burrowed into it like a prairie dog finding a soft bit of earth. The roof and third floor of the big house shuddered and sagged over the hole the war machine had made.

Watching from the trees, Troy held his breath and waited for the explosion that he prayed would come.

Burleson wished a lot of things. He wished he'd listened to the Brigadier-Justice, or that he'd listened to that squirrelly woman who'd barged into his parlor this morning. Wished that maybe he'd never taken Reginald in as his manservant. The man would still be alive, at least. The Forever Free would surely be needed now more than ever in San Antonio, if what he had been told was true. Moctezuma himself at the front of his zombie army. But most of all, the President of Texas wished he'd decided to run, or at least fight, rather than allowing himself to be captured in a failed hanging attempt by a squad of belligerent Englishmen and their bizarre cadre of trained coyotes.

Burleson hadn't even known coyotes could be trained.

They had him on his knees now, in chains on the front lawn, right in front of the flagpole. Pincher had been there for a moment or two, close enough to sneer at, but too far away to hear anything the traitorous son of a bitch had to say to the English officer in charge.

They told him he'd be waiting there for a good long while, that their General, Lord Something-or-other, would be there shortly with a treaty of unconditional surrender. Tonight, a Queen's man would be sleeping in the Presidential bed, probably screwing one of the Presidential whores, and capering about drunk on Burleson's private stock of bourbon.

What happened to the proud young Burleson, the man who'd made the black heroes of the Alamo into the Forever Free? When had be become so soft and insulated from the threats around him? At what point along the way had the perks of office become more important to him than the duties? Reginald, poor man now dead with his throat cut in bed, had said it best: *You have to act on what your best people tell you, not what you'd rather they tell you.* If he could only get close enough to Pincher, he would rip the spy's heart out with his teeth. But there was no way the Redjack guards would let him move even an inch in that direction

Burleson winced at the sudden sound of timbers cracking behind him. He heard booted feet running, coyotes howling, the sound of his gorgeous front window–imported all the way from Chicago–shattering behind him.

He could not bear to look.

Troy watched and waited, the look in his eyes daring Smoke to say a word.

Finally it came.

Right before, men in red could be seen fleeing from around the front of the house. *Leviathan 212* must have made it in one side of Burleson's home and out the other. The flagpole with the Union Jack listed to one side, the big steam vehicle having mowed it down like nothing more than a colorfully tipped blade of grass.

And then the flag, the fleeing men, the house itself were gone, replaced by an eruption of flame so intense Troy yelped and turned his eyes away. The shock of it hit him in the back and Darla begin screaming again. The explosion had sounded like two freight trains colliding head on, and the rattle of timber and glass joined the din as bits of the former Presidential home began raining down around them.

Troy turned back, saw what remained of the house engulfed in flames, the area around it a black ruin, the Leviathan nothing more than a twisted cylinder of charred metal supporting a nightmare column of billowing smoke. Bits of the landscape burned, and bodies of men and animals alike lay crushed in the wake of the explosion. Nothing moved but the flames.

"I reckon that'll do," said Troy.

"Come on," said Smoke, stroking Darla's head, trying to sooth her. "That ain't going to distract them too long and there's still plenty of Brits wandering around ready to kill us for–well, dealer's choice. Deserters, spies, or saboteurs."

Troy took one last look, savoring for a second the little tremors he could still feel vibrating through the air and through the ground. "Maybe all three," he said. "Give me that rifle."

Lightning Dove rode the waves of heat rising from the ruined remains of the white chief's home. Bodies burned in the grass, English and Comanche alike, and he cursed the British general and his men for allowing this to happen. He'd seen the clunky machine as it struck the house, and watched his people's futile attempts to flee before the eruption of flames. It was a British vessel that had caused the destruction, and that was the worst of it. These men who made such bold claims about their military might could not even control their own war machines.

The sunlight was emerging again, and with it, Lightning Dove could see the entirety of their victory. Austin was theirs, and apart from the English stupidity, very few of his people had given their lives. He longed to turn his wings south, to move on San Antonio immediately. But he knew Broken Lance would preach patience, and given the wonders that the old man had unleashed, Lightning Dove felt it wise to heed his council.

Still, it would not be long. She-Who-Is-Alone would be returned to them. Perhaps this glorious victory would be proof enough to the Great Spirit that they were worthy of that charge. And when she was returned to them, when her *power* was returned to them, they would no longer need unreliable allies in their quest to regain their land.

They would strike down the arrogant British and the upstart Texans alike.

The Comanche would have their lands again.

And they would have them soon.

CHAPTER 16

A FEW WAGONS HAD ALREADY PASSED THEM, hurrying away from Austin, but none with the room or the inclination to accommodate twelve weeping children and their caretakers. They were a mile south of the river and still halfway soaked from the crossing when Audrey finally found a ramshackle buggy during a search of what she figured might be the last farm before reaching open country. It was old enough to have carried her grandparents in their swaddling days, but the wheels looked sound and a pair of reasonably healthy horses were stabled in the same barn. Audrey had called on the farmhouse and searched the grounds, but no one was about. Probably already escaped to safety with a better wagon. She wasn't given to thievery, but under the circumstance, she figured the Lord would forgive her.

Now the open-backed wagon was loaded down with kids, while she and Willie sat up front, bracing themselves against each shake and shudder as they made their way through the rocky country between Austin and San Antonio. She couldn't imagine a less suitable pair of escorts. Audrey had never thought much about having children, and having no siblings, her experience with them was limited. And Willie ... well, Audrey had no idea what to think of the woman. Certainly they'd all be dead if it wasn't for her timely assistance, but there was a great deal of violence in her soul, and she frightened Audrey.

Still, the choice between escorting the children alone and having Willie's gun along for the ride was no choice at all.

"I'm sorry about your cousin," said Audrey.

Willie stared ahead, like she hadn't heard. She snapped the horses' reins.

Audrey had managed to get enough answers out of the woman to learn she'd been escorting the school teacher and her charges away from impending danger in San Antonio. It called into question the direction of their flight, though Audrey couldn't imagine where else they'd run. Besides, as far as she could tell, the Mexican threat was still a rumor. The Comanche and the Brits were all too real.

"Just wanted you to know," said Audrey. "I don't think I told you. Don't think I told you thanks for saving us either."

"I wouldn't know how to write my own name if it wasn't for that woman," said Willie, eyes still fixed on the southern horizon. Now that the eclipse had passed, the sun burned downed with the whole of its fury. Trails of sweat carved their way down Willie's filthy cheeks. Audrey felt her dress sticking to her back.

"Well, I'm sure she'd be pleased to know you're still taking care of her students."

"She'd be more pleased if that bastard hadn't stuck a spear in her chest."

"They finally came," said Audrey.

"What's that mean?"

"A man I used to work for always said the Comanche would come to take back the land we stole. Now they did."

"We didn't steal nothing," said Willie. "There's more land out here than anyone can use. There ain't no call to go killing people for it."

"I didn't say it was right what they did."

"I know you didn't, 'cause if you did I'd have to stop and let you out here. See how far you got on foot."

Audrey bristled. "I'd get a hell of a lot farther than you think. I'm no weakling. I run my own business and shoe my own horses. I can do any damn thing a man can do, including find my way to San Antonio if need be." She felt blood rising into her face as the curse words left her lips. It wasn't like her. She prided herself in her restraint. Once she and Jeb had been lunching by the river when a snake had slid right up under the blanket and chased them both away from the food. She'd cursed the thing and it had taken Jeb the bigger part of an hour to stop laughing about it.

Willie finally looked at her, a slight smile on her face. Willie would never be a pretty woman, but the smile softened her, and she no longer looked altogether mannish. There was a woman somewhere underneath her bluster.

"Calm down," Willie said. "I didn't mean to get you all riled up. I know you're just trying to smooth things out a little. I just ain't in much of a mood for pleasantries. Sam's dead, and we're riding right back into the mess I already left. Mexicans marching north, Indians marching south. And here we are without many options. I just hope to hell Mr. Marin gets there quick enough to help stir up some sort of defense."

"You think the Comanche are coming this way?" Audrey felt her blood rising again, remembering the horror of the assault on Austin. Neither of them had spoken about the way the Indians had *changed*. There was nothing natural about it, and it was something Audrey would rather put out of her mind. That and the horrible spectacle of all the steam gear they had riding with them.

"Course they will," said Willie. "You think they just come for Austin and now they've got their fill? No, they'll want it all. They have a big enough force to keep on moving south and put an end to this whole country. I don't see anyone stopping them, except maybe the Mexicans. Either way, it don't look like we'll have much to look forward to."

Audrey heaved a sigh that carried with it the entirety of her defeat. Life had not been perfect in Austin, but it had been better than life in Minnesota. She'd been a young fool with visions of children and true love in her head when she'd married Jim Bill. And when he got to drinking and smacked her around from time to time, she was assured by a whole passel of women that such was to be expected. Men often found themselves under stress and it was a woman's job to relieve it, no matter what form that relief took.

Then came the baby, or almost anyway. The little girl (and Audrey was certain it was a girl by the way she was carrying the child) was still in her belly when Jim Bill cut loose with a tirade that busted her jaw and left her bleeding out on her grandmother's quilt and crying over the two lives he'd taken–the baby's and what remained of hers.

She'd decided then that she wasn't cut out for marriage, but when she showed up on her parents' porch with her belongings in tow, they'd been scandalized. How could she leave a good man like Jim Bill? Him a man of means, and her nothing more than an up-jumped farmer's daughter who hadn't learned her place in the world yet. Their anger and confusion were more painful than Jim Bill's fists, and when she turned her back on the house she'd been born in, she shut her past in a dark box and threw away the key.

What money she had went for passage south, and with all the talk of people making new lives in Texas, she decided that was the spot for her. And it had been, at least until the Indians came and burned it away.

Austin was gone. Jeb was gone. She was back where she started, terrified and aimless, headed south. Eventually she'd run out of south and then where would she be?

Jeb. She had been ready to marry that man, no matter what his Daddy thought about her past. Then Laredo and the little girl. It wasn't the little girl's fault, of course, but on her loneliest of nights, Audrey cursed the child for getting kidnapped. Cursed her for dying. If it wasn't for her, Audrey and Jeb would have been married. Would probably be living somewhere far from Austin and Indian attacks and the endless hardship of life in such a rugged country. Everything had gone downhill after Laredo, and it seemed to her now that the moment Jeb left Austin was the moment she started making plans for leaving. Nothing remained for her in Texas. And even if there had been something for her here, the Indians had burned it all up and danced on the ashes.

The worst part was, she believed Jeb. He told her it was an accident, that he'd shot the girl trying to save her from a zombie. The kid, Little Bo, had confirmed this and that asshole (no other way to describe him) Troy Tanner had shuffled his feet and halfheartedly concurred, but her daddy was Andrew T. Sheppard, and a man like that would have his pound of flesh.

Jeb figured his own daddy was coming to arrest him, and he wouldn't have that. He broke off their engagement, left Audrey shocked and too saddened for tears, standing in the street with a mouthful of unvoiced protests as he rode into the dust cloud rising from the west, disappearing from her life for good.

She hated that man, no matter how much she still loved him.

Audrey glanced back at the kids, saw Gretchen and her brother sleeping in each other's arms. The rest of the children had either joined them in sleep, or sat studying the far horizons with weary eyes. Her little one would have been about that age, and would have looked very much like Gretchen with her long blonde hair and peaceful smile.

"Do you have any children?" asked Audrey.

Willie laughed. "What the hell do you think?"

"You ever want to have any kids?"

"No, I don't think so. For that I'd have to get me a man, and I ain't much on men."

"Surely there's someone chasing you," said Audrey. "Or someone you fancy."

"One time there was," said Willie. "When I was a little girl. I used to chase that boy and try to knock him to the ground. Did it too, a couple of times. Then he threw dirt at me and I laughed."

"Well, there you go" said Audrey.

"I know it sounds funny, but I knew that was the boy for me. Then we grew up and he joined the Rangers and rode off and I never had a brave enough tongue to tell him I loved him. Hell, I don't even know if I do. I ain't spoke a word to him since we was fifteen. But somehow there's no one else that's caught my fancy. And I'm too busy to look for one."

"Men aren't too hard to find," said Audrey.

"Good ones are."

"Yes, you're right about that. I courted a Ranger and I can sympathize. They're wanderers. It's in their soul. Most times they'd rather be on the back of a horse getting shot at and eating bugs than spending time at home. But then he'd come back and sometimes he'd be carrying a fistful of dead flowers he'd picked somewhere out on the Llano. Flowers that don't grow anywhere around here. And they'd be ugly and they'd smell but he'd be so proud of those flowers you couldn't help but smile and thank him–

Audrey choked off a sob. "We were gonna get married."

"What happened?" asked Willie

"He had to leave town."

"So where's he now?"

"I wish I knew."

Willie looked away, found something to focus on in the distance. "I just hope to hell Mr. Marin gets word through to Mr. Smoke. He's a capable man. He'll know what to do."

"Titus Smoke?" Jeb's father. The man who'd done everything he could to get between the two of them. He'd probably been as pleased as pigs in slop when Jeb left Austin for points unknown.

"Yeah. Titus Smoke."

"You know him?"

Willie broke into a rueful grin. "Sure do. His son's the man I love."

CHAPTER 17

NATURAL NIGHT HAD COME AT LAST, and Jeb Smoke was thankful. That meant he could no longer see the great plumes of smoke, rising to the north as what remained of Austin burned to the ground. And the few British scouts planning a route to San Antonio and shooting fleeing Texans would have a harder time spotting them. Occasionally, they encountered others on the run, but the contact was fleeting, as if no one could be trusted, and Smoke was content to ignore them and press on.

He kept hoping to see Audrey, or his daddy, but never did.

Darla was awake again, and trotting beside them with a big grin on her face like this was nothing more than a bracing trek through the countryside. Like maybe they were hunting up bull snakes or dandelions. Troy wore a satisfied smirk, and Smoke knew he was still thinking about the President's house, going up like Hell on holiday.

It had been enough of a distraction at least to get them out of town. It was obvious that the Comanche and the Brits wouldn't stop there, and there was only one other target worth marching for.

"Why do you reckon the Comanche joined up with them Englanders?" asked Troy as they pressed though a tight nest of cedars.

"Hell if I know," said Smoke. "You know how my daddy was always going on about the Indians and the Mexicans and even the damn United States all salivating over this place, like it was someplace nice. Which it ain't. I guess I can see the Indians coming for it, but I don't see where the Redjacks fit in. Maybe they just like war. Way I hear it, they're real big on anything that gets them more land. Maybe they're planning to split the winnings with Lightning Dove."

"Lightning Dove ain't gonna split nothing," said Troy.

"I don't reckon he will," said Smoke.

"You think your daddy was in Austin when it fell?"

"How the hell should I know?" said Smoke, suddenly enraged. "You've seen him since I have."

"Look here," said Troy. "Let's just come clean on this. Your daddy paid me to come look for you, but he didn't say he was gonna put you in jail. He just figured you'd get yourself killed running all over Comanche country. Might be he wants to help you hide out."

"The Brigadier-Justice ain't got no plans to hide me anywhere but in a jailhouse and you know it. That man don't have any give when it comes to the law."

"Except maybe when it comes to his son. He knows it was an accident."

"Well, good of you to fess up about that much," said Smoke. "I figured you'd be holding one end of the hanging rope."

"I told everyone what I saw like I saw it."

"Yeah, and you didn't waste no words defending me either."

"I said it was an accident! That you just got cocky and thought you were a better shot than you actually were! What more do you want?"

Darla squealed and snatched up a little grass snake. It curled around her finger. "Look how pretty and green this one is!"

"What's she saying?" asked Troy.

"She says you're an asshole," said Smoke.

They trudged southward in silence.

A few miles more and they came across two dead ranch hands, killed the old fashioned way with a bullet to the head. Their horses grazed not too far off. Troy found their hats on the ground nearby and placed them over their faces.

"Redjacks done it, probably," he said.

"Let's get them horses," said Smoke.

Troy nodded, and within minutes, they were saddled up and riding hard, Darla clinging to Smoke's back, her hair billowing out behind them like a river of night.

You Ranger long enough, you learn to catch moments of sleep in the saddle. Smoke yawned, urged the horse on faster with a soft touch of his spur, then the night closed in like a smothering blanket and there was Audrey, surrounded by a nest of rattlesnakes. They were all coiled, ready to strike, and somewhere in the distance he could hear one of those haunting Aztec chants that always spooked him when he rode too close to the Mexican border at night. His daddy was there, and of all people Bigfoot Wallace was with him, chopping off the rattlers' heads with old colony-issued sabers, but for every head they chopped, two grew back again and it was only a matter of time before one of them sank its fangs into Audrey's ankle. British drums boomed and a circle of flames rose up around the proceedings, baking the world in heat and casting the scene in a hellish light. Then Darla began to sing. She wasn't anywhere to be found, but Smoke recognized her voice, rising above the chanting, the drums, the angry rattles, like a prayer to some unknown god that Smoke hoped to hell could save them. Birds, glowing with the light of creation, lit the sky with their sudden appearance, chasing away the darkness and the flames. A great eagle flew among them, circling, guiding their approach. When he drew near enough, Smoke could see the flowing white hair trailing behind it. The eagle screamed, fell from the sky, and took Audrey in its massive talons, rising her up, away, out of reach forever. She continued screaming, and it became the only sound Smoke could hear. The flames leapt to life again, and the last thing Smoke saw before they swallowed everything was Audrey, rising into the heavens in terror, leaving him for good.

Smoke woke with a start.

Darla still clung to his back; her soft breathing assured him she was sleeping. Troy rode beside him, looking angry as usual.

"Pick up the pace!" he said. "No time for sleeping."

"Just tired."

"Like I ain't," he said. "We got to ride as hard as we can until San Antonio. You can sleep then."

"Somehow, I doubt that."

"Either way, the only other choice is getting caught or killed. Neither one appeals to me."

"How far have we come?" asked Smoke, ashamed he'd fallen asleep and lost his bearings.

"Not far enough," said Troy, then he put heels to his horse and set a galloping pace for San Antonio.

Audrey had been strangely quiet since their talk about men, and Willie wondered if she'd said something to make the woman uncomfortable. It seemed she was always making people uncomfortable, yet she never understood how. Usually, she didn't mind, but something in Audrey's manner had won her over. She didn't look at Willie like some heathen woman without enough sense to be a normal girl. Audrey spoke to her like normal folks, and if she thought Willie's manner strange, she kept it to herself.

"Not too much farther," said Willie, hoping to engage Audrey in conversation. They'd traveled through the night, and much of the following day, and Willie had kept the reins the whole time. She'd have already been to San Antonio on horse back, but the wagon was slow going. She judged they'd reach the city by the next morning.

"That's good," said Audrey. "I've never enjoyed traveling by wagon much."

"I prefer horses, myself."

"I prefer staying put in one place."

"That's good too."

Silence settled in again, lonely and uncomfortable. Only the complaints of fidgety children broke the monotony. They rode for several miles, then Willie couldn't stand it any longer.

"Did I say something to anger you?" she asked. "I'm real good at that but I don't mean to be."

"No, you didn't," said Audrey, looking Willie in the eye for the first time in many hours. "I'm afraid you're going to be mad at me. Here we were, getting along and then ... well, I think you're not going to like me much."

"What for?"

"That Ranger I was engaged to?"

"Yeah?"

"His name is Jebediah Smoke. I think you know him."

Willie grew instantly hot and wondered how long it had been since she'd felt embarrassment. Audrey looked at her hopefully, but Willie had to look away. What a fool she was, going on about Jeb while this woman already had him. Not that it was Audrey's fault. Willie blamed herself. If she'd have tried a little harder to be womanly, or maybe if she'd had the guts to mention to Jeb just once out loud the way she had felt about him, maybe he'd have taken a liking to her before meeting a beauty like Audrey. But that was the way of the world. Men like Jeb married women like Audrey, had kids, made a life. And women like Willie peered into their world from a distance, eventually rejecting the better things they knew life would deny them.

"Please don't hate me," said Audrey.

"You ain't the one I hate," said Willie.

They found their silence again, and continued with their charges toward the uncertain sanctuary of San Antonio.

CHAPTER 18

THE MORNING HAD SEEN TITUS' COMPANY engaged in reloading drills and formation marching. In the afternoon a squad led by Sgt. Wallace would be headed out for their turn patrolling the southern fringes of San Antonio. It had been more than a dozen years since Titus had spent this much time in Bigfoot's company, and the experience brought with it no end of memories, good and bad.

"What ever happened to that old nag of yours?" Bigfoot asked, as they slumped down in the scant shade of Military Plaza.

For a fleeting second, Titus wondered if the giant was referring to Cecilia, before remembering that Bigfoot and he had once been rewarded with two fine specimens of horseflesh by a rancher grateful they'd brought in a pack of rustlers. Either way, the answer was the same.

"Long passed on. But not before birthing a stubborn male."

Bigfoot nodded, scratching under one of his offset beady eyes with a thickened gray fingernail. "Reckon there's any other kind?"

Titus barked out a short laugh. "Probably not, since you mention it."

One-eyed Hadley shuffled over, a sour grin plastered across his face as he watched the younger soldiers pouring canteens over their heads and passing around bottles of more energetic spirits. "Bad news, Bigfoot," he said, pretending *Private Brown* wasn't there at all. "Lieutenant says we need to cut your patrol so we can support the folks fortifying the Alamo mission."

Bigfoot's lower lip poked out a little more than his upper as he considered this. "How many do I get?"

"Lieutenant says no more than four, and no steam mares, neither."

Titus choked back a startled curse. Hadley glared at him with his one good eye. "Private Brown, I know what you're thinking. But God help you if you say it out loud in my unit."

Titus nodded. "I understand, Corporal."

Hadley arched his back, and the crackle and pop from his spine could have been mistaken for a gunfight. "Good man, and good work out here in the drills today," he said, then turned his attention back to Bigfoot.

The oversized sergeant took off his hat and wiped his forehead with a stained sleeve. "Reckon we need someone we can trust to stay behind in charge of things."

Corporal Hadley nodded and scowled at the same time. "I see where you're going–"

"In my unit we don't interrupt the Sergeant whilst he's noodlin, Hadley."

Hadley scowled harder, but remained silent.

Bigfoot picked up where he left off. "And we need really reliable men out there to make sure that we don't step in any zombie cowpies and drag that stink home with us. Or worse yet, that we run into Moctezuma himself and nobody is able to get the word back."

Hadley nodded. He had resumed ignoring Titus again. Titus, for his part, was content to return the favor.

The corporal dug into the hardpan soil of the plaza with the toe of one boot. "So who's going on patrol? And who should I tell the Lieutenant is in charge?" It seemed a foregone conclusion to Titus, and apparently to Hadley as well that Bigfoot was going, and Hadley would be in charge.

Which left them both a bit surprised at the giant's verdict. "How about us three go on patrol? We all got our own flesh and blood mounts and all three of us have killed our share of zombies–" At this, Hadley turned his head quickly to glare at Titus with a newfound curiosity and respect.

"Who are you leaving in charge then?" Hadley said. "Not–"

Titus coughed in a way that almost sounded like a laugh.

"I thought Slippery Dave would do."

"Lieutenant Babb ain't going to like that much."

Bigfoot rose, brushing dirt from the seat of his pants with both meaty hands. "Then I reckon we ought to be gone before he gets the word." He offered Titus a dusty hand, and helped him up. "Get your kit and saddle up. I'll talk to Dave and tell him not to spill the b– not to tell Lieutenant Babb 'till we are an hour gone. Meet you at the end of Delgado soon as you're ready."

Titus snapped him a quick, "Yes, Sergeant!" and hustled off to the stable for Nebuchadnezzar.

When he looked back, Corporal Hadley was still standing there, shaking his head and grinning.

It was nearly dark, but the moon hung low and golden-bright as fresh cornbread, so they kept roving south and then east along their assigned route. Crickets and scorpions scuttled about beneath their horse's hooves. Every so often Titus would catch the odor of coyote spoor, or hear the lonely skittering of horny toads in the brush.

They took turns leading and when Titus was in the lead Nebuchadnezzar was sure-footed as ever. Hadley had begun warming up to him on the ride out of San Antonio, and by the time the town had fallen out of sight behind them he had already switched from calling Titus 'Private Brown" to 'Jeter.' He wasn't so bad, once you got him away from the military foofaraw.

Along about eight o' clock by the pocket watch Cecilia had given Titus on their tenth wedding anniversary, Bigfoot called a halt on the top of a hilly knob that was bald as a banker. They made what passed for camp with Hadley taking the first watch. Neither Moctezuma nor his dead soldiers had made it this far north, at least not yet. But there was something uneasy in the wild sounds of the Texas night; even the stars seemed to be trembling in dread and anticipation. Titus tried not to think about the handful of odd stones pressing through the doubled over blanket into his back and found himself thinking about all the critters living in unnatural harmony in Sylvester's mud house instead. Somehow, he managed to relax his saddle-sore muscles enough to sleep.

He hadn't been out for long when he became aware of a great buzzing coming from all around him. It threatened to swallow him like a sinkhole, the way it rushed in to fill up his ears. The noise closed in and lulled him on peaceful locust wings, until some part of his brain stirred itself to action and the noise became at once serpentine and terrifying.

Titus felt his eyes snap open and his hands clawing for his pistol, his rifle, his knife—anything at all that he could use as a weapon. He launched himself to his feet, blinking and pivoting his head left to right in search of the rattlesnakes he had been certain were approaching on all sides.

Hadley flinched at his sudden movement, then resumed poking at the fire with the end of a skinny branch. They had dug a little pit for the fire, in hopes that its light would not give their position away. "Not your turn for another hour, Jeter."

Bigfoot rolled over lazily. The sound had been so *real*. Titus swore. Hadley used the burning end of the branch to light a slim little cheroot. The burning tobacco added a tang to the still air, blending with the spicy aromas of mesquite and sage.

"Thought I heard something," Titus said.

"Just nerves."

Titus restrained a modest laugh. "Maybe so, Corporal."

"Call me Darren."

"Maybe so, Darren."

"You don't seem much like the type to spook easy, if you don't mind my saying. And if you've got Bigfoot's respect, you've got mine. At least on credit till you prove you don't deserve it."

"Fair enough."

Titus settled back onto his blanket. They listened to the night sounds for a few minutes. "If this blanket was as sure to find gold as it was to find rocks underneath it, I'd be a rich man."

Hadley snorted. "You've done your bit of soldiering or something like it, haven't you?"

Titus grunted.

"That where you know Bigfoot from? Were you in the Rangers with him, or at Goliad? He won't talk about it, ever."

"I wouldn't either," Titus began, but he was cut off by the beginning of a low buzz from the south that was steadily growing louder. Hadley was already on his feet, scanning the midnight horizon.

Titus rose and moved next to him. "That's what I thought I heard," he said. The noise was getting louder by the second. "It sounded like rattlers in my dream. At first anyway."

They both checked the ground around them, relief hidden on each man's face when they found no snakes waiting there, beady eyes glittering and poised to strike. The sound thickened the air around them. Titus wondered if this was some strange new magic of Moctezuma's, and wondered how in creation Texas would be able to survive it, assuming the zombies didn't bring down the Republic first.

Bigfoot rolled over to face them. "Ain't snakes. It's hummingbirds."

"Hummingbirds?" Titus repeated.

Before Bigfoot could explain, they were surrounded by tiny ruby-throated birds, so many of them perching and roosting and filling up every bit of space in view that Titus thought for a moment that he must be in a dream. Nebuchadnezzar and the other horses balked at their presumption.

Hadley's cheroot dropped from his open mouth to the ground.

"They migrate at night sometimes. I seen it once when I was living off the Llano them years." As Bigfoot spoke, over two dozen of the hummingbirds settled right on him. He cooed at them and held his body so still it was impossible to see the large man as anything but a gentle, simpleminded man-child.

Bigfoot kept making baby talk at the birds, some of which scattered around him while others pecked at things too small to be seen in the air. The hummingbirds remained all around them for less than a minute, all of them still and silent like children too skilled at hide-and-seek. Then, as if guided by one mind, the thousands of them took wing as one and buzzed away.

"They come from the south, I reckon?" Bigfoot asked, his voice no longer sounding like a woman goo-gooing over a bassinette full of babies.

Hadley nodded, too stunned by the bizarre spectacle to say anything.

Titus cleared his throat, feeling the thump of his pulse beginning to slow. His fear was giving way to wonder too late to appreciate the miracle he'd just been privy to. He ached to tell Cecilia about it.

Bigfoot was all business now. "Moctezuma won't be far behind them."

"How do you know?" Hadley asked, reaching down to pick up his burning cheroot.

"I was dreaming of snakes too."

After the incident with the hummingbirds, Titus expected to have a hard time getting back to sleep. It came as a surprise to him when Hadley nudged him a few times, made sure he was up and alert, and then promptly curled up in his own blankets, broad back positioned to soak up the meager heat of the flames.

The night had become chilly and almost silent. Titus alternated staring south and listening to the night sounds of the horses with hunting for bits of wood to keep the timid fire going in its pit. He kept thinking about Sylvester, trying to remember what the old hoon-gan had said. Jeb bringing a gift. Moctezuma weakened and on the march to do something about it. Gods dying.

And the thought of gods dying brought Cecilia's concerned face into his head. The way that woman had kept after him to attend services, to be respectful of the preacher–she had wanted more than anything for him to believe it all, same as she did. And he'd tried his best to give her that, but in the end her "saved" husband was nothing more than a Trojan Horse, and not even one that held a bunch of Greek soldiers. After seeing the things he had seen at the Alamo–Davy Crockett lost in a voodoo fervor and dead Mexicans animated and on the march–after seeing so much evidence of so many heathen gods and never coming across even one simple sign of Cecilia's Lord Almighty, believing was just not something he could bring himself to do.

He'd been washed in the blood alright. Just not the blood Cecilia thought. He'd been washed in the blood of comrades and victims he couldn't save. In the blood of rustlers and crooks and men with bounties on them to match his bullets. Now here he was, a private in the last army Texas would likely ever have, serving under the only other man who would understand.

He stalked away from the fire, aggravated with the maudlin turn of his own thoughts. Was it true, though? Was this coming battle the last hope for Texas? He groped around in the dark for more stray branches and clumps of dry grass, more than a little cautious of any critters that might be using them as a hiding place. The moon had already set, leaving the pitiless stars shining all the more brightly down upon him.

Returning to the makeshift camp, Titus squatted down by the fire and began feeding it wood and grass.

"You giving up?"

Bigfoot's voice startled him. Titus stared across the dancing yellow flames at him. "Sure can't afford to."

"I don't reckon we can."

Something popped in the flames as Titus rose to check the horizon.

Bigfoot cleared his throat, stood and wandered into the dark. A moment later Titus heard the sound of the big man urinating. Bigfoot talked over his shoulder as he did so.

"You know they're wrong about me. At Goliad."

"That so?"

"It is." The splash of urine stopped and Bigfoot returned to the dimly lit circle of camp, suspenders hanging down around his knees.

Titus had heard the stories of Santa Anna demanding a human tax in the name of the fledgling Lord Presidente Moctezuma, how the Generalissimo had poured a hundred white beans into a sack and twenty black beans in a gruesome sort of lottery; Every resident of Goliad older than six or seven would draw a bean from the sack and whoever came up with a black bean would be going back to Tenochtitlan with Santa Anna. Ranger Wallace had been there at first as a defender, but when bested by a flood of zombies he had become just another potential tax payment. In most tellings, Bigfoot had gone first. Some said this was so he could plunge his hand all the way to the bottom and grab a white bean. Others said it was just dumb luck that he had drawn a white bean. It hadn't mattered at all: Santa Anna had changed his mind and killed everyone there but Bigfoot and the youngest children, whose muddy understanding of the day's events formed the basis of all the gossip and legends surrounding "The Black Bean Affair." Everyone just assumed it was either this moment of cowardice or survivor's guilt that had led Bigfoot to turn in his star and live out on the Llano as a hermit for all those years.

"What part?"

Bigfoot hitched one arm and then the other underneath his suspenders. "I never got no white bean."

Titus felt his face grow cold with shock. Was his old friend supposed to have died that day? And if so, how had he escaped the fate of every other person in Goliad? It was hard to speak through the whirlwind of thoughts spinning in his head, but somehow, Titus managed to say, "How?" and that simple word was enough to convey all of his questions and bafflement and surprise at once.

"It's true what those kids said about Santa Anna putting so many beans into a burlap sack. And about white ones meaning you were safe and black ones meaning you'd be taken. I saw him put them in, all the white first, then the black on top, and I asked to go first."

The night had grown preternaturally still, as if Bigfoot's tale were conjuring up the specters of all those who had died that day in Goliad, and they hung just outside of the flickering firelight waiting to judge him. His voice was strained and his too-small eyes seemed to cross more than usual, giving the man an even more feebleminded appearance than the one wore most other times.

"I asked to go first and he let me, and I stuck my hand in at the top and grabbed out the biggest fistful of black beans I could. And when I yanked my hand out, I stuck those beans in my mouth and swallowed them all whole and dry.

"The Generalissimo, he fancied himself a man of honor, in his own strange way, so he told all his zombies to back away from me and let me be. He said I had done a very manly, heroic thing, and out of respect for that he could not take me to Tenochtitlan."

That matched what Titus had heard about Santa Anna, about his machismo and strange morals. Titus reached up to put a comforting hand on the giant's shoulder, but Bigfoot stepped away.

"You need to hear this, Titus."

A third voice interrupted. "Titus?" Hadley rolled over suddenly, his good eye communicating as much betrayal as his voice. "Brigadier-Justice Titus Smoke? God damn, I thought you looked like somebody. And enlisted as a private in my unit to boot!" He caught himself then and shut his trap.

Titus wondered if Bigfoot was going to go on, and how much of a problem Hadley was going to be. He'd have to explain himself and hope the man could respect his choices. But that would come after. Bigfoot could have been the giant statue of Sam Houston they had erected in Austin, for all that he was moving.

Finally, he continued. "He said he wasn't going to take me to Moctezuma as the tax, but that I had eaten all the black beans. He said he wasn't going to take a living soul to Moctezuma, and all the folks of Goliad started whooping with joy.

"And then ... "

Titus waited, his upper lip drawn back in a snarl that dared Hadley to say a word.

"And then they tied me up and he had the zombies slaughter every single one of them that was over seven, while me and the younguns watched. He had his zombies stack the corpses up like lumber on wagons and haul them out." Bigfoot was openly weeping now, and there was a lump the size of a good smoothing iron in Titus's throat.

"I couldn't do anything to stop them. And all I'd done was make things worse. I might as well have killed the town of Goliad myself." The last words came out in an anguished rush that seemed to dim the stars above.

The little fire had calmed itself down to embers while Bigfoot spoke. Hadley just sat there with his jaw propped open like a cold, dry well. Titus shivered and stepped into the darkness, looking for something to burn.

A sky pink as fancy curtains greeted Titus when he awoke. Bigfoot had some sliced potatoes frying with summer sausage and a pot of coffee steaming nearby–Titus recalled the man never did make it strong enough–while Hadley tended to the horses. Titus got moving as quickly as he was able, his achy joints complaining about the night of broken sleep on broken ground more than ever. *You're the one wanted to be a private.*

"Good, you're up," Hadley said, betraying no hint of his surprise from the night before. "Figured we'd let you sleep in, sir."

Temper flaring, Titus all but shouted back at him. "Damn it all to hell, Corporal! You are senior to me in this army, and you best not forget it. And you, Sergeant, you ought to know better than to go treating this private with kid gloves." He stood there, nostrils flaring, while the valley below them echoed with the timbre of his commanding tone.

Bigfoot laughed out loud. It wasn't half a minute before Hadley cracked a smile as well and Titus, hard as he tried to keep fuming, just couldn't.

"Told you he'd get ornery over it," Bigfoot said.

Hadley just cackled in response.

"Sons of bitches," Titus said, stalking off to piss in the tall grass. That just set them to laughing harder.

"Did ya'll see that?" One arm extended out toward the southern horizon, pointing. His voice had lost all trace of aggravation, good-natured or otherwise. He wasn't quite sure what he was giving away now, but the taste of old peso coins in his mouth told him all he needed to know about his own emotional state.

Hadley and Bigfoot stepped up to join him, squinting into the distance with hands to their foreheads as if in salute.

It was hard to make them out, because the Mexicans were just cresting a wide flat hill far off and about as high as the one they now stood on. And they seemed impossibly tall, until Titus realized they were wearing towering headdresses of colorful feathers and glittering bits of metal. But there was no doubt about it.

"How far off you reckon they are?" Hadley asked, never taking his one eye off Moctezuma's advancing army.

"Maybe three and a half day's march from San Antone for a normal army," Titus said. "But for an army that doesn't need to eat or sleep ... "

"They'll be there by dark tomorrow," Bigfoot finished.

Hadley shifted on his feet, reached a hand out as if his horse's bridle weren't on the far side of camp. "We need to get back there and give the warning."

"Agreed," Titus said. "But first, we need to be able to give a good report so they know what exactly is coming."

Bigfoot muttered to himself. His eyes darted left and right over the ghoulish horde. The giant seemed to be lost in concentration.

Hadley had gone as pale as his dark skin allowed at the sight of them. Even from so far away, the zombie army seemed to radiate the stink of death and old, merciless magic. He began to stutter something out, but Titus slapped the back of his hand across the one-eyed man's chest. "Shhh ... Let him count."

The Mexicans kept coming over the hill, dozens of ranks and files bearing long spears and short swords and rifles. On either end of the formation and scattered throughout the middle were small cannons mounted on wheeled carts being pulled by unadorned dead.

As he stared at the columns, Titus felt his stomach falling. There was something different about the ones pulling the cannon. He couldn't make out just what it was that struck him so different about them, but he knew it gave him an uneasy sense of dread to look at them. But nowhere near the queasy gut-clench he got when he stared at the ornate golden pyramid being carried along at the rear, and the royal figure silhouetted atop it.

"There's nearly three thousand of them," Bigfoot whispered.

Bigfoot sent Hadley galloping toward the Alamo with the news, while he and Titus remained behind on the hilltop to watch and count the sections of Moctezuma's army they expected to break off, just as they had under Santa Anna so many years ago. But would Moctezuma repeat his dead general's tactics?

And that was just assuming the rumors were true about Santa Anna having been killed by Moctezuma for failing at the Battle of the Alamo. Looking at Bigfoot, who kept counting and recounting the zombie horde, it made Titus feel a little better to think of the former Generalissimo now just another unflinching agent of the Lord Presidente's unholy will. But only a little better. Without the full power of the Forever Free, even the lowest ditch digger in Moctezuma's undying army could be a serious threat.

What would Moctezuma do? He declared himself an Aztec god, risen from the grave to restore his empire to its former glory. But all he had really done was grab land and empty it of bodies. He said he had bested Cortez, but was tricked in the end and buried alive for hundreds of years. Someone like that would not let himself be tricked again. Someone like that would have a trick or two up his own feathered sleeve.

Titus and Bigfoot ducked there in the scrub grass, with the horses secluded on the far side of the hill, hoping the undead god would tip his hand where they could see it. Titus nervously put his rifle to his shoulder over and over, waiting.

From out of the darkness behind them came a disembodied voice. "So here's dem two men dreamed about rattlesnakes, heh?"

Titus jumped and nearly pulled the trigger when he heard the singsong voice behind him. Relief that he hadn't done so puffed out of him in one sharp breath. Bigfoot pounced to his feet, the long steel blade of his "Arkansas toothpick" in an evil underhanded grip.

"It's okay, Bigfoot," Titus said. He swallowed the lump in his throat. "It's Sylvester. One of the Forever Free."

"That I am Mistuh Smoke. And pleased to make your acquaintance Mistuh Wallace. You gentlemen plan on letting those dead men march right over you?"

"No," said Titus. "We're counting."

"No need for that," said Sylvester. "I can tell you there's three thousand one-hundred fourteen of them, counting man and zombie."

"And how do you know that?" asked Bigfoot.

"The loa whisper it to me. And they whisper something else. That's what I come to tell you."

"What's that?" asked Titus.

"Your boy gonna ride into San Antonio today, bringing that gift we talked about. I suggest you go now so you meet him."

Titus felt his stomach lurch. Jeb in San Antonio? He'd dreaded seeing his son again, ever since he'd hired that ex Ranger Tanner to hunt him down and bring him home. He still hadn't decided what to do with the boy. Help him hide out in the United States or just whip his wandering ass, but there needed to be some sort of accounting, and it would never come with Jeb out roving the Llano.

They needed to have a talk, father to son.

Titus just hadn't expected it to come so soon.

"What gift?" asked Bigfoot.

"Something *real* special," said Sylvester, smiling. "Something gonna turn this whole world on its head."

"Let's go then," said Titus, afraid that if he stalled too long he'd lose his nerve.

One way or another, it was time for Jeb and he to come to terms.

CHAPTER 19

JEB HAD ANTICIPATED AN UNCOMFORTABLE ARRIVAL in San Antonio, but reality far exceeded his expectations. He'd imagined a hundred scenarios where he was spotted as he approached and immediately clamped into handcuffs, or where Andrew Sheppard saw him coming and put a bullet between his eyes, or where his own father tossed a rope around his neck and ran the other end over the nearest oak limb. But in all his wonderings, he'd never imagined San Antonio to be preparing for a siege.

Save for a few sideways looks at Darla, they were all but ignored as they rode wearily in from the scrub land; they weren't the first to arrive with news of the fall of Austin, and they wouldn't be the last. Just a few questions on the street and they'd learned that the British and the Comanche weren't the only imminent threats. The Mexicans were marching too, just like his Daddy had always predicted they would some day, and by all accounts they'd be here soon.

The Alamo was garrisoned again, and solders went about errands in the streets, dressed in mismatched uniforms, armed with rusty guns and swords, all of them in a kind of hurry that only reinforced the tense state of affairs. As if all the trials of the last week hadn't been enough, now Smoke and Troy would have to take up arms against Mexico too.

Jeb was beginning to dread the day he'd decided to come back. Part of him wished he'd headed out for the California Colony when they'd escaped from Lightning Dove. Texas was going to fall either way, and Smoke's presence wouldn't make a lick of difference.

Darla clung to his shirtsleeve--they'd left their red coats on the outskirts of town for fear of being shot as Englishmen. Troy strode confidently beside them, his obvious pleasure at returning to civilization outweighing the exhaustion they all shared.

"I don't even care if Moctezuma is coming," he said. "I'm just glad to be in a town that ain't burning."

"Not yet anyway," said Smoke.

"The Alamo held once," said Troy. "It'll hold again."

"The first time we had the Forever Free and their magic on our side. And there were only the Mexicans to contend with. How well you reckon the Alamo walls will hold against three armies? Hell, them coyote Indians will just scamper over the gate. And the Redjack flying machines will rain down hell, or have you already forgot?"

"I ain't forgot nothing," said Troy. "Damn if you can't ruin a man's good mood quicker than shit."

"Well, I don't see any reason for a good mood. The way I see it–" Smoke froze. Darla took another step, realized he wasn't coming and yanked at his sleeve.

"What is wrong, Wind-at-Night?" she asked.

"Nothing, child," said Smoke, staring at the battered old buggy full of children clattering down the dusty road into town. "Not a damn thing." He couldn't be seeing what he thought he was, but he changed course and headed for the wagon, walking slowly at first and then gaining speed. Darla stayed right beside him.

"Where you going?" yelled Troy.

The words hardly registered. Smoke kept his eyes locked on the wagon, and the woman stepping down from the sideboard. She hadn't turned to face him yet; only a slice of her profile was visible thorough the fall of blonde hair. But Smoke knew without hesitation that it was Audrey. It seemed an utter impossibility that she was here, that she'd survived Austin, that she was traveling with a wagon load of children. But it was her.

"Audrey!" He meant to scream her name, but someone had stolen all the air and it came out a strained croak. Still, it caught her attention. She turned, saw him, started. Her eyes widened and she began crossing toward him, leaving the children with her thin companion.

"Jeb?"

They came together in a rush, and Smoke nearly crushed her in his arms. He kissed her forehead, drank in the scent of soap that lingered in her hair, and the faintest touch of flowery perfume. She was covered in road dirt and sweat, yet the smell of her was like something from his dreams. He'd spent whole nights on the plains trying to recall the way Audrey smelled in every minute detail. Now here she was and she was alive.

Audrey pushed away from him. She wore a severe expression and her eyes brimmed with tears. "You take far too much liberty with me, Jeb Smoke."

He started to remind her that they were betrothed, but of course they weren't. He'd seen to that. Smoke backed up a step, searching for a proper distance.

"I'm sorry. I just didn't think you...I didn't think I'd see you again."

"I'm surprised myself," said Audrey. "I thought you'd lit out for good. You said so yourself. Left me standing there. So what business do you have coming back now?"

"Audrey, I've got–"

"Don't start talking," said Audrey. "You talked enough on the day you left. Now you listen. It's my turn. I didn't know what to say then, but I've had a long time to think on it and you're going to hear it."

He swallowed and felt his head nod of its own accord.

"You don't make promises like that to a woman and then leave her behind. And don't tell me you were running from the hangman, because you told me yourself it was an accident. Two men lived to back you on that, and maybe you got scared of that little girl's father, but he's not the law. He's just a man. So that's no excuse. And if you were running from *your* father, that's an even worse excuse.

"But let's say all the hounds of Hell were chasing you down, wanting vengeance for that little girl. If you planned to run, you should have taken me with you. I'd have gone. I'd have followed you wherever you went because that's what you do with your husband, or the man who claims he wants to be. You don't leave a woman standing in the middle of the street like a fresh horse pie while you slink away from everything you know and everything you love like a coward."

"It wasn't like that."

Audrey slapped him full on the face. "It *was* like that. You made promises to me Jeb! And when your world got hard, you didn't think of me as someone to help pull you out of it. You left. You didn't even think enough of me to take me along. I was going to be your wife."

"I'm sorry."

"Don't think that now you're back, things are going to pick up where they were." Audrey turned and headed back toward the wagon. Half of the children were milling around in the street, while Audrey's companion, a lightly built man with a bloody cloth covering half his face, lifted the smaller ones out one by one.

Smoke felt like he'd been kicked in the stomach, and it took him a few seconds to gather his wits and realize he should go after her. Help her with the kids. Figure out how she'd come to be here. Figure out what he was going to do to win her back. Because now that he'd seen her, the love he'd kept tucked away in the dark corners of his heart had burst loose again, and he realized what a fool he'd been to leave her. He'd spent a long time blaming it on circumstances, but Audrey knew exactly where the blame needed to be placed.

He had to go to her and fix this.

"Jebediah."

Smoke turned, recognizing the voice at once. Troy came toward him in a steady clip, trying his best not to look guilty and failing miserably. Beside him walked a graying man in a faded military outfit that looked salvaged from the days when Moctezuma last marched this way. But despite that, the old man moved with an air of command, the same natural leadership and resolve that he'd spent more than twenty years trying to instill in his son.

It had never taken, but that hadn't stopped the man from expecting it to.

"Hello, Daddy," said Smoke.

"Hello, Jeb," said his father. "Long time, no see."

Titus and Bigfoot had returned to San Antonio only a few hours after Hadley, but already word had spread that the Brigadier-Justice had been masquerading as an enlisted man. Titus hadn't been confident that Hadley would keep his secret, but he'd at least have liked to ease into the truth at his own pace.

It was too late for that now. Men clapped him on the back and cheered at his return, and before he'd had a chance to splash the dirt off his face and get the horses settled, they were already trying to put him in charge. It seemed the impromptu forces of San Antonio had a great many officers but no real generals. Most everyone but Titus thought he was the man for the job.

Titus was a real live veteran of the Alamo, not that there weren't plenty of other men around that could claim that honor too. But not so many who could claim to have traded saber blows with Santa Anna himself. In truth, it had been little more than a random incident amid the chaos of the Mexican retreat. Once the battle had turned, the Forever Free took the fight to the zombies and fool that he was, Titus had ridden out into the bloody throng. He and the Mexican general had only locked eyes for a second, lashed out at each other twice, then the horde had separated them. Santa Anna was carried away to safety. But men had seen their quick exchange, and that's how legends were made.

Titus had built quite a life on those two seconds, though he'd never really felt he deserved it. He'd done far more in service to Texas in his days as a Ranger, but what people remembered him for was that unnaturally cold March day in 1836 when he'd touched sabers with Moctezuma's finest general.

Hell, he hadn't even realized who Santa Anna was until somebody told him. In that instant, he'd been thinking about his son, and trying to remember that no matter how brutal and horrible the moment at hand became, it was all in service to that little boy. So that little boy would grow up in a country not governed by a ridiculous religion and its human sacrifices, a country not patrolled by zombies and strangled by dark magic only the ancient Mexican ruler himself could understand. That boy would be free.

That boy stood before him now, in the bustling streets of San Antonio, back from wherever his ranging had taken him. A little Indian girl gripped his pant leg like a manacle, and he stood with a wagon load of children and two familiar women. One of them was Willie. And it looked as if the war had already treated her harshly.

"Mr. Smoke!"

Titus started and saw Troy Tanner standing not two feet away. It seemed the money he'd paid the man had not gone to waste.

"Well, I see you found him," said Titus, without preamble. The sight of his son brewed up a mixture of joy and nerves that didn't set right in his stomach. Half of him was thankful the boy was back, and the other half wished he'd waited long enough to avoid the Hell that was due to descend on the town within hours.

Titus started walking, and Troy followed after.

"He was out there on the Llano," said Troy. "Just like you figured."

"Uh huh."

"Some fellow paid him to take a letter to Lightning Dove. You believe that? Craziest thing I ever heard, treating with that sort. Liked to have got us both killed too."

"Uh huh."

"I figured he was running off, but that letter was the reason he left."

"That letter was his excuse, maybe. But not his reason."

"Same thing," said Troy.

"Not hardly."

They were close now and Titus could see who Jeb was talking to. It was that married woman he'd somehow been planning to take as his own bride. Audrey something. Her presence was yet another irritating piece to a suddenly overwhelming puzzle.

"Jebediah!"

His son turned with a stricken look, finally got up the nerve to speak. "Hello, Daddy."

"Hello, Jeb," said Titus. "Long time, no see."

They stared at each other for several long seconds, then Titus took his son in his arms and crushed him with a hug. Jeb was stiff, unaccustomed to such affection from his father, and Titus pulled away hurriedly, unsure what had driven him to such spectacle.

"Well, it would seem you've inherited a mess of kids since I last saw you," said Titus.

The barest trace of a smile crossed Jeb's face. "These ain't mine."

"Well that's *some* good news," said Titus. "Willie, I see you found your way back into the frying pan."

"Yes sir, I did," she said, looking unaccountably bashful as she helped one last child from the back of the wagon. "Them Comanches burned Austin to the ground. And they had help. The goddamned Englanders have tossed in with them."

"So I hear." Willie and Jeb were far from the first refugees to report on the fall of Austin. The news had been almost impossible to believe. Everything Titus had been predicting for years was coming to pass. He'd just never expected it all to come at once. And he'd certainly never expected the British to add to their troubles.

"You got that message to the President for me?"

"Yes sir, I did. And he wasn't having any of it."

"That's not too much of a surprise."

"I reckon he's dead," said Willie. "He said you'd quit."

"A technicality. Regardless, I thank you for your trouble."

"Weren't no trouble," said Willie. "At least until they attacked. You recall me speaking of my cousin, the school teacher. Well, these is her kids. Her and Mr. Marin got them all the way to Austin just in time to turn back around. Audrey here helped keep them all safe. Sam got herself killed. I got my face cut up. Mr. Marin rode hard for San Antonio and I hope he made it."

"And you?" Titus turned to Jeb, who stood with a slack expression, as if he found it impossible to believe that his Daddy had actually hired someone to track him down and bring him home.

"We were in Austin. We put up a fight then headed out once everything went south. Don't know a thing about the President's house exploding, so don't ask."

Titus cocked an eyebrow. "And this Indian girl?"

"Long story."

"Longer than the story of why you were carrying messages to Lightning Dove? Word like that gets around and you ain't likely to be too welcome around here."

"I didn't know he was planning to attack! He locked us both up in a goddamned cactus trap. People can think what they want about me but I ain't no Comanche spy!"

"I never said you were," said Titus. "And I've never taken much stock in what *people* think."

Jeb grunted.

Audrey stood fuming nearby, and Titus could not continue to ignore her and retain what remained of his manners. "I'm pleased to see you again, ma'am."

"And you, Brigadier-Justice." Audrey was no more sincere than Titus, but at least they understood each other.

"I'm pleased to learn that you were able to flee the city. Is this a reunion of sorts? Are you and Jeb renewing your courtship?"

"Mr. Smoke, your son is a fool. And a woman can only take so much foolishness in her life."

"Well, we agree on something, then."

"So are you here leading the charge?" Jeb couldn't quite keep the contempt from his voice.

"That wasn't my plan, but it seems it's going to be the case anyway. As long as the troops are on making me boss, I might as well use that clout to get you some cots inside the mission barracks. All of you. The children too, of course. The Mexicans will be here by morning, and the Indians shouldn't be far behind and somebody's got to figure out what the hell to do about it. Jeb, I would appreciate your help to that end."

"Before or after you march me to a cell?"

Titus sighed. "There won't be any cells, Jeb. If you weren't so goddamned stubborn, you'd know that. You'd have known it before you lit off across the plains like some idiot. We have things to talk out. And assuming we survive what's coming, we'll have that conversation. But right now, I'm asking you to help me get these kids and these women to the Alamo, and help me form a defense. Can you swallow that pride of yours and do that?"

Jeb nodded, looking scolded.

"Let's go then," said Titus. "Anyone who doesn't want the protection of the Alamo is free to seek shelter elsewhere."

Willie and Audrey formed the children into a line. The little Indian girl kept her grip on Jeb's pants. He didn't try to dislodge her, and Titus could only imagine what kind of trouble she was going to bring. He couldn't envision a scenario in which Lightning Dove would be pleased to find a young Warhawk young'un in their captivity.

Jeb cast a curious look at Willie. "Where do I know you from?"

Willie shrugged.

"You ain't old enough to lose your memory yet," said Titus. "That's little Wilhelmina Wontshee, all growed up. You remember? Ya'll used to play together when you were kids, and that wasn't so long ago."

"Wilhelmina!" said Jeb with a grin. "I ain't seen you in a month of Sundays."

"Well, I don't stay in one place much."

Not to mention that she didn't remotely resemble the little girl in dresses that Jeb would recall from childhood. They both suddenly looked uncomfortable. Titus couldn't imagine what made Willie so shy around Jeb, but he figured Jeb's discomfort grew from her mannishness. Though that hardly made sense. He had, after all, been engaged to a woman who made her living shoeing horses.

"We ready?" asked Titus, bending over to address the pretty blonde haired girl at the front of the line.

"Yes, sir," she whispered.

"Well then, we've got our orders, children" he said. "Let's march to the Alamo!"

CHAPTER 20

JEB SMOKE WAS HOPELESSLY CONFUSED.

He'd expected Daddy to hang him on sight, and instead he was being invited into the Brigadier-Justice's counsel, trusted with planning the defense and quite possibly changing the future of Texas itself.

Smoke might well have preferred the hanging.

The Alamo compound teemed with activity: men positioning the few cannons that would still fire at strategic points along the palisades; reinforcing bits of the crumbling mission's walls with lengths of freshly hewn lumber; pulling all the supplies and refugees they could from the city proper into the aging sanctuary that had once stood strong against Mexican invasion. Hopefully it would again. The chapel and the attached barracks overflowed with civilians and soldiers, and they spilled into the yards, interrupting any possibility of weapons drills. Whatever skills the sorry defenders of these walls brought with them would have to serve. Smoke couldn't imagine defending the place. It was hard enough to walk through the mass of people, let alone to fight.

He saw to Audrey and the children; the kids went with a gaggle of nuns who'd ridden their donkeys all the way from the Rio Grande, and they made Audrey a cot in the relative quiet of the impromptu infirmary. Soon, it would be overrun with the injured and dying, but until then it was among the most peaceful places in the mission. Audrey hadn't spoken another word to him, hadn't responded to his apologies or his pleas. She'd simply put her head on the cot and closed her eyes. Jeb left her there to find his daddy again.

While he'd been tending to Audrey, someone had made a ragged job of fixing Willie's face, sewing up a nasty gash on her cheek that had apparently been made by a Comanche knife. Smoke didn't know what to make of the woman. She'd never been particularly girly, even when they were children, but now she'd taken on the aspect of a dime novel gunfighter, and based on what his daddy told him, she had the weapons skill to support the image. She seemed nervous around him, and gave little more than mumbled responses when he spoke to her.

All the while, Darla clung to his leg. Smoke wasn't sure what the next few hours held for him, but he knew it wouldn't be safe for her. He'd tried to send her off with the nuns and the other children, but the girl wouldn't have it. Finally, he'd given in. Now Darla sat cross legged beside him on the floor in a cordoned off room that his daddy had claimed as the command center for the nation's defense.

Daddy sat opposite him, studying a stained map of Texas, and one of Daddy's old partners, Bigfoot Wallace, sat beside him. Smoke knew all the tales of Bigfoot, of course, but he'd never met the man before today. He was a large man, that much was certain, but somehow Bigfoot, in person, didn't live up to the image he'd conjured in his mind. Beside him, an angry looking man who'd hurriedly introduced himself as Colonel Kuykendall stood fuming, an expression of pure hatred aimed at Daddy. Something was brewing in the man's mind; that much was plain. Finally he took a formal step forward, and hammered the table with his fist in a melodramatic attempt at outrage.

"Listen here," said Kuykendall, pointing a finger at Daddy. "You can't just come in here and start making plans and ordering everyone around. General Williamson is on the way with half the army and he's ordered me to hold this place until he arrives."

"That's what we're planning to do," said Daddy. "And you might not want to put all your faith in General Williamson. He had good intentions the last time the Mexicans came marching here too."

"I'm telling you I'm in charge. Those are my orders!"

"Well, you have new orders," said Daddy. "Case you haven't heard, I'm the Brigadier-Justice."

"Word is you quit!"

"Don't believe everything you hear. The Vice President is abroad and as far as we know, the President is dead, so I'm assuming that role. Somebody's got to save this country and by the looks of you, I doubt you're the man to do it. If you want to keep barking at my heels, let me know so I can take you outside and whip your disrespectful ass real quick and get back to business."

The fact that none of the others assembled came to his aid convinced Kuykendall to settle into the background and shut his mouth, but he kept his fiery expression trained on Daddy. Another soldier, a one-eyed black man named Hadley something or other, stabbed a finger at the map, reminding them all exactly where they'd last seen the Mexican army and precisely how little time they all had left to live. A few other nameless observers grumbled and fretted until Daddy shut them up with a grunt and took over proceedings.

"No one's arguing that the Mexicans are close. I need useful information. I need a plan. We figure they'll be here in a few hours time. Hell, advance scouts might be riding up on us right now. I survived this place once, but I can tell you it was magic that saved us that day. It was the Forever Free turning back that damn death magic, else none of us would be sitting here. I'd be dead and the rest of you'd be Mexican citizens. Probably sacrificing your sisters to heathen gods."

"I seen a few men with the Fs on their foreheads out there," said Hadley. "More's probably on the way."

"A few won't do us much good," said Daddy. "We need a bunch. But they're just as spread out as everyone else with any zombie fighting experience. Burleson let our defenses go to hell and now we're all going to pay for it unless we figure something out. We can't plan on magic to help us out this time, and that lot out there won't be able to hold these walls a day, let alone drive back the horde."

"There's Indians and Englanders coming too," said Bigfoot. "Don't forget."

Daddy gave his old friend a sour look. "How exactly could I forget that?"

"I'm just trying to help."

"Well, then get us more guns. More cannons. Give us some time to train soldiers. Cause that's all that's going to help."

"What if we did have magic?" asked Smoke, tentatively. The men in the room were older than him, save for Hadley, and they all had more experience as soldiers. Smoke didn't count himself an equal; when they all turned their eyes his way and regarded him with a mix of irritation and exasperation, he felt like a child who'd spoken out of place and interrupted the grownups.

"If we did have magic, we could fly away on magic carpets," said Daddy. "But we don't, so why don't we stop daydreaming and find a real solution."

Smoke bristled. He hadn't wanted to be there, but Daddy had insisted. He was in no mood to be mocked. "Maybe you want to listen to what I have to say, before you go back to fumbling around in the dark. You're the one said you wanted my help."

Daddy sighed, crossed his arms. "Say what you have to say."

"The simple truth here is, there ain't no way to defend this place with the people we've got."

Daddy nodded. "I believe that's the point I was making."

"We need manpower, we need weapons. How far out is Williamson?"

"At least three more days," said Kuykendall.

"Then we need magic. I only know one place right now we can get it."

"And where's that?"

"From the Comanche."

Tense silence settled on the room, and Smoke met every man's hard stare with one of his own. Daddy didn't betray what he was thinking, but he leaned forward, his shadow flowing across the map of South Texas like creeping death.

"The Comanche," he said.

"The Comanche," repeated Smoke. "We need them on our side."

Bigfoot barked a laugh and Kuykendall hissed through his teeth. The others stood frozen, as if waiting for Titus Smoke's verdict.

"You talking about the same Comanche that put that cut on Willie's face?" said Daddy. "Same ones that chased the woman you love out of town, killed the President, and left you in the desert for dead? Same ones that burned the whole fucking city of Austin down to the dirt?"

"I'll be damned if I ever take help from an Injun," said one of the older soldiers, a graying man with a pot belly that stretched the limits of his mud-stained uniform. His face was an overgrown tangle of hair, and Smoke was fairly certain he'd spotted a louse or two along the man's cheek bone.

"No, you'll be dead," said Smoke. "Because this place is lost if we can't convince them to help."

"It's a foolish notion, Jeb," said Daddy.

"I didn't come up with it. You did. How many years have you been telling me that one day we were gonna have to cede the western part of Texas to the Comanche? You've been telling that *foolish notion* to anyone who'd listen for as long as I remember. You've always said there were too many people willing to come and take Texas away from us, that we needed to find us some allies. The Comanche were always at the top of that list, weren't they?"

"Yes, but that was before they burned Austin."

"That don't change things," said Smoke. "I'll admit, it won't be a popular decision. At least not until the Indians sweep down and save all our asses from Moctezuma. Lightning Dove ain't a fool. He knows if Mexico takes this country, they'll have to put up with a lot worse neighbors than we've been. He hates the Mexicans more than he hates us. We offer him half the country to help us out and I think he'll take it."

"He'd have taken it before, but not now," said Daddy. "We don't have much to bargain with anymore. Particularly since he's marching with half of Queen Victoria's army."

Smoke shrugged. "You may be right, but unless anyone has a better idea, I think we need to try. If they turn us down, we won't be any worse off. Might even manage to stall them a bit."

"Yeah, that way the Mexicans can kill us all first and save them the trouble," said Hadley.

"Might be they will," said Smoke.

"So somebody just rides up to Lightning Dove's camp and sits down with him for a chat?" said Kuykendall. "Who you reckon is going to volunteer for that job?"

"I figure I'll go," said Smoke. "I've done it before."

Daddy grimaced. "Jeb–"

"Daddy, it's my idea. I ain't going to send anyone else out to do it. Besides, worst thing that happens is he kills me. He can stick me through with his lance or I can stay here and catch a bullet. Or get eaten. Maybe sacrificed. What difference does it make which way I die?"

"What about the Brits?" asked Daddy. "What're you going to use to turn them to our cause?"

"I figure if they're joined up with the Comanche, then they must have similar ambitions. If the Comanche can be persuaded our deal is to their advantage, then it should serve the interests of the Brits as well."

Daddy shook his head. "You can't know that, and you can't assume. We have a pretty good idea of what motivates the Indians, but the plain truth is we don't have a clue why the Brits are involved."

"No matter," said Smoke. "We still have to go through with this. Way I see it, this works out one of three ways. First, we ride up and they kill us. Second, we win over the Indians and the Brits follow suit. Third, we win over the Indians and then have to help them fight it out with the Brits. I'm not saying this is easy, just that it's the only thing I can think of to do. Anyone else with a better idea, speak up."

Daddy leaned back in his groaning chair, studied Jeb for an uncomfortable few seconds, as if seeing his son as a grown man for a first time and trying to determine if he was someone to be proud of or someone who'd gone loco from too much desert sun.

Finally, he pushed back from the table, turned and spoke to Kuykendall. "You get your wish, Colonel. I'm putting you back in charge of the defense of the Alamo. Get every man and boy here as ready as they can be and hold off the enemy as long as you can. I'm going with Jeb."

"The hell you are!" said Kuykendall, looking suddenly terrified. "You can't bring the Indians here."

"They're coming whether we bring them or not," said Daddy. "Get this bunch ready. I'm putting Bigfoot here as your second in command. He'll be an asset."

"He's a sergeant," said Kuykendall.

"Yes he is, and by the looks of it he's done more to bolster this place than anyone else, including you."

"That ain't a real good idea," said Bigfoot. "I don't know nothing about running a whole army."

"That might matter if there was any sort of strategy involved in our defense. Or if we had a whole army, which we don't. But you know how to direct men. I saw you do it enough in the Rangers all those years breaking in the youngsters, teaching them how to stay alive. That's what you need to do here. Teach these men who ain't soldiers how to stay alive. Once the horde arrives, it gets real easy. Shoot anything that tries to come over the walls right in the damned head."

"You ain't going with me," said Smoke.

"Yes I am. You can speak Comanche and you've at least seen Lightning Dove before, so I'll admit you're the best man for the job. But you can't authorize treaties on behalf of the Republic of Texas."

"You can't either."

"The President is dead and I don't see any other government officials here. They're probably all hiding out until the dust settles. So I'll do what I've got to do and if they don't like it, they can be the ones to go to Lightning Dove after the fact and tell him we were just fooling."

Daddy allowed a small grin to form on his weary face, and Smoke couldn't help but smile back. He'd never admit to his daddy how glad he was not to be marching off to probable death by himself.

Darla tugged on his pants leg. He'd almost forgotten she was there. "I'm hungry, Wind-at-Night. Do we eat soon?"

"Yes we do," said Smoke. "Then I'm afraid I'm going to have to leave you with Barking Spider for a while."

Darla scowled. "Why?"

"Because I'm going to see Lightning Dove."

"Can't I go with you?"

"No, but if things go right, we're going to bring him here."

"What's she saying?" asked Kuykendall.

"She was calling you a white demon."

"Sounds about right," said Kuykendall before storming out.

Daddy put a firm hand on Smoke's shoulder. "If we're going, we should go now."

Smoke nodded, began steeling himself for what came next. Finding Lightning Dove would be the easy part. What he really dreaded was telling Audrey he was leaving again.

Audrey stood in silence as Jeb and his father made preparations to leave, cinching their saddles, filling dented canteens with sandy water and trying to pretend they weren't about to ride off to their deaths.

She'd fallen asleep, reluctant to embrace her hope that Jeb had changed. But there was something different about him and the way he looked at her. He carried himself like a man who'd had his fill of chasing hardships and was ready to sort out the mess he'd made of his life. She hadn't forgiven him–possibly she never would. But the feelings she'd bottled up inside were stirring, and it was hard to keep them down. If Jeb was truly back for good, then was what they had worth finding again? As much as she hated to admit it, the thought brought her a happiness that had been missing since the day he'd left her. It brought a sense of *rightness* and–though she'd long sworn off depending on men for her well being–a sense of safety. With all the enemies of Texas bearing down, she felt like having Jeb near would keep all horrors at bay.

She'd fallen asleep, allowing a giddy sense of relief to take her. Jeb was back. Her Jeb.

Then he'd woken her with a gentle shake to tell her he was leaving again.

Troy and the little Indian girl they'd rescued from the prairies stood with her, and Willie milled about, doing what she could to help the fools make ready. Jeb had explained their reasons for leaving, and the worst part of the whole mess was that they made sense. There weren't many chances for survival, and if this was one, somebody needed to ride out and grab it. She just didn't want that somebody had to be Jeb.

"Audrey?" His voice shook her. She'd been trying to avoid looking at him. Instead, she stared north, hoping maybe she'd see the Comanche coming. Then it would be too late to bargain, and at the very least they could die together.

"What?"

"I love you, Audrey."

"I know that," she said. "You're the fool here, not me."

"I'm going to come back."

"With an army of Englishmen and Indians."

"With an army of Englishmen and Indians to fight off the zombies," he said. "Can you help Troy look to Darla? He's not exactly the fathering sort."

"I can handle the girl fine," said Troy, softly. Under normal circumstances, he'd have hurled his words like barbs, but he knew as well as any that Jeb and Mr. Smoke would likely never see San Antonio again. He'd argued for going along, but Mr. Smoke had shut him down. Arguments never lasted long with Titus Smoke.

"I'll look to her," said Audrey.

Jeb nodded, backed up like he was going to just ride away without another word. Audrey grabbed him, ashamed of her sudden terror and the tears forming in her eyes. She kissed him and squeezed him tight in her arms. Her face pressed up against his shoulder and she could smell the leather and the sweat and the trail dust that never seemed to disappear entirely from men like Jeb.

"You come back," she said firmly. "Soon. I'll expect you tomorrow, and when all this is finished we're going to have a talk. A serious talk."

"I'd like that," he said.

Titus Smoke already sat in his saddle, casting impatient glances back at the two of them. Audrey knew this whole idea had been Jeb's, but she couldn't help but hate his father for it.

Jeb kissed her head, and then he was gone, one boot in his stirrup, the opposite leg over his saddle. Riding north into quickly falling darkness. The morning would bring the Mexican army to San Antonio, or so everyone believed, and though no one liked to admit it, the two men riding north were the city's only hope.

"Have faith," said Willie. The woman stood pale beside her, looking even more miserable than Audrey felt. "They'll bring Lightning Dove."

"I'm sure they will," said Audrey. "One way or another."

PART the THIRD

※»»※«««

MANIFESTING DESTINY

CHAPTER 21

IN HIS TINY QUARTERS aboard *H.M.S. Indomitable*, Pincher hummed as he daubed lather first onto one pink cheek and then the other with a stubby badger-hair brush. He shaved carefully, gazing a bit too long into the familiar silver backed mirror. Joan had given it to him over a decade ago in Scotland, and soon after that, they'd eloped and crossed the gaping yawn of Atlantic together, in search of the things an unlanded man could find only in America: universal suffrage by secret ballot and the right to sit an office. He'd almost not brought the mirror–this particular assignment brooked no room for some stranger recognizing him–but one look at the crushed expression on Joan's songbird face had been enough for him to withdraw the very suggestion of leaving it behind.

And she was right after all. He'd taken it with him on all of his "assumed role" work, and in every case he'd come home safe and successful. So what if the mirror had his initials on the back? It just meant he had to choose his roles accordingly and none would be the wiser. Besides, Texas was a long, long, way from Chicago.

And good thing!

He was up to his bonny ears as it was, juggling monarchists, Indians, the madman in Mexico–not to mention the Texans themselves. Imagine tossing in a few bad fellows with a bone to pick into the mix!

He finished scraping his cheeks smooth, grabbed a scrap of scratchy British flannel and dried his face. A moment later the *Indomitable* jerked into motion.

Still humming, he rubbed his hair oil in, appreciating the shine more than the medicinal aroma. Even the cloying smell of cloves and menthol was beginning to grow on him. That was the price of becoming someone else, or one of the prices, anyway. One had to endure and assume the personal habits of an imaginary persona, and the longer one wore that mask of foreign mannerisms, the more likely it became that parts of the mask would never quite come off.

Satisfied that Mr. Adolphus Pincher was dressed and ready for the day, he launched himself out of the cramped stateroom, down the narrow ladders and passageways and through a stony pair of Her Majesty's finest prison guards to stand before the cell of his favorite deposed President. The man wasn't nearly as grateful as a man whose life had been saved twice should be. Pincher wondered how long it would be before that changed.

"Good morning," Pincher said, thumping the brim of his bowler hat against one thigh as if it were his old billystick. "I trust you slept well? No further attempts to hang yourself or swallow your tongue, I would hope?"

"Go to hell," Edward Burleson spat. "And take your *peace treaty* with you. I may die a coward and a fool, but I won't die a willing traitor."

Pincher took that in with a practiced air of professional briskness. The man was noticeably thinner in his jowls already, his haunted eyes ringed underneath with sleepless brown smudges. He hadn't shaven or bathed since the morning his mansion was razed (if then) and the nightsoil pot had gone thus far unchanged since departing Austin–a collection of facts which made Pincher even more pleased with his hair oil's strong scent.

"I won't trouble you with the treaty anymore, my good sir. General Lord Thackeray has received new direction from the Queen," he lied. "Her offer of exile in Tanzania has been withdrawn."

"Good, then get me a gun or some rope and let me be done with this. I am shamed to my mortal core before God."

"Oh, that won't do either. You see, Her Majesty has decided that you would do the Empire more good remaining in place–rebuilding Texas as her Governor. Lord Burleson. Has the ring to it, quite?"

Edward did not move or speak for nearly two minutes. Pincher watched the man's posture change as he digested it. He waited.

When Edward Burleson finally spoke, his voice shook with barely contained rage and desire. The man clearly wanted a chance to redeem himself, to turn the rubble he'd made of Austin and the nation around it into a stronger, more secure land. But he was not about to give up Texan independence for the chance.

"I don't hear a ring about it at all. You know what I hear? A slave collar. And not just for me, but for every man, woman and child in Texas." His voice rose with each word until he was thundering every syllable. One of the Redjack guards peered down at them questioningly. Pincher waved him back.

"Are you quite certain, sir?"

"Am I quite certain? Am I quite certain? I FREED SLAVES, YOU SON OF A BITCH! I freed them and you want me to chain up an entire nation and hand it over? I may not have been the most diligent or the bravest President Texas has had since Sam Houston, but I ain't about to get a red streak painted down my back just to cover up the yellow." Burleson stood straight as a church steeple now, and his voice rang like a bell on Sunday morning.

Pincher flared his nostrils deliberately. An abolitionist himself, he could only respect the fallen leader's conviction on that subject. This would do nicely, when things came to a head. This would do nicely indeed.

He nodded curtly at Burleson, donned his hat, then turned on his heels and headed for the topmost decks. As he passed the guards, he said, "Let's get him cleaned up. But no shaving yet, or anything else he could hurt himself with. If he manages to murder himself on your watch ... Well, you had best follow his example. You get me, boyos?"

The soldiers, not quite sure of Mr. Pincher's rank apart from being a personal guest of the General and holding some nebulous standing within the Empire's inner offices, saluted in unison and scurried to obey. Pleased, he headed for the topmost decks, noticing with every upward step how much more the steam gear seemed to sway from side to side as he ascended.

His confederate, a nearly hunchbacked man with one of those unpronounceable Welsh names, met Pincher's gaze as he stepped into the Flagship's bridge. Pincher looked past him to see the white haired Comanche and his toothless shaman in heated conversation with General Lord Thackeray while several of his staff looked on. Pincher made himself unobtrusive near one of the great opened brass shutters and listened. News had finally reached the Indians that the Mexicans were marching toward San Antonio. The chieftain didn't sound like he relished the prospect of going against the Mexican dead near so much as he had been aching to drive out the Texans. General Lord Thackeray wore a serene expression, but a vein pulsed beneath his jawline that betrayed his own surprise at, and perhaps a sense of the historic import of, this turn of events.

Voices rose and faded into a background buzz as he surveyed the scene beyond the enormous brass shutters. A warm breeze brought with it a constant stream of fine rust-colored dirt that made the fresh air taste somehow tainted. Pincher took it as a reminder to close his mouth and focus upon the facts presented to his eyes and ears instead. He would need to report things soon, probably tonight. It would be his last opportunity until the affair to come in San Antonio had played out.

Austin was far behind them, and honestly they had been making quite good time, considering the girth of the steam gear involved. The war party had suffered only the most superficial of losses. Two dozen men, one of the steam angel catapults, a handful of mechanized cavalry, and one steam angel that had been clipped by holdout gunfire and suffered a nasty landing, rendering it nothing more than an especially bulky collection of spare parts. And of course the Leviathan unit that had driven pell-mell through the President's House before something set off all the gunpowder it had been carrying. The Redjack army appeared to have shrugged off their casualties with their customary British stolidity. How he hated their disregard for the common man! Look at them, marching in perfect rank and file, every weapon shouldered, every button shining in the desert sun.

The Comanche had lost no more ... *men* than the Queen had, but those losses bit far more deeply given the relative smallness of their force to start with. He would have to make special note of their battlefield transformation and slow return to near humanity this evening. He made an effort not to turn around and look at the hunchbacked Welshman. Instead he stepped into the wide-eyed circle of debate.

Thackeray was upon him in an instant. "What word did the Empire have of this?"

"Word?"

The General snorted. "Montrazulu or whatever he calls himself! The ruler of Mexico and all his zombie hordes, converging on San Antonio. The Queen must have known. And you as well, given your–" he caught himself, but just barely. " ... position," he finished weakly.

"Indeed, I've been kept in the dark until only just lately, General. But you have no need to fear." He said the word deliberately, enjoying the way it made the assembled soldiers and savages bristle. "She knows Lord Presidente Moctezuma is marching, because she arranged for him to be."

Silence reigned throughout the command deck. Pincher sniffed once for sincerity, then told the biggest lie of his career.

"Her Majesty has led the Mexican to believe that her forces are allied with his, and that the spoils of Texas will be shared between our two countries." He stared pointedly at the white haired chieftain. "But Her Majesty has already allied herself with the Warhawk Council. It has been her intention all along to crush Mexico as well as Texas."

Someone coughed. An enlisted man said "Cor!" in an aghast whisper loud enough to be heard by all. It might even have been the Welshman, but Pincher could not tell for sure.

"She's certain you are up for the task. Aren't you, General?"

Thackeray blinked and cleared his throat. He looked like a man who was already being measured for a larger-than-life white marble monument. Pincher kept his face straight.

"Of course I am." Thackeray stared at Lightning Dove. "Can our red-skinned allies say as much?"

Pincher thought he saw something pass between Lightning Dove and Broken Lance. He hoped it was the unspoken realization that the British would as quickly turn on them as they would Moctezuma. Everything depended on chaos and distrust at the Alamo. Lightning Dove gave an eagle's shriek before he spoke. "The Great Spirit cries out against the wrong being done in the south. Breathless Men fighting when their bodies should be returned to the Earth. He is like the panther that returns for a different child every night. My people will not be safe in our own lands until he is killed."

Broken Lance's brittle hands squeezed his medicine stick. He rapped it once on the teak deck and began chanting something under his breath in his own language.

"I trust you do not need me to plan your order of battle, General?" Pincher did not wait for a translation before walking away, and none came. General Thackeray and the Indian Chief were both summoning the elders of their particular tribes. It was time for an even greater council of war than they had imagined.

The Welshman held the door for Pincher, trying very hard to catch his eye as he passed through it. Pincher ignored the man almost entirely until he was in the portrait-festooned passageway beyond. He pointed at the one closest to him, a reluctant favorite.

"Did you know this was supposed to have happened at midnight?" he asked the Welshman. "Precisely at midnight, if I recall correctly."

The Welshman nodded understanding, but said, "Nay sir, I didn't know that. No end of surprises in this world, I'd say." He laughed.

Pincher took hold of the handrails and bounded down a skinny ladder to the deck below, looking for something to settle his famished stomach, and thinking of the painting he had used to give the man his signal.

It was a scene from the Opium War. Proud British warships giving bloody hell and broadsides to a gigantic Chinaman made of bamboo and silk and wooden gears that had fallen to one knee while wading out into the stormy black waves to meet them. Flaming rockets arced from its disproportionately broad shoulders into the sea. An idiot grin stretched between fat brass cheeks; inside the mouth, the piloting crew displayed various expressions of near comic defeat and alarm. *The Pe'king Giant Bows to English Might*, it was called.

Pincher wondered how long it would be before the English learned to bow. He hoped it would not be long.

In his room that night, with a belly full of English mush and a few sips of whiskey from a barrel that had been "liberated" from its Austin oppressors by a trio of stalwart, rambunctious steam angel pilots, Pincher carefully pried the cap from the handle of his mirror. Yes, it had come in handier than Joanie would ever realize. He winked at his image in salute of a rather fine idea.

Beneath the cap, a hole had been drilled. He turned the opening toward his bed. More of a cot, or torturer's rack, really. It had not been made up in the two days of travel since Austin. He refused to allow the stewards or anyone else to enter. And since he envisioned Mr. Adolphus Pincher as a far less tidy sort than Joan would have allowed him to be at home, he forced himself to revel in the slovenliness of it.

As the contents of the mirror's secret compartment fell onto the rumpled sheets, a knock came at his door. Momentarily flustered, he pulled the blankets up over everything, then stood with his face almost touching the frame.

"Yes?"

There was a cough on the other side, but no response.

"Yes?" he said again, angry at the trill of fear he detected in his own voice.

"It is not customary for an officer in command to be kept waiting on his own flagship-even by Her Majesty's favorite Texan agent."

Pincher's eyes widened. "My apologies, I was undressing, General." He hastily collected the mirror and all its contents, dropped them into the trunk at the foot of his bed and snapped it closed. Soon as he opened the door, the General strode in with a military man's disdain for mess instantly visible on his face.

It was at precisely that moment Pincher saw the end cap of Joan's mirror laying on the floor just beneath the bed. He cursed himself for falling too far into his slipshod character's inattention to detail. Ice in his heart, he turned to General Thackeray.

"To what do I owe the pleasure?"

His answer was direct, and perhaps it should have been expected. "Why did the Queen not trust me enough to know her entire plan from the beginning? You, a runaway Scotsman and a traitor to your own republic, she allows to know every twist and turn of her Machiavellian scheme. But her own third cousin she tells nothing?"

Pincher began to laugh, stopped himself, then carried on with it. Thackeray looked at him like something a German would eat. Pincher raised one hand.

"Don't you see?" he said, feeling the role of Adolphus Pincher, spy for England, rising up in him. "If you had known Moctezuma would be on the march instead of resting quietly at home atop his bloody pyramids, you would have handled Austin differently. You would have handled the Comanche differently. And we have no idea whether, or rather *how many*, spies there are among our own. Can you be so sure a few of those bestial Indians are not secretly allied with Mexico, telling them our every move? Are there no Texan sympathizers among your own, plotting even now to free Edward Burleson?"

Thackeray boggled, but only for a second. "I see."

Pincher made his voice sound worried. "Even what was said today may have been better spoken behind closed doors. If word gets to Moctezuma that we come with a tribe of Comanche, he may become wise to the fact that we intend to quash his own army as well ... "

Thackeray plopped down upon the unmade bed, forgetting his earlier disgust at the lack of order. He rubbed his eyelids with two stubby thumbs. The mirror cap was just inches from Thackeray's spit-polished boot. Pincher's breathing quickened.

Finally, the General sighed and stood up again. "You are correct, sir. And much more careful a thinker than I have given you credit for."

"You are too kind, General." He looked Thackeray in the eyes, adamantly refusing his own desperate urge to glance at the mirror cap beneath the bed or at his steamer trunk.

"I do not like underestimating my allies any more than I enjoy underestimating my enemies, Mr. Pincher."

"That is most wise, I would think."

"And it is even more distressing when I am not one hundred percent certain that a man is my ally."

Pincher became distracted by the saliva collecting in his mouth. *If I were to swallow it now, while he is staring at me, it would be an admission. He would know the truth and I would find myself swapping noose techniques with Burleson down in the brig.* He nodded smartly and waited.

"Lightning Dove worries me. When will the Crown allow that I turn on him?"

Relief washed over Pincher. He swallowed. "She wants their magic on her side, at least until Moctezuma and his army are dead. Permanently, that is."

"After that?" The general made it to the door in two long strides.

"Yes," Pincher said. "After that."

With the Queen's witless third cousin gone, Pincher latched his door and grabbed the mirror cap from under the bed. His hands shook as he opened the trunk and removed the mirror and its erstwhile contents: a long strip of tin with a pattern of one to six tiny holes going along its length as if they were the jumbled-up pips on a lunatic's die. He produced a pin from his hat and tore yet another thumb-sized piece of onionskin paper from the back pages of his Bible.

He set to work with his hatpin and code stencil on the message.

COLUMBIA, it began. TEX WARH ENG MEX IN PLACE. Pincher labored over the stencil for nearly two hours, encoding a cordial but informative letter to the man who had asked him to take on his most precarious assumed role ever: that of a Texan traitor loyal to the Queen. ALLIANCES CRUMBLING.

It had been hard, being away from Joan for so long. But he knew she would understand. The power of one more free state—and such a large one—in the United States would mean an end to slavery all the sooner. DESTINY MANIFESTS TWO DAYS HENCE.

He looked at his pocketwatch. It would want winding soon. After midnight, when he met his hunchbacked Welshman and sent this message winging off attached to the leg of a carrier pigeon, he would wind it up good and tight. TELL JOAN I WILL BE HOME SOON AND PROMISE NOT TO LEAVE HER EVER AGAIN. He'd turn that spring so tight it wouldn't need wound again till there was nothing but dust and rubble in San Antonio, and all four enemy armies had weakened themselves to the point that they'd be no more threat to Polk's dream of an American continent than the sort of petty thug he had put away back in Chicago.

Pincher rolled the coded letter up and was about to head back to the *Indomitable's* afterdeck to wait for the Welshman and his bird with its miniscule oilskin pouch. He stopped himself and unfolded the paper. Certainly, the President knew who had sent the letter, but that was no reason to be impolite.

He poked the holes that signified his name, his real name, into the paper. Satisfied, and perhaps a bit giddy with anticipation and the stress of not quite knowing when or how he would make his hasty departure from Texas, Allan Pinkerton checked the time once more and then rushed out of his stateroom and up three ladders into the starry night.

CHAPTER 22

IT WASN'T THE FIRST TIME Jeb had ridden toward incredible danger, but it was the first time he'd done so with his father beside him.

Daddy kept pace beside him, their horses' hooves thumping at the dry packed earth in unison. Daddy's hat rode low on his brow and he kept his eyes on the horizon, looking for the first sign of Comanche movement to the north. He looked old. Jeb had grown up viewing his father the way the world viewed him–a bigger than life hero of the Alamo, a laughing, fighting, wilderness-taming force of nature who'd been instrumental in carving out a new nation from the stuff of destiny. It seemed impossible that such a man could ever grow old or weak. But since Jeb's mother died, his father had been winding down. Whether from age or grief, it was impossible to tell. The end result was the same. Titus Smoke was weary to his soul, but the fact that he rode alongside Jeb now meant he was not yet beaten.

"So what's your plan when we spot them?" asked Daddy.

"Surrender."

"Unless they shoot us first."

"They could do that," said Jeb. "I figure they'll have an outrider or three and we'll come up on them first."

"You aim to spot them before they spot us?"

"I'd prefer it," said Jeb.

"And I'd prefer to be home in bed," said Daddy.

Jeb and his father had both spent more then their fair share of time peering across desolate horizons for any sign of movement. Hoping to hell they'd spot any Comanche before the arrows began to fly. They were likely two of the best Indian hunters in the country. But that didn't mean they'd be able to sneak up on an advancing army. They'd have to press on and hope for the best.

"We may get lucky yet," said Daddy. "Maybe it'll be one of your Indian pals."

"What do you mean by that?"

"You carried that letter out to Lightning Dove. Got out of a cactus cage, Troy says. Speak Comanche like a native. You mean to say you never made friends with an Indian?"

The insinuation rubbed Jeb the wrong way. "I already explained that to you!"

"I don't recall an explanation," said Daddy. "Just an excuse."

"A man needed a message delivered to Lightning Dove. He knew I was a capable sort, that I knew the Llano and had hid out among one of the outer tribes for awhile. So he hired me to carry it. And I did. That explanation enough for you?"

"Not really. Sounds like you lost what remained of your common sense."

Jeb wanted to argue, but he knew it would be an empty attempt. Before Austin had even fallen out of sight behind him, he'd known it was foolish to accept such an errand, no matter how much money was involved. With a little distance, he understood it was his best excuse for leaving town, and that was something he'd desperately wanted. His world hadn't fallen in around him yet, but it had started wobbling like a house of cards and Jeb didn't want to be around when the crash came.

It was also an easy form of suicide, and though he wouldn't admit it, Jeb had never entirely dismissed it as one of his underlying motives.

"I just wanted out of there," Jeb finally said. "Away from every goddamned thing. How long do you think it would have been before old Sheppard sent some man to hang me?"

"The hell he would have," said Daddy. "I wouldn't have allowed it."

Jeb cast a sideways look at his father. "You might not have had a say. They might have come for me at night, with a lynching party. Besides, ain't you the one sent Troy Tanner to hunt me down and drag me back?"

"Yes, but that was to save you before you got yourself killed. I had no intention of hanging you."

"Just throwing me in jail."

"Son, I never believed that little girl dying was anything more than an accident."

Hearing his father speak of the incident out loud caused Jeb acute discomfort. He turned away, heeled his horse, and picked up their pace. He felt sick to his stomach, so he wound the reins around his fist until it threatened to cut off all the blood to his fingers and got back control of himself. Thoughts of Annabelle Sheppard were for those terrifying nights when he was all alone with nothing else to think about. They couldn't be escaped. But talking about it was something he wasn't prepared to do.

"Listen here," said Daddy, pulling up beside him again. "Anybody that knows you knows you're no killer. I've heard every report from that day, including the boy's and Tanner's, and they both swear it was an accident. Tanner likes to go on like maybe you were too reckless, and maybe you were, but you know that man's always been jealous of you. That's no secret. When it gets to the meat of the matter, he knows same as everyone else that you were doing what needed to be done to save that girl. Things didn't work out, but when do they ever?"

Things didn't work out. That was a hell of an understatement.

"I don't think Mr. Sheppard is going to accept that excuse," said Jeb. "Coming back here don't change the situation. I'm still a marked man."

"I reckon you don't have much to worry about from Sheppard," said Daddy.

"Why's that?"

"He's not liable to find support for a lynching now that he's turned coat. He joined up with Moctezuma."

This news was enough to pull Jeb from his sulking and make him take an interest. "The hell he did! What reason could he have for doing that?"

"Well, he didn't fill me in on his plans beforehand," said Daddy with a grin. "I reckon he's a man who knows when to cut his losses. He owns more of Texas than any one man should have a right to. If Moctezuma rolled through he'd lose it all, and there's a better than even chance of that happening. He probably thinks by ceding his loyalty to Mexico, they'll let him keep some of it. If that's his reasoning, the man doesn't know a hell of a lot about Moctezuma. That old boy never learned how to share, and Sheppard will be just another of his zombies. Whether he's dead or alive won't make any difference."

Jeb hadn't realized just how heavy a burden his fear of Sheppard finding him had been until it was lifted. He laughed, then caught himself and tempered his enthusiasm. Annabelle Sheppard was still dead; this new information didn't absolve him from that guilt. Still, he couldn't help but feel there might be some hope for him beyond their immediate circumstance, should they survive. Maybe he and Audrey would find a way to work things out, and maybe he could earn back some of the respect he'd let slip away.

Daddy reined up, held a hand out at Jeb and said, "Hang on." He pointed to a small rise on the horizon, and squinting, Jeb saw two men watching them approach. Comanche, beyond accurate rifle range, but Jeb didn't plan on there being any shooting anyway. Daddy had spotted them first, a fact that galled Jeb. He looked around for more Indians but saw none–which didn't mean they weren't there. He thought of all the coyotes and other creatures running wild through the burning streets of Austin, and the astonishing accounts from Audrey and Willie that made it plain the creatures were actually Indians under some kind of horrible spell. Jeb was thankful that these men appeared to be just men, and he hoped to hell they'd stay that way.

Daddy pulled his rifle gently from his saddle scabbard, then held it above his head with both hands, making sure the Comanche men saw. Then he heaved the gun behind them and onto the ground, raised his hands again and demonstrated that they were empty. Unsure how else to proceed, Jeb did the same. Both men still wore their pistols, but Jeb was hanging on to his until Daddy showed him otherwise.

"Ride slow," said Daddy, heeling his horse into motion. They rode at a leisurely pace toward the two Comanche. Daddy wore a grim expression on his face, like he'd suddenly decided this was a really bad idea. Jeb was fine until they came within reasonable rifle range and he saw the bare-chested men both held bolt action Winchesters. So far, they weren't aiming this way, but they might be waiting for a foolproof shot. Both men rode spotted mustangs, but neither gave their horse any rein. They simply waited in inscrutable silence as the two Texans approached them with growing trepidation. At last, Daddy stopped his horse about fifteen feet away from the man and Jeb did the same.

"Tell them why we're here," said Daddy.

Jeb didn't hesitate. "We represent the Republic of Texas and we're here on behalf of the President." This wasn't strictly the truth, but neither of the men appeared disposed to helping them, and he needed as much leverage as he could get. "We have news for Lightning Dove."

The men seemed momentarily taken aback that Jeb had addressed them in their own language, but the surprise didn't last long. The bigger of the two, a broad shouldered man with a handsome face and heavy black boots that looked like they'd once belonged to an American soldier offered the thinnest of smiles. "Have you decided to surrender so soon?"

"We can only talk about that with Lightning Dove. That's what the President says."

"Your president didn't send you. He's our captive."

Jeb's face burned. That was the last goddamned thing he'd expected. Burleson alive and in captivity. What little credibility he'd had with these men had evaporated.

"This is the Brigadier-Justice with me," he said, trying to keep the situation from deteriorating further. "He's acting President. We figured the real one was dead."

"If only he were," said the Comanche. "I've never heard more noise and protest from one man. I'd gladly kill him myself just to shut him up."

"What's going on?" asked Daddy. "Is he taking us there or not?"

"I'm just making friends with him," said Jeb in English, then he reverted back to Comanche. "Listen, we've got to talk to Lightning Dove. We have a proposal to end this whole war and give every bit of the Comancheria back to you. Can you take us to him?"

"You'll *give* us back our land?"

"We'll *return* what we *stole*."

"I'll take you to Lightning Dove, because he'd be angry if I did otherwise with the *acting* President of Texas," he said. "But don't expect any mercy from him. Our course is set, white man."

He raised his rifle and his companion did the same. Jeb and his father stiffened but knew better than to reach for their hips.

"Take off your pistols and hand them to me," said the Comanche.

They rode forward, did as requested, then proceeded at gunpoint toward the massed might of two hostile nations.

CHAPTER 23

LIGHTNING DOVE RECOGNIZED THE TWO PRISONERS approaching in the dusk immediately. The young one was the man who'd been bold enough to deliver a message to him on the Llano, one of the pair he'd left behind to die by the sun. He couldn't imagine how the man had escaped, or by what path he'd found himself captured again. The older man was none other than Brigadier-Justice Titus Smoke, and the sight of him at gunpoint almost brought a smile to Lightning Dove's eternally stoic features. Titus Smoke had been a scourge to the Comanche in his brief days with the Rangers, and he'd risen far in the Texas government because of it. Now here he was, a beaten-looking man, stumbling through the brush, weaponless and without hope for escape. In a week that had seen many triumphs, this was not least among them.

The two Comanche riders halted their captives when they saw Lightning Dove approach. Broken Lance walked with him, but the old man was speechless. He simply stared at the two white men as if they were of little importance. Lightning Dove knew better.

"Where did you capture these men?" he asked the riders.

The one called Brittle Bone eased from his horse and nudged the two men in Lightning Dove's direction with the butt of his rifle. "We didn't capture them. They surrendered. They claim the old one is the new President and that they want peace."

"What are they saying?" asked Titus Smoke, addressing the other man.

"I was asking where they captured you," said Lightning Dove. Surprise was evident on the Brigadier-Justice's face. He obviously hadn't considered the notion that an Indian could speak his language.

"You didn't tell me he could speak English!" he said.

"Forgot to mention it," said the younger man.

The Brigadier-Justice turned back to Lightning Dove. "Well met, Chief Lightning Dove. I am Brigadier-Justice Titus Smoke, acting President of the Republic of Texas. This is my son, Jebediah Smoke. I believe you've met." Titus Smoke cast a weary look at his son before continuing. "I've come here on good faith and would appreciate the opportunity to speak with you about a mutually beneficial arrangement to end this conflict."

"I know who you are," said Lightning Dove. "A man who's killed as many of my brothers as you is difficult to forget. You've been an enemy of the Comanche for many years, and now that the tide has turned against your pretender nation, you've come to sue for peace? You are a bold man."

"Bolder than most."

Lightning Dove knew this wasn't boasting but a simple fact. There were few men as capable as Titus Smoke drawing breath in the world these days.

The Brigadier-Justice continued. "I'll admit some mistakes in my past. Certainly I worked to keep Texas safe from those who would kill her citizens, and I'll admit that our claim to this land in the first place was tenuous."

"Tenuous? The Kiowa may steal our horses, but we steal them back. At least we acknowledge our thievery and don't hide behind weak words."

"You seem like an intelligent man, Lightning Dove. You know this war will end poorly for all. You've heard that the Mexicans are massing to the south?"

"I've heard more than you, I suspect."

In truth, the lack of information about the Mexican march was maddening, but Lightning Dove wouldn't concede the point to Titus Smoke. He was already embarrassed by the fact that information of Moctezuma's movements had reached him from that odd-smelling English spy, Pincher, and not his own scouts. What was to be one last march and assault to claim back everything they'd lost had become a strategic problem he wasn't sure he could solve. Assuming they could take San Antonio and turn back Mexico's army too, they would still have the British to contend with. Lightning Dove had never trusted them, and had given up even the remotest hope that they'd keep their word once Texas had fallen. They weren't honorable men. They did not honor themselves with their actions, they did not honor others with their dismissive, superior attitudes, and they did not honor the Earth Mother for all of her gifts.

Yet for all of that, Lightning Dove was afraid they could not take the Alamo, and thus San Antonio, without them. He'd thought his tribe was finally being rewarded for its service to the earth when the creatures in their souls had emerged during the battle for Austin. After years of manipulating plants and healing with gentle touches, at last they'd tapped the true power of their spirits and struck back at an enemy of the People. But the change had been temporary, and in the waning hours of that grand day, the men had returned to their former selves. Even Lightning Dove had been forced to return to earth as the feathers at his back began to smoke and burn away. He'd consulted with Broken Lance to determine why the magic he'd claimed for them had disappeared, but the old man was without answers. The men tried to find their animal forms again, but the totem spirits had fled back into the depths of their souls.

Lightning Dove prayed that the magic would return when they once again fought the Texans, and that it would remain to help them destroy the British. But he sensed that he was being punished for being so careless with the Earth Mother's greatest gift. He'd nearly given up hope of finding She-Who-Is-Alone. Surely the girl was lost to the wilds forever. Yet he held out hope for forgiveness, and prayed each day that she would find her way back to the tribe. With the girl, he knew the People's way of life would continue to prosper. Without her, he feared that the bones of every brave and squaw would be picked at and scattered by the myriad scavengers that had come to infest his lands.

"Then you know his army numbers in the thousands," said Titus Smoke. "Just like the last time he brought siege to the Alamo. And it took a whole lot of the Forever Free to win that day."

"It makes no matter to me if they kill you all. I'll just as gladly conquer Breathless Ones as Texans."

"No offense, but I don't think you're up to the task. You haven't seen the force they're bringing to bear. You'll need allies."

"We have allies," said Lightning Dove distastefully. The British didn't deserve to be called that, but it wasn't a sentiment he wished to share with the Texan. "Your compatriots in Austin learned that. Surely you didn't come here expecting us to help you fight off the Mexican army. I took you for a bold man, but not a fool."

"I'll tell you my expectations," said the Brigadier-Justice stiffly. Lightning Dove was glad that he'd managed to ruffle the hard fellow. "But we'd prefer not to share our reasons for being here with your *allies*."

The Texans eyed a group of British infantrymen milling about a few yards away, and the overt display of steam technology rumbling by and soaring overhead, with a mixture of awe and nervousness that pleased Lightning Dove. It was good that these men feared the combined force of Englanders and Comanche, even if the bonds that held them together were becoming whisper thin.

"There's nothing else you have to say that I wish to hear. Siding with Texas against Mexico is unthinkable. My people would not have it, and there's no advantage to it in any case. Your people are beaten. I would have you killed now if you did not hold a rank. You will be jailed with the weak-backed man you call a President until I determine there is no possible further need for you, and *then* I will have you killed."

"We have something you want," said the younger man, who he had left to die in a cactus cell. He had yet to speak and Lightning Dove had all but dismissed him from the conversation. He wore a desperate look, as if he could feel his country's last breath of hope being exhausted. Lightning Dove understood how that felt, but he had no sympathy for the man.

"You have nothing I want," he said.

"We have Darla."

"Darla?"

"A little girl. A little Comanche girl. She ran away from your camp and I've tended to her and now we have her safe. She's one of your people, and we've kept her fed and well. We've treated her nice. I think she'd like to come home, but if you want to see her again, we're going to need to make a deal."

Lightning Dove felt hot winds stir up around him, and blood thundered through his heart, pounded in his skull. He stared at the father and son, haggard and bleak in their desperation. They could not know of the girl unless what they said was true, and he wondered just how much they knew about her. Surely they had not been able to use her gifts. They could not understand such magic, and in any event, the Earth Mother wouldn't allow such blasphemy.

No other girls had disappeared from camp, and Lightning Dove knew it must be She-Who-Is-Alone. His doubts and reservations fled in an instant, and he knew that all of this had only been a test. He had led the tribes of the Warhawk Council well. He had taken back much of their land. And now, as enemies of the People converged on all sides, he would regain the instrument of their destruction.

"Bring them to my tipi," said Lightning Dove to his horsemen. He glanced around, but none of the British seemed to be paying attention to them. "And avoid our friend, the General. No need to bother him with such unimportant prisoners."

Bringing up Darla had been a desperate ploy, and Jeb was as surprised as his father that it worked. What would a man like Lightning Dove care for one child wandering lost in the fog of war? But he'd seen the look in the old man's eyes, the resignation, and he knew certain as sunrise that if he didn't find a way to convince Lightning Dove to keep talking to them that very instant they'd never come out of the Comanche camp alive.

He hadn't been sure what to expect, but the expression that appeared on the Indian's face before he banished it with composure told Jeb everything he needed to know. Lightning Dove knew exactly who Darla was, and he wanted her back. She was more than just some child; possibly she was his daughter. Regardless, they had his interest.

Jeb had grown fond of Darla, and using her as a bargaining chip didn't really sit well with him, but it might be the only way to save them and more importantly, to save Texas. He felt responsible for her, and though he wouldn't admit it to anyone, he felt maybe taking care of her made up in some small way for what happened with Annabelle Sheppard. He consoled himself with the fact that these were her people. Giving her back might actually be the best thing for her.

But before he could give her back, he'd have to have something in return.

They sat in the stuffy confines of Lightning Dove's tipi, just Jeb, his father, and the old, white haired man, who despite his age still looked as fearsome as all the stories claimed he was. Two guards pointed Jeb and his father's own pistols at them. This was the man who united the Comanche under the banner of one great tribe, the Warhawk Council, the man who'd chased every Apache north of the Rio Grande into Mexico, the man who'd killed more Texas Rangers than any ten other Indians. This was the man who'd burned Austin to the ground. His eyes were set deep in his skull, and they bored into Jeb as if searching for the perfect weakness to exploit. Jeb didn't intend to show any.

"Tell me about the girl," said Lightning Dove.

"I call her Darla. She says her Comanche name is She-Who-Is-Alone."

Lightning Dove hissed air through his teeth. "Why did you kidnap her?"

"I didn't kidnap her! We found her wandering on the Llano and took her to safety."

"You should have brought her to me. To her home."

"I wasn't interested in being taken prisoner again."

"Yet here you are."

"Yeah, here I am."

"What are you proposing?" asked Lightning Dove.

"A truce. The girl for an end to all this."

"I wouldn't sell my people for the life of one girl."

"I'm not asking you to sell your people," said Jeb. His father sat quietly beside him, allowing Jeb to speak. He half wished Daddy would take the reins and negotiate, but this was his show now. Daddy's silence was acknowledgment enough of that. "We're proposing to give you back your lands."

"We've already taken them back. Would you give me my own horse too? Or this tipi?" Lightning Dove did not seem like a man who smiled much, but Jeb sensed an underlying amusement to his tone.

"Daddy–I mean Brigadier-Justice Smoke here–has been trying to convince the President to make peace with the Comanche for a long time. We're here to finally do that. I know you have an advantage, and you might win if you march on San Antonio, but what then? You don't think the Mexicans will just let you have all this, do you? What do you think they're marching for?"

"As I said, we have allies."

"You don't trust them," said Jeb. "Else we wouldn't be here. We'd be sharing all of this with the Redjacks."

"You are the one who requested privacy."

Jeb sighed. "Here's how we figure this. You can kill all of us and let Moctezuma take our place, spreading into your land with his horde, setting up shop all the way out to the Llano and god knows how much farther. Or you can help us beat them back and we'll stay the hell out of your way from now on. I can't honestly tell you that we'll all up and move back to wherever our people came from to begin with. A lot of people here now was born here and there ain't nowhere else to go. But we can stop moving west. We can be content with the land from Austin east to the border with the U.S., between the Rio Grande to the south and the Red to the north. We'll keep our people there and the Comancheria is all yours. And you won't have to worry about the Mexicans marching to take it. We'll turn them back at the Alamo, like we did before. And if they come for you later, we'll be there to help beat them back again."

"We can have peace," said Daddy, speaking up at last. "If everyone can just swallow their damned pride, we can do this. There's more than enough land to go around, and with our people standing together, we can protect the whole mess of it from anyone that wants to take it. Including the British. They aren't helping you out of the goodness of their hearts. What have they asked of you? A portion of the land? What are they holding over your head?"

Lightning Dove did not reply, but stared intently at them both. It was hot in the tipi, and sweat coursed down Jeb's cheeks, but Lightning Dove seemed not to notice, as if he were too great a man to be affected by such things. The two Indians guarding them shifted restlessly behind, no longer pointing their pistols directly at the prisoners, but holding them at the ready nonetheless.

It was maddening. Jeb wanted to know what the old man was thinking, wanted to know how the magic worked that turned them into animal men, and why they'd changed back to their former selves. He wanted to know what the British were up to, what sort of deal they had with the Comanche, and most of all he wanted to know if Lightning Dove was going to take them up on their offer or bind them to the nearest pecan tree and use them for target practice.

But Jeb kept his quiet and allowed the old man his time to think. The silence seemed to draw on forever until at last Lightning Dove leaned toward them and spoke again.

"What of the girl."

"She's in San Antonio," said Jeb. "With my fiancé. In the Alamo."

"If she is in the Alamo, she is not safe."

"I guess you're right about that," said Jeb.

"What possessed you men to come here?" asked Lightning Dove. "Was it madness, sheer desperation, or a measure of both? These promises you make are worthless. They're no more than words. White men's words. White men have been making promises to us since the first day they began moving here from the east, and they've only been true to their word once. They promised they'd take our land, and they did. I've heard little to convince me that you are any more trustworthy than your brethren."

"We're more trustworthy than the British," said Daddy. "And I guarantee we're far less land hungry. We just want a patch to live on and, given the chance, I promise you they'd take it all and still not be satisfied. You may have been lied to, but not by me. I'm not an American anymore, I'm a Texan. And if I make you a promise, I will not change my mind when the situation suits me. Hell, that's one of the reasons I moved away from there in the first place."

"You will give me back the girl."

It wasn't a question, and it didn't acknowledge any sort of victory on their part, but Jeb was heartened that Lightning Dove hadn't made any more outright refusals. "We'll give you the girl. Of course."

Lightning Dove stood quickly and the guards trained their pistols on the Texans again as if expecting the kill order to come any moment. But Lightning Dove motioned for Jeb and his father to stand, so they did.

"Perhaps it's time for you to spend time with your President."

"Do we have a deal?" asked Daddy.

"Take them to the other prisoner," said Lightning Dove to his men, ignoring Daddy's question. "And tell the General I must speak with him."

"What are you going to do?" yelled Jeb as they were hustled from the tipi.

"Take back the girl," said Lightning Dove.

Jeb and his father were led away at gunpoint, and he began marking time. They were done, Texas was done. He'd been a fool to even suggest coming here.

He thought of Darla and he thought of Audrey, and he prayed they'd both make it through the coming days alive.

As for himself, that was simply too much to ask.

CHAPTER 24

TITUS HAD EXPECTED that Burleson would take the news of their proposal badly, but instead the President received it in dignified silence, nodding occasionally to confirm that he was indeed listening, but otherwise allowing Titus to fill him in on the state of the nation since his captivity and the deal he and Jeb had conceived to pull them from the brink of defeat.

"I should have listened to you, when you attempted to resign."

Titus did not bother pointing out that he'd considered the attempt successful.

Burleson wasn't the hale and hearty man he'd been. Titus had never seen him unshaven or with stains on his clothes. He'd never even seen the man with an untucked shirt. And yet the Burleson sharing a cell with them on the British prison conveyance was defined by his humility. At last, the old bastard was willing to listen to what Titus had to say.

"It seems a good plan," said Burleson, when Titus finished. "I should have listened to you before. We could have avoided all of this."

Yes you should have, thought Titus. But what he said was, "No one knew it would get this bad. And we damn sure didn't know about the Brits."

Burleson scowled. "That's what gets my blood boiling the most. At least the Comanche have a reason for hating us. What the hell business do those foreigners have to meddle in our affairs? I've met a few of those fellows, including their general, and I've wanted to strangle every one of them to death with my bare hands."

"What about the Comanche?" asked Jeb. "Are they at odds with the Brits?"

"Hard to say," said Burleson. "I've hardly seen an Indian yet. I was in my home when the Englanders stormed in with a band of wild dogs. Course, you tell me those were Indians and I'm not exactly sure what to make of that. Well, they take me prisoner in my own home and then some fool blows the place up. I'd be dead in pieces if it wasn't for that great big old marble table in the study shielding me from most of it. Still got cut up but I'm better off than most of those fellows who came for me. That's cold comfort at this point, but I'll take it."

Jeb shifted uncomfortably in his seat. "Yeah, well good thing they pulled you out of there then. Though it ain't gonna really matter. We're not exactly in any shape to take advantage of being alive." Jeb shook the chains on his wrists. They'd both been outfitted with handcuffs before being tossed into the cell with Burleson. Could be worse. The President wore a set of chains on his ankles as well.

"Don't be so quick to give in," said Titus. It was obvious that despite Jeb's convincing plea for a treaty, the boy didn't believe he'd won over Lightning Dove to their way of thinking. Titus wasn't so sure. Lightning Dove wasn't the kind of man to make a snap decision, and even if he was inclined to their cause, he'd likely discuss it with the skeletal looking medicine man that had accompanied him. Titus also did not discount the value of the little girl Jeb had cared for. He had no idea what spurred Lightning Dove's intense interest in her, but it was something he hadn't been able to hide from them. Little Darla might well be the high card in their deck.

"He threw us in jail," Jeb was saying.

"Yeah, but he didn't kill us," said Titus.

"Gentlemen, mine is a grievous sorrow," said Burleson. "That my vanity and inaction brought us to this is inexcusable. Should we win out, I'll be resigning from office and may Texas find a better man than me to lead her."

"No, if we win this you'll be an integral part of it," said Titus. He doubted Burleson had much to offer in the way of battle skills or even diplomacy at this point, but every man was a potential asset and he didn't need to lose this one. "We're on the inside here, so if they decide to turn on the Brits we'll have to help out. Shackles or no."

"How will the Texans know if the Comanche are friends or foe?" asked Burleson. "They'll shoot them on sight and then ask questions."

"There's that," said Titus. "I suspect we'll have to pray for a little luck."

Burleson chuckled. "Well, that's in short supply lately. Let's see how much luck we need. First, we have to hope that Lightning Dove agrees with what you're proposing. Then we have to hope the Texans don't kill too many Indians before they can make their good intentions known. Then we have to hope the combined might of the British, the Comanche, and the Texans, can whip a whole army of zombies and Lord knows what else. And finally, we hope then that there's enough scraps left to send the Englanders running back to their Queen. Does that about sum it all up?"

"Sounds about right," said Jeb.

"The Smoke clan raises 'em bold and foolish," said Burleson, settling back against the metal wall with a rueful smile.

"So we've been told," said Titus, hoping that the powers that be had one more miracle left to spend for the sake of Texas.

Titus woke to the rattle of keys. Light split the gloom and there stood a weary eyed British solider in the doorway, flanked by the two Indians who'd delivered them to camp.

"Step up you lot," said the solider. "You've finished your stay here."

They all rose, but the soldier motioned for Burleson to sit. "Not you, your majesty," he grinned. "You're a prisoner of the Queen and as such we'll be enjoying your company a while longer. You other two were brought in by the savages and now they want you back. And glad to be rid of you, make no mistake."

"Here now!" said Burleson as the soldier gripped Jeb's arm and ushered him toward the waiting Comanche. "I'll not have this! These men are the blood and life of Texas and must be treated in finer fashion than this. You can't just take them off to be murdered by these people."

"Makes no matter to me what's done to them," said the soldier. "Keep quiet, old man, or you'll get no food. No matter what orders say."

"Keep the peace," said Titus, looking back at the President. The man's face was a violent shade of red but he bit off another protest. "If they wanted to kill us, we'd already be dead I reckon. This may be the luck we're looking for, right?"

The cell door slammed shut before Burleson could respond, leaving Jeb and Titus in the hands of the two Comanche men. The British soldier eyed them suspiciously and shook his head. "God cursed savages. What would the Queen think of us consorting with their lot?"

"They might not take kindly to being called savages," said Jeb. "I'd keep my council if I was you."

"They don't speak a real language," said the guard, disdainfully. The Comanche obviously didn't understand him because they hustled their prisoners away. Titus could hear the soldier laughing under his breath and he took strength from it. Such obvious disdain for ones allies could not bode well for a long-term relationship.

Jeb rattled off something in Comanche and one of the men answered.

"What'd you say?" asked Titus.

"I asked him why he's taking us and he said Lightning Dove says it's time to go!"

"Go where?" asked Titus.

Jeb spoke again and received an answer.

"San Antonio," said Jeb, wide eyed. "He says we're riding hard for San Antonio."

Jeb and his father were led to horses and their cuffs were removed. They bobbed in a sea of horseback Comanche braves, of lumbering war machines breathing threats and steam into the morning, of marching Redjacks with spotless uniforms and polished bayonets pointed at the sky. Leviathans crafts like the one he and Troy had destroyed rolled steadily on, and with them came great catapult-looking devices which Jeb assumed were the launchers for the British steam angels. Where the army had been advancing at a deliberate pace, now it moved forward with all possible speed; even so, the mounted men from both forces looked restless as they were forced to hold back in order to not outpace the slower landships.

It was obvious to Jeb that something had changed. This was not an army content to wait for an attack that best suited their timing. This was an army making for San Antonio with a speed bordering on desperation. Hope welled inside him. Lightning Dove must have ordered this, must have convinced the British General that haste was needed. What else could have precipitated this change? Jeb knew in his gut that Lightning Dove wanted to get to Darla. Whether or not he'd taken them up on their offer, the fact remained that she was in the Alamo, and as a result, in imminent danger. They were marching to save her.

He shared his thoughts with Daddy and he agreed. "Yes, that makes sense. And I reckon them letting us ride free in the middle of all this can't be a bad sign."

"Well, what's to stop us from running off and warning everyone besides a few hundred arrows in the back?" said Jeb.

Daddy laughed. "Whatever the reason, I'm glad to be breathing fresh air. I swear I don't know how men can live cooped up inside them metal monstrosities. Speaking of, don't get too comfortable. The President is still captive in one of them, and no matter how this goes down I reckon we're going to have to figure out a way to spring him at some point."

"If we live that long," said Jeb. "Things are liable to get confusing when we get there. Might be we get shot by the good guys."

"It's a distinct possibility," said Daddy.

They topped a rise to the south and Jeb could tell by the landmarks that they were an hour's ride from San Antonio at their current pace. They'd been gone long enough now that it seemed impossible that the Mexican army hadn't already begun their assault on the Alamo. He thought again of Audrey, and Darla, and the rest of them. He even thought of Troy and took some comfort in the fact that no matter his shortcomings, Troy was generally a capable man. He and Bigfoot and the rest wouldn't let that place go without a fight, and if his take on Willie was correct, she'd probably be able to hold off half the Mexican army with her orneriness alone.

Jeb had faith in his friends, but he still wished he was there to stand by their side.

"Let's ride, white man."

The big Comanche who'd taken them captive and then brought them to their horses rode up beside them. His rifle was stowed in a feathered scabbard, and his face was painted with violent swaths of red and blue paint. His grin showed red-stained teeth and Jeb was momentarily terrified of him.

"Go where?" asked Jeb in Comanche.

"Lightning Dove says you're to ride with me," he said. "We're going out ahead."

"What for?"

"What's he saying?" said Daddy, looking concerned.

"Hold on," said Jeb, waving his father off.

"Lightning Dove has considered your offer," said the Comanche, keeping pace beside them. "He allows that you may be correct about the British and their motives. This does not mean that he feels the Texans are his friends, and he's asked that I make that point particularly clear."

"I understand," said Jeb.

The man nodded. "Good. Lightning Dove plans to turn on his former allies."

The news shook Jeb with hope, and he couldn't help but grin. "I think that's a real good idea."

"First, we take down the Mexicans. Lightning Dove has convinced the idiot that leads the British army that this battle must be fought on two fronts. The Comanche will flank and rout the Mexican army while the British lay siege to the Alamo."

"I'm liking this less and less."

The Comanche shrugged. "I doubt Lightning Dove cares."

"What if the Mexicans and the Texans are already trading shots?"

"The plan remains, though I'll admit things get more complicated."

"So assuming your people turn back Moctezuma and we can hold off the British army long enough for you to do it, then Lightning Dove will order you to help us against them."

"He's considering this part, but he'll factor the girl into his decision. The most important thing is that she remains alive. That's why we're riding ahead."

"You and me?"

"That's what I've said. We ride ahead to let the Texans know that the Comanche will not be attacking them, and to secure the safety of the girl. You and I will take possession of her and deliver her to Lightning Dove. And then, he will determine whether or not he'll suffer your nation to live."

Jeb bristled at the man's attitude. Basically, if they went along with everything Lightning Dove wanted, the chief would *consider* keeping his end of the bargain. Jeb tried to think up another angle for bargaining, but they'd run out of time and options. It was a minor miracle that they'd convinced Lightning Dove to the extent that they had. Jeb saw little choice but to go with this man and trust that Lightning Dove had an honorable soul.

Jeb translated for his father who seemed less irritated than he had been at the man's cavalier attitude. "That's as good a shot as we'll get," he said. "And about the same terms we've ever given them. Ask if they're letting me ride out with you. And ask what happens to Darla if the Alamo is already under siege."

Jeb asked the questions, the man answered, and he translated. "They figure you're more important than me, so you've got to stay put. As for Darla, if the battle's already started, we fight our way in and protect the girl with our lives until it's done." This much, Jeb could agree with. He'd had his fill for one lifetime with letting people down, particularly little girls. He envisioned himself standing side by side with the big Indian, blasting away at Zombies and Redjacks and anyone else that saw fit to try to harm Darla. He kind of liked the idea.

"I'm Jebediah Smoke. People call me Jeb. If I'm riding with you, I'd like to know your name too."

The man considered this for a moment then answered in English. "I'm called Many Scalps."

"Good to meet you then," said Jeb. He held out his hand for several seconds then at last Many Scalps clasped it and shook, the hint of a smile on his face.

"I'll see you at the Alamo," said Daddy. "Soon. And leave some of the fighting for me." He wore an expression of pride that brought a lump to Jeb's throat. Jeb peered into his father's eyes for several seconds, then chased away the emotion with a wild grin.

"See you there, Daddy. Keep an eye on the President. He's liable to piss somebody off and get his self killed."

Daddy laughed as Jeb and Many Scalps spurred their horses. Jeb waved back at his father, then turned to race for the horizon. When he looked back again, Daddy was nothing but another speck in the advancing force.

A mile ahead, Many Scalps returned Jeb's pistol then slid a saber loose from another saddle scabbard and handed it to him. Jeb received them with thanks.

"You will need that gun," said Many Scalps. "But you will need that sword more."

Jeb knew he was right. Might be they'd have to fight through a whole army of zombies just to get to Darla. If so, that's what they'd do.

He whispered a prayer to Audrey and his mother's god, and he hoped to Hell there'd be something left of the Alamo and her defenders by the time he reached them.

CHAPTER 25

"**S**EE IF YOU CAN FIND HIM."

Newly minted as a Warrant Officer, William A. A. "Bigfoot" Wallace accepted the spyglass from Colonel Kuykendall. Crouched next to them on the wall, Lieutenant Babb barely covered up a look that threatened horsewhipping. Bigfoot cursed Titus for putting him in the role of an upjumped officer. The men in the ranks now greeted him with frosty military respect, and the other officers and warrants spoke to him with a kind of detachment bordering on suspicion.

He squinted one eye and had the devil's own time not closing the other as he held the worn brass and rosewood contraption in both hands. It was the same here on the north as it had been on the south. Rank after rank of dead soldiers holding an assortment of weapons from Brown Bess muskets and Sharps rifles on down to long pig sticking spears and crude axes made of some black mineral that glittered in the morning sun. On each face of the Alamo, cannons squatted in place manned by as many dead white men and women as Mexicans. There were a number of long-armed timber constructions in the mix and this side featured the rolling stepped pyramid Bigfoot had seen before. He counted again, adding the sums while doing his best not to wonder how many of the white zombies had grown up in Goliad.

The wind kicked up a little from out of the north, bringing with it the smell of corrupted flesh. Something evil rode on that scent, Bigfoot was certain of it. His hands tightened on the spyglass as a wave of terror washed over him. He heard Lieutenant Babb asking as if from far away, "Lord Jesus, what's happening?" Down the wall, someone began crying and begging not to die.

Bigfoot fought down the panic rushing through him with every lungful of air. He was dimly aware of drumbeats hammering in the courtyard as loudly as his heart. Somewhere out there, Moctezuma worked his dark magic against the Republic of Texas, turning the steel resolve of her men into mayhaw jelly. Where was he? They had not seen the Lord Presidente of Mexico to the east, west or south. He had to be here somewhere among the silent standing army to the north.

Colonel Kuykendall and the Lieutenant had gotten themselves under control as well. The pair of them scrambled down the rough wooden ladder, shouting hold-fire orders and encouragement in every direction. Bigfoot watched them go down into what used to be the chapel, taking great care to avoid a circle of fire about six feet across. It was constantly being stoked by a pair of Forever Free while another half dozen writhed around it. *Is that all that's left of them?* It had to be. A one-legged white man was responsible for the drumbeats. He pounded an empty watering trough with a hickory crutch. The sound of every impact seemed to get louder, crowding out other noises and oddly enough, the smell of the dead men. Old Sylvester stood all but in the center of the ring of fire shouting unintelligible things at the one-legged man, the other Forever Free, and even the fire itself. Bigfoot wondered if this was what it had been like before, tried to remember from the stories how many more of them there had been that time, not counting Davy Crockett.

A Tejano boy of fifteen with a rifle of about the same age laid one trembling hand on Bigfoot's arm. "Is that him?"

Bigfoot wasn't sure which him the boy meant, 'till he looked back out across the surrounding army. One side of the pyramid had unfolded and a man about five feet tall stood in the center of it, wearing a hat of feathers and plumes and bits of gold that nearly doubled his height.

He swallowed, raised the spyglass. Lord Presidente Moctezuma had an ugly, squashed face, with a hatchet-like nose. His lips moved as if he was in conversation with someone, but Bigfoot could see no one near enough to hear him. Dead eyes seemed to stare back at him through the spyglass and Bigfoot quickly jerked it downward so as not to experience that lifeless black gaze even a second longer. What he saw next sat in his stomach like a lump of Appalachian snow from his youth. Moctezuma wore armor of bone and metal and glinting minerals over his desiccated skin. A leather belt bit into a nerveless brown waist. Something awkward dangled from the belt, something hairy and round like a giant spider that Bigfoot could not quite make out.

"Is it him?" the Tejano boy asked again.

Bigfoot croaked out a yes as Moctezuma turned and set the thing dangling from his belt spinning wildly. In that instant, Bigfoot nearly fainted. As it was, he dropped the spyglass over the side. Not waiting to hear it break in the dry moat below, he reached for the boy's rifle.

The boy stared at him with wide eyes but held on to his weapon. "What did you see?"

"Santa Anna," Bigfoot said, blinking the vision of it from his eyes. "He has Santa Anna's head on his belt and it's talking to him."

Troy was ready to shoot someone. A Mexican zombie, Jeb Smoke, anybody that wanted for shooting. Being barricaded into what amounted to a freshly dug root cellar with the women and Darla was not the way he'd ever planned on dying. Damn Jeb Smoke for saddling him with Darla. The girl was barely coherent; the only words to pass her lips over the last hour had been Comanche mumbo-jumbo unless he stepped too far away from her. Then she'd break the looming silence with the only English words she knew: "Barking Spider! Barking Spider!" and scurry over to clutch at his legs.

Apparently, Smoke had told her that was Troy's name. Yet another reason to skin the son of a bitch if they both managed to make it through the week.

The women were contentious, each in their own way. Audrey hung by herself in a corner, hands clasped and eyes hard and shiny in the flickering light of an oil lamp. She prayed with an air of angry fervor that seemed to dare the Lord Almighty Himself to cross her. Willie loped across the tiny cellar like a caged coyote, stopping every so often to cock her head and listen, fingering the plain walnut handles of her pistols like a holstered set of worry beads.

When she spat on the floor for about the eighteenth time, Troy snapped. "Is the whole room your spittoon, woman?"

She snarled at Troy and pounced, surprising him. She had him in a hold faster than he would have given her credit for. She jerked his arm up behind him and stretched his neck out until she was whispering right in Troy's ear. He imagined he could feel the soft down of her upper lip grazing his jawbone and a part of him he hadn't thought much about lately stood up and took notice. "Don't you ever disrespect me again, Mister Tanner. Got it?"

Troy grinned like the first cat into a barn full of mice, but whatever he had been about to say was cut off by the boom and pop of gunpowder weapons starting up on the walls. Willie let him go. Over in the corner, Audrey started sobbing. It almost sounded like she was cursing in the middle of her prayers. Troy reminded himself to be scandalized later and turned his face to the boards blocking the entryway to the root cellar. Willie had her guns out. Troy itched to do the same, but not with Darla hanging–Darla?

Where'd she got off to? He spun and there she was, curled into the corner opposite Audrey. Her eyelids flickered like a deck of cards being shuffled and her tongue lolled out of her mouth. In the shadows behind her, some darker shadow was sidling up the wall past her.

"What the hell?"

An explosion overhead left Troy's ears ringing as he rushed over to Darla. The shots were coming fast and loud as a hard rain on a tin roof. "What's going on with you, girl?" he all but screamed at her, scanning the wall behind her. Whatever he had seen before was gone now, probably just a trick of the light.

A ragged cheer went up briefly from somewhere near one of the southern watchtowers, but it was short lived. He heard a wrenching sound and looked back from Darla to see Willie prying open the door. Audrey scrambled to her feet, murder in her eyes.

"You're going to get us killed!"

Willie shrugged and kept at her work, despite Audrey clawing at her arms and shrieking.

Darla started to spasm. With each tic and jerk she seemed to be gaining strength.

Willie threw the first of the barricade spars across the room. It landed a few inches away from the lamp. Audrey ran for the spar, shouting "You're not going out there! You're not!" She grabbed it by one end and slammed it crookedly back into place.

Willie slapped Audrey hard across the face, sending her reeling toward Troy and Darla. She jerked the spar out of the catches and tossed it again. This time she made sure it went away from the lamp.

Troy was doing his best to keep Darla from slamming her head against the packed soil wall, but with every slam of her body against it, more and more of the wall crumbled away behind her. Too much of it was crumbling away to be accounted for by a little Indian girl's fit.

He heard another wrench of wood, then smelled the blue smoke of battle brought in on the wind. The lamp sputtered in its corner, but did not go out. In the courtyard, someone was chanting and a drumbeat kept fast, erratic, time.

Willie grabbed Troy by the shirt collar, pointedly doing her best not to look at Darla or Audrey. "You keep them safe as you can. Best bar this back up behind me."

Then Willie sprang up the narrow stairs, slamming the wooden hatches closed behind her. Troy looked at Audrey, wanting to smack her one more good time to get her to quit sobbing and help with Darla, but she just lay there on the ground as still as if the zombies had already come in here and shot her dead. Darla kept shaking against the wall. Dirt flew around her like a dog was digging a hole out behind her. He went to the girl, attempting to hold her shaking limbs steady.

Troy shouted at Audrey to bar the goddamn door back, but she did not respond. He looked from the swinging door up into the fracas to Darla foaming at the mouth in his arms and back at the door again. If he let Darla go long enough to go rig it shut, she was liable to hurt herself. But if that door stayed unbarred, the sooner Moctezuma's armies would come swarming in after them.

Troy spat. He could hardly hold Darla now, her fit had gotten so strong.

"Audrey?" he said, then yelled it. "Audrey!"

Her head rose blearily and she blinked at him. "Jeb asked us to care for this girl, and I need you to help me with her." Overhead, a man screamed horribly.

"Try to keep her head from knocking the wall too hard. If Jeb gets back–*When* Jeb gets back, we don't want her to have her brains all splattered on the floor of this root cellar, do we?"

Audrey shook her head, but it was as if she were doing it from somewhere far away. Troy would just have to hurry. He charged up the steps with both wooden bars in his arms and set to securing the door with wedges and stake hammer. He wished for all he was worth that he was on the other side of it, facing the enemy head-on with Willie and the rest.

The dead men fired upon the Alamo from well-formed ranks, cannons booming, an assortment of muskets and rifles popping just enough to keep the defenders' heads down on the wall while others of their filthy horde struggled silently to keep ladders propped against the wall long enough to gain access. Two dozen others battered at the iron-backed gates with a pair of limb-stripped oaks capped with some kind of stone. But the worst were the ones trying to use lengths of hooked wood to launch powder-bomb laden spears over the wall. They just kept coming.

Bigfoot grunted, took aim at one of the spear throwers as it came within range, squeezed the trigger and missed. A second later the zombie shuddered and fell to the ground anyway. Someone else along the wall had got him. The shot had come just in time to skew the spear's arc, leaving it stuck in the side of a lumbering brute with what looked like an old Brown Bess. The creature pivoted from side to side to shake the spear and its explosive payload free, but failed. A geyser of fire and noise erupted, dismembering the zombie and most of the surrounding squad. Only half of them got back up. *Thank Heaven for small blessings.*

In the courtyard at Bigfoot's back, the Forever Free danced around an enormous pillar of smoke and flame. There weren't many of them, but they were dancing to beat the band and shame the Lord. Sylvester moved with a feline grace that belied his age, bouncing against the flow of the other dancers, pulling rattlers out of a burlap sack and draping them on the oblivious shoulders of black men. The one-legged white who had started off beating the drum as steady as a pendulum clock was pounding it in a frenzy now. As Bigfoot watched, the snakes crawled to the ground on one side of the fire and seemed to be tying themselves in a knot and burrowing into the ground underneath.

Sylvester had told Titus Smoke and the others that the spirits weren't strong enough to keep the zombies dead like they'd done ten years ago, so he was just going to ask them to provide whatever aid they could. Bigfoot couldn't tell that the Forever Free's magic was doing any good. He was just glad no one had asked him to do any voodoo dancing.

Someone gripped his arm and he looked back over the wall, feeling the beat of that dance in his bones. The heat of their fire on his back made him sweat more than the uncaring Texas sun overhead. It was the boy, what was his name? Had he even asked? The rascal had stuck his head up just a little too far, a little too long and taken a bullet through the left eye. His young mouth gaped open in confused wonder before he fell backward. Bigfoot stifled a sob as the boy's body crunched into the ground below. Something unhitched itself in his chest and a fierce anger enveloped him.

He reloaded, aimed, and fired over and over, mechanically. Tried his damnedest to land a shot in Moctezuma–or better yet the skull of Santa Anna riding at his belt, but they were too far off. He heard someone screaming orders, the thud of the gates shivering under the assault, and then crack and a whoosh as the odd beam and bowl contraptions snapped in the east, filling the air with dozens of sprawling backlit shadows.

"What the hell is that?" a throaty voice asked. Bigfoot turned his head to see that mannish woman who'd come in with the kids, her pistols drawn and hat pulled down low.

He squinted at the pinwheeling forms as they arced through the sky, thoughts of asking her what she was doing out of the fortified cellar forgotten.

"Zombies," he said. "And they are going to land inside the walls."

Troy finished pounding the second bar back into place and let the mallet hang from his wrist by a leather thong. He wiped sweat from his forehead with the other shirtsleeve and turned to check on Darla.

Who wasn't there.

Wasn't there.

How in the hell did a girl just disappear from a locked room while his back was turned? Audrey stared dumbfounded back at him. The place where the wall behind her had taken such a beating from the girl's fit rippled like a tall grass in a soft wind.

"Did–" Troy began.

Audrey nodded, her eyes drier and wider than they had been a moment ago, her panic replaced by an expression of awestruck bafflement.

The wall shuddered and trembled, then vomited a writhing knot of rattlesnakes out onto the dirt floor. Troy whimpered involuntarily. At the sound, Audrey very calmly slipped the revolver out of Troy's holster and started shooting.

She-Who-Is-Alone erupted in a brown shower from the arid soil. She brushed clumps of it from her eyebrows and hair, then pulled her waist and legs free. The Great Spirit had come to her again, in the company of nearly twenty lesser animal spirits, all of them whispering things at her that she could not hear. But the Great Spirit she understood. He told her she was needed, that she must not remain in the ground with Barking Spider and the white woman. She had felt the world growing empty around her, saw the spirits dancing like the shadows of a hundred dying flames, let them carry her along the secret tunnels of the earth until she saw the sun and a fire and men with skin burnt even darker than her own twirling and chanting.

· She felt great pain in her stomach and knew that if she were to look she would see dozens of close-set puncture wounds. The snake spirits had bitten her as she passed through the earth, she realized dreamily.

One of the dancing men greeted her like a friend returning from the hunt, and she felt the Great Spirit moving her to trust his silver-laced hair and gap-toothed smile. He threw both hands into the sky, exultant. The men surrounding him stopped dancing, staring upward as well.

Are you here to save us? The voice in her head was startling and comforting and awestruck all at the same time.

She answered honestly. I do not know. The Great Spirit brought me to you.

The old burnt man clasped one of her hands in both of his. The fire crackled loudly at her back. White and black and brown skinned soldiers buzzed everywhere she looked in fearful uproar, their firesticks popping like the drippings of a roasting hare.

There was a meaty slapping sound behind her and she turned to see what had happened. Her entire field of view was taken up by Breathless Ones. Broken Lance's tales had been meant to frighten her, and they had. But not like the sight–and smell–of the monstrous creatures of unliving flesh and sinew before her now did. Some landed in the tall flames, disrupting the burnt men's dance. They did not seem to care that they were on fire as they staggered after black and white men, struggling to capture their prey in fiery embraces. As if led by one mind, half of the Breathless Ones suddenly turned on the defenders at the splintering gate with long sharp metal and firesticks of varying lengths.

She-Who-Is-Alone tucked her head against the old burnt man's chest as a white man's insides poured out onto the dirt before him. Behind, another swung his firestick around like a club until the horde swallowed him up.

Should we be dancing to make the magic strong? Or running? She asked him, using the words inside her head.

He studied the chaos around them briefly. She-Who-Is-Alone stared up into his face, wrinkling her nose at the weird pink scar drawn upon his forehead before turning her gaze in the direction he was looking. Two of his dancers had collapsed, and the white man with one leg grappled desperately against a dead man who had him pinned against the big wooden circle that the white men's wagons rode upon. The man with one leg ripped a dead arm out of his enemy's socket with a sickeningly dry slurp and pop, but that small victory only served to let the dead Breathless One's mouth near enough to tear out his throat.

The old burnt man nodded at her in a way not so different from how Broken Lance might have. *Sometimes running is a kind of dancing.* He grabbed her up in his arms and carried her toward the closed doors of the root cellar.

Not there!

The old man stopped, already huffing, and set her down, oblivious to the destruction and murder going on about them. *Then where?*

She pointed at a squared-off building with an out of place looking burst of bluebonnets in a clay pot beside the door.

The chapel? He thought at her. *Well, why not?* He grabbed her up again in his bony arms and sprinted to the door as madness engulfed the fort of the white soldiers.

The defenders lost all sense of military discipline when the zombies landed inside the Alamo. Colonel Kuykendall, Lieutenant Babb, and few other officers were shouting orders, but the men weren't listening. Shot after shot went wasted as the onslaught of dead men continued, and near as many soldiers had given up already, screaming and crying. One of the men just down the wall had shot himself when a Mexican ladder appeared next to him with zombies perched near the top. Bigfoot ducked down the best his big frame was able and ran to that position, the woman right on his tail. The two of them pushed the first zombie back over the wall, turquoise ornaments clacking on his antiquated armor the entire way down.

"We've got to stop them from throwing anymore sonofabitchin' dead Mexicans inside the walls," the woman said. Hadley must have got the same idea. Bigfoot saw him yelling orders and directing one of the Alamo's light cannon crews to fire on the catapults.

Bigfoot nodded, firing a shot directly into the forehead of the next zombie. He loosened his cutlass in its scabbard, and reloaded as fast as he could while the woman shot and kicked another down.

"You got a sword, miss?"

"Willie. Don't need one." She placed another perfect shot into the next zombie as it groped its way up, then kicked the ladder down.

"No, I suppose you don't," Bigfoot huffed.

He looked across the massed army of dead men. His ears rang from the constant gun and cannon fire, not to mention the black powder bomb spears. A bone-shaking explosion pulled his attention down the wall to where Hadley and the cannoneers lay in bloody pieces all around the ruins of the big gun. Santa Anna's head was probably cackling like a schoolgirl at that and giving Moctezuma moment-by-moment advice.

"I think it's time we take the fight to the enemy, Miss Willie," he said as a platoon of zombies clattered the ladder back into place.

She scowled. "Just Willie. And if you're thinking of going out there you're a damn fool."

A bullet whizzed by. In the courtyard, a burning man sprinted in search of water, hollering like all of Hell was behind him. Far as Bigfoot could tell, it was.

She smiled at him. "But you're my kind of damn fool." She waved a hand at the ladder. "Ever see a man getting off his stilts after the Alamo Day parade?"

"I have."

"Well, what are we waiting for?"

Willie reloaded her revolver while Bigfoot swiped his blade at the first two zombies coming up the ladder till they lost their balance and fell onto their silent comrades below. Right as they hit bottom, she asked Bigfoot whether he had a name he cared to share.

Bigfoot touched two fingers to the brim of his hat. "Bigfoot Wallace, pleased to meet you, ma'am."

"You ain't," Willie declared flatly, doing her level best not to appear startled.

"I am."

Willie flashed him an awkward smile, "Well ain't you somethin'?"

"Like to think so," Bigfoot replied.

The two of them grabbed on to the top rung of ladder, tucked their legs behind them and kicked off as one into the dry Texas air, aiming for a gaggle of Moctezuma's zombies to break their fall.

Troy bit back a few of his choicest words as one of the rattlers sunk its fangs into the meaty part of his calf. He swung the mallet at its head which flattened with a satisfying squish. Audrey had missed the snakes with all but one of her shots, and there were still a handful of them to contend with.

"Get behind me," he snapped at her. Troy let the heavy mallet fly, catching another one a foot behind its head. They reared on him, the dry rattle that gave them their name crowding out all other sounds. There wasn't much room down here, but Troy Tanner was damned if he was going to let them get past him to Audrey. He had failed in keeping Darla safe, whatever was behind the dirt wall had taken her away and it most likely meant any hope of Jeb's plan working had gone with her.

The mallet thunked down over and over again in fury. He felt the pangs of venom working through his system, the ache of too many bites to survive. He swung and he swung until he had no power left to move his own muscles and his bowels had emptied, his vision so blurred he could hardly make anything out at all, but he killed every last one of the rattlesnakes and kept Audrey safe. If he was going to die, he was going to die like a Texas Ranger, by God.

He felt cold and then hot, his skin tight and slippery with sweat, peppered with gooseflesh. His ears rang like there was a child somewhere wailing and then another and another. The dirt floor rose up to meet him. Audrey grabbed the mallet from his hand, saying something about getting help as she started unbarring the door. Troy felt a touch of crankiness, wanted to tell her not to open it, to stay in here where it was still safe, but he was fading in and out of consciousness and couldn't muster up enough voice to bark at her.

A blazing light set his eyes to watering as she shoved the cellar doors open, screaming for a doctor. Blue and gray smoke colored air thick with the terrified cries of dying Texan soldiers. A Tejano man with dour, heavy, cheeks bowled past her and down into the cellar, slamming the door shut behind him. Audrey jerked it open and slapped him hard across the face. "Help him!" she implored.

The man clicked his tongue as he took in Troy's condition, then crossed himself. Over the man's shoulder, Troy saw a flight of long white wings encroaching upon the blue sky above.

He tried to spit the acid chunks of vomit from his mouth so he could speak, but his tongue was too swollen to cooperate. He wanted to point at them, to give everyone a little hope, but the effort of raising one arm set his entire body shaking out of control. "Angels," he rasped, but no one understood him.

The Tejano extended two fingers, whispered a short prayer in Spanish then gently closed Troy's eyes.

CHAPTER 26

WHEN JEB REACHED SAN ANTONIO, he nearly gave up hope of reaching Darla. There was fighting in the streets, zombies tearing into homes and businesses as ill-equipped civilians fought them back with rifles and knives. Many of the buildings were ablaze. Mexican cavalry, living men all, helped the zombies with their destruction, riding men down with sabers or crushing them beneath the hooves of their massive war horses. They did not appear to be killing women and children, but the same couldn't be said about the zombies.

Cannons and undead infantry surrounded the old mission, and it was evident that Moctezuma didn't share General Santa Anna's sense of patience. Where the living Santa Anna had weakened the previous defenders of the Alamo with a prolonged siege, Moctezuma had unleashed the whole of his force, and already the place looked in danger of falling. Zombies climbed ladders while Texan defenders fought to push them back from the walls. Many of them had tossed aside their guns in favor of sabers and long knives, knowing that only the most well-placed bullets would fell a zombie.

Great catapults hurled zombies into the courtyard. Black smoke billowed up from the place as if the mouth of Hell had opened inside those crumbling walls. The Alamo had never been built to withstand such a force–its first defenders had learned that lesson well–and Jeb feared he was at last seeing the old Spanish mission in its death throes, despite years of miserly fortification.

Pieces of the wall, rebuilt after the last assault, lay in ruins where zombies clawed their way through. The boom and whistle of cannon fire directed to and from the Alamo was a constant presence, as were the screams of men and the wooden creak of catapults as they whipped their gruesome cargo into the sky. The odor of rot and burning flesh caused Jeb to choke and cover his face with a shirtsleeve, and the despair he felt was almost too much to bear when he thought of Darla and Audrey, and even Willie and Troy, mired in the middle of all this carnage.

He might have given up if it weren't for Many Scalps. Jeb's horse slowed to a stunned trot as they reached the outskirts of town, but the Comanche pulled up beside him, shook him by the shoulder. "The girl is in there?"

Jeb nodded. "If she's still alive."

"She's still alive," he said, then he burst into flames.

Jeb yelped and his horse sidestepped the flaming Indian. He watched in horror as Many Scalps tumbled from his terrified horse, his skin melting away. Seconds later, the flames were gone and an oversized coyote rolled out of a bed of ash and peered up at Jeb with human eyes.

"Make for one of the broken places in the wall," the coyote said in a gravelly voice. "Whichever we can fight our way to first."

"What happened to you?" asked Jeb, backing away. He knew what had happened–he'd heard the tales from Austin and seen coyotes just like this roaming her streets. But it was difficult to comprehend the reality of it.

"I'm blessed again by the Great Spirit," said Many Scalps. "The girl is alive. We must hurry."

"Over the wall's our best shot," said Jeb, struggling to gain his composure back. He'd been in many a skirmish, but never a full scale battle like this. He'd heard all of his Daddy's stories about defending the Alamo in '36, but he'd never imagined it in such horrible detail. "They're plugging up the holes best they can and there are plenty of ladders lying around. We just got to hope they don't try to shoot us getting in there."

"I might have problems climbing a ladder," said Many Scalps. Was he smiling? It was hard to tell.

"Hadn't thought of that."

"Maybe we should keep close," said Many Scalps with an almost imperceptible smile. "They're more likely to shoot you than me."

"Stay tight then," said Jeb. And before he could lose his nerve entirely, he spurred his horse and rode hard into the fray. By the time he'd beheaded his first zombie, the blood lust was on him and all fears and reservations had fled. Many Scalps howled his fury and Jeb joined in, screaming for all he was worth as they battled toward the Alamo.

There were two girls he loved in that falling mission, and Jeb Smoke intended to find them.

The Comanche war party galloped beneath a blazing sun, three hundred strong, faces painted and souls ready for war. The sound of their passage was all Lighting Dove could hear, and he rode at the vanguard, a feathered lance held defiantly over his head and a shout of righteous anger forming in his throat. He could feel the blood of war rising in him, but he wondered if he'd chosen the right enemy.

He could only follow his conscience, and that told him that She-Who-Is-Alone must be retaken at all costs. If that meant fighting the Mexicans, so be it. And if that meant abandoning General Thackeray and his men, then all the better. He'd come to the conclusion that allying the People with land-hungry British had been a mistake, and they'd been paying the price for it ever since. With a clean break from their influence, Lightning Dove was convinced they would have the girl again and the Great Spirit would favor them with her power.

By now, Many Scalps and the younger Smoke would be fighting to secure her safety, but Lightning Dove could leave nothing to chance. Every minute she remained in the Alamo she was in peril. He knew she hadn't been killed--the Great Spirit would make that plain to him if it happened–but the risk of losing her hung heavily on him. They must drive back the Mexican army as quickly as possible and bring her to safety.

That the British did not agree with his methods mattered little.

He'd taken pleasure at the look on Thackeray's face as they'd mounted up and ridden off to war, leaving the slower moving procession of metal monstrosities to lumber behind them in frustration. Lighting Dove thought for a moment that Thackeray might send his cavalry in pursuit, but the man was not so great a fool. The Comanche would make short work of the lesser horsemen without the support of their machines.

But the British would not be far behind, and Lighting Dove was not sure if they could prevail against their technology without the Great Spirit's blessing. Rescuing the girl was paramount.

He'd have left with Many Scalps and the younger Smoke, but he'd had two tasks to attend. First, he'd needed to rouse the other war chiefs and convince them of his plan. The fact that it might result in a treaty with the Texans was not well received. Though Lightning Dove's power wasn't absolute, it was respected, and with Broken Lance agreeing on the dire importance of saving She-Who-Is-Alone, they grudgingly fell in line.

That accomplished, he'd ordered two of his men to kill the soldiers guarding the Texas President and spirit him away out of the Queen's reach. It was a simple task, and likely the deed had yet to be discovered. Lighting Dove was not certain of the day's outcome, and he had little trust for the Texans. Better to have that prize in his possession than leave it for another to exploit.

He allowed himself a moment of joy at the thought of Thackeray when he discovered that Burleson was gone. Then he banished all thoughts of the Redjack army and set his mind on the south, on the Breathless Ones, on the Texans and their brittle promises.

Lightning Dove sang a prayer to the Great Spirit, and rode hard for his salvation.

The feet of the ladder dug into the mess of zombie parts, blood, soil and fallen Texans at the bottom of the moat as Willie and Bigfoot (*Bigfoot Wallace his own self! Imagine that.*) sailed through the empty air above. When the ladder's midpoint came to rest on the far side of the moat, they shuddered to a stop and hung there dangling in the air over an army of angry dead. She wiggled her boots, grunting a little as she kept herself in place. Bigfoot made a face like he was considering dropping down onto the zombies below, but he never got the chance.

With a pair of cracks that went mostly unnoticed amid all the gunplay and mayhem, the ladder beams gave in to their combined weight, splintering the ladder into uneven sections. She felt a lurch in her stomach that wasn't entirely due to the fall. One of the

Mexican soldiers had begun to react, bringing his rifle to bear on her. She twisted enough as she fell to collide with him and send the gun spinning, but two others were on her now. She kicked and squirmed her way between them, barking her shin on one of their muskets and cussing a blue streak as she rolled off. Bigfoot was already swinging his sword around in wide arcs as he ran toward the zombie launcher to the northeast. Willie broke free of a grasping white hand and sprinted after him.

She struggled to keep up with Bigfoot, but the man's bigger than life stride and surprising speed all but guaranteed she would never catch him. Best she could do was try to pick off anybody that dared to aim at him, and keep herself from getting shot or stabbed in the process. The battlefield's orderly nature had dissipated in the few short minutes since she had been on the wall looking out. Or maybe it was just that she was now in the thick of it and not getting a bird's eye view.

They were winding up the zombie launchers again, but the machines might as well have been miles away for the riot of soldiers between her and it. And there were three others just like it. By the time they got to the first one and put it out of commission, all four of them would have fired again, putting the number of zombies inside the Alamo up over thirty. And that was assuming Willie and Bigfoot didn't die on the way to the first one. *What was I thinking, following a true life hero out into the middle of an army that's already been killed once? You ain't got a lick of business out here, Willie Wontshee. Not one damn lick.*

But they fought their way closer, and the farther from the moat they got, the less the zombies seemed to even realize they were there. It was like every bit of their attention was on the Alamo, and the two crazy Texans in their midst could be dealt with at any time. Halfway to the zombie launchers, the wooden contraptions thumped again in unison, filling the cloudless sky with sprawling shadows.

The zombies were ignoring them now and Bigfoot had slowed to a trot as he started to realize that the creatures were actually moving out of their way, clearing a path through their ranks that doglegged off to the left just ahead. Willie came up beside Bigfoot, tasting the beads of sweat on her lip as she tried to get her breath under control.

"I ain't liking this," Bigfoot said, as under his breath as a voice like that was able.

The leather string that was supposed to be holding her hat on had gotten cut somewhere between the wall and here, but the hatband held it firmly on her head. As Willie slowed down, she began to feel the ache in her shin. A dozen other little scrapes and cuts started acting up to get her attention, but she ignored them as best she could. The dead soldiers lining the impromptu path around them weren't even looking their way. It felt like a chill wind was blowing across her nethers. She looked at Bigfoot.

The man's mouth was set, his slightly crossed eyes hard and sharp as shoeing nails. He focused on something around that bend. Willie had seen that look one time before on a man, the unblinking desire to take a life with no compunction whatsoever. Lucky for her, she'd killed him first. She stared with Bigfoot across the ranks of the Mexican army, over their heads to see what lay in wait for them just past that bend.

A tall crown of feathers, glittery with scraps of gold-flecked bone and turquoise all through it, rustled toward them down the cleared out path. Beyond, Willie could see the zombie launcher getting wound back into place to throw another mess of enemies into the heart of Texas.

"They ain't clearing this path for us," she said, feeling the pressure change in her ears like a Blue Norther was coming in fast. Even the sun seemed like it was dimming, despite the lack of clouds.

"No, I reckon they ain't," Bigfoot rasped back at her, then brandished his cutlass and charged off across the throngs, yelling with all the air and anger his big lungs had in them, over and over: "Goliad! Goliad! GOLIA-A-A-D!"

Far, far above, great white stink metal birds circled. Next to She-Who-Is-Alone on the ground, the man with burnt skin and silver in his hair rapped on the door while smoldering Breathless Ones lurched about like blind men. Others plummeted from the sky, picked themselves up and staggered this way and that, some of them on broken limbs. The faster moving ones took firesticks or knives of stone and metal from whoever they could and set about using them to deadly effect on the paleface soldiers. Clutching her poisoned stomach, She-Who-Is-Alone plucked a blue flower, her favorite kind, from the big clay pot they were growing in and put the flower in her hair. This made the burnt man smile for just a moment at her before he set to pounding his fist against the door.

He shouted in the white man's tongue, heard a response from within and shouted more. He cocked his head as he listened, but no further response came. He shook his fist at the door, scowled at it and kicked dirt onto the bottom of it. *The White Chief is afraid to open the door. He says he is safe from zombies in there because it is a holy place.*

She-Who-Is-Alone felt a heat in her chest. The scorpion sting on her foot no longer throbbed. Somewhere, she had gotten a spider bite on her neck that had felt like it was about to explode with pus, but no more. The snakebite her foot had suffered in the river might have never happened. And already, the purple and black marks around the bites on her stomach were fading.

But her heart felt like vultures were rending it from her chest bite by bite to feed to their young.

If their gods keep them safe from the Breathless Ones in there, why do they fear to open the door?

The burnt man made a face. *I think they know that the gods are dying, even their own, and no one is going to protect them.*

She-Who-Is-Alone took another flower and gave it to the burnt man. *The Great Spirit is not dying.* He took the flower from her as if it were supposed to be proof, looked at it a moment, then realized that was exactly what she had intended. *He says that only the Gods who take and do not give back are dying. But if they would only learn to give back to the people who love them, they might live forever.*

It was silent inside her mind for a long time, and the silence was louder than all the fighting and fearsome shouts and explosions that surrounded them. Finally, *What else does he tell you?*

He says we should go inside this holy place and wait for the one who comes for me. He says I should not be afraid.

The burnt man raised his shaggy silver eyebrows as if to ask how they were going to get in there, but before she could think at him that she did not know, a shiny metal gourd bounced across the courtyard to land at their feet. It simmered like it had a venison stew boiling within it, and made little clicking noises besides. The burnt man grabbed her hand

and the two of them ran away from the door of the white man's holy place before the little gourd made all the noise and light of a hundred thunder strikes. When the thunder strikes had ended, the door they had been standing beside and most of the hardened adobe that surrounded it were gone.

Where did that come from? The burnt man thought at her, looking around the blood and body littered courtyard like he expected some new enemy to have appeared out of nowhere. She pointed one stubby finger straight up to where a pair of long white wings circled. Content that it was answer enough, she marched through the gaping, smoky hole the metal gourd had made, into the white man's holy place.

Jeb lashed out with his saber and beheaded another zombie, this one with so little flesh left on the face it was hardly more than a skull. The head toppled from the creature's shoulders and both bits fell among the others choking the moat. Beside him, Many Scalps worried at the neck bone of another zombie as Jeb pushed on toward the breach in the Alamo's wall.

His shirt was shredded and he'd been clawed by the creatures in at least a dozen places on his way through the madness. The wounds ranged from tiny punctures to freely bleeding gashes. Every one of them itched and ached like he was wearing a suit of poison oak. One zombie had three teeth in his thigh, and a second had seized his ankle and wrenched him around so hard it was a miracle no bones had snapped. He'd taken the thing's head off with little problem, but that didn't keep his ankle from swelling and hurting like hell.

He stepped painfully over bodies, zombies, and those more recently dead, wincing each time one of Moctezuma's cannons chewed up another chunk of the wall or exploded against some building inside the mission. Bullets whined past at such a rate that he was amazed one of them hadn't managed to clip him yet, and smoke from countless fires blackened the air, setting him off on a coughing fit.

Many Scalps brushed against his leg, then with a series of nimble steps he was over the bodies and staring back at Jeb from the Alamo courtyard. He'd made it through the breach and his expression seemed to chastise Jeb for being so slow.

"I'm coming!" he said, swinging absently at a zombie all but enveloped by smoke. "Ain't all of us have four legs."

Jeb took hold of a crumbled bit of adobe, pulled himself forward and joined the coyote inside the Alamo. Many Scalps looked up at him expectantly, as if Jeb knew instinctively where to find Darla. Unfortunately, even if he knew exactly where they were keeping her, it would be tough to go anyplace directly in the middle of such chaos. Most of the courtyard was ablaze, as if someone had started a giant bonfire and let it rage out of control. Zombies stumbled about on fire while more fell from the skies every minute. Texan defenders fought them back, and even some of the living Mexican soldiers were beating back zombies who seemed to have abandoned any allegiance to Mexico in favor of an easy meal.

Jeb hacked at a burning form that stumbled into his path, Bigfoot had mentioned something about hiding any last women and children in a root cellar, and he figured Troy and Audrey might have taken Darla there, but he had no idea where to find it. He moved alongside a band of Texans and helped them hack the legs off a zombie. A human soldier stabbed at him with his bayonet, but Jeb sidestepped and shot the man in the chest. He hadn't even realized he was still carrying the gun–the shot was a reflex–but he quickly shot the next two living enemies he saw. Both fell and the Texans with him gave a tired cheer.

"Where's the root cellar?" yelled Smoke.

"What the hell you want with the root cellar?" asked a heavyset, red-faced man a good foot taller than Jeb. "You don't look the hidin' type."

"There's a girl in there who can save us all. I have to get to her."

"There's a root cellar next to the barracks. Little pantry unit off it and a stairway inside goes down to the cellar. You need help?"

"No, but I need a favor."

"What kind of favor?" The man lashed out at a zombie with a huge Bowie knife and the thing's head lolled to the side. It began circling, hands on its cheeks trying to keep the weight of its loose head from snapping its neck and ending its existence.

"The Comanche are coming. My name's Jeb Smoke and my daddy is Titus Smoke. The Brigadier-Justice."

"I know who Titus Smoke is."

"Yeah, well we made a deal with the Indians. They're riding here fast and they're going to help us fight of these zombies."

"I ain't no simpleton," said the man. "Indians won't help us."

Behind him, Many Scalps growled around a mouthful of dead throat.

"Yes they are," said Jeb. "Don't believe me, that's fine. But when you see 'em with your eyes and they're attacking Mexicans, I want you to spread the word to everyone that they're here to fight with us, not against us. And they might not look like Indians. They might look like coyotes and birds and things."

The man gave him a sour look and backed up a few steps. "War's gone to your brain, boy!"

"Just keep an eye out and if you see it, spread the word." Jeb sprinted off toward the barracks. Then, remembering one more thing he wanted to tell the man, Jeb spun and called back. "And after we beat the Mexicans, we're going to have to help them fight the Redjack Brits. They're on their way too. Feel free to shoot all of those assholes you want."

The man waved irritably in Jeb's direction then resumed killing zombies. Jeb saw him wedge his sword in one of the monster's cheekbones, then another wave of smoke rolled past and obstructed his view. The world was dark again, lit only by fires and brief glimpses of sunlight. Jeb and Many Scalps turned and began fighting their way toward the barracks.

➤ ●● ◀

Bigfoot Wallace plowed right through the zombie ranks, with Willie in tow behind him. He charged up to Lord Presidente Moctezuma–who seemed to Willie like he'd be a whole lot less impressive without his big hat–and pointed his sword level at the man's withered chest, then down to the human head hanging from his belt.

A *head?* Morbid curiosity made her wonder whose head it was. Just now, the face pointed in toward Moctezuma's armored left thigh. The ruler of Mexico may not have been a physically imposing man–Bigfoot had him outsized by nearly three feet–but the Lord

Presidente radiated a kind of presence, a raw ill-will that came off of him like a branding iron's heat. Being this close to him made Willie feel like his mark was burning into her soul. She imagined she could smell charring flesh, then realized in this crowd that was not necessarily her imagination. She heard a *thunk* sound repeat itself four times. More of the ghoulish troops passed overhead.

"You think you have it bad now? It's time for you"–he jabbed the point of his sword at the human head hanging from Moctezuma's belt–"to pay a price for what you done in Goliad."

Moctezuma's leathery face betrayed no emotion. His beetle-like eyes might have been staring at Bigfoot, or a million miles past him, or directly at his tender soul. Wind rustled the Lord Presidente's head dress, sending the bits of bone and metal dangling within it to clattering. With one scarred hand, Moctezuma reached down and twisted the head around so that the face came into horrifying view. It looked fresh enough to be a recent kill, Willie thought, like maybe the Mexican god-king had seen his zombie army getting their heads lopped off and decided fair was only fair. The face had a familiar quality, like Willie might have recognized this man, if there'd been more of him to look at. She studied the head intently, wondering what Bigfoot was planning.

What happened next nearly caused her to faint dead away like a nancy in church. It was only the reassuring heft of a pistol in each hand and the surrealness of being in the middle of the Mexican army with Bigfoot Wallace facing the Lord Presidente himself that kept her on her feet.

What happened was, the head on Moctezuma's belt blinked twice, and then answered him. Willie was so taken aback that her understanding of what was said lagged a bit behind the actual words like sick cattle.

"I treated you fairly," the head said in a raspy whisper. "And as for *having it bad*, I am the servant of a god. A god who will soon reclaim these lands!" Moctezuma's mouth cracked open then in silent laughter, the first time his stony face had betrayed any sign of life. Willie could hardly drag her eyes away from the weird spectacle of it.

The tip of Bigfoot's long blade wavered, then rose toward Moctezuma's gaze. Willie had a hard time meeting those eyes, but if Bigfoot Wallace was able to do so, then so could she. She took a few steps closer, just to prove the point. In the distance, zombie launchers ratcheted up for another throw. She didn't dare consider how many Mexican zombies were running amuck within the walls of the Alamo by this point, or whether they had gotten the gates open, or how well the army of the Texan republic was handling the situation. She didn't dare because the very thought made her feel helpless and weak, at a time when she'd much prefer to let her anger take the reins.

"We can take him," Willie muttered, hoping Bigfoot heard her and no one else. "He ain't even got a weapon."

Moctezuma's mouth cracked open wider, but still he said not a word. Santa Anna's head tutted at her. "A god has no need of weapons, stupid boy."

Her ire up and burning hot and out of control as a grassfire in the dry season now, pretending she did not see the way Bigfoot tried to wave her off with one hand, Willie spat on the ground in front of her. "I got two bits of advice for his godliness."

She took a big step forward, coming even with Bigfoot. "First, Don't call me a boy–stupid or otherwise. I'm not just a woman, I'm the toughest woman you're ever going to meet." Her voice rose with every syllable. Even in her own ears, she sounded strong and hard. "And Second? Always bring a gun to a gunfight."

Willie emptied both pistols into the Lord Presidente and his vile little pet, hoping the close range would make up for her weak left-handed aim. Bigfoot must have known where she was headed with this, because soon as she ran out of ammunition, he bounded toward the Lord Presidente with a powerful two-handed sideways slash that might have taken Moctezuma's head off, if his saber hadn't rusted away to nothing in midair.

Willie stood there gawping. Her shots had passed right through the flesh wherever there was any showing and ragged holes littered the bronze chest piece. Santa Anna had taken one right between the eyes.

None of which appeared to have had any effect at all.

None. At. All.

Willie heard a keening noise that threatened to swallow her up but she couldn't tell whether the noise came from somewhere on the battlefield or inside her own mind. Moctezuma kept on smiling, a hideous toothless grin that looked out of place and almost good-natured on his malicious squashed face. He reached out one hand toward Bigfoot in a friendly, soothing gesture, like a man pulling fat blood-filled ticks off a beloved hound.

Bigfoot just stood there, momentarily befuddled as any sixty-year-old man, and let Moctezuma's long, dead fingers stroke him on one cheek. Willie tried to move, tried to scream, but found herself rooted to the Texas soil, her voice chained up inside her chest.

As Moctezuma withdrew his hand, Bigfoot's skin turned the color of ashes where the Lord Presidente had touched him. That smudge of gray spread out quickly to cover his whole body while Willie damned her uncooperative eyes for not shutting, her muscles for not moving to beat the Mexican god with the butts of her pistols till one or the other of them was dead.

Bigfoot crumpled to the ground. Despite all the racket of war and emotions that enveloped her, she heard two things clearly: The last air Bigfoot Wallace had ever breathed sighing out of his lifeless body and Santa Anna's raucous, hoarse laughter.

The sounds threatened to rip away her sanity. She tried to move, to get away, to go someplace where what she had just seen had never happened, but she was trapped like a caged animal inside her own skin.

Santa Anna broke off from his gleeful chortling long enough to say to her. "Right or Left, *stupid girl?*"

Willie did not understand, couldn't make herself respond even if she did.

"Cat got your tongue, *girl?*" he asked her, cruelty riding behind his words like a stagecoach passenger. "Then the Lord will take the right-hand path for now, but later we will savor your womanly charms piece by piece until you are just like me. My mate, in fact."

Willie felt the river of fear she'd been swimming in rise up to flood her senses as Moctezuma drew close. In an almost gentle way, he took the gun from her right hand. It turned to rust in his grip and he dropped it to the ground, never taking his eyes off Willie. He clasped her right hand in his own ancient flesh as tenderly as she imagined a suitor might, if she would have ever allowed herself to be courted. She watched in paralyzed horror as the skin on the back of her hand turned cold and gray and numb, then her wrist followed suit. She felt a numbness spread up underneath her shirtsleeves. A tear rolled down one cheek and Willie hated that tear nearly as much as she hated Moctezuma. Bigfoot's corpse lay rapidly decomposing on the ground just inside her peripheral vision. Willie knew for certain that she was going to be next.

The burnt man with the silver hair huddled with She-Who-Is-Alone against the smoking ruin of a wall. Paleface soldiers with yellow buttons and trimmings all over their coats and hats lay strewn about the floor of the little room. Some were scattered across long benches, smoldering and moaning. Many did not move at all. Against one wall, more benches had been stacked to make room for a big table in the middle of the room that had many large papers arranged upon it. The biggest of the papers had bits of wood and metal scattered upon it in a most confusing fashion.

The walls rose high within the white man's holy place, with tiny openings set so far above the ground that She-Who-Is-Alone wondered who was meant to be able to look up at their Sky Father through them. One of the wounded soldiers said something to her, but she did not understand the words.

He's asking for help.

She felt sorry for the man, but she did know what she could do to help him. The Great Spirit had called her into this place to wait for the one who would come for her. She hoped that meant Lightning Dove, or perhaps even her paleface friend Wind-at-Night, but she knew better. She could feel the one who was coming, and she was sure he could feel her as well.

She swept the little pieces out of the way and climbed up on the table and lay there with her hands holding her aching heart, feeling the coolness of the smoothened wood beneath her. The papers rustled as she brushed them to the floor. The burnt man, attempting to bandage one of the soldiers, sent a panicked thought message at her, and then another, asking if she was ill.

But the Great Spirit did not want She-Who-Is-Alone to answer.

Audrey sat on the floor of the root cellar, holding Troy Tanner's hand in hers. The Tejano man, who'd introduced himself as Manuel Salazar, had covered the body with a burlap bag. He stood with his back to the doorway, a long muzzle-loading rifle cradled in his arms. The muffled sounds of war sounded outside, but inside was a stifling silence as the reality set in that this hole in the ground would be her grave as well.

Audrey cursed her own uselessness. She'd watched Troy killing rattlesnakes by himself and (apart from wasting ammo) had made no effort to help. Worse, she'd spent the last few hours all but screaming in terror as the Mexican army tore down the mission above them. She'd been terrified in Austin, but she'd managed to pull her weight. She and Willie had made sure the children made it out of town alive with those nuns. So why had she frozen this time? She'd sat beside Troy's still form for the better part of an hour thinking about it and realized it was because now she had something to lose. In Austin, it had become obvious the town would burn to the ground and her business with it. There was nothing to be done. And Jeb had already been gone long enough that she'd convinced herself he was never coming back. There had been little enough left to live for, so why fear death?

Yet, upon seeing Jeb again, she'd bought back in to the silly notion that maybe he was ready to stop wandering and keep his word to her. Although he'd ridden off again on a mission she doubted he could survive, she clung to that notion for all she was worth. She didn't want to lose him again.

Audrey wondered what he would think of her when he learned she'd lost Darla, and let Troy get killed. She wanted desperately to go find the girl, to make everything better somehow, but she didn't know where to look. How do you follow someone who disappears through a solid dirt wall?

Something scratched at the doorway and Manuel spun around, his rifle aimed at the warped plank of wood and the sacks of flour stacked ineffectually against it. A knock followed the scratching and a voice called to them. "Audrey! Troy? Open up the damn door!"

"Jeb!" Audrey scrambled to her feet and began moving away the flour sacks. "Jeb, we're in here. Just hang on a minute."

Manuel looked at her like she'd lost her mind, but began helping her with the sacks. "Who exactly are we letting in?"

"A friend. Maybe one that's going to save us all."

Manuel pulled aside the last sack and Audrey pulled open the door. A giant coyote rushed past her leg and she screamed, but it simply ran around Troy's body a few times and settled back on its haunches. Then Jeb walked into the room and all her other fears vanished. He looked as if he might collapse any moment. His body was ravaged with open wounds and one half of his face was covered in ash and blood. He limped toward her, all but supporting himself with a cavalry saber. Audrey put an arm under his, steadying him, then gave him a furious hug that made him wince.

The coyote whined then began to speak. "I don't see the girl here."

Manuel raised his rifle in shock but Audrey screamed, "No!" If this creature was with Jeb, that could mean only one thing. He'd somehow gotten through to the Comanche and brought them back, just like he said he would. She'd seen enough of these transformed Indians in Austin to recognize them. She was just happy this one was walking on four legs and not still half human. Somehow it made the strangeness easier to bear.

She tried not to think about how Indian magic might fit into God's plan.

"Where's Darla?" asked Jeb, heaving for breath.

"You're back!" said Audrey. "How did you make it back?"

"Audrey, I love you to death but I need to find Darla. If I don't get her to Lighting Dove real soon, things are going to get even worse."

"Is that possible?" Manuel asked.

"It is," Jeb answered.

How could she explain it to him? She'd seen the girl simply disappear into the wall. She began telling how Darla's fit had started, about the snakes, then Jeb's battle-dazed stare fell on the length of burlap covering Troy's body. He pulled away from Audrey, knelt by the body and pulled the burlap back just enough to see who was beneath it. If he was shocked or saddened, he didn't allow it to show. He just sat on both knees next to Troy, staring blankly at his closed eyelids, no longer seeming concerned about Darla's fate or anyone else's.

Audrey knelt beside him and explained how Troy had died after Darla got sucked into the wall. Jeb absorbed the knowledge without a sound, and his coyote companion whined impatiently and paced in circles.

"We have to find the girl!" said the coyote. Audrey took that in stride as best she could.

Jeb turned and looked her in the eye for the first time since his return. He looked so much older than she'd remembered him looking when he'd left her Austin, older even than the nervous but hopeful man that had ridden north just yesterday.

"So he watched after Darla and you best as he could?"

"Yes he did," said Audrey.

Jeb climbed to his feet with a grunt of pain and Audrey once again took some of his weight on her shoulders.

"Audrey, I don't want to leave you again, but I have to find Darla. If she dies...Lord, if she dies we all do."

"I understand that," said Audrey, though she wasn't entirely sure she did. All she wanted was to bar the door again and hide out with Jeb until the battle passed. But that was just more foolishness. "You have to find her and you can barely walk. So what's going to happen is we'll find her together."

"You ain't going nowhere," said Jeb.

"You're in no position to boss me," said Audrey. "I'll go wherever I please. And right now it pleases me to keep you alive. So you hang on to me and we'll go."

"I've got your back," said Manuel.

"Who're you?" asked Smoke.

"Manuel Salazar," he said. Audrey noticed that he hadn't taken his eye of the coyote yet, as if certain he might need to end the creature's life any moment now.

"You just got that one muzzle loader?"

"A pistol, too." He patted the pocket of a faded suit coat.

"Thank you," said Audrey, then she helped Jeb back up the stairway. It was only seconds before Manuel was shooting and battling off the horde behind them.

"I have this," he yelled. "Hurry!"

They hurried.

Titus kicked Nebuchadnezzar a little harder than usual as the war party climbed a red-brown hill ringed with sage and the occasional bluebonnet. Lightning Dove, white hair streaming, rode beside him at the center of one long rank of mounted Comanche braves. Far behind them, the Redjack war machines fumed and groaned along. The British General had to have been angry as a wet hen that Lightning Dove dared to strike out on his own, but he had not chosen to impede them in any way. A pair of steam angels went up and flew a big swooping circle overhead before heading farther south. Titus assumed they were assigned as aerial scouts.

Not too bad a thing to have here in Texas. If we ever get a chance to rebuild.

At the top of the hill, a sorry sight greeted them. San Antonio proper was as close to a smoking ruin as you could get with one brick still on top of the other. The Alamo hadn't fared much better. It was surrounded on all four sides by haphazardly ranked zombies, wooden catapults like out of a schoolboy's tale of knights and castles, well placed cannon crews, and a bizarre stepped pyramid on wheels. An empty pathway curved its way through the Mexican troops, like a well marked trail, bordered on every side by Moctezuma's troops. From this angle, Titus could see the whole path clearly, from the wheeled pyramid all the way to the bashed-in North Gate.

A soft wind blew from east to west across the battlefield, which Titus appreciated. For one thing, zombies smelled to high heaven. For another, he wasn't ready to hear the sounds of dying Texans that were no doubt being carried along on that wind.

"Do you think many of your people will attack the Comanche?" Lightning Dove asked. "They knew of your errand, did they not?"

Titus waved the staff he carried with the patchwork flag attached to it. He'd made it by hastily sewing the sleeve of a British red coat to one of his own white shirt sleeves with buckskin string, then attaching a square of thin, mostly blue Indian blanket embellished with Titus's own freshly shined Ranger star. If he wasn't riding, the thing hung like a heavy curtain, but with Nebuchadnezzar in a canter, it flared enough to be seen.

Cecilia would have done a better job of it, but the thing would suffice. *And how long before I'm seeing your sweet face again, my lovely?*

"I can't promise they'll all get the word, even if Jeb was to shout it out at morning muster. But we can hope that enough of them see us riding in together killing zombies under the Lone Star flag that they figure it out."

Lightning Dove did not reply. From the look on his face, it seemed like the Titus's answer had disgusted him.

Peeved, but remembering his place here in the custody of a barely allied Comanche war party, Titus added, "Best anyone could do."

But Lightning Dove did not listen. He glared at Titus a moment as if the man had suggested they get off their horses and dance a waltz, looked up and down the rank of braves, then out at the mayhem surrounding the Alamo. Something odd was happening to the man's face, Titus realized, as it began to stretch.

Lightning Dove shouted triumphantly in Comanche, raising one fist into the air. As one, the Comanche braves stopped their horses and burst into flame, leaving Titus in such surprise that he hardly noticed his jaw hung open farther than he generally cared to let it.

When Lightning Dove and his war band started turning into animals and monsters straight out of their legends, he spurred Nebuchadnezzar again, waving the flag of the Texas Republic as hard as he could over himself and his country's strange new allies.

Darla felt a coldness pass across her, as if she had stepped suddenly into the great shadow of a mountain. It was cooler than the underground place where Barking Spider had died, and the cold penetrated deeper now, chilling her spirit. He was here.

She opened her eyes, not quite sure how long she had been laying on the broad table of war in the white man's holy place. The burnt man stood before her, with his back to her, holding a dirt-caked sack in front of him and shouting things at the imposing figure before them. The dead chieftain of Breathless Ones bent over at the waist, but he was not bowing to the burnt man, merely keeping his tall feathered head dress from touching the remains of the wall as he entered.

He was not truly a god, she decided. Just an ugly man filled up with evil. But She-Who-Is-Alone knew that she was wrong as she watched him step softly from one paleface to the next, paying no attention to the burnt man's cries and chants. As he touched each of the white men, their skin turned the color of a terrible storm approaching. Their eyes rolled around in their head for a moment like ants were upon them, then they trembled hard and breathed no more. The dead chieftain wore a living head upon his belt as if it were merely a scalp. The terrible thing hissed words she could not understand to each of the men as they died. She did not need to understand the words to know that they were cruel and filled with hate.

She-Who-Is-Alone wept as he took the life from the last paleface and placed his hand upon the burnt man who had called her up through the ground. The burnt man fell into dust immediately as if all along he had been made of ashes. The dead chieftain turned his shiny black eyes toward her.

You hold much power. The voice in her mind this time felt timeless and set apart from the world. The thought words came unbidden on ripples of suffering and stony indifference. She begged the Great Spirit to keep those words out of her head. But if the Great Spirit was listening, he did nothing to aid her.

My own power wanes.

She-Who-Is-Alone waited. The hard, flat wood pressed into her shoulder blades and the backs of her thighs. She heard someone shouting her name outside, not her true name but the one Wind-at-Night had given her: Darla. Wind-at-Night? At the sound of his voice she tried to rise up but discovered that she could not.

Was she meant to go with Wind-at-Night, and not the dead chieftain? Would he rescue her from the Breathless Ones' god? Hope bloomed for only a moment before it was swallowed up. The dead god unsheathed an obsidian knife and cut at the buckskin of her shirt until it fell away exposing the pale puckered bite marks on her stomach and the purpling bruise of her heart. She felt his cold hunger wash over her all at once.

Am I to be nothing more than food for a dying god? she demanded of the Great Spirit. Am I meant to give my life to him that he may live on and continue to harm the people–all the people of this land?

In her heart, she knew the answer. The black knife rose and fell, then rose and fell again, but she felt nothing. She-Who-Is-Alone listened to the cries of many birds, great and small. They seemed to be coming from very far away, but she knew they were getting closer.

Back in the courtyard, the smoke was thicker than ever, but there seemed to be a lull in the fighting, as if Jeb and Audrey had found the eye of a storm that had already swept everyone else away. Gunshots still cracked all around and men still died with noisy screams, but there were no immediate enemies to attend to, no zombies within sword range, no Mexican soldiers to be seen at all.

But there *were* bodies, more than Jeb could count, littering the ground save for a wide swath cut through all the carnage, as if someone had drug a plow from one of the Alamo's collapsed walls, through the courtyard, and toward the chapel. The bodies piled at the edges looked to have been melted, and as Audrey and Jeb followed Many Scalps through the smoke, he saw that they were in fact mostly ash. Many still retained some characteristics of the flesh, but those at the edge of the smoking path had mostly crumbled away, and bits of feathery gray matter lifted up and away in each gust of wind.

Whatever had passed this way, whatever had used this path, was an aberration. It had burned all the men in its way and left no doubt where it was headed. Jeb thought for a moment that the British had arrived. Maybe this horrible trail was the result of one of their war machines, one they'd never unleashed on an enemy before today. But another look convinced him that there was magic involved, dark magic based on the human remains that he was already sure would haunt him the rest of his days. He'd seen what the Indians were capable of, and it was a far more human use of magic than this.

Jeb hurried along, sure now that this was Moctezuma's doing. He had no idea where Darla was and no idea what he'd find if he followed the path of destruction, but he knew one thing. If that little girl was at the end of it, she'd need his help more than ever.

"What did this?" asked Audrey, shaking beneath his weight.

"Lord only knows," said Jeb. "Has to be that goddamned blood magic." Jeb expected Audrey to scold him for taking the Lord's name in vain, but she was either too shocked to notice, or to stunned by the atrocity to react.

Jeb hurried best he could, limping as he was. With every step, pain lanced up his leg and he wondered if he'd broken something after all. Thank God for Audrey. He doubted he could stumble along by himself for long. He hated bringing her into this kind of danger, but truth be told no place was safe in the city of San Antonio. And if she was by his side, at least he could do his best to defend her.

They followed the trail to the face of the chapel. The venerable old structure with its arced façade still bore the scars of the first Battle of the Alamo. And on top of those, new ones. The heavy wooden doors had been blown off, and all along the rooftop perched hundreds–no, thousands–of birds. Many Scalps, wide-eyed, shook his head at them all and bounded inside. A moment later, an awestruck Jeb and Audrey followed.

The air within was icy cold, and the stench of spilled blood was pervasive. Outside, it had been all smoke and rotting flesh and burning wood–the smell of blood was lost amid more prominent odors. But in the chapel, blood held sway. It covered the floor and was spattered against the walls. Bits of matter that might once have been human lay strewn to all corners of the room. Jeb could make out several ruined heads, each halfway burned to ash like the bodies outside, various limbs and a few men still mostly intact, but the greater part of those who'd been defending the chapel had been reduced to little more than discarded meat and ash.

In the middle of it all, beneath a slightly crooked wooden cross was Darla, lying on her back upon the altar, head cocked toward the door just enough so that Jeb could make out who she was. Eyes closed. Face pale. Dress gone and chest torn apart. She'd been slit from chin to stomach and blood leaked freely from the open cavity. Jeb stumbled, dropped to one knee and put a hand on the ground to steady himself. Audrey was screaming and Many Scalps howling, but the sound of blood rushing in Jeb's head soon drowned them out. It beat a maddening rhythm in his skull, as if it wanted to escape his body and finish decorating the walls.

A bloody figure stood beside her, hands lifted over its head, holding something. The figure wore an impossibly tall headdress of feathers, golden bones and beads, and when it lowered its hands, Jeb saw they held Darla's heart. It looked like it was still beating, but

Jeb knew that could only be a product of the shadows that were swirling around him now, threatening to take his mind and deliver it somewhere no one would ever be able to find it again.

The figure–*Moctezuma, goddamn it! Who the hell else could it be but the evil old bastard?*–Moctezuma lifted the heart to his mouth and took a greedy bite, chewed, then took another. It was too much for Jeb. He joined Audrey in her screaming and unloaded his pistol into the Lord Presidente of Mexico. It wouldn't do Darla any good; he'd failed another little girl and nothing could be done about that. But it might do Texas some good if he could kill Moctezuma, and it would damn sure do Jeb some good.

When Moctezuma turned a lazy, curious eye his direction, Jeb realized he'd missed. A split second of consideration and he corrected that assumption. No way he'd missed, not in such close quarters, not with his considerable skill. His bullets had hit their target, and they hadn't done a thing to slow him.

Moctezuma took another bite of the heart as he began a slow approach, coming for Jeb and Audrey, coming for all of Texas.

Many Scalps began burning, his coyote skin chewed away by the flames and replaced by human flesh. He knelt on his knees, staring at his hands as if hoping they would explain why his magic had abandoned him at such a crucial moment.

Jeb stood, dropped his useless pistol and held his sword at the ready. It wouldn't kill the monster–all he'd seen here had convinced him of that. But what else could be done? He would die, Audrey would die, Many Scalps would die. Probably every man and woman who'd woken up in San Antonio that morning would die.

Knowing that gave Jeb a kind of resolve. If death was a certainty, he intended to meet his fighting with all he had for everything and everyone he loved.

CHAPTER 27

GENERAL THACKERAY SURVEYED THE RUIN OF SAN ANTONIO from the swaying deck of *Indomitable*, fingers curled around the iron railings in barely controlled fury. Lighting Dove and his heathen traitors had already engaged the enemy and it appeared that they'd once again assumed their bestial forms, unwilling to go to battle as men. Zombies grappled with grizzly bears and fought mindlessly with snake-headed Indians while the battered Texans, who looked all but defeated already, fired useless bullets at the Mexican dead and fell victim to Moctezuma's saber-wielding cavalry, living men who swept through the battle like avenging angels, cutting down anyone who wasn't already dead.

It seemed the Mexicans had the upper hand; they might already have taken San Antonio. Thackeray was certain his men could have taken the town and routed the Mexicans besides if Lighting Dove hadn't dashed their plans with his treachery. Thackeray hadn't a clue what the savage war leader had in mind, riding away from the slow-moving camp in a storm of hooves and smoke–possibly the coward thought he could make peace with the Mexican and save his worthless skin–but Lighting Dove's actions had relieved Thackeray of any responsibility he had to the Queen's temporary allies.

Despite his anger at being tricked, Thackeray felt almost thankful to the man. The British army had a storied history of conquest without the aide of heathen magic and the General would prove once and for all to his detractors in London that the men under his command were more than equal to this task. The Texans were nothing more than land-squatters, holding this foul piece of dirt until Her Majesty came to claim it. And the other factions were likewise mere pretenders. The Comanche had shown him little but parlor tricks, and Thackeray was confident that they could be crushed with little effort. As for the Mexicans, however distasteful it might be to war with dead men, it appeared that Moctezuma's vaunted army had little in the way of conventional firepower, and what artillery they did have was devoted to raining endless salvos at the rapidly falling Alamo. By the time they realized the greatest army in the history of mankind was in their midst, they'd already be defeated.

Thackeray's vanguard reached the fray and rolled over the rear of Moctezuma's north line just as a fresh squadron of steam angels passed overhead and began firing rockets at strategic targets. Three went off in the main body of the mission, while another collapsed a stone clock tower. Huge river rocks rained down, killing several Texans and crushing at least two zombies.

His landship reached the battle and he pulled his saber. It was doubtful any of the zombies could scale the landship's steel sides, but if they dared, Thackeray would show them the skills of a British swordsman. On the battlefield below, his dragoons fought valiantly, killing the living with careful aim and felling zombies with their bayonets. Like Thackeray, they understood the strategic importance of the battle. The Queen reigned supreme west of the Rocky Mountains, but if Thackeray and his men could deliver her Texas, the rest of the continent would be within Her Majesty's easy grasp.

An Indian with the body of a man and the head of a panther ran past in pursuit of a British soldier with a gaping wound in his chest. Thackeray drew his silver plated pistol from inside his jacket and fired one shot, killing the beast in an instant.

Routing this lot would be a simple matter. Already his men were pressing their advantage. Then, all around him on the battlefield, two hundred Comanche men burst into flames and emerged from them as nothing more than confused, naked men, ready for the sword.

Thackeray, a stoic Briton if ever one walked the earth, allowed himself a satisfied grin.

Twenty feet above the earth, Lighting Dove caught fire and began to fall. Unlike the times before, the pain was intense. When the change had come upon him again, his spirit had rejoiced. It meant that She-Who-Is-Alone was alive and that her power had been returned to the People. As long as she was close, they would prosper.

He'd taken to the skies and all the men scrambling below had feared him. His war song caused zombies to flee and Mexican soldiers to race away on their horses, desperately trying to outrun a predator they could never hope to escape. Lightning Dove was the embodiment of all the People's wrath, and his fury would not be denied.

And then, the power abandoned him again.

He plunged like a star falling from the sky, red flames tailing behind him and all too quickly the ground came up to meet him. He struck hard, heard bones in his body snap. If he'd been any higher, he would have been dead, and perhaps that would have been better. At the very least, he would not have to live with the confirmation that he'd failed once again.

He tried to stand and found he did not yet have the strength. Pain came at him from all quarters, so much that he couldn't tell exactly where he was injured. He pushed up with his arms, found they worked. When he raised his neck, white hair spilled in front of his eyes, but not before he saw the advancing zombies, teeth rotting in their mouths.

The last of the flames flashed into shadows and Lighting Dove was left broken on the battlefield, alone with his fate.

He sang a song of death and pushed his hair to the side so he could meet his end with open eyes.

Titus rode Nebuchadnezzar through the swarming hordes, driving them back with his boot heels and taking off as many heads as he could with his sword. More often than not, his blows only served to loosen their heads, and the zombies would stagger off in confusion. Long shadows crossed ahead of him and he glimpsed Redjack steam angels passing overhead. Like thunder following lighting, huge explosions erupted in the wake of their passing. Zombies he could handle, but how was a man supposed to fight enemies a mile above him?

A few of Lighting Dove's men who'd assumed bird forms harried the air machines as they passed, but as Titus watched them circle around one of the crafts, trying to disable it, they suddenly burst into flames and spiraled down to earth. Likewise, the Indians that fought at his side and all across the battlefield caught fire, and when the flames died, Titus realized they'd reverted back to their original forms. Their magic must have failed them. He didn't understand what had happened, but he knew the chances of surviving the day had grown slimmer.

Amazingly, word had spread that the Indians weren't to be feared, and only a few of the Texan defenders had attacked the Comanche. The animal men had torn into the zombies, pulling them to bits with claws and talons and teeth, leaving grateful Texans unmolested in their wake. It had been obvious to the uninitiated that these animal men, however terrible they might appear, had not come to kill San Antonio's defenders. Now that they'd reverted to normal Comanche again, they seemed stunned, and the zombies quickly turned the table, advancing on them before they could recover from their loss. It was the Texans' turn to come to *their* aid, and they did so with fervor, putting themselves between Indians and zombies wherever possible, buying the fallen men time to regain themselves.

And in short time, they did. The Comanche were fierce warriors *without* supernatural assistance, and when they'd gathered their wits, they pulled themselves up from the piles of ash that surrounded them and fought for their lives and their nation.

The ground began to shake and Nebuchadnezzar bounced nervously in a circle. The Queen's war machines had arrived, rolling down the gently sloping hill and onto the battle plain. Titus pulled the horse around and made for the Alamo, hoping there was still at least one working cannon that could be directed at the creeping steel beasts. Rockets exploded behind him, and chain gun fire chewed deadly ropes through living and dead flesh alike.

Nebuchadnezzar reared up in terror, then caught a belly full of bullets. Titus leapt free from the saddle, barely managing to avoid the half ton of horseflesh as it fell to the earth. More bullets hissed overhead. Titus scrambled away from Nebuchadnezzar's corpse on all fours, miserable about his companion's sudden death and angrier than he could recall being in his life. Mexicans and Comanche wanting this land were one thing, but what goddamned business did the British have here, killing a man's horse right out from under him?

Titus crawled, kept his head down. He realized he'd lost his sword, cursed under his breath and pulled his pistol. Little good it would do against zombies–Willie might be able to aim well enough to pop their necks every single time but Titus had never been that skilled. Maybe he'd get to use it against one of the Queen's cavalry. If he did, he might just shoot their fiddlestickin' horse instead.

Then he saw Lighting Dove, supporting his torso with both arms, legs kicking behind him, screaming out in words that Titus couldn't understand. And yet their meaning was clear. A zombie reached down, pulled the old war chief up by the hair, and it was obvious that Lighting Dove didn't have the strength to resist.

"Mr. Smoke!"

The voice distracted Titus. When he turned to see who'd spoken, he barely recognized Willie. She was bloodied and beaten, and one of her little four shot pistols hung limply in her left hand. As for her right, it looked like her arm was missing entirely. No blood leaked from the socket, but she'd damn sure lost it. Willie stumbled toward him and he caught her weight before she hit the ground.

"God damn, Wilhelmina, what happened to you?"

"Moctezuma happened," she said, her eyes glassy. "And would you mind calling me Willie?"

Lighting Dove wailed. He was about twenty feet away and the zombie had him by the hair, chewing at his scalp, trying to work the hair loose with tooth and claw. Titus wanted to move to help the man, but Willie leaned against him, yelling in his ear, crying now about what had happened to her, something about Moctezuma melting her arm, turning it to nothing more than ash, killing Bigfoot, killing everyone and everything he touched. She was raving.

Lighting Dove grabbed at the zombie, but the monster stood and lifted him up, spun him around and drove his teeth right into the back of the war chief's head. Titus began moving toward him, supporting Willie and doing his best to bowl through the carnage and make it to Lightning Dove. Willie quieted, as if she finally understood there was still a battle going on around her. Lives to be lost and lives to be saved.

Titus felt her grow taut against him and suddenly Lightning Dove slipped free from his attacker. The zombie stumbled back as its head tilted sideways then fell free from its shoulders. The creature's body wound in a circle, then crashed down at Lighting Dove's feet. Emboldened, the white-haired Comanche began kicking the lifeless thing, screaming out until his voice cracked and he dropped to his knees, no longer able to stand.

Willie still held her pistol at arm's length, one eye closed, hand beginning to tremble. Titus tightened his grip on the girl, afraid she might drop any second.

"They killed Bigfoot," she whispered. "They took my arm."

"I know, Willie," he said. "We'll pay them back. I promise."

She grimaced and lowered her arm. Titus led her to where Lightning Dove was kneeling. He'd need medical attention and so would Willie. Titus couldn't understand why the girl hadn't bled out yet; he could only guess that the amputation had been cauterized. Blood coursed down Lighting Dove's face, but he was smiling. Titus held out his hand and helped the man rise uneasily to his feet.

"I am still alive," said Lighting Dove, as if trying to convince himself.

"You are at that," said Titus.

A pair of rockets exploded in succession. Stampeding zombies pressed in and the Redjack cavalry thundered around them like a sea of boiling blood, the vanguard of Her Majesty's horrible army. The hissing and rumbling of approaching steam gear drowned out the shrieks of the dying and the moans of the hungry dead. Titus, Willie, and Lighting Dove stood back to back as hell closed in on all sides.

Lighting Dove raised his voice in a song of war and Titus Smoke and Willie herself joined in, whooping a rallying cry for all they were worth.

Acrid blue smoke hung in the air around him, but Jeb only saw red. Audrey stepped in close to him, trying to slip her shoulder under his arm, take some of the weight back off of his ruined leg. He pushed her away as gently as he could manage, launching himself in a cruel, painful, limping parody of a charge at Moctezuma instead.

"No!" Audrey screamed. She tried to hold him back, keep him outside of the dead god's reach, but Jeb shrugged her off. Many Scalps was on his feet now as well. Nude and weaponless, the brave grabbed weapon after useless, rusted out weapon from the ash corpses on the ground.

The Lord Presidente of Mexico plopped the remainder of Darla's heart into his mouth like the last bite of a jam-covered biscuit at Sunday breakfast, then casually removed a human head from his belt and placed it on the altar next to Darla. The hideous trophy twitched and jumped as if it had just come off of some living man, maybe one of the dead soldiers from this very room. The half smile Moctezuma wore remained in place as he took a step toward Jeb and Audrey, then stopped. Jeb swung his Ranger cutlass high and hard for Moctezuma's neck.

It never made it there. The sharpened edge turned brown and then orange before falling into flakes of rust that might as well have kissed Moctezuma for all the good they did. Feathers rustled in Moctezuma's head dress, the only thing that seemed to be able to move in the cemetery stillness of the chapel. The head on the altar blinked and made a staccato rasping sound, as if it were trying to laugh, but certainly that couldn't be the case. Could it?

Moctezuma reached one hand out like a preacher inviting sinners to come forward and repent. Jeb felt the stiffness of the dead overtake his body. He could not move, and the dead god's bony fingers and ragged nails were only inches from his face.

Many Scalps, red-toothed, pounced from his position on the floor. His face held more feral rage now than it ever had as a big coyote. The Comanche's attack fell short nonetheless as he staggered suddenly and landed awkward and immobile on the gore-spattered floor just inches from Jeb. Audrey whimpered something from out of sight behind him. Jeb imagined how she must look, terrified out of her mind, held in place by Moctezuma's dark magic and forced to watch those life-taking hands do their despicable work.

Moctezuma's outstretched fingers approached Jeb's face so slowly he wanted to scream at the dead god to get it over with, to take him, take Many Scalps–but leave Audrey be. The little hairs all over Jeb's body began to twitch and stand up on end. He felt a tear roll down one cheek, stinging in the first open wound it came to. A faint smell like surgeon's ether crept into the air. The bits of metal in Moctezuma's head dress clinked, softly at first, then louder and louder, against the gilded bones and shards of turquoise nestled in it.

The long middle finger touched Jeb first and he started backwards, surprising himself with his own motion and awareness. Jeb landed against Audrey and the pair sprawled to the ground. Wind rushed into the chapel through the gaping remains of the front door and through every window and crack. The smell of blood slowly gave way to an overwhelming ether-like aroma that tingled in Jeb's nose and made Audrey flat out sneeze. There was something familiar about this smell. It reminded him of the way the air around *Leviathan 212's* steam engine seemed to be made of molten metal. And something else, something Jeb could not quite place.

Moctezuma took one, then another shambling step toward them, as if he were becoming unsure on his sandaled feet. Many Scalps, discovering the dark spell binding him had dissipated as well, made as if to trip the Lord Presidente, but found his arms too short, his fingers too stubby, every inch of his naked skin blackening and bubbling, as if an invisible flame were scorching the man where he crouched. The wind kicked up again, stirring the rust and ashes of Kuykendall, the other dead men, and their weapons into dozens of miniature dust devils.

Moctezuma bent toward Jeb and Audrey as if the bones of his back were held in place with rivets. Jeb put himself between the dead god and Audrey, who wanted to kick him in the back for his chivalry. With one hand on his shirt collar and the other around his bruised, bleeding ribs, she pulled him away from Moctezuma.

Something was wrong. The air kept coming in to the chapel, but it didn't seem like any was leaving. Jeb could not see Many Scalps, but he heard the man's anguished cries as if they were coming from the bottom of a well.

Moctezuma's fingers wrapped themselves around Jeb's throat and held him there with all the ease of a cat picking up a kitten by the scruff of the neck. Jeb marveled that he was still alive and not a dust pile like the officers who had already died in this room.

He took in the scene over Moctezuma's shoulder, as he jabbed at the god's beetle-eyes with both hands, clawed the feather head dress from his head and sent it sprawling across the floor. When would it happen, what would be the very last thing he saw before this darkness enveloped him? Would it be Many Scalps on all fours, skin boiling? The fluttering maps borne on medicine-smelling air? The head that was somehow magicked alive rolling side to side on the floor beneath the altar? Darla, getting up, innards trailing down around her knees as she walked silently toward them?

Jeb blinked, and she was still there. Behind her eyes, a faint blue light crackled like butterflies caught in the glass of a gas light.

Her lips did not move, but the words came from every corner of the room, every swirl of ashes and decay in a hundred languages at once. Jeb made out snippets of Spanish, Comanche, English and other tongues he'd never understand.

"You have eaten the poison of my heart, a gift to you from all gods and men."

Moctezuma released Jeb's throat and pushed him away, spinning to face Darla. Jeb landed with all his weight on his bad leg, which collapsed beneath him. He moaned before he could stop himself. Audrey, face wet, crab-walked over and held him tightly in both arms. If he had not been so focused on the weird prickled skin sensation in the air and the spectacle of Darla's awakened corpse speaking in tongues, he would have kissed her and hugged her back.

Moctezuma stalked toward Darla, for the first time his expressionless face betraying a human sort of emotion: rage.

It felt like Jeb's ear drums were going to pop from all the building air pressure in the chapel. Audrey's hair stood on end, as did Darla's and no doubt his own. Many Scalps had begun a slow motion transformation back into his coyote form and the standing tufts of fur on his lean frame gave him a spiky cactus-like appearance. He yipped at Jeb and Audrey now, tugging at their clothes.

"Get out of here, palefaces," he said. "Now."

Jeb tried to rise but found he could not, even with Audrey's help. The two of them scooted backward along the floor toward the open sky, facing Darla and Moctezuma the entire way out.

Moctezuma raised a hand at Darla as a parent might threaten to slap a back-sassing child. She gave him a look with those blue-limned eyes, daring him.

The Lord Presidente swung his open hand at her face as Jeb and Audrey cleared the plane of the missing doorway. As his hand gathered speed in the air, everything else seemed to slow down. The tang of metal in the air built and built as the dead god's hand approached her face.

In the moment before it struck, Jeb heard three things:

A long, low sizzling sound like steam escaping a kettle that's sat too long by the campfire.

Darla's voice of many tongues saying, "What I take from you, I give back to all of the People, brother. In the name of love."

A brilliant blue thunderstrike crashed inside the Alamo chapel so hot and bright that Jeb could not see or hear or smell or feel anything for a long, long time. Anything, that is, besides Audrey.

Lightning Dove shook off the assistance of the Texan war chief and the tall, one-armed paleface boy with him. That one seemed afraid to touch him. Why the whites were so afraid of nakedness was one of the Great Spirit's deepest mysteries. Lightning Dove doubted even Broken Lance understood it. He forced himself to stand on his own feet, knowing in his heart that the day was lost. No amount of fighting would stop the red-coated men and their metal beasts. The dead army from the south were even at this point too numerous to overcome. They had destroyed the gates, scaled the walls of the white men's fort. The remaining Warhawks and Texans were barely enough to hunt the buffalo.

He saw the same truth clearly in the bold man's eyes. He nodded, showing respect for the man's bravery. The Texan war chief nodded back at him somberly, holding his gaze. The one-armed boy held his gun in front of him left-handed, quivering as a ring of zombies began closing in upon them. As if they knew one another's thoughts, the three of them kept their backs together, standing shoulder to shoulder against the gathering horde. To his credit, the Texan war chief did not shy away, but the tall boy did.

"Ow, damn it!" the one-armed boy said, in a high-pitched voice that betrayed his youth. "Why is your skin so hot?"

Lightning Dove turned his head from the slowly gathering mass of dead men, quickly, to see the face of one so afflicted with the brain fever of war. His attention was pulled past the boy—or could it be? A woman in man's clothes?—to the black cloud that rode over the Texan fort like blankets placed over the sun to block out its light. The last time the sun had been darkened, he'd been fighting against these men, not beside them. How quickly a man's destiny can change.

Broken Lance had claimed it was the moon that caused the unnatural darkness in Austin, but it seemed to be a writhing mass of smoke and storm clouds causing it this time. Regardless, the result was the same. The day grew dark and Lighting Dove felt a change coming on him as well. He felt the same sensation he had that day, the first time he–

The earth shook beneath them so hard the fierce woman fell to her knees. Most of the dead men fell to the ground as well, a fact which seemed to cheer the Texan war chief.

The cloud above the white men's fort erupted in jagged streaks of lightning, colored blue as the bird who cries jay. Dozens of glowing spears of light flew from the fortress, leaving no part of the building visible above the wall, but tracing a familiar figure in the false twilight above.

"What in the blue blazes is *that*?" the Texas war chief asked.

"Blue blazes is right," said the one-armed woman. "Whatever it is, the zombies ain't getting back up from it."

Lightning Dove noted with satisfaction that the woman's words were true; the dead men seemed truly dead. He felt the change coming on, the ache of his broken bones becoming lighter and knitting themselves whole again as they did so. His nose became a long sharp beak even as his skin was replaced by flames and then feathers. He beat golden wings against the choked air of battle until he rose above it all, closer and closer to the Thunderbird.

Titus didn't know whether it was Cecilia's God or Lighting Dove's that had saved them, but for the first time in several days, he believed he might live to see another.

Lighting continued to erupt from the Alamo, making jagged patterns in the sky like giant blue spider webs. Every hair on Titus' body stood at attention and he could practically taste the heat in the air. Whatever was causing the phenomenon had laid the Mexican army low. All the zombies had dropped in place, delivered to the true death that Moctezuma had denied them. Many of the Texans continued stabbing at the corpses with swords and bayonets, either driven by blood lust or unwilling to believe the bastards would stay dead. But one look at the rapid decomposition taking place all around him was all it took for Titus to understand they had no more to fear from zombies.

Once again, the Indians had found whatever power it was that brought on their animal forms, and they emerged from the flames with a righteous fury. They attacked the confused Mexican cavalry, suddenly vastly outnumbered without their dead counterparts, and the arriving waves of Redjack dragoons as well, taking full advantage of their animal attributes as if afraid they might revert back to men any second. A bear ripped the throat out of an Englishman's horse while a pack of snake-headed Comanche pulled the rider down to the ground and gutted him. A joint force of Comanche and Texans scaled the nearest steam frigate, tossed the shocked British solders off and turned the lumbering ship's chain guns on the Redjacks' own mechanized cavalry.

"What the hell's going on?" asked Willie. She was staring upward as if trying to spot the circling figure of Lighting Dove in the crackling air.

"We're winning the day." Titus knelt down and robbed a dead Englishmen of his rifle. He checked that it was still loaded, then passed the man's pistol to Willie.

Blue light gashed the skies overhead and moments later, pieces of a shattered steam angel rained down around them. Titus seized Willie and made for the opposite side of an approaching steam transport, seeking some sort of shelter. Bullets chewed the ground behind them and bits of metal sang against the machine's steel hide. They hung close enough to the slow-moving transport that the on-board guns couldn't target them, and from that cover, Titus and Willie began shooting anyone in sight wearing the Queen's red.

"You sure we're winning?" asked Willie. "Because it's awful hard to reload with one arm."

"Oh, we're winning all right," said Titus, "Hand me that revolver."

His mission all but complete, Pinkerton checked the contents of his go-sack again, making sure it contained everything he would need when the time came to run. He'd taken on the identity of captured spy Adolphus Pincher, ingratiated himself with the fledgling government in Austin, and used every resource and scrap of information in his possession to help President Polk engineer a decimating blow to not one, but *four* rival nations. The letters he had written to Moctezuma on Queen Victoria's behalf promised a lion's share of Texas in trade for a coordinated attack; the risen Aztec had no intention of sharing any part of his land with the British, Indians, Americans or Texans. No living ones, at any rate. It amused Pinkerton to think of the Lord Presidente's naiveté in matters of diplomacy. Luring him north had been like calling a hungry dog into the butcher shop.

In the passageway outside his room, Pinkerton heard the tramping of men's boots running this way and that, bells ringing, horns blaring, shouts and explosions and gunfire. The tenor of it all seemed to have changed subtly over the last few minutes, the surety of Her Majesty's victory now laced with panic. As it should be. It was America's manifest destiny to see her flag waving over every stitch of this continent, from the Atlantic to the working gold mines of the Pacific coastal colonies. From the ice fields of Canada to the southernmost tip of Mexico. It would not all come easily, but the rapid western expansion would find little to hinder after this masterpiece of stage-setting.

An empire of free peoples, Pinkerton had explained to Joan, would save the world from its own tyranny, lifting every man into a better world. *But aren't there men and women who do not wish to be lifted up, or–like Texas–already revere liberty? What of them?* she asked him. His answer had not quite satisfied her: *Freedom requires a watchdog, my dear. On this continent, the District of Columbia intends to have the most fearsome bark and bite, lest some despot come and take away all of our bones.*

And what of the Negro slaves in our own southern states? she pursued. *Should America not clean her own house before looking outward?*

I find the practice as despicable as you, Joanie. You know that. But what use is a clean house, if it be surrounded by dirt and wolves and flame?

She had pressed him no further, knowing his mind was set.

Putting his wayward thoughts to rest, Pinkerton looped the go-sack about his shoulder, feeling something hard within jamming into his ribs. His silver mirror. Better it were a hand gun to get him through this day. He took one last look at the tiny stateroom, smirking at the tight bedsheets. It was the first time since he'd occupied the cabin that he'd made the bed. The part of him that was no longer Pincher felt a stab of satisfaction at the irony.

Grinning, he shut the wooden door behind him and made for the afterdecks. In the passageways, Redjack soldiers betrayed an uncharacteristic lack of discipline. "What's happening?" he asked one of them. The man did not reply, only barrelled past on the way to some crisis or assignment. The next man, he grabbed by the collar and asked the same thing.

"The zombies all fell down dead and the Indians turned coat," he said, huffing and pale with fear. "And on the top of it all, the Texans have some kind of lightning magic they've launched into the air. It's headed this way!"

The man shook himself free of Pinkerton's grasp and darted up a ladder at the end of the narrow passageway.

Lightning was not the sort of weapon anyone had pegged the Texans for. They were considered all but modern primitives with their scarce steam gear and heavy reliance on horse and black powder weapons. But if it were so, the last place Pinkerton wanted to be during an electricification attack was aboard a metal landship. He raced to the afterdeck now, dodging soldiers with firefighting kits of sand and heavy blanket, occasional water hoses flaked out in preparation for use.

As he emerged from *Indomitable's* hull, the heaviness of the air outside startled him. It was nearly as thick as the most closed up air within. It felt wet in his lungs like the foggy mornings of his Glasgow boyhood. Not at all the usual dry heat of Texas he had grown accustomed to. Far off to the north, there was blue sky. But not here. Here the sky roiled with malignant dark majesty. Even leaning out over the rail, he could not see much of the Alamo and battlegrounds ahead, blocked as it was by the great landship's bulk. But he heard the cheers of decidedly Texan voices, the cries of eagles, the crash of thunder and cannon and chaingun.

The victory of the Texans and even the Comanche over the Britons pleased Pinkerton, he was surprised to note as he twisted his body beneath the rails and threw a ladder of rope and yew down the landship's stern. Almost as if Thackeray knew of his treachery and intent to escape, *Indomitable* lurched hard to port, sending Pinkerton's feet swinging out behind him and scrabbling for purchase on the rungs again. His arms ached but held true, even as his go-sack dropped down around an elbow. It spun there beneath him in neat tight circles as Pinkerton negotiated the remaining distance to the bottom, took a steadying breath and let go.

There were virtually no British troops or equipment to be found in the rear. Seeing the collected enemies as an easy target, Thackeray had sent them all ahead of the command vessel to participate in the turkey shoot. Which made Pincher's departure all the more simple.

He ran briskly, waiting for the deserter's shot in his back, but it never came. He saw an abandoned steam mare and made for it. When he'd mounted the thing, and mastered its clumsy articulation, he rode up the hill away from San Antonio and surveyed the destruction below.

Steam angels, piles of still bodies, and all the debris of war littered the ground on every side of the Alamo. The sky was still oppressive and blackened with thunderclouds. The plain below was a study in fire, iron, adobe, and death.

The Texan weapon, a creation so incredible it had to be magic rather than technology, soared through the haze, the fearsome outline of a gigantic bird made up of constant jags of blue-tinged lightning. As Pinkerton watched, the enormous creature terrorized mechanized cavalry, ripped the treads off of leviathan units, electrified steam angels and sent them plummeting to earth. Their pressure bombs exploded on impact, adding to the noise and smoke. Indian shapeshifters and their new Texan allies made short work of whatever foe they got their hands, claws, or talons upon. But the worst was when the enormous electrical raptor fell upon *Indomitable,* turning the several-ton landship on its side with the ease of a man sweeping table crumbs to his dogs below.

The ship groaned and buckled while men screamed and animals and Texans converged upon them. Pinkerton thought of General Thackeray, all puffed up in the wardroom the night before, declaring that the conquest of San Antonio would be accomplished with twice the leisure as Austin had.

"Where is your leisure now, General?" Pinkerton said softly.

He watched a while longer, till he had seen his fill, then turned the clumsy steam mare and followed the ripped-earth tracks of the war party back along the way that he had come.

EPILOGUE: REBUILDING NATIONS

WISPS OF WHITE RACED ACROSS A PERFECT BLUE SKY north of San Antonio as Titus shouted encouragement to another of the gangs hard at work righting the big English cruiser. "We certainly do appreciate the steam gear," he said to the shackled man walking behind him. "You sure the Queen ain't going to need it?"

Thackeray harrumphed at him. "The way you are treating me is absolutely insufferable. My cousin–"

"Third cousin," Burleson put in.

"My cousin, the Queen, will come for me with the whole Empire in tow. You, my good man, and your entire wretched backwater nation, will soon be quite sorry for the way you've treated me."

"Really?" Titus asked. His voice almost sounded sincerely worried.

"Indeed." Thackeray shook his manacles in front of Titus. "I *demand* you have these removed immediately."

Titus eyed Burleson. "You want to tell him?"

"No, why don't you?"

"Tell me what?"

"He ain't going to like it."

"Don't reckon he will."

"Tell me *what?*" Thackeray all but screamed at the two of them. His guard took a step closer, but Titus waved the man away.

The shouting had drawn the attention of the nearest work gang. They turned their attention from the mess of chains and pulleys to wipe their brows and listen.

"Your cousin," Burleson began.

"Third cousin," Titus interjected helpfully.

"Your third cousin, the Queen," Burleson began again. "She said we could keep you."

The veins appeared to be on the verge of bursting from General Lord Thackeray's forehead.

"She said *what?*"

"You heard me," Titus said.

"Don't be ludicrous! I am a peer of the Realm. She would never–"

"Lighten up, Courtney," Titus said to the sputtering Briton.

"You will address me as General Lord Thackeray-upon-the-Thames, or I will not respond."

"That so?" Titus grinned, rubbing the itchiness of a new beard coming in.

"Indeed."

"Have it your way, Courtney. But it's going to be a long, long, time before you see California or the Realm again."

"What does that mean?" he said.

"Just what he said," Burleson said. "We've set your ransom awful high..."

"How high?" General Thackeray asked, his ego piqued.

"Well, the Republic of Texas has sent our Ambassador–Sam Houston–have you heard of him?"

"Of course I've heard of him! How much is my ransom?"

"Money to cover the return to service of all this gear Her Majesty abandoned out here–"

"It was most certainly *not* abandoned."

"And training to be provided by you and the other prisoners on how to operate and maintain it. Once you become guests, I mean."

Thackeray stuck his chest out. His nostrils flared imperiously. "Texans operating Her Majesty's land frigates, leviathans and mechanized cavalry? Your Sam Houston is a fool, if he thinks my cousin–the Queen–will agree to that."

Titus nodded at the guard, who popped the general in the nose with the butt of his rifle.

"You don't disrespect Sam Houston," the man said in a matter of fact tone.

Thackeray held his manacled hands up to his face, trying to stanch the flow of blood by pinching his nose.

"She won't," he said in a thick, twangy voice.

Burleson nodded his head. "She will, unless she'd rather us let the French come over and see if maybe *they* can help us figure it out."

Thackeray turned white, realizing the strength of their argument. When he spoke next, the resignation in his voice was thicker than just a bloody, pinched nose. "I will of course follow any written instructions Her Majesty may send. For now, though, I think I'd like to return to my quarters."

"Indeed," Titus said, waving the guard to usher Thackeray thataway. He started back toward the other side of the enormous *Indomitable*, where other gangs endeavored to shove pry-gears into every inch of open space that the teams on the other side made available.

"What do you think we should name her?" asked Burleson.

"*Darla*," said Titus. "I was thinking we'd name her *Darla*."

On the last night before the Comanche were to return to their lands, Titus took Burleson and newly promoted Colonel Babb with him out on the Llano to where they had made their camp. They ate silently for nearly an hour, hardly speaking, before adjourning to a tipi to smoke the peace pipe. Colonel Babb, cursing his weak lungs the whole time, barely kept from a coughing fit. Titus and Burleson managed to partake without amusing or offending Many Scalps, Broken Lance, and most importantly, Lightning Dove.

After smoking and eating, Lightning Dove spoke in the slow deliberate way of his people. Titus and Burleson both knew enough to wait a spell before responding, and to give Many Scalps a chance to translate when necessary.

"She-Who-Is-Alone Again has not returned to the People, in flesh or in spirit."

"Texas feels great sorrow that she is not among the People," Titus said.

Blue smoke curled around Broken Lance's head as he exhaled toward Colonel Babb. The man was all but turning green.

"Who is chief of Texas? You?"

Burleson cleared his throat. "I am still President, for at least the next month, given the death of our Vice-President not too long before the battle of Austin. But our people will be electing a new chief soon."

"Will it be the bold man?" Lightning Dove asked, looking Titus in the eye.

"I am not running. My place is making sure Texas can defend herself." He took the pipe from Many Scalps. "As well as answering the call of our friends in the Comancheria, when need be."

"Who asks your people for the place of chief?"

Burleson worked that one out before Titus, and responded. "There's a piece of work named Anson Jones thinks he can do a better job. May be that he can. But my money is on Davy's boy, Sylvester Crockett." He turned to Titus. "And your old friend Sheppard aims to run, too.

Titus raised his eyebrows. "Didn't hear that."

"Fellow brought a stack of news sheets from the Rio Grande. He just announced he's going to run too."

Many Scalps interpreted that for the other Comanche in the tipi, which brought a moment of confusion. After some back and forth in Comanche, Lightning Dove addressed the white men again.

"My people do not understand why it is that paleface men who want to be chief must 'run' by standing still."

Burleson thought before answering. "Our people have a bad habit of saying one thing and doing another." He looked at them each in turn. "But we're going to try to do better than that here in Texas, no matter who it is that becomes President."

It was silent in the tipi for a long while after that, except for the rustle of Colonel Babb rushing out of the tipi to void his stomach upon the earth. The retching sound made the Comanche laugh. Titus and Burleson grinned behind their mustaches.

When the Colonel finally stopped gagging and vomiting, Broken Lance shook his medicine stick in mild annoyance at all of them till their faces became somber again. "What of the dead lands below the great river?"

"Mexico?" Titus asked.

The shaman grunted.

"Saw something about that, too," Burleson said. "Folks down there have been working against Moctezuma from inside for a long time. Their leader–fellow named Juarez–claims he can reform the whole damn country. Says the first step is respecting your neighbors' right to keep living."

Passing the pipe, Lightning Dove said, "That is a good first step."

Shirtsleeves up and sweat coursing down his back, Jeb Smoke hammered another board in place on the side of the new President's mansion. All around him, hammer blows sounded and men shouted orders at one another. Thunder rumbled in the distance, momentarily freezing many of the workers, but Jeb continued his labor. He knew these were garden variety thunderstorms approaching, and he hoped they'd get some rain out of it. Maybe cool the place off a little. Anyone scanning the skies for the Thunderbird would be wasting their time. She'd gone somewhere they couldn't find her.

Salazar worked beside him, hammering as quickly as he could to keep up with Willie's demands. Willie hadn't let the loss of her arm slow her down, and with the exception of a few quiet moments where Jeb had seen her wandering by the river alone or staring at the place where her arm had been, you wouldn't know the woman was even bothered by the fact that she'd lost it. She carted planks back and forth under her left arm and fed them to Salazar faster than he could attach them to the side of the building.

"You're the slowest man I ever met," she said.

"I can only hammer one board at a time," he said, grinning. Salazar didn't seem to mind her irritation. He didn't seem to mind much about her at all.

"Hell, I just got one arm and I could probably finish this job quicker than you. Good thing you're a better soldier than you are a carpenter or your working pace might have cost us the battle."

Jeb chuckled. "Willie, why don't you leave Captain Salazar alone? You've got him working twice as hard as anyone else here."

"You wouldn't know it, to watch him with that hammer."

Jeb finished the board he was attaching and stood back to admire the new mansion rapidly growing before their eyes. "I believe I'll break for lunch. Can I invite the two of you to join me?"

Salazar shot him a hungry look but Willie handed the man another wooden plank. "I believe we'll keep working," she said. "Plenty time for eating when the job's done."

Jeb slapped Salazar good-naturedly on the back, willing the man strength. Ever since the return trip to Austin, Willie had attached herself to the man and it didn't look like she was going to let him loose any time soon.

He walked down the gentle slope of the President's new front yard and into the ruined streets of Austin. Just clearing the debris was a monumental chore, and piles of splintered wood beyond reuse burned like funeral pyres all around him. Lightning Dove had offered the assistance of his People to rebuild Austin, but Burleson had rightly turned the man down. It was a kind offer, but not one they could accept. Siding with the Indians to beat back zombies was one thing, but looking them in the eye while you picked through the burned remains of your life was quite another.

Walls were going up on a handful of new buildings, and a wide assortment of tents had been erected to host businesses and provide temporary shelter until houses could be rebuilt. The largest of the tents was a church, built by a preacher that had wandered up from New Braunfels. It offered a place to worship and a makeshift home to some of Texas' displaced citizens, particularly to children who'd found themselves without parents. Audrey spent much of her time there, volunteering and helping to find homes for the children. She planned to rebuild her business, but didn't seem to be in a hurry about it. She felt it was more important to make sure all the kids got sorted out, and she'd taken a liking to the ones she'd delivered to San Antonio with Willie.

Jeb and Audrey had tents down near the river's edge, set side by side beneath the shade of two huge pecan trees. She was kneeling by a fire, heating up some coffee and cooking some biscuits when Jeb arrived. He squatted on a rock across from her and poured himself a cup of the coffee.

"How's the work going, Sheriff?" She smiled softly at him, then gave a tug at a fishing line that ran into the river.

Sheriff. Half the time Jeb forgot he'd accepted the position. He pulled absently at the star pinned to his chest, so much like his old Ranger star and yet something else entirely. Jeb didn't feel like he deserved the office and wasn't even sure he wanted it. But his Daddy was a difficult man to argue with, and Burleson was worse still. Jeb was convinced he'd only been offered the job as a way to keep him from leaving again. And maybe some part of him had accepted for that very reason.

Regardless, Austin would need someone to keep the peace. Once word got out that Texas was free from Mexican and Comanche threats, Jeb figured people would come west from the U.S. in droves. He'd serve; at least until they grew tired of him or he decided there was someplace else he needed to be.

"Going well enough," said Jeb. "When do you think we should start on you a stable? I think they've got the President's house under control."

"Maybe after we have a real church and some houses for everybody. The stable can wait."

"I reckon it can," said Jeb.

Audrey stared at him across the fire, her face worried. "Jeb, have you heard about Sheppard?"

"Yes I have," said Jeb, keeping his voice even. "I hear he means to run for president."

"How does that man expect to win any votes? He deserted the country and threw in with Moctezuma."

"That he did," said Jeb. "But I'm sure he's got an explanation he can sell to folks. What happened and what people will think happened ain't always the same thing. I know something about that."

"It won't be good for you if he wins," she said.

"Audrey, we have enough to contend with today. I wish you'd quit borrowing problems from tomorrow."

"I just don't want you running off again!" she said, yanking at the fishing line and pulling it back without a fish.

"I ain't running again," said Jeb. "Not if I can help it. And if I do, I'll take you with me this time. I promise that, Audrey. We'll go together."

"What makes you think I'll go with you anywhere?" said Audrey. "We aren't married."

"I just figured–"

"I don't care what you figured. We aren't getting married. Not any time soon anyway. I've got a business to rebuild if that's what I decide to do. Might be I want to teach school instead. There's plenty of kids around here and not many teachers. And I've got work down at the church too. Plenty to keep my days filled without worrying about you. If you're still around when I get through with all of that, then maybe we'll talk about getting married."

Jeb stood up, circled the fire and sat down beside Audrey. He took her hand in both of his and they sat together without speaking, listening to the crackle of the fire and the slow creep of the river passing.

"I think maybe I want a couple of those kids," said Audrey after a time. "You remember that little blonde girl that rode into San Antonio with me? Gretchen. Her and her brother don't have anyone left. The girl's a sweetie. Her brother's a little rascal, but I think I can tame him."

"You've had practice."

Audrey smiled at him. "Yes I have. You don't think it's a bad idea, a woman alone taking in a pair of kids?"

"You ain't alone, whether we're married or not. As for the kids, I reckon you'd make a better mother than most. You kept the whole mess of them alive during the fighting."

"I had help."

The thought of Troy came with a strong sadness that Jeb feared would never leave him. He'd never liked the man, but he'd taken on the opinion in recent weeks that maybe he should have. After the battle, Jeb had loaded Troy's body up in the wagon and brought it back to Austin. He'd dug the grave himself, on a little hill out west of town that overlooked a particularly pleasant stretch of the Colorado. Troy had never spoken of his family, so Jeb didn't know who to notify. But despite having no relations to attend, it seemed like the whole town had turned out for his funeral.

"I think you should take them kids," said Jeb.

"I think I should too." Audrey put her cheek against his shoulder and squeezed his hand. "You were a good man, helping that little girl. I hope you know that."

"I love you Audrey."

"I guess I love you too. But I'm still not going to marry you."

"Well if we ain't getting married, I suggest we eat so I can get back to work. Austin ain't gonna rebuild itself."

Allan Pinkerton was glad to have done with the Adolphus Pincher alias, though the smell of the man's hair oil might have grown on him enough to be adopted into his own persona. After four days on a stolen British steam mare with a decidedly annoying lean to the right, he'd arrived in Galveston, saddle-sore and in dire need of a razor and bath. The next day, he stepped aboard a tramp steam wheeler to Mobile, freshly bathed, shaved, and wearing a new suit of clothes provided by a Baptist preacher of no small repute who just so happened to serve as President Polk's eyes and ears in town–when he wasn't too busy shaming sinners.

A few days of bad weather and good fishing had delayed the boat and there was nothing Pinkerton could do to convince her captain to hurry on to Mobile. Apparently, the man was far less worried about the train to the District of Columbia than Pinkerton. But finally, the boat wove its way into a sleepy port town, and Pinkerton found that he was actually grateful for the chance to consider how best to phrase his report to the White House. He wrote it out carefully and presented it to the telegraph operator. The Morse-man gave him a puzzled look and read it aloud to him:

DEAD AND MAJESTY WOUNDED SORE STOP.

DOVE FLIES WITH STAR STOP.

STAR DIMMED NOT EXTINGUISHED AS PLANNED STOP.

"Is that right?" The Morse-man spoke in a tone that begged for explanation.

Pinkerton gave him a brisk nod and laid the fee down on the counter in lieu of any such satisfaction.

"It's more than right, it's destiny."

With that, Allan Pinkerton departed for his train. Through the window glass, he saw the Morse-man cock his head to one side and begin clacking away at his machine, looking even more puzzled than before.

Comanche Legend

Long before the palefaces took part of our land and named it Texas, the People faced a time of great famine and no rains. They danced and prayed and asked the Great Spirit what they had done to anger him. But he sent them no sign and no rain. Their shaman traveled to the top of a nearby hill to pray, and when he returned he said this: "The People have grown selfish. They take from the earth, and they give nothing back. The Great Spirit demands that the tribe's most valuable possession be burned up in fire. Only then will the Great Spirit return the rains and make the earth green and full of buffalo again."

The People went back to their tipis, saying, "Surely my special beads are not the most valuable" and "Surely my favorite bow is not the most valuable." One little girl had lost her mother and father and grandparents to the long hunger. The only things she could call her own were a warrior doll and her new name, She-Who-Is-Alone. The warrior doll was beautiful, with the blue feathers of the bird who cries "Jay! Jay!" in its hair and tiny beads on the leggings. The little doll was the only thing that She-Who-Is-Alone had left to love.

That night, she lay thinking about the shaman's words while everyone slept. She thought about the ones who had given her food and taken care of her even after her own family had died. She thought of the tribe's suffering and wanted to help them. She pulled a stick still red with embers from the fire and went away from the tipis to burn her doll so that the Great Spirit would ease the People's suffering. When there was nothing left of it but ashes, she gathered them up and offered them to the Four Winds so that the Great Spirit would know of her gift. The little girl was so tired after this that she fell asleep there on the ground.

When the People awakened, they were amazed. She-Who-Is-Alone lay sleeping in a field of flowers as blue as the feathers of the bird who cries "Jay! Jay!" The shaman said, "The Great Spirit has accepted your gift and sent this sign to show the People that they are forgiven." The tribe danced and rejoiced as warm rains began to fall upon the land. Ever since that day, the little girl has been known as One-Who-Dearly-Loves-Her-People, and every spring, even in the lands that are now called Texas, the Great Spirit makes the blue flowers bloom to remind the People of her sacrifice.

THE END

About the Authors

Josh Rountree is a sixth generation Texan, a descendant of Texas Rangers, horse thieves and other shady types. His short fiction has been published in a variety of magazines and anthologies including *Realms of Fantasy*, *Electric Velocipede* and *Rayguns Over Texas*. His short story collection *Can't Buy Me Faded Love* is available from *Wheatland Press*. Learn more at www.joshrountree.com

Lon Prater has worked in the Reactor Compartments of USS Enterprise, edited the military's textbook on arms deals, and kept things safe in the produce and laundry industries. He lives, writes, and games in Pensacola, Florida. Visit www.lonprater.com to find out more.

www.ingramcontent.com/pod-product-compliance
Lightning Source LLC
Chambersburg PA
CBHW070756280626
47162CB00016B/1066